CW00842050

THE G......
TATTOO

Catriona King

Copyright © 2016 by Catriona King
Photography: art_zzz
Artwork: Jonathan Temples:
creative@jonathantemples.co.uk
Editor: Maureen Vincent-Northam
Formatting: Rebecca Emin
All rights reserved.

ISBN: 978-1539675112

Hamilton-Crean Publishing Ltd. 2016

For my mother

About the Author

Catriona King is a medical doctor and trained as a police Forensic Medical Examiner in London, where she worked for some years. She has worked with the police on many occasions. She returned to live in Belfast in 2006.

She has written since childhood and has been published in many formats: non-fiction, journalistic and fiction.

The Craig Crime Series

A Limited Justice
The Grass Tattoo
The Visitor
The Waiting Room
The Broken Shore
The Slowest Cut
The Coercion Key
The Careless Word
The History Suite
The Sixth Estate
The Sect
The Keeper
The Talion Code
The Tribes

Acknowledgements

My thanks to Northern Ireland for providing the inspiration for my books.

My thanks also to: Maureen Vincent-Northam as my editor, Jonathan Temples for his cover design and Rebecca Emin for formatting this book.

I would like to thank all of the police officers that I have ever worked with for their professionalism, wit and compassion.

Catriona King
Belfast, September 2016

Discover the author's books at:
www.catrionakingbooks.com

To engage with the author about her books, email:
Catriona_books@yahoo.co.uk

The author can be found on Facebook and Twitter:
@CatrionaKing1

The Grass Tattoo

Chapter One

Monday 3rd December 2012. Belfast.

Joanne Greer stared venomously at the phone before she spoke.

"Persuade him, Bob. It's what you do all day."

The man's voice was quiet but firm. "We need to cut our losses."

"I'm not losing anything because of you! You have one week, and then London gets involved."

She slammed the phone down and stood completely still, her decision already made. London was getting involved today.

****

Wednesday 5th December. The Stormont Estate.

The first rays of the sun broke through the wet Ulster sky and the man sighed, already regretting his next action. He had no stomach for it anymore, if he'd ever really had.

He looked up at the cloudy sky, wishing himself elsewhere, and then his shoulders slumped as he resigned himself to the task.

He measured the distance again in his mind, and waited for them to appear, convincing himself that it was a computer game, that none of it was real. At least his distance was a shield: he didn't know how they coped with their part. Too close.

Gradually the wet sun lifted, and the jewel-coloured grass came into view, each blade's edge sharp in his sight. Any minute now. Then they appeared. Two blonde heads. So different in life, so differently fated now. He watched their exchange sadly. His sorrow had deepened with every year and it was unbearable now, watching her tears and begging. It tore at his heart and made him hate his orders, and the one who gave them.

He quickly raised the sight to his eye, turning off the voice in his head that said that this was all wrong. He shut out the faint winter breeze and the fresh hum of traffic on the comfortable street below, and he focussed.

The steel mechanism responded smoothly to his touch as he readied himself. And then, with one hard pull the bullet left the barrel, cutting through the air. Twisting, arc-ing, angled perfectly for the light wind, until it reached its destination, just as she turned.

It was strange how they always turned. After the bullet had gone, while its trajectory curved and twisted, but before it had even hit them. It was almost as if they knew what was coming, but they couldn't know, could they?

The bullet skewered straight through her, shutting out her daylight completely, causing her knees to buckle and then to fall.

The moment of impact was different for all of them. With this one a surprise, with that one a gaze, their eyes turned upwards, locked in time like a DVD on pause. With some, quiet resignation. Or indifference, as if they'd had enough of this world.

She fell now; perfectly vertical, kneeling down urgently, arms arching through the sky, towards the steps. He thought he could hear the soft tap of her knees upon the ground…imagination. Then forward, her kind face buried in the gentle grass, finally coming to rest.

He hated that moment more than he hated the whole thing, and vowed again that this would be his last. His anger this time at their orders, and disgust at the victim's innocence, was almost too much for him to bear, needing alcohol to bury it every night.

He unscrewed the sights, quickly placing the gun in the car, and left the rooftop at speed, collecting the second blonde by the gate. Then they drove to the one place that he could find peace, in alcohol, at any time of day.

****

The Belfast Chronicle Newspaper. St Anne's Square, Belfast.

Maggie Clarke stared across the white portico-ed square, bored. Wednesdays always bored her; they lacked the prison-break excitement of a Friday or even the long-suffering martyrdom of a Monday. They were just boring.

Added to that, it was a cold, wet morning and she would happily have stayed in bed, reliving last night's dream of Christian Bale, mask and all. Why they expected her in for eight o'clock she would never understand! Nothing worthwhile ever happened this early, every journalist knew that.

She pulled the soggy pencil from her mouth, examining it slowly for an un-chewed portion; then she popped it back in, satisfied and returned to her view. At least *that* wasn't boring.

A full wall of windows extended her cubby-hole of an office via a trompe-l'oeil, across the wide piazza of St Anne's Square. A little known gem set deep in Belfast's city centre, behind its namesake Cathedral.

What had once been elderly banks and offices had morphed into the city's buzzing Cathedral quarter, with a myriad of new additions to the arts and entertainment scene. There were hotels and restaurants, theatres and galleries, clubs, and coffee houses in the old style. It was a western Mecca for the tourists who poured in from all over the world. Belfast was booming, and this time for all the right reasons.

She glanced idly across the elegant vista, planning her next coffee break, and noticed a lithely handsome man entering the Metropolitan Arts Centre opposite, its lean, arrowed stone and glass slotting perfectly into the square's smooth design.

The man looked...well, she wasn't actually sure what he looked, but he looked something, and he made her feel shy somehow, without knowing why. Then she realised what it was - he looked arty. Arty men had always attracted her, and made her shy. There was something so uncontrolled about them, and she liked to be in control.

He sensed her gaze and smiled up at the window, in a reckless, Christmassy way. She could feel her blush rising, but before she could react by hiding or waving, her desk phone rang noisily, reminding her that she was at work.

She grudgingly removed her pencil and lifted the receiver, just as he disappeared through the centre's sliding door. Another failed romance.

"Hello. Derry..."

She stopped herself abruptly, remembering that she'd left the Derry Telegraph two months earlier, and then started again.

"Belfast Chronicle news desk, Maggie Clarke speaking."

The line was quiet, apart from a faint clatter of crockery and murmured voices in the background. She imagined the caller in an up-market cafe.

She tried again. "Hello, news desk. Can I help you?"

Again, quiet. But now there came the sound of breathing and it occurred to her that it might be a prank: her kid sister 'nuisancing' her during a free class. She was just about to say "Kim" accusingly, when the caller finally spoke. The voice surprised her. It was a man's voice, strong and deep, and at another time, she might even have said sexy. But the main surprise came from its accent, formed many miles from Belfast.

"You will find Irene Leighton at your Stormont."

'Your' Stormont, not mine.

She was leaning forward now, the hairs on her journalist's neck standing on end. Something exciting was coming next. Not nice, but exciting. It was what she lived for.

For a moment, the man didn't speak, and neither did she. Fighting the urge to question, each listening to the other's breathing. Then again, the clatter of crockery, this time with the unmistakable sound of ice hitting a glass, and an optic emptying. He was in a bar. At eight a.m.!

He spoke again, and Maggie was sure that she heard sadness in his voice. "She found the grass, I think. Her

14

husband bought it for her."

It didn't make sense, but there was no explanation forthcoming, just more silence. She couldn't fight her need to speak any longer.

"Who are you?" Not the most elegantly framed question she'd ever asked.

"It is not important who I am. You have what you need. Tell your police."

The background noise rose suddenly, and she heard the voice murmur something indecipherable. Then without another word the line went dead, leaving her staring at the receiver.

She sat for a moment, confused about what she'd heard, and about what to do next. Her journalist's nose was pulling her towards Stormont, the seat of Northern Ireland's government, to see for herself. Before the other papers got the call, if they hadn't already. There was a story here, and she knew it. Not some dopey two columns on the fifth page, but a real front-pager. And it was her story.

But somewhere in her 'normal citizen' past she could feel a conscience stirring, boring her with 'duty' and all that it implied. Call the police. But that was what he wanted, and Maggie didn't like giving people what they wanted, not until they deserved it, and often not even then. Calling the police would be the responsible, moral thing to do. But even she would admit that they weren't words often used to describe her.

Her brief tug of war was interrupted by the heavy thump of files on her desk, dropped so close that they caught the edge of her hand. She let out a yelp and swung her arm back at the newsboy who had dumped them, catching him on the nose.

"Ow, that hurt."

Maggie grabbed her bag and phone and stood up, waving a sore finger in his young face. "And so did that." And then without further discussion, she left her office, stomped across the newsroom floor and yelled. "Tell Ray I'll be at Stormont, following a lead."

She took the lift to the car-park and gunned her

V.W. Beetle down the Dunbar Link, past the Albert Clock and over the bridge, her mind made up. Of course she'd do the responsible thing and phone the police, but not until she was sitting outside Stormont's front gate.

Chapter Two

Marc Craig was sitting outside Belfast's City Hall, stuck in the dense morning traffic. It was even worse than usual, people still confused by the new road system after three months, and Christmas adding to the crowds.

He smiled, watching as the crowds milled by on the pavement, waiting for the Christmas market to open, and tapped his fingers on the wheel in time to a carol playing from its tannoy. He was late for work. Well, not late by anyone else's standards, but by his, he was late.

He blamed it on his sudden urge to regain his fitness, without which he would never have been in the gym at seven, pounding away on the rowing machine. But he had to admit that he felt better for it, after only two weeks. So he was late, but not really.

His car-phone vibrated loudly. 'Liam'. He quickly pressed answer and Liam Cullen's gruff voice boomed over the line, waking him up.

"Morning boss, nice day for it."

Craig looked out at the drizzle, smiling sceptically. "Nice day for what? I'll be there in five minutes. Can this wait until then?"

"Aye, well, that's why I called. Don't go to the squad, come here. We've a case."

"Where's here?"

"Stormont. You'll see why when you get here." Then, without ceremony, the line clicked off. Liam was being mysterious again, but Craig knew better than to dismiss it as a tease, he was a good detective. Whatever it was, it was important.

He accelerated down Chichester Street and cut through the Lagan Courts, preparing to show his badge if challenged. Then over the Albert Bridge, and up the Upper Newtownards Road faster than was strictly legal, reaching the Stormont Estate within ten minutes.

As he pulled into the concrete semi-circle outside the Estate's main gates, he noticed an incongruous, lime-green Beetle nestling amongst the liveried police

17

cars. It had a giant sunflower on its dashboard that gave it a 'hippy' air more common in Berkeley than Belfast, and a pink furry toy stuck to its back window.

He climbed out of his car and strode across to a uniformed officer, quickly showing his badge. "Morning, constable. D.C.I. Craig."

"Good morning, sir."

"Is Inspector Cullen around?"

"Down there, sir."

The young red-haired constable turned, pointing through the black wrought-iron gates into the distance. Craig could vaguely make out the very tall, very pale figure of Liam Cullen, standing a mile away down Prince of Wales' Avenue, in front of the white-stone edifice of Parliament buildings.

He nodded his thanks and was about to get back into the car when he remembered the Beetle. He walked over to it, expecting a female occupant, and knocked lightly on the passenger window.

The young, dark-haired woman inside jumped, staring at him, startled. Craig smiled amiably and indicated to roll down the window, but instead she jumped out, storming around angrily to where he stood.

"What do you mean banging my window like that? You scared the life out of me!"

The constable stepped forward indignantly. "That's D.C.I Craig."

"I don't care who he is."

She looked up at him challengingly and Craig smiled, half-amused for a moment; whoever she was, she certainly liked drama. Then he recognised her, and instantly looked less amused, sighing inwardly.

"What are you doing here, Ms. Clarke? You know journalists aren't allowed at crime scenes. You'll get a briefing later."

Maggie was taken aback by him knowing her name. Then she shrugged: journalists in Northern Ireland earned their own sort of fame.

"Who are you to tell me where I can be? I gave the police this murder."

A curt response sprung immediately to his lips, but he bit it back out of politeness, looking down at her more coldly.

"So you 'gave' us this murder, did you? Enlighten me."

She completely missed his froideur, and obliged. "A man called the news desk and told me that Irene Leighton was here. Then he told me to call the police, so I didn't imagine she was opening a fete."

Her sarcasm reminded Craig of Ray Mercer at the Chronicle, so he asked the question. "Are you at the Chronicle nowadays, by any chance?"

"Yes."

Her quizzical look asked for an explanation, but he merely nodded. It figured.

"What exactly did this man say? Please tell me anything you noticed about his voice, any background noise, anything."

She reluctantly detailed her conversation with the anonymous caller as he listened, storing it away for future reference. Then he nodded, turned on his heel and waved her goodbye, throwing "please escort Ms. Clarke away from the area" over his shoulder to the constable.

Maggie's face burned in a combination of embarrassment and anger, and she stormed after him, yelling. "I gave you this murder. You owe me the story."

Craig wheeled round to face her, and she saw his barely controlled anger. There was no love lost between the murder squad and the Chronicle, but that had been Ray Mercer's irresponsible coverage of the Adams' case, not her fault. She'd been in Derry then and she wasn't taking his bloody blame.

She decided to try another tack, her voice softening. "Look, I know that you hate the Chronicle. Ray's coverage of the Adams' case wasn't good, we all know that."

Craig's eyebrows rose at the understatement, but she ignored his scepticism and kept going. "I was on the Derry Telegraph then, and I covered the story responsibly. Ask Inspector McNulty at Limavady, she'll tell you."

He softened slightly at the mention of Julia McNulty's name. They were sometime 'friends with a future' and she had mentioned Maggie's account favourably. He nodded her on.

"Look, how's about I leave for now?"

"Good idea. After giving your statement to the constable."

"Of course."

"OK, and?"

"When you're ready to see the Press, I get an exclusive interview. Say...six hours before the main briefing?"

He gazed down at her shrewdly, knowing her game. Six hours meant that she'd make the early edition, with the others losing out to the 'late'. But he could turn the request to his advantage. If he could control what she wrote and it hit the newsstands first, the others might have to behave better. 'Might' being the operative word.

He nodded slightly to himself and Maggie caught the move, smiling inwardly. Her smile was short-lived.

"OK, Ms. Clarke. I'll give you an exclusive. But I want to see your copy before printing. And if you play games with me, I'll make life very challenging for you in the future. Do you understand?"

The look in his eye showed that he meant it. There would be no messing.

Maggie nodded grudgingly. "Agreed."

Craig turned to go and she moved to give her statement to the constable. Then she remembered something important.

"Chief Inspector."

"Yes?"

"You do know that Irene Leighton is the wife of Bob Leighton, don't you?"

"Who?"

"The Energy Party M.P. for West Antrim."

And with that his normal day went to hell.

Chapter Three

Parliament Buildings. The Stormont Estate.

D.I. Liam Cullen was kneeling back on his substantial haunches, wearing a much too-small forensic suit. Its seams were struggling, and so was he. He stared at the grandeur around him in a mixture of sadness and anger. And then reluctantly back at the body of the blonde woman, face-down in the damp grass beside Parliament Buildings' steps.

She was fully-clothed in black trousers and an elegant beige-silk blouse, tucked loosely into the trousers' narrow waistband. Her slim body lay in the unmistakable shape of a cross; her arms at right angles to her body and her legs set tightly together. She looked so vulnerable that even Liam's world-weary heart broke.

He couldn't see any obvious trauma, apart from some faint grazes on her left hand. But that didn't mean that there wasn't any, he knew his limitations. The crime scene investigators had just arrived, so thankfully his view wasn't the last. What he could see were clumps of new grass clasped in both of her hands, and a small dark area below her left shoulder blade, clearly visible through the blouse's thin material.

A shape above him blocked his light unexpectedly, and he knew it was Craig without looking. "Hi, boss. What kept you?"

It was said tiredly and Craig immediately heard the fatigue, so he smiled at Liam's cheek, lifting the mood. He had no intention of explaining his lateness, and Liam didn't really want him to. He was just filling-in the silence in the way that he always did.

Craig looked down thoughtfully at the woman on the grass, and then spoke quietly. "She's the wife of an M.P."

Liam looked at him, surprised. "How do you know that? There's no I.D."

"I've just met one of our friends from the fourth

21

estate."

He filled Liam in on Maggie's information and his bargain with her, and Liam let out a low whistle. "Shit, that's all we need. The press will be all over this like a rash."

Craig nodded. "Let's solve it quickly then. I called John and he's agreed to take it. He'll be here in ten minutes."

Just then, a bright blue car pulled up on the elegant avenue, and Dr John Winter extricated his long limbs from its interior, loping towards them. His brown hair blew randomly across his eyes and he pushed it away absentmindedly, adjusting his glasses and dropping his briefcase in the process. He looked like the stereotype of a youthful nutty professor, because he was. He was also Director of Forensic Pathology for Northern Ireland and Craig's long-time friend. They often worked together, when time and the system allowed.

He speedily donned a suit from the C.S.I.'s pile and ambled over to them, scanning the body expertly. "The traffic was dire. I nearly had to send Trevor."

"I thought he was in the north-west, John?"

Winter gazed intensely at the body as they talked.

"Nope. He moved down here last month, and I'm pleased to have him. He's good."

"Limavady won't like you poaching their staff, Doc."

Winter looked over his glasses at Liam, half-smiling. "I think you'll find that as Director they're already mine, Liam."

Craig smiled benignly at his friend's unfamiliar ego. John had never pulled rank yet, and Liam understood his bluff immediately. "Trevor asked you for the move, didn't he?"

Winter smiled as his cover was blown. "Oh, OK then. He has a new woman in Belfast. I just thought I'd try acting the boss for a day."

"Give it up, Doc."

They laughed together for a second, and then Winter turned seriously towards the woman and started reporting.

"No sign of blunt force trauma anywhere on the

22

posterior aspect of the body, except..."

He leaned in, peering at the woman's back through the thin fabric of her blouse.

"There's a tear in the material, here." He pointed at a miniscule rip that Liam had missed. "And this dark area below the left scapula might be a bruise, or congealed blood. I'll tell you more when we get her back to the lab."

"What can you give us quickly, John?"

Winter stared at the woman for a moment longer, before speaking.

"Right. The victim is thirty to forty years of age, well nourished, and judging by her skin and hair, not deficient in nutrition or vitamins. Definitely not a smoker. She's wearing a wedding ring so probably married. She has new abrasions on her left knuckles and torn clumps of grass in both hands. The cruciate positioning of her body is interesting."

"It's deliberate."

"I agree. It might have significance; perhaps even tell us something about the murderer."

"Definitely a murder then, Doc?"

Winter sat back on his haunches, surprised by Liam's question. 'Natural causes' hadn't even occurred to him, and it always should. But this was definitely a murder.

"I'd say so, Liam. She could have lain down in this position herself I suppose...but the way the grass is clasped in her hand, and torn out from the earth..."

"How do you know it's torn?"

Craig interjected. "The roots are still on the grass, Liam. The abrasions on her hand could indicate a fight or a struggle. Can you see her nails, John?"

He leaned forward and gently opened the woman's left hand, finger by finger, carefully removing the strands of torn grass. Her nails were long and oval, painted with a tasteful, beige varnish, and he wondered if she'd deliberately matched it to her blouse, touched by the small detail. Her death had been so obviously unexpected.

The nail on her left index finger was half-torn from

the cuticle and he opened her palm to examine it. Then he gasped audibly. Craig leaned forward quickly to see what had caused the reaction. John was very familiar with death, so whatever made him gasp had to be something unusual. It was.

In the woman's small, hurt hand lay a clear zip-locked bag, like a miniature freezer bag. Inside it lay a square of white paper. Winter held the bag up to the newly-appeared December sun, examining it from every angle. But the view yielded no new information - the paper was folded tight.

He lifted a pair of tweezers and opened the bag slowly, cautiously removing the square. Then he laid it on a sterile glove, unfolding it gently. A tiny figure '10' was written on the white paper, in black ink.

The three men looked at each other, puzzled. Then, with a quick look, Craig asked him to examine the other hand, but there was nothing. No broken nail and no hidden note. Just a few thin blades of grass.

Craig broke the silence. "Ten? Ten days...ten thousand?"

Liam looked blankly at him and then at the paper, uncharacteristically silent. Finally John interjected. "There's no rigor and she's not cold yet, despite the weather. I think she died in the past hour, Marc."

Craig's dark eyes narrowed, they'd just missed her murderer. Whoever had called Maggie Clarke had phoned from nearby.

John Winter turned the woman's body over carefully and the three men saw her face for the first time, making everything more real. She was lightly tanned and blue-eyed, and her shoulder-length fair hair was lightly streaked with grey. A pretty woman; in a mummyish way that made her pleasant rather than striking. She looked as if she had been nice.

Craig looked away from her face sadly and noticed a fine gold cross on a chain around her neck. Below it hung a longer chain, holding a tiny, engraved bracelet, identical to one that his sister Lucia had worn as a baby. It was marked clearly with the initial 'R'. It wasn't Irene Leighton's.

He thought for a moment. In his experience there were only three reasons for murder; love, power or money. Everything else was just a combination of those. He wondered which one applied to Irene Leighton. John's soft baritone broke through his reverie, signalling the woman's removal to a discretely parked mortuary van, and onwards to his Saintfield Road lab.

Craig looked at his watch, scanning the area quickly. The morning work-crowd was gathering rapidly outside the Estate's gates, and from the look of some of their suits, it probably included politicians. Damn. Then he realised that Liam was talking.

"The Doc says there's blood on her chest, from a wound. The C. S.I.s will need another hour or so here, but they'd better get their skates on, apparently we're stopping five thousand civil servants getting to work." He snorted. "You'd think they'd be grateful."

Craig half-smiled at the comment, already preoccupied with questions. He waved the investigators on vaguely, thinking. Why would anyone have killed this innocuous looking woman? Was she Irene Leighton? And if so, was her husband involved in her death? The husband always had to be the first suspect. But she'd been left outside the seat of Northern Ireland's parliament, so could there be some political aspect to her killing? And why tell a journalist to call the police, when you could just call them directly? Unless the murderer wanted publicity for some reason...

John interrupted his thoughts. "I'm going to the lab now, Marc. We're not busy so I'll do the post-mortem this morning. If you call down about two, I should have something for you."

"I'll find the husband, boss."

Craig nodded, sighing. "And I'll call Chief Superintendent Harrison, tell him that an M.P's wife might be dead, and then listen to him try to find ways to look important."

Chapter Four

Joe Watson was knackered and it was only ten a.m. The night before's meeting of the Strategic Finance Foundation had been a late one, and he wasn't young any more.

Added to that, he hadn't been able to get near his office until ten minutes ago, because the police had locked the whole of Stormont down, with no bloody explanation. He threw his briefcase tiredly onto the desk and yelled for his special advisor, ready to shout about something.

Michael Irwin popped his head around the office door warily. His boss was a politician and they were tricky at the best of times. But S.F.F. had gone on until midnight, so tired would be added to tricky today.

He fixed on his best smile and entered quietly. "Good Morning, Minister. May I get you something?"

"A gun would be good, after last night."

Watson was leaning red-faced over his laptop, and by the way that his fingers were tapping, Michael knew that he wanted a cigar. He'd only quit yesterday. Again.

"Sorry, no guns. Would a white coffee do instead?"

Watson smiled grudgingly. "It'll have to, I suppose."

Irwin turned, and had nearly made good his escape, when Watson added to his burden. "Then find me the Commissioner for Public Conduct. We need a little chat..."

****

Kaisa smoothed the expensive body lotion down her slim, tanned legs and smiled to herself. He'd been quite good on Monday night, not that it mattered; it wouldn't make any difference to the final outcome. Still, if you had to do something it was always better if it wasn't repulsive, and he'd certainly been energised on Monday, about heaven only knew what.

She pulled on her designer lounge-suit and brushed her soft blonde hair; one hundred times, just like her mother had said, stopping mid-stroke to remember her. Her worn brown hands, even though she'd been young, romantically entwined with their father's. Her soft, kind smile when she'd looked at them, as if they were everything important in her world. And more than anything, her strength. Never crying, not even when *they* came.

Kaisa scrutinised herself in the mirror. Her hands were white and smooth, and when she smiled it wasn't soft at all. But just like her mother, she was strong. Always.

****

West Antrim.

Bob Leighton, or The Right Honourable Robert Leighton, Member of Parliament, as he preferred to be called, was sitting in his West Antrim constituency office, bored and angry. Bored because his next meeting was on road drainage, and angry because of the previous evening's Foundation meeting, and the latest threatening phone-call, received four hours earlier. He was getting fed up with them now.

He had plenty of ideas on how he could make his day more tolerable, but only one of them was available now, so he walked speedily to the door, checking that his secretary was busy outside. Then he locked it, reached into his desk drawer for the small tinfoil wrap, and sat down eagerly on the dark-brown sofa in the corner.

He placed the foil on the coffee table, unfolding its edges cautiously, careful not to spill any of its contents. Then he took a credit card and a ten-euro note from his pocket, and began his favourite ritual. He spread and chopped the white powder rhythmically with the card's edge, then rolled the note into a tight funnel, with one end at his nostril and the other poised to inhale. He'd always known that Euros would prove useful for something.

He inhaled sharply and waited for the chemicals to hit his brain. The buzzing in his ears made him

27

momentarily deaf and his head fell back against the sofa in slow motion. Then the familiar warm, tingling sensation spread first through his arms and fingers, and then flowed like water through his thin thighs, arousing him as it passed.

He closed his eyes in pleasure for a moment, imagining her dancing between his legs, moving sinuously back and forth, up and down, while he slipped high-value notes into her G-string.

A knock on the door pulled him harshly back to reality. He rose slowly and reluctantly, his legs weak, and opened it just a crack. His young secretary's wary face appeared.

"Your ten o'clock is here, Mr Leighton"

Shit.

"Oh. Alright, Sarah, I'll be right out. Give me a minute."

He closed the door too quickly in her face, and hurriedly scraped the remaining powder back into its wrapper, running a wet finger across the residue and rubbing it into his gums for one quick, final buzz. Then he prepared himself to face the most boring men in Antrim, and talk about the drains.

****

They'd been halfway through the surveyor's report when Sarah had rescued him, or so he'd thought until Craig and Liam had entered noisily, flashing their badges and ensuring that their visit was common knowledge in Antrim by lunchtime. Leighton's hackles rose angrily. He had enough of the local cops without Belfast's heavies barging in.

"You should have made an appointment, Chief Inspector, instead of interrupting an important meeting. The Chief Constable will hear of this."

Craig had intended to deal sensitively with Bob Leighton. After all, the man had just lost his wife, whether he knew it yet or not. And Craig believed firmly in 'innocent until...'

But he'd just had a ten-minute phone-call listening

28

to Terry Harrison's unctuous self-promoting, severely straining his courtesy. Plus, the politician's overly-bright eyes had alerted him to his drug habit on sight, so his natural politeness was already tempered with suspicion.

"Mr Leighton, please sit down. We have some news for you."

They'd agreed in the car that while Craig told Bob Leighton about his wife, Liam would watch his reaction, so Liam was watching the scrawny M.P. very carefully now. They'd both seen his flushed face and eyes when they'd entered and now Liam could see white powder inside his nostril, knowing that Craig was at the wrong angle to catch it. The man was on coke, and untidily at that, and it was only ten-thirty in the morning! Liam had a grudging respect for his stamina.

Leighton was still talking. "What sort of news?" Then alarm crossed his face, and what he said next surprised them both.

"Kaisa? Is Kaisa alright?"

Craig said what they were both thinking. "Who is Kaisa, Mr Leighton?"

"My nanny." The look on their faces told Bob Leighton that he'd slipped, and he tried to cover it quickly, digging an even deeper hole. "My son Ben's nanny, he's three."

Embarrassment made the M.P. hostile, and his next words were nearly a shout. "She's new here, OK. Is she all right?"

It told them a lot about the Leighton's marriage, and made the man in front of them more likely to be a killer than a victim. But he was still innocent, until...

"I don't know anything about any Kaisa, Mr Leighton. But...we have found the body of a woman..." Leighton's eyes widened.

"We believe that it may be your wife, Irene."

Bob Leighton stared at him, uncomprehending. So Craig restarted, softly. "We need you to come with us...to help with the identification."

The politician didn't move at all, his expression

unchanged. In shock? Then he surprised them both, by laughing, hard.

"Don't talk rubbish, man. My wife? Load of nonsense, she's fine. She's at her mother's in Fermanagh. Look, I'll call her now."

He reached quickly into his jacket for a mobile, and pressed some keys, until Craig could see 'Irene' dialling. It rang out with no answer. Leighton just shrugged.

"She's out shopping somewhere. She'll be in touch when she sees that I've called."

Then he rose again, angrily. "You should check your facts before you frighten people."

He really didn't know what they were talking about, or was pretending that he didn't. Craig motioned quietly to Liam and he reached into his pocket, withdrawing an envelope full of photographs.

"Please sit down again, Mr Leighton."

"Now look here, this has gone on long enough." But the look on Craig's face told him to sit, so he did, grudgingly.

Liam selected the least gruesome picture from the envelope and placed it slowly on the desk. Leighton looked at the picture in front of him and his mouth opened slowly, then he froze, immobile. The room fell silent and for a moment none of them moved, until Craig finally lifted the photograph gently from the desk, certain that the man had seen enough.

Then, completely without warning, Bob Leighton banged his head hard on the desk, again and again. Until blood started to trickle from his nose and smear across his mouth, and his lower lip ripped open. Liam grabbed him before he knocked himself out, and Leighton emitted a single deafening yell, several seconds long. Then he sat rooted to his chair, staring ahead, the blood dripping freely down his face.

Craig watched him for a moment, puzzled, re-thinking his earlier quick assumption about the nanny. He could spot pretence in a heartbeat, and Leighton wasn't pretending. He was genuinely bereft, so why the concern for this Kaisa? Maybe it was just kindness.

After a few mute minutes he took his arm kindly and they led the bloodied official to the car, and then on to John Winter's Lab. To confirm what they both already knew, that his wife of twenty years was dead.

****

The Pathology Lab.

John felt genuinely sad about the woman's death, and that didn't happen often. All death was sad of course, whether from the waste or for the victim's loved ones, or from the sheer indignity and ignominy of the demise. But occasionally, even when all of those things were accepted, and when age and circumstance had been taken into account, occasionally there was another dimension that made death even sadder. Strange or unnatural death, and Irene Leighton's death was both of those.

He was touched by her suburban 'mummy-ness', signposted by her sensible mid-heel shoes and 'slacks' from M&S, and echoed in her minimal adornment. No garish earrings, no loud rings and no multi-coloured nails. Just a simple gold wedding band, the cross of some religion, and a child's bracelet on a chain around her neck; a memory of someone, or some other time.

John gazed down at the woman respectfully for a moment, then he sighed, reaching for his scalpel to uncover Irene Leighton's story, as gently as possible.

Chapter Five

Kaisa played gently with Ben's dark curls and smiled affectionately at the little boy. At midday, she would go to the supermarket for fruit and yoghurt for his coming week's breakfasts and then she'd pop into Castle Court shopping centre. It was only two streets away and she needed a new lipstick, now that she had an appreciative audience.

She strolled over to the mirror and admired her image, smoothing down her white vest top and turning to assess her rear view in jeans. Everything was where it needed to be for best effect. Good genes. She laughed at her own pun and at the English language, where one word could have so many meanings; jeans, genes, Jean's, there, their, they're. How complex did they need to make it?

Still, even if their language was sophisticated, their men often weren't. And that, she smiled, was to her advantage.

****

Docklands' Coordinated Crime Unit (The C.C.U.). Pilot Street, Belfast.

Craig was sitting in a boiling relative's room on the second floor of the Coordinated Crime Unit. Boiling, courtesy of a broken thermostat; cut-backs. He was working himself up to interview Bob Leighton. Working himself up not because he was nervous, or because the interviewee was special. He was no more or less special than any victim's spouse, where his instinctive sympathy was always tempered by the knowledge that in thirty-percent of cases when a wife died, the husband had actually killed her. No, he wasn't working himself up because of that. It was a situation that he'd dealt with many times, too many times recently.

And he wasn't working himself up in anticipation of

being lied to, because people nearly always lied to the police, even when they didn't mean to. He probably lied to himself at times.

No, he was working himself up because the man in front of him was a professional liar, calling it politics or diplomacy or pragmatism, or necessity. The man in front of him could probably lie without breaking a sweat, even in this heat. After all, he promised people things every day, most of which he knew that he would never deliver.

He was working himself up because he knew that he had to look beyond the clues that gave normal people away. The sweat, the refusal to make eye contact, the nervous tics and kicking at the table legs. The 'tells' and inaccuracies and inconsistencies in their stories. The sudden need to embellish everything to fill the silence. 'So there I was, walking down Edgar Road to buy milk. It's a lovely road, full of trees and flowers...etc.' Too much information.

No, the normal signs of nervousness and lies wouldn't apply here. This man wouldn't show any signs that he was lying, because he really believed his own lies. This one was tricky. And then of course, he wasn't under arrest. He was a relative, and there was grief, real or otherwise. And there was always the possibility, large or small, that he might just be innocent. Until...

****

Craig re-entered the squad-room just after one and threw the file down on a vacant desk, frustrated. Nothing! He'd got nothing. Leighton had seemed genuinely grief-stricken, but he'd also refused to answer most questions until his solicitor arrived, and then he wouldn't answer any at all.

He sighed and cast a look around the large, open plan office. There was no one there but Liam and himself. No Annette, no Nicky and no Davy. It was just like the airline advert.

"Where is everybody? Did I miss a bank holiday?"

Liam flung himself back in his chair and swung his

33

long legs onto the desk, half-laughing.

"Nope, something much more important. A girl on the sixth floor is selling jewellery, cheap. They all went for a look."

"Davy as well?"

"Oh, aye. Apparently, EMOs are into body piercing. Although God knows which part he's looking to adorn."

Craig shrugged and smiled. The young could get away with anything, he knew he had. He pulled off the jacket of his modern suit, loosening his tie, and sat down.

"What did you make of Leighton at the viewing?" Liam had volunteered to take the politician into the mortuary with John, while Craig talked to Trevor about the upcoming P.M.

"Rough enough, boss. He went white as a sheet and the Doc had to sit him down. Then he started crying and calling her name out. I felt sorry for him." Liam immediately looked embarrassed by his own compassion, as if he'd admitted a flaw.

Craig nodded. He agreed with him. Much as he hated politicians, Bob Leighton's grief was genuine, he was certain of it. But that didn't mean that he was innocent.

"He's guilty of something, Liam, but I'm not sure it's murder. Did you see the size of his pupils? In a bright room too."

Liam nodded. "He didn't stop sniffing all the way to the lab. Big coke habit. I thought his nose would never stop bleeding."

"I'd like to bet that it isn't his only vice. He showed a bit too much concern about that nanny."

They needed to speak to Kaisa 'whatever her name was', now that Leighton had formally identified his wife. There'd been little doubt that the body they'd found had belonged to Irene Leighton, but the formalities still had to be observed.

"That Dublin trip of his was a handy little alibi. I'll check it out after lunch. But I'd say presenting to the European Energy meeting would be hard to fake. Five hundred witnesses and a T.V. show to prove it."

34

Craig thought for a moment. "Yes, but…"

"But, what?"

"It doesn't prevent him being involved in some other way. Even if he didn't kill her himself, he's up to his eyes in this death, somehow."

They lapsed into silence, thinking, and then Craig remembered that he hadn't eaten since seven a.m., so he slipped-on his jacket and stood up.

"We can't do anything until his brief arrives, so let's go to 'The James' for lunch."

A sudden thought struck him. He had a pile of paperwork waiting in his office; Nicky had been tutting at him about it all week. He pushed the thought away guiltily and turned to go and Liam swung his long legs down from the desk, never one to refuse food.

"Good idea, I'll need a full stomach to have a go at the nanny."

"You're going nowhere near the nanny. Annette's taking that one."

Liam feigned offence for a second and then grinned, acknowledging his reputation for giving pretty women a free pass, and for putting his foot in it.

"Just give me a minute to check for calls."

Craig pressed the number for the main desk and listened to his messages. There were two. Nicky telling him that they were all on the sixth floor and would return about one thirty; and Julia McNulty asking for a copy of the public prosecution file on Jessica Adams. He smiled quietly, making a note to ring her back personally.

They headed for the lift and just as they were leaving, the arriving lift's door opened, and Craig's heart sank at the sight of Terry Harrison. That was all he needed; their earlier conversation had been bad enough.

Harrison's uncomfortably high-pitched voice rang out across the floor. "Ah, D.C.I. Craig. Just the man." He turned his head slightly and caught Liam ducking into the stairwell, waving him back, in an order, not a request.

Without any debate, he oiled his way towards

Craig's office and pushed open the door, seating himself behind his desk with an attitude that brooked no discussion. He swung Craig's chair round to face the river, and started talking with any preamble.

"I'm not happy, D.C.I. Craig."

Before Craig could ask 'what about', he continued. Craig already knew what about in any case, and that Harrison was about to tell them again, at great length.

Terry Harrison was a political operator with a small 'p' and he fancied himself as a player. Sucking up to politicians was one of his many dubious skills, and he was both good at it and proud of it, although in Craig's book it was definitely nothing to boast about. Politics should be left to the politicians, and solving crime to them – the force had been used by vote-hunting bureaucrats before.

Harrison was still talking. "I'm unhappy for many reasons, D.C.I. Craig. The main one is that you are treating Mr Robert Leighton, Member of Parliament for West Antrim, as if he's a criminal. The poor man's just lost his wife!"

Craig was standing in his own office in front of his own deputy, being asked to explain himself by the fat, pompous prick in his chair, and Liam could see his temper flaring. It didn't go often, but when it did, it wasn't pretty.

"It would be useful if you would turn to face us, sir."

His tone was barely civil and Harrison heard it, swinging the chair around sharply. Craig really hoped that his obesity wouldn't ruin the suspension; it had taken him years to wear it in.

"I don't like your tone, D.C.I. Craig."

"And I don't like either myself or my men being accused of things that we haven't done...sir!" The 'sir' was definitely an afterthought.

"Explain yourself."

"I will!"

It was half-shouted and Craig knew that he needed to wind his neck in quickly, before he reached over and grabbed Harrison by the throat. He looked around for a less violent way to even the power-balance, quickly finding one.

The only free chairs in the room were in the low coffee area to one side of the office. Craig groaned inwardly. They were for visitors, and his and Liam's height made them murder to get into and out of. But he was damned if he was going to stand there like some school-boy being told off by the headmaster, so he gestured Liam to sit down, taking them both out of Harrison's view.

It had the desired effect. Harrison had to walk around the desk to see them, getting him out of Craig's chair before he completely ruined it, and throwing him momentarily off topic. Craig kept talking without skipping a beat.

"Robert Leighton is not under arrest. He expressed a wish to find his wife's killer, so he's helping us with our enquiries."

Harrison went to speak but Craig ignored him.

"He's being afforded every courtesy and we've only had brief sessions with him. One to inform him about the death, and the second of which yielded information as to his whereabouts at the time of Mrs Leighton's death. We're currently checking that information to eliminate him as a suspect."

Harrison's mouth kept opening to speak, and then shutting again as Craig ignored him, deftly. Liam stifled a laugh. He looked like a Guppy.

"Mr Leighton identified his wife initially from a photograph that we showed him from the scene, and later confirmed that I.D. at Dr Winter's laboratory on the Saintfield Road."

Harrison wagged an overweight finger in the air, and Craig quickly added. "The photograph was of her face, which was completely uninjured."

The finger dropped and Liam laughed aloud at the pantomime. Craig shot him a quick warning look; there was a time to push it with Harrison and this wasn't it.

Craig could see the D.C.S. hesitating and decided to play his trump card. He was in the mood to wind him up. "John..."

This time Harrison did interrupt. "John?"

Craig looked at him coldly. "Dr Winter."

The police hierarchy viewed John Winter with a wary respect, knowing that he could make their lives easy or hell. But Craig had the familiarity of a thirty-year friendship and it irritated Harrison immensely. That and the Chief Constable's attempts to make Craig superintendent, doing Harrison out of a job at the Docklands. He'd resisted the rank so far, too many meetings and not enough crime scenes, but Harrison knew that he couldn't resist it forever.

Craig could feel the conversation's power balance shifting. "The post-mortem is being rushed through and we'll have his preliminary findings after lunch. We already have lines to pursue."

Harrison leaned forward eagerly, forgetting to be angry. "Have we indeed?"

Craig nodded curtly and Harrison looked pleased. "Yes. Good, good." He crossed to where they were sitting and half-smiled: it was like a Malthusian gap. Then he started back-peddling with Olympic skill.

"Well Marc, I know I can trust you to be diplomatic with Mr Leighton. Politicians are a tricky bunch, not to be trusted really. Not like us. They try to interfere in policing, you know. Not good enough."

He reached swiftly for the door handle, pulled the door open, and with a wave and a falsetto "keep me up to date" he strode across the floor to the lift. Ready for his brief journey back to the isolated luxury of the C.C.U's twelfth floor.

Craig thrust himself immediately out of the low, soft chair, as Liam grabbed for the door handle, pulling himself vertical.

Craig watched him ruefully. "That's why my handle keeps falling off! Nicky blames me every time."

Liam grinned and Craig knew that he was about to launch into a diatribe about Harrison, so he quickly checked that he'd gone, and then waved him on.

"When was the last time he worked a case? Twenty-ten?"

Craig shrugged, his temper subsiding as quickly as it came. "Earlier than that. He's been in the 'political wing' since I came back in two-thousand and eight, and staff posts long before that."

"Here, is the political stuff why they call him 'Teflon'?"

'Teflon' had been Terry Harrison's nickname for as long as Craig had known him -nothing bad ever stuck to him, although there'd been a few near misses. Everyone knew he was aware of his nickname, but Liam still would be in trouble if he heard, so Craig reluctantly said so. Liam just shrugged, after twenty-eight years in the force he'd said a lot worse than that and survived.

Liam's stomach rumbled loudly and they were reminded of their original destination, heading quickly back to the lift before anything else stopped them. They strolled out into the wet December sunshine, across the wide expanse of Dockland's Barrow Square and past the tram-lines in Princes' Dock Street, heading for The James' bar and a very well-earned lunch.

Chapter Six

By two o'clock Craig was accelerating down the narrow length of Pilot Street, then left onto Garmoyle Street and on towards the A55. He was heading for the pathology labs, set in a high-tech science park on the Saintfield Road.

Annette and the others had re-appeared with their booty just as they'd returned from lunch and she'd already left to interview the mysterious Kaisa. Liam was busily checking every inch of Leighton's alibi, but Craig already knew that he'd find nothing there.

He parked randomly outside the labs and pushed through the opaque PVC doors nearest pathology. He headed straight for the dissection room, knowing that John would be in there, having a sandwich and a game of solitaire in his cluttered, corner office.

He was there exactly as expected, the only change to his habits today was that he was playing chess with himself instead of solitaire, and winning. Craig drew an espresso from the machine, needing the caffeine, and sat down heavily at the desk.

"The way you sat down says that it wasn't a perfect morning."

"You mean apart from the murder?"

John smiled and his fine-boned face creased-up like an accordion. He took off his black-wire glasses, rubbing them gently on his lab coat. "Harrison?"

Craig nodded.

"You'll cope."

They both laughed at his lack of sympathy, and then lapsed into a minute's relaxed silence. From the day they'd met at school, they'd been friends, and the friendship was a real one, based on common values and wicked humour. Expedience had played its part at times too, a pre-growth-spurt John trading the protection of Craig's physicality and sportiness, for his understanding of quantum mechanics. At other times, circumstances had threatened them, such as when John had briefly dated Lucia. Thankfully, she'd dumped him after a week, saving Craig's protective brother intervention from jeopardising their close bond.

They were very different. Craig's warm, half-Italian fieriness balanced John's placid shyness perfectly and it had worked for thirty years, although Craig had lived in London for fifteen of them. It worked even better now that he was home.

John cleared the chessboard abruptly, declaring it a draw. "I was playing Des but he's on holiday until Monday. I'm not much of a challenge" adding with a smile, "I always know my opponent's next move."

Des Marsham was the lab's Head of Forensic Science and he worked closely with both of them. He was bearded, benign and a father twice over, contrasting with their terminal bachelorhood. And he was almost as eccentric as John, almost.

"Your body is very interesting, Marc."

Craig laughed loudly. To anyone else the remark would have sounded strange, but he knew exactly what John meant. Irene Leighton's body was very interesting, but until they'd solved her murder, it would feel like theirs.

"What have you found?"

John took a hurried bite of his sandwich and motioned Craig towards the cold dissection room, where their victim's body was lying covered, on the lonely, steel table. He pulled on a pair of sterile gloves, motioning Craig to do the same, and then lifted a pointer and moved to the body, gently lifting the sheet down to the woman's neck, revealing only her face.

He began reporting concisely and quickly, knowing that they were both uncomfortable in the presence of their innocent victim.

"I'll just give you the main points."

"Thanks."

"Starting from the top. There are no marks, abrasions or bruises on her face, or in the mouth, pharynx or neck. There's nothing on the scalp or in her hair. She's a generally well-nourished female of between thirty and forty."

41

"Nearer forty would fit; they'd been married for twenty years."

"OK, fine. Moving down the body - I won't lift her but there's the entry wound of a bullet on her back, just beneath the left shoulder blade, co-linear with her heart. There was no exit wound because the bullet lodged in her fifth rib anteriorly."

Craig nodded. Shot. At least it had been quick.

"What's the bullet like?"

"Unusual. Not one that I've seen before. Des is away so I'm getting the north-west labs to look at it, but it's certainly not standard issue. The bullet penetrated the trapezius muscle on her back and went through the interim structures. It ruptured the pericardium, the heart envelope, on entrance and exit, traversed the heart, and lodged anteriorly in the rib. Most of the blood tracked down internally."

"The mark we saw on her back was the entry wound? And bruising?"

"Yes, but not only that." He paused and a mix of disgust and confusion flickered across his face. "There was a tattoo at the entry site."

"What?"

"Around the wound. Healing indicates that it was about two to three days old."

Craig was taken aback; this was something new, even for them. "What sort of tattoo?"

John turned to him, the professional now. "If you let me finish, Marc, I'll show you. I have photographs of everything."

Craig nodded, conceding that he wanted everything yesterday. John smiled benignly and moved on.

"There was no sign of sexual assault or recent intercourse. She'd had at least one pregnancy, and I'd say probably more. Normal deliveries. The rest is unremarkable, apart from her right foot and left hand.

First, her hand. We saw that she had abrasions on the left knuckles and that one of her nails was torn away, almost from the nail bed. The angle of its avulsion would say that it was torn in a struggle, rather than deliberately, with pliers, for instance."

42

Craig winced, reminded of nails that he had seen 'pliered' in London, during gang disputes. It required a particular sort of callousness. At least Irene Leighton had been spared that horror. He realised that he'd been too optimistic after John's next words.

"I believe the injuries were caused in a struggle, while she was still alive, possibly to insert the note. I think the left was her dominant hand, so she used it to fight with. Her husband can confirm that."

He closed his eyes for a minute, as if preparing for the worst.

"Her feet tell the rest of the story. As well as the tattoo on her back, there's a fresh one on the sole of her right foot. We didn't notice it at the scene because she had her shoes on. It might be linked to the tattoo on her back, but it's much newer."

Craig tensed, already guessing what came next.

"It was tattooed within thirty minutes of her death, Marc." John paused and cleaned his glasses, like he always did when he was unhappy. Craig said nothing, just looked down at their victim sadly, waiting for him to restart.

"The tattoo was so fresh that it was still bleeding, while she either walked or ran barefooted onto an area of grass. It was probably the grass at Stormont, but we're awaiting confirmation of that. Her shoes were on when she was found, but her killer could easily have replaced them after she died."

Then he delivered the words that outlined Irene Leighton's final ignominy too clearly.

"The grass attached itself to the tattoo as the blood clotted."

As he talked, he lifted the sheet to reveal the sole of Irene Leighton's right foot, and Craig could clearly see the mixture of ink, blood and grass, combining to form exactly what John said next. "It's a grass tattoo, Marc."

Craig looked at him horrified; this was something that neither of them had seen before. Irene Leighton's back had been tattooed two to three days earlier, and then her right foot tattooed thirty minutes before she'd been brought to Stormont that morning. There, she

43

had either walked or run bare-footed across the grass, so that its wet blades had embedded in her fresh wound. She'd been shot and lain face-down in front of Parliament Buildings in the shape of a cross, or lain down and then shot through the back. Her shoes had been replaced, and finally, a note had been forced into her hand as she was dying. Craig shuddered. It was chilling.

Neither man spoke as they returned to John's office and sat there in silence for several minutes; thinking about Irene Leighton's suffering. Craig formulating scenarios and questions for her husband, and John wondering about the bullet.

Finally, John removed a cardboard file from his desk drawer, setting it in front of his friend. Craig stared silently at it for a moment and then removed the photographs inside, spreading them across the desk. They both stood, looking down at them. Two were of special interest. One, of the area below Irene Leighton's left scapula, the other, of the sole of her right foot. They were tattooed in the same ink and style.

The image on Irene Leighton's back was easily recognisable, a Madonna and child, a symbol of many Christian and orthodox religions. The excoriated image on her foot was less clear. John had magnified it and Craig could see that it was writing, but it wasn't made up of English words, and it wasn't in any script that he recognised.

«Я здесь и я жду».

What did it mean?

John interjected, reading his thoughts. "I'm pretty sure it's the Cyrillic alphabet. Used in Russia and some other eastern countries. I've sent it off to be translated, so we should have it back later. The design on her back is interesting, and so is the note."

Yes, they were. A Madonna and child. And the number ten. But what was the connection? And what had they to do with Stormont? Craig was more puzzled than he'd been in a long time, but at least he had more to go on than before, so he stood up quickly to go, ready for another session with their victim's husband.

"Will you be back for the translation?"

"Davy will call you. What time suits?"

"Any time before six. I've a squash game at seven, up at Queens."

"Who's your victim?"

John had competed in squash for the university and had won every match that he'd played. Every other sport had been Craig's domain, but squash wasn't called 'jet-propelled chess' for nothing, and what John lacked in strength he made up for in strategy. It was perfect for him. Craig just wished that his coordination on the court carried into normal life, but one glance at his office was coffee-stained proof that it didn't.

He immediately looked shy, and Craig knew who he was playing.

"It's Natalie Ingrams, isn't it?"

He nodded, embarrassed. Not because there was anything wrong with Natalie, but because everything was right about her. He was falling hard and Craig knew exactly how that felt.

"She's not bad at squash, you know." It was high praise, but Craig decided not to tease him, turning back to the case to save his friend's blushes.

"Davy will call you later. Liam's busy checking Leighton's alibi, and Annette's at the house interviewing the nanny." He paused for a second.

"It's unlikely that Leighton did this, John. He's been in Dublin for days."

John nodded. "He was very cut-up when he I.D.ed her. I think he really loved her. But where did he think she was all week?"

"At her mother's in Fermanagh. Of course, he could have arranged for someone else to kill her, but why, if he loved her? You were right about children, they have a son."

"I'd be surprised if there weren't more, Marc. The bracelet around her neck was the right size for a baby girl."

Like Lucia's. Craig nodded briskly and headed quickly for the door. "I'll call you later." Then he turned and smiled. "And let Natalie win a game this time."

****

The re-interview with Bob Leighton yielded some more information, although how useful it would be in finding their killer remained to be seen.

He had a son, Ben, three-years-old, a precious baby after many years of trying. He was at home with the nanny, Kaisa. But there were no other children and Leighton had never even asked his wife about the bracelet around her neck. It indicated a level of indifference that took Craig's breath away.

Yes, he'd been away for the past four days, in Dublin for the last two, back for a meeting of the Strategic Finance Foundation at Stormont last night. But he wouldn't disclose his location for the first two days; 'no-commenting' Craig into frustration. His solicitor was briefing him well and Craig couldn't insist on Leighton telling them. He wasn't under arrest. Yet.

Yes, his wife often went to stay with her elderly mother in the Fermanagh Lakelands, in a small village near Enniskillen called Belleek, where the porcelain came from. Craig knew of it, his mother had a set.

No, he hadn't spoken to her that week, but then that wasn't unusual. They often went for days without speaking, more often now that he was in Westminster.

Of course their marriage was fine, absolutely fine, why wouldn't it be? And do you really need to ask such personal bloody questions when my wife has just been killed, D.C.I. Craig? I'm a victim here too.

Craig was astounded at his selfishness, insisting on equal victimhood with a dead woman. But they'd exhausted every option they had without charging him, so after another wasted hour he headed for the lift, taking it the eight floors back to the squad. He was fitter, but not that fit yet.

Annette McElroy, his sergeant, was still out, so when he entered the floor only his personal assistant Nicky, and Davy Walsh their technical analyst, were there. He strolled past Nicky's desk quietly, praying for temporary invisibility. No such luck.

"Good afternoon, sir. Your diary says that you have half an hour free, that's if you haven't booked yourself something."

She gave him her best 'head-teacher' look for daring to fill his diary himself, a frequent sin that led to double–booking. Then she looked up at him pertly, her pretty, darkly-tanned smile holding a challenge. "Can I come in?"

Craig sighed, mock-heavily. "I haven't booked anything else, Nicky. But just give me five minutes to grab a coffee please, before you hit me with your 'list'." He said it fondly but his need for caffeine was urgent and genuine. It had been a very long hour since his last fix.

Nicky had invented her 'list' of tasks years before, and now it was infamous. It hadn't been Craig's problem until he'd inherited her full time from Terry Harrison, but now it was, and it was still a small price to pay for getting the best P.A in the Docklands C.C.U.

It detailed the tasks, dates and progress of every file that needed to be completed, every memo that hadn't been actioned, and every letter that lingered unsigned. He knew that she was planning mini-versions for Annette and Liam, and he wanted a ringside seat when she told them.

He dumped his briefcase by the floor-to-ceiling window that gave his office one of the best views in the building, and poured a coffee from his ever-hot percolator, allowing himself a brief look across Belfast's winter Docklands. The new Titanic building was shining in the mid-afternoon light, its textured silver exterior rippling like the water beside it, reflecting the City's maritime history. Further up-river he could see the redbrick Odyssey Arena, home to exhibitions and concerts, movies and clubs, gearing up for another good night. There was no shortage of entertainment in Belfast nowadays.

The morning's rain had morphed into a beautiful afternoon and it lit up Sailortown, the historic area that they worked in. Its narrow streets and old buildings nestled below the C.C.U.'s glass shard and he knew that if they could speak, three hundred years of stories, including his family's own, would come flowing out. The seasonal feeling made him want to join the pre-Christmas social scene, and all at once he felt sad at the certainty that he'd be spending the evening alone again.

His thoughts were broken by Nicky unsubtly dropping a file on his desk, and he turned away from the view and smiled at her, resigned to his fate. She sat down, crossed her festive red leggings, tucked into what could only be described as pixie boots, and handed him a warm copy of her latest list.

Craig smiled quietly at her eclectic fashion sense. He'd given up being surprised by what women wore years before and had learned not to comment long before that. Lucia and his flamboyant Italian mother Mirella had trained him well, but Nicky's style managed to raise even his eyebrows. She mixed old and new, Goth and punk and emerged with something like early Madonna. Well, whatever it was, it suited her, signposting her quirky personality even before she spoke.

She lifted her pen ostentatiously and they started. The session turned out to be like many things in life, not half as bad as he'd dreaded. It was twenty minutes of 'this is what needs to be done, and here's how we can do it' requiring only an occasional nod from him. And not for the first time he reflected that she should be running the whole police service - it would definitely be more efficient.

Craig watched her as she talked, quickly and in a loud, deep voice that belied her thirty-seven years and slight build. Dockers and sailors had inhabited Docklands for hundreds of years, but he doubted if many of them had had a louder voice than Nicky.

She could feel his attention wandering and waved a chastising finger at him. "You're not paying attention, sir. And we'll never get through this unless you do. You don't want me back tomorrow, now do you?"

48

They both laughed. She'd always behaved like his mum, despite Craig being five years older, but it had got worse since her recent holiday in Venice. Now she behaved exactly like Mirella - she'd be listening to opera next.

He was rescued by his mobile phone ringing, and with a mock-apology, he answered it gratefully. "Marc Craig."

"It's Maggie Clarke, Inspector Craig. What have you got for me?"

He didn't know whether to be surprised or annoyed at her cheek, so he opted for neutrality. "Absolutely nothing, Ms Clarke. I told you this morning that I would call you when we were ready."

"But there are other reporters sniffing around your press office, and you promised me an exclusive."

He sighed. She was right; it was never going to take the hacks long. A dead body anywhere was hard enough to keep quiet, but in a place full of five thousand civil servants, there was no hope. He shrugged silently, conceding defeat.

"OK, Ms Clarke."

"Maggie"

"Ms Clarke. Leave it with me. I'll be in touch later."

"But..."

"Later. Now, goodbye."

He clicked the phone down and looked at his watch, feigning surprise.

"Is that the time, Nicky? I have something for Davy to chase-up with John, and I need to catch Liam."

She looked up at him sceptically, tapping her long painted nail on a file. "Dr Winter has already called Davy, and Liam is still checking Mr Leighton's alibi, so we have at least ten more minutes."

He gave up on the escape, smiling, and slumped back in his chair, adjusting it very deliberately, at some length. At least he could control that.

****

The Leighton Residence. Stranmillis Road, Belfast.

Kaisa Moldeau didn't look like a nanny to Annette, well, not one that any sensible woman would want anyway. She was nothing like Mary Poppins. She was barely thirty, barely eight stone, and barely dressed at all.

When she'd first answered the door at the Leighton's opulent home on Belfast's prosperous Stranmillis Road, Annette had thought that she was going clubbing, wondering who the mini-skirt was for, certainly not the giggling three-year-old hiding behind her tanned legs. She was stunning.

Annette had always thought 'stunning' was a much overused word, beloved by women's magazines. This stunning reality star, that stunning pop star, always applied to perfectly ordinary looking girls with extraordinary egos. Stunning had never applied to any of them that she'd seen. But it did apply to the girl making the coffee.

She had white-blonde hair that looked unfeasibly natural, and a lightly tanned perfection that made Annette conscious of her own forty-something flat shoes and bitten nails. When she smiled it was through even, white teeth, and her clothes, what there were of them, were moulded to her. Irene Leighton must have been a saint or insane to hire this girl, while her husband had a pulse.

Kaisa returned with a tray of coffee and sat down opposite her, with the magnanimous charm of a woman who knows that she's perfect, faced with another one that she knows isn't.

"Can I ask you a few questions, Ms Moldeau? Just to clarify timings, and get a picture of life with Mr and Mrs Leighton?"

The girl leaned forward to pour the coffee, and although Annette couldn't see the expression in her eyes, she could have sworn that she was smiling. When she sat back again the smile was no-where to be seen, a fixed sadness in its place.

"Poor Mr Leighton, poor Mrs Leighton." Interesting order. "They are both so kind."

One more than the other, if Bob Leighton's earlier outburst was anything to go by.

"They bring me to care for leetle Ben five month ago. He is lovely boy."

"May I ask where you're from, Kaisa?"

"Ah yes, I am from Estonia. I come to Ireland six month and type, but now I love the children."

"Can you tell me when you last saw Mr and Mrs Leighton?"

"Ah yes, Mr Leighton was saw on Saturday evening. And Mrs Leighton, she leave for Mama house on Sunday noon."

Irene Leighton had been there on Sunday. She'd disappeared less than three days earlier.

"Did they often leave Ben with you?"

"No, but Mrs Leighton Mama very sick. She got phone-call, so she rush to see."

"Had either of them called you since Sunday?"

"Yes, Mr Leighton he call every day, and Mrs Leighton she call when she reach Mama, Sunday night-time."

"Not since then?"

The girl shook her head once, firmly. Irene Leighton had last called home nearly seventy-two hours before. Annette thought of her own children - no mother would leave their child that long with anyone without calling. Not unless something was stopping her.

"Weren't you surprised that she hadn't called?"

"Her Mama sick."

The girl's eyes clouded unexpectedly at the mention of...what? Mrs Leighton? No, she'd mentioned her before. Her mother? Yes, she looked sad about Mrs Leighton's mother. Annette made a mental note to interview her next and turned back to Kaisa. She was still talking in her high, light accent.

"Mr Leighton call, and I call him. He tell me take Ben to his parents for few days, so I take him Monday. There was no worry."

She smiled down at the toddler by her side, in what

seemed like genuine fondness. "Ben and I have fun, we go to park. We go for burger and chip."

Very few chips in your case, Annette thought ruefully.

****

Liam was loping back across the squad-room just as Annette returned from her interview, and by the look of him she'd had the better deal. Craig met them in the middle of the open-plan floor, beckoning both of them and Davy into his office for a briefing.

As usual, Liam and Davy took the walls. Liam for comfort, his six-feet-six making standing easier than sitting in low chairs, and Davy in imitation, always copying the detectives, but preferring the safety of his high-tech computers. Annette sat-down opposite Craig at the desk and dropped her enormous handbag by her feet. He wondered idly what she kept in there. What did any woman? It was more than his life was worth to ask.

"OK, where are we?"

As he asked the question, he rose to make coffee, holding the glass percolator out in silent offer, answered by three quick nods.

"Liam?"

Liam ran a large freckled hand down his face and sighed. "Absolutely nowhere, boss, as far as I can see." He paused for a moment before continuing. "I just checked on Leighton and he's crying again. Can't we let him go home?"

Annette looked at him, surprised, it had sounded remarkably like sympathy, not something that Liam was known for. He caught her look and continued quickly, correcting her assumption with macho defensiveness. "He's blocking the relative's room and drugs want it."

She hid her smile as Craig continued. "Did he say anything more?"

"Not a dicky-bird. Either he's a brilliant actor, or he's genuinely upset. He fell apart at the lab when the

Doc said how she died."

Craig stopped mid-pour, thinking. "When exactly did he fall apart, Liam, really fall apart? Was it when he knew it was his wife, or when John told him how she'd died? It's important."

Liam knew what he was getting at and he had noticed, but he hadn't registered its importance at the time.

"When he saw her face he went a bit pale and there were a few tears, quiet ones like. But when the Doc told him about the note and tattoos..."

Annette leaned forward, shocked. "She had tattoos, a lady like Irene Leighton?"

Liam turned to her, half-amused. "Not the tramp-stamp type."

Now Craig was puzzled. "What's a tramp-stamp, when it's at home?"

"You know those ones women get on their lower backs, flashing them when they bend over, trying to look cool." He snorted. "Mostly middle-aged housewives as far as I can see." He paused and then grinned cheekily. "Here, Annette, have you got one?"

She bristled immediately. Craig wasn't sure if it was being called middle-aged that did it, or solidarity for women everywhere, but before he could admonish Liam, Annette had let rip, taking them all by surprise. Their mild rivalry had definitely been increasing lately.

"And you're the arbiter of good taste now, are you? Who died and made you King?"

"I'm just saying that you might be a secret raver for all we know." He looked at Davy conspiratorially. "Take my word for it, lad. It's the quiet ones you have to watch."

Before she could retaliate, Craig shot them both a look that said 'zip-it' and handed out the coffees, sitting down thoughtfully behind the desk.

"Go on, Liam. What did Leighton do when John told him?"
"Buckled completely and started crying. We had to get him a chair. It took ages to calm him down, and all my powers of diplomacy."

Even Davy, their gentle computer expert snorted at that one and Craig smiled. Liam wasn't known for either his diplomatic skills or his political correctness, and after his 'tramp-stamp' comment, there was another equality course looming in his future.

"At what point did he buckle? The shot, the tattoos or the note?" Knowing that John would have staged the information very precisely.

Liam looked at him, confused for a second, as if the distinctions hadn't occurred to him. And they hadn't, at the time. But his powers of observation and recall were legendary and they didn't disappoint him now. He closed his eyes for a second, ordering his thoughts, and then started.

"When we went in, the first thing that happened was that the Doc exposed her face, and Leighton cried a bit and I.D.ed her. Then the Doc told him that her death had been caused by shooting, and he cried a bit more, but it was still for her at that point. You know what I mean? He was still crying for her, not himself."

Craig and Annette nodded at him; they'd seen the difference many times. Tears for a loved one had a very different feel to tears of self-pity, and to tears of fear.

Liam kept going, his face screwed up in concentration, remembering. "Then...the Doc took us into the office and told us about the tattoos. He didn't show us, just told us, but right then Leighton's eyes widened. I mean really widened, like one of those cartoons where the eyes pop out."

"Fear?"

"Nope, not fear exactly. More shock I guess. Aye, shock. But he looked a bit puzzled too. Until the Doc showed us a copy of the note – that was when he really lost it. Totally freaked-out."

They were unconsciously leaning forward, awaiting Liam's punch line.

"Did he definitely react less to hearing about the tattoos, than to the number ten?"

Liam thought for a moment, Craig was right; there had been a major difference.

"He howled about the tattoos all right, but it was

54

definitely when he saw the note that he buckled. He was scared rigid, boss, and he didn't look puzzled by anything after that. He just wanted to get the hell out of there."

"And did he?"

"Aye, he bolted out of the office saying he needed some air, and by the time I caught him he was on the phone. He wouldn't tell me who to...and I couldn't make him."

Liam's last comment was said with regret and they all smiled. Liam never crossed the line but his opinions on suspects' rights were well known.

Craig thought for a moment. The '10' on the note had scared Leighton stiff. Why? Ten what?

"How is he now?"

"Nursing a coffee and scared stupid."

Craig nodded. The tattoos might be a clue to their killer's identity, but the figure ten linked to Leighton himself.

"I think the tattoos are significant – they link to the I.D. of our killer. But the ten means something special to him, something that he's afraid of."

"His brief won't let him answer anything."

Craig nodded. "I'll try again when we finish. He may not have killed her but he definitely knows who did, or why. OK, thanks Liam. Annette?"

Annette looked up from the file on her lap and started reporting, by the book. She was efficient and intuitive and Craig knew that it wouldn't be long before she was ready for her inspector exams, then she'd really keep Liam in line. That's if he was allowed to keep them both. Maybe if he became a superintendent?

He was torn from his thoughts by her words. "Kaisa's the nanny. She seems nice enough, came over from Estonia six months ago, and she seems very fond of the little boy, Ben. But I wouldn't have her as my nanny, that's for sure." She pursed her lips and looked at Craig. "Far too pretty. The girl should be on a catwalk."

Liam and Davy both leaned forward, staring at Annette's notes, as if a picture of the nanny would miraculously appear.

"Here, boss, you should have let me interview her. Seniority has to have some perks."

Craig smiled ruefully. "After your tramp-stamp comment, you'll be interviewing men for the next six months." He turned back to Annette. "Did you get the sense that there was anything between her and Leighton?"

Annette smiled. Senses were her territory, honed by years of nursing before she'd entered the force. "Possibly. She didn't give anything away, but there were lots of phone-calls from Leighton when the wife was away, ostensibly about the boy.

In the four days that he was away, Ben was at Leighton's parents for two of them and Ms Moldeau wouldn't be pinned down as to where she was for those days, especially on Monday night. There were some vague comments about shopping, and visiting friends, but nothing solid. I'd be surprised if she wasn't with a man for at least part of that time. I suppose that it could have been Leighton."

"Couldn't have been him, boss. He was in Dublin 'til last night."

"When did she collect the boy from his grandparents, Annette?"

"This morning about eleven, sir."

"Thanks. Where did you say she was from again?"

"Estonia."

Something was gnawing at him, as if he'd forgotten something. "Was her accent strong?"

"Yes, sir. Very, in fact. Is that important?"

Craig looked thoughtful. "I think it is, but I'm not sure why yet. We'll come back on that. Thanks, Annette. Davy?"

Davy Walsh was their tall, handsome twenty-five-year-old, reed-thin, technical expert. He was an EMO, and his height, uber-tight dark clothes and black floppy hair made him look like long black chimney-brush, soon to be adorned with piercings by the sound of it. He had a wicked sense of humour and an occasional stutter on 's' and 'w', turning both to his own benefit when swearing. Nicky and Annette mothered him mercilessly and he loved it.

"Dr W...Winter e-mailed over the photos of the tattoos earlier. The text on Mrs Leighton's foot has just been translated, and I've got information on the tattoo on her back."

Annette looked at him quickly and Craig realised that she didn't have the full detail. He nodded a promise to brief her later, and waved Davy on.

"The one on the victim's back is of the Madonna and child, a common icon in Christian and Orthodox religions, Greek, Russian etc. But if you look at the images." He handed out copies of the photographs as he spoke. "You can s...see that the child is overly large in comparison to the Madonna."

He was right, and neither Craig nor John had noticed it.

"Is that important, Davy?"

"In the context of other things, yes, it might be s...sir. I'll come back to that in a moment."

Craig smiled to himself at Davy's confident delivery. When he'd started with them a year before, he'd been so shy that he would hardly look at Craig. Now he was flying.

"The other tattoo, the one from her right foot." Annette looked shocked again, but Davy kept talking.

"That image contains text, as you can s... see." He pointed to the photograph of Cyrillic text in front of them. The '«Я здесь и я жду»' that Craig had seen earlier.

"The translator came back earlier than expected."

Liam was puzzled, but interested. "What does it say?"

"It's Cyrillic and translates as 'I'm here and I'm waiting' "

"What the hell does that mean?" Liam hated anything cryptic, far too much like hard work.

"You could look at it literally, that they're w...waiting for her, but there's another link between the text and the tattoo on her back. And maybe with the position of her body too."

Davy took their silence as assent, and continued. Craig was already making the connection.

"The Madonna and Child is known as an apotropaic, intended to fend off evil, as is a cross, and s...she was laid out in the shape of one. They're both common in eastern countries. The letters are from the Cyrillic alphabet, used in Russia and a few other eastern countries. I can narrow that down for you later. But w...with the Madonna and cross, and the Cyrillic text, I think we're looking at the killer coming from either Russia or an eastern country. Perhaps one that used to be part of the s...soviet republic."

Liam and Annette stared at him open-mouthed.

"The phrase 'I'm here and I'm w...waiting' is commonly used by a criminal group known as the Vory v Zakone, usually from Russia."

Craig nodded, he'd heard of them. In a recent movie he'd seen, the actor Viggo Mortensen had played a Vor, covered in tattoos. But what were they doing in Northern Ireland?

"They often wear crucifixes called Dukhs to ward off danger. Again a cross, like the position of the body. And the large child is used to indicate a criminal w...who has been one from an early age."

Davy stopped, waiting for their questions, but they all remained silent, stunned and thinking. Questions ran quickly through Craig's mind. What did the Vory v Zakone want in Northern Ireland? And what did they want with a quiet housewife like Irene Leighton? They'd left her body at the seat of Northern Ireland's government, so was it a political statement? An act of defiance by political dissidents? Were the Vors working with local terrorists?

He shook his head thoughtfully. No, this didn't feel like political dissent, this felt a criminal smokescreen, and he knew immediately that Bob Leighton was up to his political eyes in it. He leapt to his feet and beckoned Liam to follow him, throwing "Thanks a million Davy, well done" over his shoulder, and they headed for the second floor relative's room and another, much more pointed conversation.

Chapter Seven

The re-interview proved completely fruitless, with Leighton 'no commenting' to every question, particularly concerning the number ten. But one thing was certain, he was petrified, and not of them.

His alibi for the time of his wife's death had been verified. He'd arrived in Dublin on Sunday evening, before his wife had called home from her mothers. The previous thirty-six hours unaccounted-for were too early to be important, so they had nothing to charge him with. They had no choice but to let him go, with uniformed surveillance.

Craig wasn't worried. Liam would find out where Leighton had been for the lost time, and where he was going to next. He was an expert in exposing people's secrets; he's missed his vocation as a tabloid journalist.

By the time they returned to the squad it was nearly five and Annette beckoned Craig over, confirming that Ben Leighton had been with his grandparents since Monday afternoon. But she was no nearer to pinning down Kaisa Moldeau's whereabouts since then, including at the time of Irene Leighton's murder.

Nicky appeared unexpectedly beside them, coughing her presence loudly, a mannerism that always indicated bad news. "Superintendent Harrison has called a press conference for six-thirty, sir"

Craig looked at her, immediately knowing the briefing's agenda. Harrison was desperate to vindicate Leighton and feather his own political nest. Well, he'd be doing it without him; it was far too early to involve the media. Now he needed a viable excuse for absenting himself.

He went into his office and swung his chair round to face the river. The seagulls were having a party outside, swooping and cawing in front of the window like it was Christmas. He laughed to himself, remembering that in three weeks' time it would be. He always lost track of time when he was preoccupied, and it had been a busy few months for murders.

The day was abnormally 'soft' for the time of year, warm and wet; Northern Ireland's climate was definitely changing. Global-cyclical or global-warming, who knew, but the guaranteed winter snow and summer light of his childhood seemed to be morphing into a milder year-round cloud. He missed the snow.

An impudent gull had perched on the narrow sill outside and was pecking lazily at his window, with no hope of access. Craig smiled at it. The windows were heavy-duty and never opened; the force ever fearful that they'd throw themselves out after a bad day. He'd need a bungee rope for every murder.

He stared past his companion and towards the sky, searching for inspiration. What were the Vors doing in Belfast? Northern Ireland had eastern immigrants like everywhere in Europe, but they'd had no briefings to suggest that the Vory v Zakone were part of that population. Davy was putting out the feelers in serious crime. If they were here, it was odds-on that the drugs, vice or fraud squads would know about it already.

He smiled, remembering London, where practically everyone was an immigrant from somewhere, himself included. It made for a more tolerant society and Belfast could only benefit from that. He always felt protective towards anyone new; it was hard learning new ways. He wondered vaguely if Kaisa Moldeau found it a challenge, his mother Mirella certainly had.

She'd come from Rome, the Eternal City, forty-three years before, when she'd married his Belfast father, Tom. It had been a huge sacrifice, only made bearable by her twice-yearly visits home and the constant stream of Italian cousins visiting throughout their childhood, improving their rusty Italian.

They'd met when his scientist father was presenting a paper in Venice, in the same conference building where his mother had been a pianist. And, as she'd never tired of telling them, it was love at first sight, or 'amore a prima vista' as she much preferred to say. He smiled to himself; they were an old married couple now, living in the quaint town of Holywood, 'home of Rory McIlroy', one of Northern Ireland's favourite golfers.

He shook himself back to business. He still felt that he was missing something, but what? After a minute chasing the thought he gave up to try again later, knowing that he should return the phone message that he'd received earlier. He hesitated for a moment and then quickly lifted his mobile before he changed his mind. Not from any lack of inclination, but from caution.

It was answered in three rings and the familiar clear Anglo-Irish voice of Julia McNulty answered warily, recognising his number.

"D.C.I. Craig. Hello."

"Hello, Julia." Hoping that she would follow his informal lead. She didn't.

"Thank you for returning my call, D.C.I. Craig. Would it be possible to get a copy of the Adams' file?"

He knew that he deserved her frostiness, he'd hurt her. She was a beautiful woman and he'd foolishly risked a dinner that could have led to more, if his past hadn't prevented it. But it had.

She knew why. She understood that he still had unfinished business with his ex-fiancée Camille. She understood, but that didn't mean that she was happy about it.

He picked up the conversation from her lead and it became a formal call, until with all the business done, she made to go. He stopped her, gently.

"Julia, I'm sorry that I hurt you."

Her reply came quickly, and coldly. "I can assure you that you didn't." But he had.

"I just didn't want to embroil you in my mess, you know that."

"I'm fully aware of the facts, sir."

Craig could feel his frustration rising. "Oh, for God's sake Julia, talk to me."

"We have nothing to talk about, sir."

"Yes, we have. We have to work together and we can't do that if we're barely civil." He looked at his watch and made a swift decision. "I'll be in Limavady in an hour, and I'd like a meeting, D.I McNulty."

61

There was silence for a moment. He hated pulling rank, but he knew that she couldn't refuse to meet a senior officer. Finally she answered him, slowly, and feigning indifference.

"As you wish, sir. I can do five-thirty. Now I really have to go." And with a quiet click, she'd gone.

And without even planning it, he'd found his perfect exit from Harrison's press fiasco, and from Maggie Clarke's demanding gaze.

****

The Lab.

The dissection room was always cold, but John rarely felt it, much more interested in the dead's answers than his own comfort. Davy had phoned through his findings on the photographs five minutes before and they fitted perfectly with John's on the bullet. Now he just had to work out the logistics.

Normally Des would look at bullets and trajectories, but he was on leave, and John didn't want the north-west having all the fun, so at that moment he was in Des' lab on Des' computer, playing with Des' programmes, and setting up a spectacular light show for Marc Craig to solve.

****

Parliament Buildings.

Joe Watson hadn't believed it when he'd been told, dismissing it angrily as Stormont gossip. The grapevine running away with itself again. Then he'd tried her mobile, listening anxiously as it rang and rang, and then cut to her sweet, kind voice on the answerphone, entreating him to leave a message.

He'd left three now with no reply, and he thought vaguely that the police would soon know that he'd called. But he didn't care, not even a little, unable to shake off the image that while he'd been having the best sex of his life; Irene had been somewhere alone and terrified. He reached for the whisky bottle and poured himself another hit, trying to drown the pain. But he couldn't. The mother of his child was dead.

Chapter Eight

The Leighton Residence.

Bob Leighton wasn't hanging around. Once they'd told him about the note, he'd known exactly what was happening, and he wasn't waiting about for the finale. He looked around the bedroom that he'd shared for years, with the woman that he'd killed as surely as if he'd pulled the trigger. His eyes filled with sudden tears.

He sat on the edge of the bed with his face in his hands for a moment, remembering her. Her warm laugh and her shining fair hair. The scent that she'd always worn, that smelled of raspberries and summer, all year round. He smiled at the memory of her touch while tears ran freely down his cheeks, and then he sobbed rawly that their son would never feel that gentle touch again.

They'd loved each other, really loved each other, but he'd buried it under career and politics. Under the years of his infertility and trying desperately for a baby, nearly breaking them, in every way possible. None of it was her fault, none of it. She'd stayed as kind and loving as the woman that he'd married twenty years before. Never demanding, never scolding, and never giving him a reason to be cruel. But he hadn't needed a reason, it was just who he was. He loved power.

With the power came more stress and easing it with drugs, and now, what? Kaisa? He would never have done anything while Irene was still alive, but now? He needed warmth and comfort and he couldn't stop thinking about her. But he couldn't tell her yet; too soon, it would be wrong. People would think that he'd never loved Irene. But he did.

He kept packing and thinking, now and again lifting one of his wife's trinkets, tempted to put them in his case as a keepsake, already wearing her wedding ring to remember her by. He needed to get away, just for a few days. To think, and find a way out of this mess.

He'd be back, Ben needed him. Of course he'd be back.

Just then, a telephone rang and it took him a moment to decide, landline or mobile? Then he reached into his jacket pocket, and looked at the flashing screen. No number, it could be the office. He hastily pushed another shirt into his case and pressed 'answer'.

The man's voice wasn't one that he recognised. The accent was so heavy that at first he didn't understand what he'd said, so he asked him to repeat it. He understood him clearly enough the second time.

"You bought the grass for her, Mr Leighton. And you will have it yourself soon."

He froze and drops of sweat formed urgently on his upper lip. Then he shouted down the phone. "Who are you?" Silence. "Leave me alone, for God's sake. I don't have it."

"You must find it, or we will find you."

"But it wasn't my fault."

"You were hired and you failed. Then you got greedy. Ten, Mr Leighton, by Saturday. This is the last call that we will make."

The line went dead, and Bob Leighton gasped wildly for air, his throat closing over in fear. He sat down heavily on the bed, coughing, and completely out of his depth. Who the hell were these people? What sort of people had Joanne Greer involved him with?

He grabbed for his phone and was just about to dial her number when there was a soft knock on the door. It opened slowly inwards, revealing Kaisa and his toddler son. Ben's tear-streaked face looked exactly how he felt.

Kaisa ushered the boy towards his father with a sad look. "He is missing his Mama." Oh God, so am I, Ben. He put the phone down and lifted his baby son urgently into his arms, hugging him tight, to comfort both of them. Kaisa sat down primly on the bedroom chair and stared at the chaos of clothes.

"Are you going on other trip?"

He answered her quietly so as not to frighten the boy. "Yes. I need to go to London for a couple of days.

But when I'm back I'd like us to talk, Kaisa...about the future."

She smiled to herself quietly. Men often said such things to her, always talking about their future. She wasn't being arrogant, it was just the truth. But she looked at him faux-questioningly anyway; it didn't look good to be too confident. His quick look answered her question, and she smiled, gently extricating Ben from his father's arms.

"Shall we go to park, Ben? We can feed ducks. And then, when Papa is back, we can talk about the future..."

****

Parliament Buildings.

"Thank you for coming, Mr Cabot. I know it's rare for a Minister to volunteer for a meeting with the Commissioner."

Joe Watson laughed nervously and gestured the round-faced Commissioner for Public Conduct to take a seat. John Cabot looked at him curiously. He'd been surprised when Watson's staff had called his office; politicians normally avoided him like the plague, keen to hide their bad habits from his scrutiny.

But when he'd heard why, he'd been eager to meet. He'd gathered together the papers that he'd been preparing for months, in anticipation of just such a moment. As far as he was concerned, this meeting was four years overdue, but the retirement of one Minister often opened doors for another to come along, with fresh eyes, and hopefully more honesty. Now all of his preparation would come to fruition and with Joe Watson's help he would expose a national fraud that would give the Chronicle column inches for months to come.

****

Bob Leighton finally made the call to Joanne Greer just as he was about to board at Belfast City Airport. "You cow! My wife is dead because of you. Who the hell are involved with?"

Greer hissed down the phone at him. "I warned you that London would get involved."

He shook his head in disgust. "You set some bastards on me, and now they've killed Irene! She had nothing to do with the deal. She didn't even know about it! You've left my son without his mother, you bitch, and I'm going to kill you when I get back."

"I think you'll find that *you'd* already killed her, Bob, the moment we paid you half a million pounds."

"Five hundred grand! You killed my wife for a poxy five hundred grand!"

He was yelling as loudly as he could in an airport lounge without being arrested, and the coolness of her voice was infuriating him even further.

"Now some gangster calls to tell me I owe them *ten* million. *Ten million!* Where the hell do they get that from? Who are these bastards?"

Joanne ignored the question. "Your job was to keep the Minister sweet, Bob. All you had to do was finesse the Horizon Project through the sub-committees and we'd have been home and dry by now. But you couldn't even manage that-"

He interrupted defensively. "Ron Burgess was fine. We got the approval through without a murmur. But then he had to go and retire halfway through, leaving Watson in charge. Joe Watson is a different kind of Minister. He spotted that the contracts were bogus. You're embezzling public funds, Joanne-"

She cut him off in a cold voice. "And you. Let's remember that you've had half a million a year since thousand and eight. It all adds up, Bobby. Watson has been interfering in everything since he joined S.F.F. but you've had nearly a year to sort him out and you've done bugger-all. Now he's going to blow things wide open. Did you really think that we'd do nothing? We've got millions invested in this!"

"Who the hell is 'we'? You said you were in this with Declan and he would never have sanctioned killing Irene."

Joanne laughed caustically. "You're right; my darling husband's far too big a wimp for that. But did you really think he was the backer? Declan knows nothing about this. This is *my* project."

"Then who's 'we'?"

"No one you would know. The money came from my contact in London; not someone you want to mess with. I warned you last week that I'd call London."

His panic rose. "But you said that you'd give me a week! And I thought that you meant Declan was in London. Christ, Joanne, whoever these people are, they're killers! You have to call them off me."

"Sorry. It's out of my hands now." Her tone said that she wasn't sorry at all. "I sank a fortune into Horizon, and so did our backer. We had it perfect. Approval, dummy contracts, everything ready to go. Just two more months then we'd have made millions and walked away scot-free...If you'd just done your part with Watson."

"Watson can't be bought! I've tried. Believe me I've tried."

"Not hard enough! He'll be bought, Bob, everyone has a price. We're working on him right now and we'll do it. But you're out. You're out and you're dead unless you come up with the ten million."

"Fuck! Where do you think I'll get that? Where do you get the ten from, anyway?"

"Salary, plus what you stole from us to shove up your nose."

Leighton gasped audibly and she laughed.

"Did you really think that I wouldn't find out about the coke? There's nothing you do that I don't know about. Then there's the money that my contact stands to lose if Watson goes public. Ten million should just about cover it."

There was silence for a moment, and then she spoke again, sarcastically.

"At the airport, are we, Bob? I do hope you're not trying to run?"

"I'm going to London to try to borrow the money, you avaricious bitch."

"Good. I'm glad to hear it. I look forward to seeing you when you get back on Friday."

"How did you know I was coming back on Friday?"

"You can't hide from us anywhere, Bobby. Remember that."

****

The Lab.

John Winter stood by the ballistics' lab door taking one last look at his light show. He'd finally worked it out. The bullet was identified, ready to be matched with the rifle, if they ever found it. He corrected himself mentally, when, not if. And now the bullet's angle and speed of trajectory had been calculated to within half a millimetre.

He knew that he should be pleased with himself for succeeding, even once, in Des' domain, but all it showed was that they were dealing with a professional. And if they'd been that professional in their aim, they'd be equally professional in their disappearance. Marc had his work cut out on this one.

John shrugged, resigned to the knowledge that too many murders were never solved. Then he smiled. Craig's fail rate was much lower than average. He'd find their killer, if they could be found. He flicked off the light and left the safety of his clean, sterile world, to get ready for his squash match, and the much messier, less safe one of romance. He felt nervous already.

****

Joe Watson pulled off the Bangor Road into the layby outside the high wooden gates of his detached home and the gates opened slowly inwards. He was grateful that they'd been shut, needing the ten-second delay before he pasted on the smile of a devoted husband, one that he'd have to wear all evening.

He could already hear Caitlin's kitten heels crunching down the path, accompanied by the bark of

69

her small terrier, knowing that his own giant Airedale would be resting sensibly by the fire in the cool December evening. His thoughts ran frantically through the day's events, crushing-in one last moment of remembering.

Remembering what? The woman that he'd always loved but never owned, not since they'd been young, and free. Before life had ground them both down. Remembering the promise that he'd made to her; a promise that he had really meant, but that she had broken. Remembering their child; the happy, sweet girl whose loss had broken them both, and put a wall between them that he'd eventually been too weak to climb.

The gate was open far too soon and he looked through the car windscreen at his attractive wife, whom he loved, but obviously not enough. He smiled at her in reflex, but without feeling, hardly seeing her at all. And then he drove in for another evening of charades, counting backwards to Irene, and forwards to next Monday night.

****

The M2 Motorway.

Craig turned up the C.D. player and accelerated up the M2, nearing Limavady, hoping that he'd soon feel better about the call that he'd just taken. Nicky hadn't wanted to phone him, but Susan Butler, Harrison's austere P.A. had insisted upon it, and no one sensible ever argued with Mrs Butler. He smiled at the certainty that Nicky was already planning her revenge.

He wasn't annoyed by the call, just irritated with Harrison. And astounded that he thought it was acceptable to summon him back from Limavady just to placate a bunch of journalists. As if he was really going to come! Maybe he'd call the Chief Constable and accept the superintendent's post. At least it would stop Harrison being his boss anymore.

He mused for a few miles further, against a

background of 'Run' by Snow Patrol and then turned sharp right into Limavady's Victorian police headquarters, flashing his badge at the lad on the gate, and parking near the building's low front entrance.

He took the three flights of stairs two at a time and arrived at the long office corridor, still breathing normally. The workouts were definitely paying off, time to add in a few weights. He slowed his pace, eventually reaching Julia McNulty's office. But before he could knock, the door opened inwards, sharply, and she stood in front of him with a face like thunder, ready to rant.

"I've just had Harrison's office on, shouting about you 'coming to see me for coffee' when you should be at some press conference in Belfast. Thanks very much for getting me the blame for whatever you're up to!"

The words flew out without punctuation, in her crisp light accent, and Craig couldn't stop himself from smiling, both happy to see her and amused by the tirade. He looked down affectionately at the absurdly pretty, absurdly angry woman in front of him.

A red curl from her chignon was straying onto her cheek, like an escaping prisoner and he wanted to reach forward and stroke it back, already knowing that the action would earn him a slap. He wouldn't do it anyway, it wasn't fair on her, but he gifted himself a moment longer, drinking in her beauty.

Her soft blue eyes were on fire, set against flushed cheeks sprinkled lightly with glitter-fine freckles. His eyes moved unbidden down her fine up-turned nose to her curved lips, remembering their kisses that evening months ago, and his overwhelming desire to repeat the event. He was dragged rudely from his reverie by the sheer volume of her next words.

"And then, she had the cheek to tell me to send you right back. As if I'm a bloody delivery service!"

He slipped easily past her through the gap by the door, and entered the office, lifting a seat from the wall and seating himself calmly at her desk. She turned around quickly, incensed by his cheek, and sat down proprietarily in her chair. Her office.

71

She stared at him with a mixture of anger and affection, trying desperately to hide the latter, while he didn't at all.

"Mind if I help myself to coffee?" The words were only a courtesy, he was already doing it. He returned to his seat and took a sip of the too-hot drink, knowing immediately that she'd brewed it fresh for his visit, and encouraged by the sign.

"Don't worry about Mrs Butler; she's just letting off steam."

She half-smiled, and then stopped herself, determined not to be charmed. She was ex-army and war had been declared between them two months ago. She was in 'no surrender' mode today.

"Why did you ask for this meeting, D.C.I. Craig?"

He didn't answer, just smiled at her infuriatingly and she continued, flustered. "I'm very busy, and it seems that you are too." She sniffed. "Although you obviously take your duties less seriously than I do."

She'd scored and he bristled, then he spotted what she was doing. He'd read Sun Tzu's 'Art of War' as well. He controlled his temper and leaned forward, placing his cup on the desk slowly, and as he relaxed, so did she and they fell into a less hostile silence.

Finally, he spoke. "The conference is a token to appease the press, so that they can write something bland and justify their own oxygen. The D.C.S. is just flexing his muscles."

She interrupted him quickly. "So are you, and I'm getting caught in the middle. I..."

He held both hands up signalling truce and she stopped abruptly, letting him speak. "We caught a tricky case this morning that involves politicians, so Harrison is covering his back. That's all the press conference was about, appeasing the local hacks." She could see him getting angry now. "We don't have anything solid yet, and he shouldn't be going near the press, so I'm damned if I'm supporting it by standing beside him while he name-drops."

"That's all they wanted you back for?"

"Yes."

She smiled at him, then realised that she had, and turned away abruptly, towards her computer. She stared at the screen as she spoke. "Why did you want to meet me, D.C.I. Craig? I'm in a hurry to get home."

She realised immediately that her tone was too abrupt for a senior officer, even one who'd hurt her, and she rushed for a balance, overbalancing on the way.

"My brother is here. I promised to cook...We don't get to see each other often...we..."

Craig could see her getting flustered and rescued her, kindly. "Is he older or younger?"

"Younger...by seven years. He's a doctor at Peter's Hill in Enniskillen."

Then she realised that they were being friendly again, and stopped. He wasn't her friend, he was her senior officer and her...What? Possible past lover. Except he wasn't. Possible future? No, she couldn't allow herself to think that, or hope that. Back to business.

"Why did you want to meet with me, D.C.I. Craig?"

Craig sighed. She wasn't going to make this easy for him, and half of him knew that she shouldn't. So he pulled out the copy of the file that they both knew he could have posted to her, and they had their meeting. Their relationship would have to wait for another day.

Chapter Nine

Joe Watson stared at the clock tiredly. Six a.m. He still had an hour. He glanced at the empty space beside him, relieved. Caitlin had left for Pilates and he had the place to himself, just him and the dogs. He needed the time to think.

Not about Irene. No. He couldn't let himself think about her, or he'd get nothing done. Except...He wondered if he should send flowers to the funeral home. Would that be OK? Or hypocritical when her husband and he were political rivals? But did that really matter when the flowers were for Irene? For them. For Rebecca.

He pushed his emotions down and thought about Tuesday night's S.F.F. meeting, and yesterday's with John Cabot. He'd been shocked on Tuesday, although in retrospect he really shouldn't have been. Everyone had known that Ron Burgess was an idiot, and a crooked idiot to boot, there was no surprise about that.

But that the whole Foundation had been fooled, that had shocked him. Politicians and business people together, all denying that there was anything wrong with Horizon. Honestly Minister. That was where he and doubt had parted company, he was certain that at least some members of S.F.F. were up to their ears in fraud.

A last vain hope rose in him, maybe he was wrong, maybe all the contracts were kosher, maybe Horizon would be built and this was all just him being suspicious. But as soon as it rose, the hope died again. This was fraud on a massive scale: he knew it. And the Commissioner for Public Conduct agreed with him.

****

The Lab.

As Craig followed John down the ballistics' lab corridor, he could have sworn that he saw him saunter.

Yes, there it was again, a definite spring in his step. He decided that banter was in order.

"Good squash game, John?"

Winter took the bait innocently. "Yes actually, it was. I won four games to one. Natalie wasn't too pleased, though."

John was happy and Craig was pleased for him. As long as he'd known him he'd never had a serious relationship, and he'd never understood why. He was kind and chivalrous, a New Age Knight in every way, and attractive, Lucia had told him so. So Craig could only put it down to; wrong girl, wrong time or 'the job', plumping for the last.

Few women would or could tolerate their twenty-four-seven sense of duty, but Natalie seemed different, she never complained about John working too hard. She was a surgeon and even Craig didn't work the gruelling hours that they did. John's voice broke through his thoughts, his next words surprising him.

"I really like her, Marc."

Craig was astounded, it was the closest that John had ever got to saying he was in love. He was pleased he'd confided in him.

"She's great, John."

John hesitated. "I know, but I'm...I'm not great about showing it. I don't really know how. Now she...she wants to meet my family."

John had been the much-loved only child of parents in their forties when he was born. They were academics, bemused by children and childhood generally, while unconditionally adoring their small son. But he had grown up shy and solitary, until he'd met Marc Craig.

After that, he'd never been away from the Craig's lively house, with his parent's blessing, relieved that their overly adult twelve-year-old was finally behaving like a child. Now that both of his parents were dead, the Craigs were the only family that he had.

Craig thought of something. Tomorrow was Friday and that meant that his mother would insist on the full Italian family dinner, plus guests.

"Bring Natalie to my folk's tomorrow evening."

An immediate look of gratitude crossed John's face, followed by one of abject terror. Mirella Craig was quite an experience, even for him. Craig laughed, knowing exactly what he was thinking, and warmed to the idea.

"It'll be great. Natalie and my mum will get on brilliantly, you wait."

John looked at him warily, and then said hopefully. "Will Lucia be there? Natalie and she could chat."

Craig's younger sister could chat to anybody, at length, about anything. She worked for a charity and cared about everyone, passionately, so he was certain they would find plenty of common ground. He laughed at John's anxiety.

"Don't worry. Lucia will keep Mum in check. And she won't let her ask Natalie her intentions towards you."

John smiled nervously, that was exactly what he was worried about. Since his parents had died, Mirella had acted as if she was his mother as well, and they both knew that was exactly what she'd ask.

"At least it'll make a change from her pushing me to get married."

"Oh, thanks Marc." Then he smiled, blushing slightly and warming to the idea. "I'd love to come. But let me ask Natalie before you tell your mum."

"Sure." Craig turned briskly back to business. "What are we going to look at?"

He was puzzled. They were outside the ballistics' lab, not John's usual habitat. John smiled at him conspiratorially, back in professional mode and feeling much more comfortable.

"Well, you know that I sent the bullet up to the north-west for typing yesterday?"

"Did they manage it?"

"I'll tell you about that in a minute. But in Des' absence I thought I'd have a go at the trajectory myself."

Craig looked at him, surprised. It wasn't like John to leave his comfort zone; Natalie was obviously good for him.

"Go on."

"I've watched him do it plenty of times, so I worked-up the bullet's pathway, using the injuries, angle of entry and wind speed, and ..."

Craig interrupted him kindly. He was enjoying John's preamble but he had a meeting with Maggie Clarke at ten. She'd caught him on his way back from Limavady, furious after Harrison's press briefing. He'd wasted all their time by calling them in when he'd nothing to tell them, just as Craig had predicted. Now she was holding Craig to his deal so he'd grudgingly allocated her thirty minutes this morning.

He urged John on. "Can you show me, John? You know I'm better with images than words."

John startled, looking at his watch. They'd been talking for thirty minutes. "God, is that the time? Sorry."

Without further delay, he threw open the lab's heavy white door. The ballistics' lab was very different to the dissection room, with an area set aside for test-shooting bullets to match barrel markings, and another full room of laptops and screens, winking randomly. John moved quickly to a laptop in the corner.

"I'll give you a quick run through the simulation. Then tell you about the bullet."

"Thanks."

He flicked on a laptop as they spoke and it booted up, to display a simulation of Irene Leighton's shooting on the wall plasma.

"The simulation allows for the wind-speed recorded at City Airport yesterday morning, so it should be accurate. We've also allowed for the victim's height and weight, and the fact that she dropped forward when she was hit. There was no backward transit of the body on impact that we can determine - that's confirmed by the lack of blood spatter."

His words were clinical but the sadness in his eyes wasn't. Craig nodded him on, thinking.

"I've also taken into account the size and shape of the entry wound, which was slightly angled, consistent

77

with her turning to her left just before the impact. It's common for people to turn to their dominant side and I believe that she was left-handed"

Craig interrupted, nodding. "Her husband confirmed it."

"Good. There was no exit wound because the bullet embedded in the fifth rib anteriorly, but even if we didn't have the bullet the type of entry wound made it likely to be a .33 calibre." He paused and looked at Craig. "It's likely that it was travelling at over eight hundred metres per second, Marc."

"What?"

"It was a sniper round. This was a professional job."

Both men were quiet for a moment, while John let Craig take the information in. Irene Leighton, housewife and mother had been the victim of a professional hit.

"Using the speed and angle of entry, we know the likely location of the shoot-site." He flicked on a map of the area surrounding Stormont, and indicated. "I can get it more accurately for you, later."

Craig stared incredulously at the leafy streets around the Stormont Estate. Someone had shot Irene Leighton from one of them.

Something struck John. "Marc, there's no way that she would have walked voluntarily into an open space to be shot. She'd been kidnapped and tattooed; she must have known that they weren't going to let her go. So why would she go without much more of a struggle?"

"But how would she have known, John? They were taking her to Stormont for God's sake. A public place, somewhere that she was completely familiar with from her husband's job. They might have told her that they were releasing her."

"Bastard."

"Bastards. There was more than one of them."

"How do you know?"

Craig spoke quietly. "One of them must have taken her to the lawn by the steps and kept her there, long enough for the other to shoot."

"Do you think that the proximity of Carson's statue is significant?"

Craig startled, realising that it hadn't occurred to him. But, even though John had said it, his gut still said no. She'd been deliberately walked past the statue, towards the main steps to assembly buildings.

He shook his head and they fell silent, neither of them wanting to relive Irene Leighton's final moments. John focussed hard on the screen in front of him, tapping gently at a key, and the simulation started to readjust, displaying a trajectory that curved from the shot's likely origin.

"For the angle of entry to be correct she had to be facing the steps from the Massey Avenue entrance. The left side of her back would likely have been towards the killer, but for some reason she must also have turned to the left."

"Do you think she saw something at the last moment?"

"Well, she was looking in the direction of the shooter."

Craig looked down, sadly. "I think that she turned to plead with the person who brought her there. Then they forced the note into her hand as she was dying."

"God."

They sat looking at the screen for a moment, imaging their victim's helpless pleading and knowing that it had been ignored. Anyone callous enough to kill her like that would never have been moved by her tears. Eventually John broke the silence.

"The bullet is a .338 Lapua Magnum, Marc. In clear weather conditions it can travel at around eight hundred metres per second."

"I've never heard of it."

"Neither has anyone else. Lapuas are sniper rounds, usually shot from one of two rifles: SAKOs or A.I.s. SAKOs come from Finland and the one that would fire this round is most likely to be the TR-42 SAKO model. The A.I. is from a British Manufacturer called Accuracy International. Both were used in Iraq and Afghanistan.

The 338 is the only calibre designed specifically for

sniping. Its range is about sixteen hundred meters, and in the right shooting conditions, two thousand."

Craig interjected. "That means we've a range of possible shooter locations. Can you mark the outer limit on the map?"

John adjusted the map's gray scale to colour and drew an arc outwards from Irene Leighton's body in the likely direction of the bullet. The farthest point took them over a mile away from Stormont, close to a multi-storey car-park on Vernon Road.

Craig thought for a moment. "We'll search the area and hope that we can still find something after twenty-four hours. Particularly in the car-park, the height of its roof would make it a good vantage point."

"The bullet's markings don't match anything that we have on file, but we're linking up with the Irish and UK forces and Interpol."

Craig looked at the screen incredulously. Could there be a Finnish hit-man in Northern Ireland? He was even more convinced now that Irene Leighton's death was linked with her husband's political career.

He moved quickly, heading for the door. "Thanks, John. Get the ballistics to Davy please. I've a few leads to follow up and then we've a full briefing at five if you can make it." Before John could answer yes or no, he was gone.

****

Bedford Street. Belfast City Centre.

The door of the luxurious modern office swung open and Joanne Greer looked up from her phone-call, irritated. She waved her husband Declan away angrily, putting her hand over the receiver when he ignored her.

"Can't you see I'm on a conference call?"

"I don't care. Cut out of it for five minutes. I need to talk to you."

He was in one of his stubborn moods and she knew that there was no arguing with him. She interrupted the speaker at the other end and excused herself out of the four-way call, turning on him furiously.

"For God's sake, Declan, that was Buruli in New York. I'm trying to bring a huge land deal here. It looks terrible you interrupting me like that. Anyway, what's so damn important that it couldn't have waited until tonight?" Then she looked at him horrified. "God, tell me you haven't crashed the car?"

"It's not about your stupid car." He enjoyed saying it, just to see her outrage. She loved that car so much he thought she'd like to sleep with it. Unpleasant images entered his head and he shook them out vigorously.

"It's about that dickhead, Joe Watson. Apparently, he's going to pull the Horizon project. I've just found out from my mole at Stormont."

"He can't - the Approval in Principle's already through."

"He can, and he doesn't care. The exact quote was 'Minister Watson knows that the A.I.P.'s through, but he's looked at the project's return and doesn't think that it's the best use of public money', end quote. I told you that this would happen, Joanne. You should have pushed it through before Burgess retired. He was much more pleasant."

She looked at her husband, astounded by his naiveté. Thank God, one of them knew which end was up.

"Only because he was OK with taking backhanders. Watson is too bloody honest. Damn."

Declan Greer had been prowling around the office as she spoke, but her last sentence made him stop still. He turned towards her urgently. "What do you mean backhanders? What did he need to be paid for? And who paid him?"

She looked at him pityingly. He was worse than a trophy wife and even more useless; at least one of those would cook the dinner.

"To cover up the dummy companies I've put in place. And I paid him of course. Don't be dim, Declan."

He stared at her astounded, as if some alien

81

inhabited his wife's designer body.

"What do you mean dummy companies? What for?"

"To make money of course." She slowed her speech down patronisingly, as if speaking to an infant. "We needed the dummy companies to siphon off the funds."

"What?"

She watched, bored, as realisation finally dawned on him.

"You're stealing public money! You'll be caught. And why? We have all this already." He gestured around her carpeted office, aghast.

"Because as Wallis Simpson once said, you can never be too rich or too thin. You're being tedious now and I've work to do. We'll talk about this later."

"No we bloody won't. What about Horizon? When is the building due to start?"

Joanne shrugged and laughed, sarcastically. "It isn't. Don't you understand? There is no Horizon, darling. It only exists on paper. The money has been going into accounts that I've set up. And now Watson is interfering.

Bob Leighton's been worse than useless; he was supposed to be handling Watson. That's what I paid him for. Damn, damn, damn."

Her anger grew with each expletive, and her husband stayed quiet as her outrage overtook his by miles. He knew that she'd need someone to blame now, even though it was all her own fault. And he would do. So he sat down and waited.

Joanna and Declan Greer had always been a golden couple, even by Northern Irish standards, where there were a lot of high-income families floating around. Mostly floating around Belfast 9, aptly nicknamed Belfast's 'Golden Mile'.

They'd met in London in the eighties, when she was a trainee barrister doing her pupillage, already tipped for the top someday, and he was studying accountancy at one of the 'big six'. Joanne had assessed him like a portfolio investment and decided that it was a suitable match. She had no illusions about marrying for love, this was business, and Declan would make a very

82

suitable escort for a rising barrister. But he'd actually loved her.

They'd done the shacking-up thing for a while, in the little flat in Chelsea that her father had bought for her twenty-first. Until her parents had pushed for the 'big day', expressing a sudden urgent desire to see their daughter floating towards the altar wearing a meringue, or they'd disinherit her.

They'd done the deed at her parent's home church near Bangor, squeezed out a couple of puppies and then moved to the London Toast-Rack, the meshwork of parallel Victorian terraces off Wandsworth Common, costing a few million each. They'd both missed Chelsea but particularly Joanne, she was a true 'sonly', the London slang for Toast-Rackers excusing their child-burdened geography by saying it was 'sonly' five minutes from Chelsea.

The kids had been farmed out to a string of nannies with names like Felicity and Jemima until Declan opted to work from home, unable to bear their small sad faces any longer. Then Joanne had set about the much more important business of making millions, and she'd been good at it too. But her career as a criminal barrister had its drawbacks, a few too many gangsters on speed-dial for one thing, and Declan eventually used the excuse of the children to relocate them to Belfast.

God, but she'd moaned. She'd spent the first few years racking up her gold status on the Belfast-Heathrow run. It had cost them dearly for her to meet her friends and have facials in Brompton Cross, but it had been worth it for the sake of peace. Until eventually, she'd worked out that there was big money to be made in Northern Ireland, and Belfast became her new best friend. He had always appreciated Northern Ireland's rural beauty, and the fact that the grammar schools had saved them a fortune in school fees.

He rose and walked over to the window of their fifteen-storey office building in Bedford Street, looking wistfully at the view over Belfast and beyond. There

83

was a light snow on the Cavehill, giving the basalt outcrop 'Napoleon's nose' a white tip. He smiled at the image, tuning out her ranting and thinking of the Christmas skiing at Courchevel, and next summer's festival at Down Royal, where he could indulge his twin passions; racing and betting.

He'd heard that Joe Watson was a betting man, although not in his league. He'd lost nearly a million last year, but it was worth it, the adrenaline he felt as he watched his horses coming down the stretch was better than sex. Well, better than sex with Joanne anyway.

He pulled himself out of his dream to hear her still yelling; sincerely wishing that she had a mute button. She was saying something about Watson now, and it sounded ominous.

"It's just as well that one of us has a brain, and thought about this possibility when Burgess retired."

"What are you talking about, Jo?"

"Don't call me Jo, you know I hate nicknames. And stop calling Isabella, Izzy, for God's sake. It's common and she hates it."

She didn't hate it of course, she was eighteen and she thought it was cool, but he couldn't be bothered arguing.

She'd already moved on, speaking so quickly that he sometimes wondered how she breathed. Her voice always took on a harder, higher pitch when they were alone, and it had reached 'fork on a blackboard stage' now.

He looked at her distantly. She was slim and tanned, with dark hair styled like that skinny one from Desperate Housewives. Yes, she was still good looking. Yes, she'd kept her figure after two kids, but all the perfect breasts in the world couldn't compensate for that personality.

"I thought about all the risks when Burgess said that he was retiring. Even though we had the approval, I knew it could be reversed unless the contracts were signed. So I thought ahead about how to deal with your mate, Joe."

"He's not my mate."

"You've been to Down Royal with him." It was said accusingly, but he knew that if Watson had proved useful she'd have applauded them socialising. Joanne never clung to principle when there was money involved.

"No, I haven't. Yes, we've both been there, but not in the same box. It's a hell of a big place."

It didn't matter; she wasn't interested in mere details. "Well he's not going to lose us all that money."

"You."

"Whatever."

Izzy's language had rubbed off on her mother. He just thanked God that she didn't do the 'W' hand sign to go along with it. It barely looked cute on an eighteen-year-old.

"He's not going to lose me all that money then. I've been preparing a nice little dossier on Mr Watson, amongst other things."

"What? Jo...Joanne, you can't be thinking what I think you are?"

"Of course I am. I've spent two years setting up those dummy companies so that I could award myself the contracts without a trail. Do you think that was easy? And do you really think that I'm going to sit back and let some walking dick, who can't keep his eyes in their sockets when a woman walks past, lose me all that money? Well, you've another think coming then."

Her voice had reached screeching pitch now, and Declan rushed to the door to check that there was no one outside. No, of course not. It was lunchtime and the hive's occupants had escaped across the road for coffee. Good luck to them. He wished he could join them.

"Joanne, for God's sake calm down. We can't talk about this here."

She suddenly remembered her conference call, grabbing the phone quickly to re-enter it.

"Now look what you've made me do! Get out. We'll talk about this tonight. But I'm telling you now Declan; you won't stop me. I've done a lot of background research on Watson and I've already set some wheels in motion. On Bob Leighton too, useless prat. And I'll run them both over if they get in my way."

Oh, Crap...

Chapter Ten

The C.C.U.

Maggie Clarke parked her Beetle at the narrow end of Pilot Street, in the cul-de-sac by the Rotterdam Bar, and walked into the thirteen-storey glass column that housed the Coordinated Crime Unit, awaiting her escort to the tenth floor.

She'd never been there alone before, always part of a pack of journalists vying for position in the pressroom; elbowed out of the way by one of the men every time she raised her hand. She often wondered how she'd ended up in such a tough job, but she loved writing, promising herself every January, 'just one more year' and then she'd write her novel.

She looked at her reflection in the glass reception desk. She was thirty but didn't look it, everyone said so. And she wasn't bad looking, they said that as well. So why hadn't she had a date in a year? Surely she wasn't that scary.

Then she remembered the man at the MAC the previous morning, and her hiding away when he'd waved, and she shrugged, acknowledging that she didn't help herself much. Craig wasn't bad looking, of course, but too old. She didn't like men in their forties, far too old-fashioned, even if they liked to call it chivalry.

Just then, the lift-door opened and she recognised Craig's P.A. from earlier briefings, smiling to herself at her glittery top and leggings. Nicky caught the smile and made a mental note to seat Maggie at the back in future briefings, behind the lights, then she fixed on her smile and walked to where the younger woman was sitting.

"Ms Clarke?"

"Yes."

"I'm here to take you to D.C.I. Craig." It was said in a tone that left Maggie under no illusion about her disapproval.

They travelled the ten floors silently, and then Nicky showed her to a sofa by the squad's glass double-doors. Maggie looked around her curiously. It was a typical modern office. Large and open-plan, filled with desks and cubicles and computers. A few people were gathered at one end by a vending machine, and a very tall man who she recognised as Liam Cullen, was sitting with his feet up on the desk, chatting on the phone.

Just then, a young man loped through the doors past her, and over to a horseshoe of desks bearing computers. He bent over Cullen's desk as he passed and they shared a brief joke, then he turned to take his seat behind the screens. Maggie could feel her mouth opening in surprise, in a way that she'd thought overacting in the movies. He was gorgeous.

She blushed hotly, aware that she was staring, and looked away hastily. Her eyes were soon drawn back to him. He had chin-length black hair and a lean, muscled look, highlighted by his tight black t-shirt and jeans. He wore a silver chain around his neck matched by the bracelet on his pale arm and his short nails were painted in black varnish. But it was his face that drew her attention most. His dark brown eyes were shaped like almonds, with long lashes that no mascara could ever create. With his aquiline nose and full lips, he almost approached feminine beauty; the contrast with his defined biceps was nearly too much for her. What was this amazing, modern creature doing in such a formal world?

Nicky watched Maggie staring at Davy, part amused, but a bigger part annoyed. He was a shy boy like her son Jonny, and he was no match for a calculating journalist. She marched over to Maggie and deliberately stood, arms folded, in her line of sight, blocking her view of him. But it was already too late, Davy had noticed her too, and he liked what he saw. He arrived at Nicky's side quickly, and she turned to him annoyed.

"Have you no work to do?"

"No. Aren't you going to introduce us?"

88

Maggie smiled up at him, entranced, and held her hand out shyly. "Maggie Clarke."

Davy shook it and smiled. "Davy W...Walsh."

Maggie's heart melted immediately at his mild stutter and she gazed up at him, entranced. He gazed back and Nicky immediately knew that she was fighting a losing battle. Just then, the lift-door opened and Craig strolled out, pushing through the doors and bumping straight into Davy.

"Sorry, Davy." Davy smiled, not taking his eyes off Maggie. "No problem, boss."

Craig beckoned Maggie to follow him, completely missing the tableau. And while she got her exclusive interview, Davy got Nicky's 'mother's lecture' on dangerous women, making him even more determined to date Maggie Clarke. He wasn't half as shy as they all thought.

****

The eleven o'clock briefing was short and sweet, with Liam reporting that Bob Leighton had taken a flight to London the night before, and The Met were following him. There'd been no way to stop him going. He was an M.P., and he might be doing business in Westminster. Anyway, he'd be back tomorrow evening. Craig smiled wryly; Leighton wouldn't get far with Liam on his tail.

Davy had drawn a blank on the Vors. Fraud, vice and drugs hadn't had a sniff of them and that only left gang-crime and terrorism to check, but he was following up the tattoos. He'd soon be even busier with John's ballistics. Annette had left for Enniskillen unhappy. She'd gone to interview Irene Leighton's mother, reluctant to see the pain that she was suffering. She'd be back at three.

They were just wrapping up when the phone rang, and Nicky interrupted. "It's the lab, sir. Dr Winter."

Craig was surprised. He'd only left John an hour ago, but he waved her to put him through, on speakerphone.

"Yes, John?"

"Two new things have just come through. We've found a print on the plastic bag in Irene Leighton's hand. I'm sending it over to Davy now." Davy nodded at the phone. "And the tox-screen shows that she was drugged. Rohypnol."

'Roofies'. They would have made her confused and suggestible. Irene Leighton would have done whatever she was told.

"It would have been easy to walk her anywhere without her struggling, John."

Liam interjected. "The gates on Massey Avenue opened at seven-thirty, Doc. The guard reported that a woman walked through just after that, with a young man."

It was news to Craig. "What did the man look like, Liam?"

Liam saw his puzzled look. "We've just got the info, boss. The guard went off yesterday at nine and uniform have just caught up with him. He was pretty vague, but he said that he thought it was a young lad, wearing a baseball cap. He didn't stop them because the public walk through the grounds all the time. There are thousands of people up there every day, and lots of people come early, to walk the dogs or get fit."

"Any close circuit TV?"

Liam shook his head. "Wrong angle."

Craig doubted that the early morning visitors were a coincidence. "OK, thanks, John. Send the print over."

He clicked the phone off, thinking. "Liam, nip down to gangland and find out what they have on the Vors, and then ask The Met what their presence is like in London. I've got a hunch..."

****

County Fermanagh.

Annette had made good time on the M1, reaching the A4 within an hour. But it was by-roads the rest of the way and she was torn between gratitude, wanting to delay her interview, and stress, desperate to get it over

90

with. She was dreading it.

She looked at the road ahead, narrow and winding, slowed to ten mph by weekday 'Sunday' drivers and tractors full of grain. The hedgerows were quietening down for the winter but she could see festive holly growing amongst them now, and late conkers falling from the overhanging trees onto the road, reminding her of her Maghera childhood. She was tempted to stop and collect some for Jordan, and then she reminded herself that her son was sixteen, not six anymore.

The road forked into the edges of a small village that the sign announced as Belleek and she stopped, programming the sat-nav with the address of Irene Leighton's childhood home. She followed its detailed directions through the town and into a narrow country lane, which ended in an iron gate to a gravelled driveway.

Belleek was a thriving market town set deep in the Fermanagh countryside, close to Lower Lough Erne. It was part of the region's rural Lakelands, an area of almost ethereal beauty. Well known locally and to purposeful tourists, the seven hundred kilometres of rivers, lakes and canals were home to a myriad of small islands, dotted throughout. They were used by cruisers, pleasure craft and anglers, travelling the peaceful waterways, fishing, exploring and stopping-off for picnics on the tiny isles.

She remembered visiting the lakes on a school trip many years before. Their concealing mists and glass-smooth surfaces had made her romantic teenage soul imagine the 'Lady of Lake' appearing at any minute, holding Excalibur.

The town's small size was no reflection of its industry, with the oldest pottery in Ireland producing flawless Parian china. The exquisite porcelain travelled the world as expensive gifts and resided locally in every other home in Northern Ireland. Annette bet that even the unrefined Liam had a set at home, the feminine Danni's attempt at civilising him.

She parked by the gate and swallowed hard, ringing the local sergeant who was meeting her at Bridie

91

Hannigan's neat home. The voice that came through was gruff and warm and Annette liked him immediately.

"Sergeant McElroy. Hello. Are you here then?"

"Yes, Sergeant Creen. How's Mrs Hannigan?"

"Ach, as well as you'd expect when your daughter's dead. But she's a country woman for all that."

She understood the reference. Country living faced people with life and death in a different way to cities, breeding stoicism. Her own father had grown up on a farm and her mother said that it would have taken an anvil dropped on his head to upset him, offering to try whenever he annoyed her.

The sergeant was still talking. "Her son's staying with her, so that's not too bad. Anyhow, what can I do to help you?"

His emphasis was a mark of sympathy for her task and she appreciated his offer, saying so. But how could anyone make the questions easier? She sighed heavily to herself, driving on slowly until she finally pulled the car onto the paved forecourt of a white pebble-dashed bungalow.

She was still talking when the man she was talking to, arrived at the door to greet her. His round, fresh face smiled at her pragmatically, and they walked together into the small room where seventy-year-old Bridie Hannigan sat waiting for them, surrounded by memories of the loving daughter that she would never see again.

****

The C.C.U.

Liam took the lift down to the fifth floor and after two minutes meandering around the un-manned foyer he noticed the corridor marked 'detectives'. He wandered up and down it, confused for a moment, and then knocked hard on Geoff Hamill's door. At least he thought it was his – the fifth floor wasn't laid out like theirs. All the doors were solid with no hint of the occupant inside, and there was no welcoming Nicky to greet visitors. It wasn't homey at all.

The white door opened sharply inwards, and Liam fell forward from his leaning stance, nearly colliding with the man in front of him. Geoff Hamill sidestepped quickly to avoid being flattened; he was on the small side and Liam could do him serious damage.

Liam looked down at the other man, grinning. "Ach, Geoffrey. Have you never grown yet? Your mammy didn't feed you enough."

Hamill ignored the jibes. He hated being called Geoffrey and Liam had guessed it, but you never let anyone on the job know that you really hated something, or they'd get years of mileage out of it. He'd had the piss taken about his size for years, but he'd made the minimum height requirement for the force when it had existed, and what he lacked in inches he made up for in mouth.

"And she fed you far too much, Cullen. You need to watch that paunch, man." Liam stared down at his stomach, disgruntled, and silently sucked it in.

"Grab a pew." Hamill indicated a seat by the desk and Liam grabbed it, exhaling as he sat.

"Right, the Vors."

"God, don't go mad with the small talk, Geoff, will you?"

Hamill looked at him seriously "Sorry, Liam. No time. We've a gang war gearing up in Tyrone. Some dickheads fighting about who owns the streets."

"Don't you mean who owns the sheep, down there?"

Hamill laughed despite himself and it opened the door to a minute of banter, then he pulled the meeting back to the reason Liam was there.

"Vors. The quick answer is no. Not here in Belfast, not anywhere in Northern Ireland in fact, or in the Republic as far as we know. But..."

"Ah God, there's always a 'but'."

Hamill nodded. "We've heard a whisper, and it's only a quiet one mind you, that they might be investing in land here."

"Land, as in farmland?"

93

"Nope, as in development land. We've nothing else, no names and no idea where. But if you get onto George Milton at The Met, he might tell you more. That's it, as far as we know. Sorry."

Liam thought for a moment, and something occurred to him. He stood up quickly and made to leave, then turned back, smiling, determined to have the last word. "Get some glass in that door, Geoffrey, or the next one might really stunt your growth."

****

Liam took the lift back to the tenth floor, thinking. He was certain that land deals needed government permission and made up his mind to check later. He sat down heavily at his desk and called The Met, and after five minutes he set the phone down triumphantly. He smiled broadly across at Nicky, who returned his look with a scowl.

"Here, what's that look for? What have I done?"

"You? Nothing." Then she looked suspiciously at him. "Well...not as far as I know. It's Davy I'm cross with."

"Davy?!"

He was surprised. Davy was everyone's pet, especially Nicky's and Annette's. Whatever he'd done, it must have been bad. Then she told him about Maggie Clarke and the fact that Davy had spent the past ten minutes arranging a date with her, and Liam made the biggest mistake of his week so far. He laughed.

****

Craig stared at the black coffee in front of him thinking about Irene Leighton. She'd been alive between Sunday evening and Wednesday morning somewhere. Part of the time had been spent at her mother's; Annette would confirm exactly how much at the briefing. But for at least two days, according to the tattoos, she'd been held somewhere that she couldn't escape from.

94

Her killer had had access to drugs. Easy. Tattoo equipment. Easy. A secure location. Easy enough. A sniper rifle? Not so easy, but unfortunately not impossible. There were still too many guns floating around his pretty little country for his liking.

He tapped his pen absentmindedly on the desk. What did they have? The bullet, still waiting for a match. The print, perhaps a break. The husband. OK, Bob Leighton loved her, but he was a slippery bugger, and on coke.

He could search Leighton's house and office and do him for possession of course, but he was holding back on that, to see where he would lead them. For the moment, he was more use to them free, and a drugs charge on a grieving widower wouldn't do them any favours.

Then there was the man who'd called Maggie Clarke. Annette's comments about Kaisa's accent had reminded him to ask Maggie about his, but it hadn't helped. The man had said so few words that all she could give them was 'foreign' and 'European'. At a push, French. Languages obviously hadn't been her strong point at school.

And what of Kaisa Moldeau? Leighton undoubtedly found her attractive, but had he actually done anything about it? Craig would bet that if he hadn't actually committed physical infidelity, his fantasies had included her many times.

And where had she been between Monday afternoon and Wednesday morning at eleven, when she'd collected the boy?

He looked at the note that Nicky had brought in five minutes earlier. It was from Andy White in drugs, he wanted a meeting about something. He made a mental note to call him later. After ten more minutes thinking about the Leightons, he was going round in circles so his mind reluctantly turned to another area of his life where he was making no progress, Camille, his long-time ex.

She'd appeared in Belfast without warning in October, after five years absence, during which she'd moved on with another man and he'd built a wall around him so strong that no other woman could penetrate it. Their meeting had stirred up all sorts of unwanted feelings in him and he was still unravelling them.

After a week spent avoiding her in Belfast they'd finally met in London for lunch last month. He would have loved to have felt nothing for her. It would have freed him completely. But he hadn't, he'd definitely felt something, and he couldn't work out what it was.

She was still beautiful, still the same. No taller or smaller or thinner or fatter. Not even older looking, as if she'd been frozen in ice while they'd been apart. Except that he knew she hadn't, that had only been his fate. She even sounded the same, with some slight, new, east-coast inflections sneaking in on 'yes' and 'no', and 'Marco'. Otherwise, no change.

They could still laugh and talk together like they always had, remembering the years that they'd shared. And she was sorry, really sorry for what she'd done. Citing ambition and fear and...lust? Was that part of it, Camille? Was that why you chose him over me?

No! No. Her protests had seemed genuine and he thought that they probably were. This hadn't been about lust, it had been about her ambition, and he'd always known about that. Her career came first. And the man that she'd chosen had helped her; he'd made her a success. Her phone hadn't stop ringing during their meal together.

She was the same Camille that she'd ever been. Success had always been her driver, he'd always known that. It was nothing new. So what was wrong with him?

Why wasn't he sure anymore? Was he really so unforgiving? Or had something died in him during the five years of pain in between? But not everything, unfortunately.

Or had he finally just seen things that were always there in her, that his love had blinded him to? He didn't know, he honestly didn't. He knew that he still felt something for her, but what? It was like touching something through gauze.

96

His thoughts were interrupted by a shy knock at the door and he was glad of the rescue. It was Davy. Craig was surprised, and pleased. Davy normally asked Nicky to see if he was free; it was a good sign that he was knocking by himself now. Or so he thought until he noticed Nicky's annoyed face in the background. Craig beckoned him in, closing the door and indicating a seat.

"What can I do for you, Davy?"

"S...Sir, I've information on a few things, but they can w...wait for the briefing later. I just wanted to get your approval for s...something. If that's OK?"

Craig was puzzled but nodded him on.

"I'd like to take Maggie Clarke out for a meal." He hurtled on before Craig could say a word.

"I know s...she's a journalist and they can be trouble, but I promise you I won't s...say anything about the case, I promise."

Craig smiled to himself; so this was why Nicky was annoyed. She was being protective. He looked kindly at the younger man and smiled.

"Thank you for telling me, Davy. But I think that you're responsible enough not to say anything inappropriate to Ms Clarke. I saw her draft of my interview and it was fair, so I've no problem with her professionally."

He raised his voice slightly, knowing that Nicky was listening at the door. "If we barred everyone from dating people that they met through work, then none of us would ever have a relationship, given the hours that we keep." He didn't miss the irony in his own life.

"You have fun, Davy. It's what being young is about. Now, was there anything else?

The younger man blushed and shook his head, then remembered something. "Yes, s...sir. Could you ask Nicky not to be cross with me anymore? I don't w...want to upset her, but I have to live my life."

Craig nodded. "Leave her to me." Immediately thinking that his words were much braver than he felt.

****

Craig returned the call to Andy White, agreeing a quick meeting before he left for the day, so when Annette arrived back at three he called the briefing early, grabbing a chair out on the main floor.

"We'll stay out here, if everyone's OK with that?" He leaned back over the chair and smiled. "Nicky, could you join us? I'd be grateful for your insight on things."

She knew that he was sucking-up and she wasn't falling for it. But she was interested in the case, so she sat down grudgingly beside Annette, certain that she would agree about Davy, ignoring Liam's attempts to catch her eye.

"I'll summarise where we are, and then hand over to each of you for the detail."

He handed out a sheet of A4 that detailed his earlier thoughts.

"Right, Davy. What have you found?"

Davy lifted a sheaf of paper from his desk and sat down between Craig and Liam, unconsciously looking for protection. He stared down at his papers, refusing to meet Nicky's eye.

"First, the bullet that Dr W...Winter found. It's very unusual, a 338 Lapua Magnum from Finland. I've just been reading up on them, w...wait 'til you hear this." He pulled out a sheet and started to read.

"It's the only calibre designed just for s...sniping, designed to penetrate five layers of body armour at one thousand meters and kill. Effective range is sixteen hundred to two thousand meters. It's a military anti-personnel round and only a few rifles can fire it. The S...SAKO TRG-42 and the A.I."

He was about to go into more detail when Craig stopped him, updating them on John's ballistic simulation and the likely position of the sniper. And then surprising them with the information that a search of the area had just yielded something. The call had come in just five minutes before.

"There's a high rise car-park on Vernon Road and the roof provides a perfect view of Parliament Building's steps. It's in range, and when the C.S.I.s searched it they found a spent cigarette, so we're hoping that it will yield something."

Liam looked sceptical. "If they're professional enough to kill like this, are they likely to leave a clue?"

Craig nodded, smiling. It was exactly what he had thought. "I think they left it deliberately, Liam. It won't link to them but it might give us something to follow."

"Like the print, sir." Craig nodded at Annette. Just like the print.

"Keep going, Davy."

"W...well, I thought that we s...should be looking, not only for a ballistics match, but as the bullet itself is so unusual, look for any use of that bullet elsewhere at all. I've been searching under all possible parameters."

"Great idea, lad."

"I used international databases and there have been two relevant cases in London over the past thirteen months. Both 338 Lapua Magnums, but no sign of the guns. They also had a s...similar killing in Paris two years ago. The London contact is an Inspector Yemi Idowu and the Paris contact is an Inspector Chevalier." Craig smiled broadly. He knew Yemi well; they'd been friends at The Met for years.

"Paris w...was the only one outside the U.K. This may be a new s...shooter in the past two years. Or someone who graduated to it from other things."

"Or someone who usually operates in countries where death's so commonplace that it doesn't even merit an investigation."

Davy nodded slowly. "They were professional hits without a doubt. One bullet each time. To judge the distance and velocity of a bullet like that, s...so accurately that it didn't go through the victim and hit anyone else - this guy is very talented."

"We've a contractor at work, boss. And it looks like he's just been here for his holidays."

Craig looked thoughtful for a moment. "Anything on the killer themselves, Davy?"

"Only that London believes they could have had an accomplice."

The young man who walked Irene Leighton into

Stormont.

"The fingerprint hasn't traced back to anyone yet, s...sir. I'll keep going on that and on the D.N.A. from the cigarette, but..."

"Yes?"

"W...Where did they get the gun? I've never heard of anything that high-tech in Northern Ireland, even looking back at The Troubles' database. And if it isn't from here, then how did they get it into the country? And how do they think they're going to get it out?"

They were good points but Craig knew that there were illegal ports all over Ireland, and even some legal ones with limited checks in place. He could feel a chat with counter-terrorism coming up.

"Well done, Davy, that's outstanding work. Follow up the Paris and London leads and let's see what the D.N.A and print give us. Annette? How was your trip?"

Davy blushed red and Annette smiled at him, earning a glare from Nicky that she completely missed, totally unaware of the day's events. She sighed heavily before starting.

"Belleek is beautiful, sir, but I'd rather have been there in different circumstances. Mrs Hannigan is devastated, as you would expect. Mrs Leighton went down to see her on Sunday afternoon, arriving there about five. Her mother was delighted to see her of course, but didn't know why she'd come. Apparently the call saying that her mother was ill was a set-up."

Craig interjected. "Davy, run a back-trace on all the Leighton's phones." Then he remembered something. "And the Chronicle news desk as well. Maggie Clarke was tipped off and it may have been the same caller. We'll probably find nothing, but it's worth a try. Sorry Annette, go on."

"Well, once there, Mrs Leighton decided to stay for a few days. She went out to the shops for some food around eleven on Monday morning and never returned. Mrs Hannigan was frantic, calling around everyone she knew, but she couldn't get hold of Bob Leighton because he was in Dublin. And there was no answer at home.

The first she knew of what had happened to her daughter was when the local police notified her of her death." Annette looked down at her feet sadly. "She's completely distraught."

She fell silent and no one spoke. Craig gave her a minute, turning to Liam. "Liam, what have you found?"

Even Liam's voice was hoarse at the thought of Bridie Hannigan's loss and he coughed loudly to clear it. "Aye, well. I went to see Geoff Hamill in gang crime, and that was short and sweet. No sign of the Vors in Northern Ireland or the Republic as far as he knows, but..."

Craig and Davy leaned forward, interested, and Liam was gratified. "He did say that he'd heard a whisper they might be looking at land acquisition here. Development land. So I thought; land development would have to go through all sorts of planning permission, wouldn't it? And...Bob Leighton's in government and government gives land permissions, see?"

Craig saw and so did the rest of them. Liam continued enthusiastically. "Davy's just started looking for anything relevant on that. Then I spoke to The Met about two things. They've been keeping an eye on Leighton and it seems he's been spending the day visiting foreign embassies. They started to tell me the names, but he'll visit a few more before he's done, so they'll e-mail the list through when he's finished. Maybe he's visiting them for energy discussions?"

Annette snorted and even Davy looked sceptical at the comment. Liam shrugged, that's what he got for trying not to be cynical.

"Anyway, then I asked George Milton in headquarters about the Vors in London, and it seems there's a whole nest of them in the East End. He wouldn't give me any more detail and suggested a face-to-face. I thought you should do it, boss, seeing as you worked there."

Craig looked at him sceptically, certain that wasn't the only reason Liam was suggesting he took the trip.

Liam caught his look and nodded. "Aye well, the baby's due just after Christmas, and if I disappear to London now my life won't be worth living."

They all laughed. Liam had missed his toddler Erin's birth and his wife Danni had never let him forget it. Craig turned to Annette and noticed her looking a bit happier, smiling.

"OK, that's excellent work all of you. I'm going to chat to counter-terrorism tomorrow – Davy, I want you in that meeting with me." Davy beamed at him, proudly.

"I'll speak to London about the Vors, Liam, but a trip is the last resort; we've plenty to get on with here. Annette, go back and have another chat to Ms Moldeau, please. I want her exact whereabouts from Monday morning to Wednesday.

Liam, when Bob Leighton gets back I want his prints and his location for those unaccounted-for days. Davy, keep going with the prints and D.N.A. and anything more you can find on the bullet. And Nicky..."

He turned to look directly at her and smiled kindly. "Davy is a big boy. I know you care about him but you're not his mother. Better to be his friend and take care of him if something goes wrong, than sit and scowl disapprovingly at him all day. Yes?"

Annette looked at them, completely puzzled, and Nicky nodded a grudging 'yes' with a half-smile at Davy, who grinned back. Craig could hear Liam getting ready with a smart remark and he shot him a warning look, stopping him in his tracks.

"Now, I've got a meeting with D.C.I. White in drugs, and I've no idea what it's about, so..." He stood and turned quickly for the door. "Play nicely children. I'll be back in an hour."

102

Chapter Eleven

Bob Leighton lifted his case quickly from the airport carousel and headed through the automatic doors for the car-park, saddened. Irene had always met him at arrivals smiling, with Ben's small hand held up in a wave. A tear sprang to his eye but he held it back, determined to focus on his upcoming journey; his life could depend on it. There'd be time to mourn Irene later, and he *would* mourn her. He had really loved her.

He could feel tears threatening again so he dumped his bag quickly in the boot and over-revved the car in a show of self-control, pulling speedily onto the M3 towards Belfast. He'd come back a day early to fool Joanne and it was eight o'clock now. By eleven tonight he intended, no, he absolutely needed to be in a different country.

****

Craig's Apartment. Stranmillis, Belfast.

Craig dropped his bag in the hall of his apartment and pulled off his leather reefer, throwing it over the modern bronze by the front door and wondering idly why Andy White had requested a meeting and then disappeared before he'd arrived. He shrugged, understanding; something always came up to wreck your diary. Maybe he should try that excuse on Nicky.

He had just pulled a cold beer from his tall American fridge and turned on the sports' channel, when the sound of his mobile disturbed his long awaited peace. He placed the beer on the counter with a sigh and clicked the phone onto speaker without looking.

"Marc Craig. Can I help you?"

The silence that followed could only have belonged to one person. No. To one woman, Camille. He started speaking quickly, before she did.

103

"Camille, I promised to call you tomorrow."

Her soft, perfectly rounded vowels honed from years at R.A.D.A. flowed seductively down the line at him, wrapping him in their warmth, and he could feel himself about to be manipulated. But forewarned was forearmed, and he was well forewarned after nine years of her warmth, followed by an arctic winter.

"Marco..." She was the only one but his family who routinely used his Italian name, automatically creating intimacy. But instead of achieving her aim of warmth, it made him wary now. "I'd like to see you again."

He'd known that it was coming, of course. They'd left things hanging after their lunch a month before; their first real exposure five years after she'd left him for the 'Prick'. And four since he'd returned to Belfast from London.

He didn't know what he'd expected from their London meeting. A Damascene moment where everything would immediately become clear? Why she'd left him, why she'd come back, what she really thought he was going to say and do after her infidelity and years of silence? 'Lovely to see you again, Camille. Of course I forgive you. Now here's my heart, just crush it again.'

That was never going to happen, and he'd been astounded by her arrogance that it even might. And by her contrition.

Her tears had been genuine, and not just for herself, but for what she'd done to him. By the end of their few hours together, he'd berated her, punished her, and nearly forgiven her. Forgiven her for five years of pain in three hours. He was disgusted by his own weakness, and for loving her again even a little, so quickly. And yet... Something was lacking, and she knew it.

"Marco, when can we see each other again? I could come over at the weekend. I'm free and we could go away for a few days."

Oh, Camille. You live in a world of self-important freedom, never bound, except by performances when you have to be there. The rest of your life is completely unfettered. He always had duty, even when he wasn't

104

at work.

"We're in the middle of a case, Camille. I can't just drop everything and go away."

"I could come there and stay with you."

He could hear her entering the role of nineteen-fifties housewife already. Dinner prepared when his Marlowe-esque detective came home from work. And she wouldn't just play it, she'd actually believe it. It was what made her such a good actor.

His voice was firm. "No, Camille. I need to focus on the case. You would be a distraction." His tone said that wasn't a good thing and he could feel her retreating through the gauze, realising that he'd been too sharp. He softened slightly, taking no pleasure in her pain.

"After this case is wrapped up, we'll talk...maybe go away for a few days..." As soon as he'd said it, he regretted the words, said to be kind, but creating a whole world of pain in the future, and not only for him.

"Oh yes, Marco, please. When it finishes." Her eager voice confirmed it. A whole world of pain. He waited to feel happy for pleasing her at least, but it didn't come, and he knew then that something was very wrong.

****

The Home of Joanne and Declan Greer.

"I don't give a shit about the money, Joanne. You can't do this. OK. Not even if you've lost a lot of money."

"*We*. We've lost a lot of money."

Declan shrugged, knowing that although Joanne had planned it alone and planned to keep the proceeds for herself, she'd make damn sure that he would share in any losses. He couldn't be bothered arguing with her.

"You need to cut and run now. It's just a bloody project. There was always a risk they would pull it, that's business." He took a deep breath, before making another mistake. "It was illegal anyway, insider trading. So you can hardly complain now, can you?"

Joanne was sucking at her red wine like a vampire sucked blood, and talking, God was she talking. It was eight p.m. and it had been pouring out of her since they'd got home. What she'd been doing, what she'd planned, what she was still planning - it all spewed out. The wine had stained her tongue and teeth black, and she looked ugly.

Declan looked at the woman that he'd once loved. Everything about her glamorous exterior seemed hideous now, twisted out of shape by greed and spite. It made him so sad that he ached. The best he could hope for was that their daughters took after their grandparents, because neither of them was an example to follow.

It was his fault that she'd gone this far, it must be. She hadn't been like this when they'd met. Spoilt yes, selfish yes, but between him and her parents over-indulging her, and the moneyed friends she'd made in London making her desperate to keep up, she was completely screwed-up now. She was fifty, too late to change her. He could only hope to control her now, if that was even still possible. He hadn't believed his ears when she'd told him what she'd been doing behind his back...for months now...for bloody months.

"I've got a little book on Joe Watson. His comings and goings, his gambling, his tarts, every dirty little thing he's ever done. "

"Blackmail? Are you mad? There's no way I'm going along with this, Joanne. He'd never cave in any way, he's not the type."

"How do you know? He has a family and a position; he's got a lot to lose. "

"He's independently wealthy, Joanne, he made a mint working at Goldbergs'. He doesn't even take his government salary. And I'm damn sure his wife already knows about the women. Wouldn't you?" He'd never been unfaithful but he looked at her for confirmation that she would care if he had, but she was too busy ranting.

"I'll leak if to the press, then."

"Oh, Jo. Get a grip, will you."

106

"Joanne." Whatever...

"Do you really think that the press here don't know everything about politicians? It's a tiny country; you can't keep secrets in Northern Ireland. Anyway, he won't give in to blackmail."

"You said that already. But how the hell do you know? You would."

"Yes, I would. But he's not me and I know men. Watson will just tell you to 'shove it'."

She slumped abruptly in the preposterously expensive Corbusier chair he'd given her for their twentieth anniversary, and put her head down. Declan could see tears running down her cheeks and he instantly felt sorry for shouting. Then he shivered, as the white clenching of her fists said that they were tears of fury. He felt as if she was walking over his grave. No, not his...

She raised her head and looked at him and the room felt completely still. Her brown eyes were like slits and, combined with her darkened lips, the whole effect was pure movie evil. She didn't say a word, she didn't need to, Declan could see now that their argument about blackmailing Watson had just been a charade, put on for his sake.

She'd wanted him to argue that it wouldn't work, it gave her just what she wanted, confirmation that there was only one option left. And it was something much worse. She'd been planning this all along. But for how long?

He couldn't believe the thoughts running through his head, as he looked at his Malone Road wife sitting on her expensive anniversary present. Surely he must be wrong. But he wasn't.

Joanne sat back, casually, drawing her long tanned legs up beneath her to form an elegant curve, a trick learnt from her student modelling jobs. Her eyes locked onto his and she carefully rested her empty glass on the black marble lamp-table. It was as if she was gauging his thoughts, while not caring, not even a little, what they were.

When she finally spoke, she was calm, all sign of

hysterics gone. "You know I'm right Declan, you've just confirmed it." She'd walked him straight into it. "He won't be blackmailed. You said it. That means if he doesn't cave in there's only one way out of this."

He froze, willing her to stop before she said the words that would end his love for her, end their marriage, and perhaps even ruin lives. He knew with certainty that theirs would be among them.

Every ounce of him willed her not to say it, but she did.

"If the blackmail fails, I'll have to kill him."

There, it was said. But she didn't stop there. She was on a roll.

"Well of course, I won't actually kill him myself, but he'll have to be killed. Don't you worry, I've organised everything. There's no way it can be traced back to me." His eyes widened as she talked. "I've done it before so don't worry. Here's what's going to happen."

****

Bob Leighton pushed quickly through the front door, looking around for Kaisa. He found her in the kitchen. He stood hesitantly in the doorway, admiring her slim waist and pertly curved backside and instantly feeling guilty about Irene. He pushed it away quickly. There'd be time to mourn later. But right now, he had to get out of here, and he wanted Kaisa to get out with him.

She stood, washing a glass and pretending that she hadn't seen him. She'd seen him all right, pulling hastily into the wide double drive, not even bothering to remove his travel bag from the boot. He'd nearly tripped over the suitcases in the hall in his rush.

She turned to him and smiled calmly, wiping her hands on a cloth. Then she moved slowly towards him, meeting him in the middle of the room. They both remained silent, all the talk about 'the future' that she'd known was coming, had already come on the phone last night. She'd agreed to pack the cases, leave Ben at his parents and get ready to go as soon as he arrived. Just for a few days, just to Donegal, just to talk. Both of them already knowing that Bob Leighton never intended to see Belfast again.

****

Liam stared at the list that Davy had handed him, totally confused. When Bob Leighton had hit the tarmac a day early, two hours before, they'd been on him immediately, and they were on him now. He was heading to Donegal, somewhere that they could easily watch him, albeit from a distance. But that didn't explain the list in his hand.

He squinted at the paper, puzzled. It held the names of nine countries, but he had no idea what they had in common. Apart from the fact that Leighton had spent the past twenty-four hours visiting their Embassies.

International energy partners? Or maybe he was buying a holiday home. Liam looked sceptically at some of the countries listed: Leighton would need to wear a flak jacket with his sunglasses there.

He made a note for Davy to run more checks tomorrow and looked around the empty floor. Everyone else had the sense God gave them and had gone home, time that he was away too. He yawned and rubbed his eyes, catching sight of the wall clock. Ten p.m. Oh crap. Danni would kill him.

Ten was bad at the best of times, but his wife's normally placid nature had been replaced with a temper that could melt glass in this pregnancy, so he knew that he'd get it in the ear. He stood up and stretched, smiling at the thought of his five-foot-four wife yelling up at him. He'd never admit it at work but he loved her dearly, and he couldn't wait for this baby to be born. He loved kids, for their jokes and fun and unconditional affection. A sudden thought struck him and he smiled mischievously. No, he couldn't wait for this baby to be born. Then they could start working on the next.

****

109

The C.C.U. Friday morning.

Liam yawned and smiled to himself, staring out the window at the bright morning. Danni had been in a sympathetic mood the night before, even though he'd got home very late. They'd spent a pleasant few hours researching names on the internet, agreeing on a shortlist for girls, but differing wildly on the boys. There was no way his son was being called Tristan! He pulled his mind reluctantly back to work, attempting to focus.

"Here, Davy. What's the story with the print and D.N.A.? Any matches?"

Davy was twirling around in his chair energetically, and Annette was waiting for the wheels to come off, literally. He was in a good mood and they all knew why. His first date with Maggie was on Saturday and they'd all be eagerly awaiting an update on Monday. All except Nicky that was.

"Nope, nothing. Nowhere in the U.K. or Ireland, and nothing from Interpol yet. But I have news on your list, Liam."

Annette stood up and leaned on her partition wall, curious. "What list?"

"The Met have been tailing Leighton for us since Wednesday."

She looked at Liam competitively. "You told us that, yesterday." Irritated at his ownership of the information when she was stuck finding background on Kaisa Moldeau, or not finding background more to the point. And not finding the lady herself to re-interview either.

Liam ignored her sharpness, putting it down to hormones, but only inside his head. He could do without a feminist lecture; he'd learned the hard way to avoid those.

"Aye, but Leighton visited nine embassies in his London trip and Davy's looking at the list, for connections, like."

Before she could comment, Marc Craig strolled onto the floor, tiredly.

"You look exhausted, sir."

Annette said it kindly and Craig nodded at her, smiling. "Busy week." The truth was slightly different. Busy week followed by no sleep after Camille's call. He'd overheard the last part of their conversation and picked it up quickly, still blushing under Annette's maternal scrutiny.

"What have you found, Davy?"

"Nothing yet on the prints or D.N.A, but Liam's list of countries is interesting."

Craig put his hand out and Liam placed a copy of the list in it. He scanned it quickly.

"Non-extradition countries."

Davy nodded at him, smiling, and Liam looked baffled.

"None of the countries on that list have an extradition agreement with the U.K, Liam."

"What does that mean?"

Davy was sitting forward eagerly so Craig nodded him on, pulling over a chair.

"If there's no extradition agreement, then the country w...won't allow other countries to demand that people are deported back to them. S...So, if I commit a crime in Belfast and run to Venezuela, then even if the U.K. government ask for me to be s...sent back for trial, Venezuela won't make me go. Brilliant isn't it?"

Craig looked at him dryly. "I'm not sure brilliant is the right word, Davy. But I take your point." Davy looked down, hiding a smile. Extradition appealed to his wilder side.

"You're saying Leighton's looking to do a runner?"

Annette interjected. "And those countries will grant him asylum, just like that?"

Craig yawned. "I imagine that he's made some useful contacts through his job, but he'll probably still have to pay them. I can't see them going through the hassle just for love."

"But why's he gone to Donegal, boss?"

Craig looked at Liam, interested. "Since when?"

"Since two hours after he landed last night. He landed a day early at the City, belted home, collected

Kaisa Moldeau, and then ran."

Annette smarted; Liam had located the girl and she hadn't. Then she smirked knowingly. "Oh, did he now? Was the little boy with them?"

Davy shook his head. "He's at Leighton's parents."

"Leighton nipped over the border into Donegal, boss. We're keeping a loose eye."

Craig looked at Liam sharply. He should have called him last night with an update, but then, he really should have called-in to check. Camille had distracted him and he wouldn't let it happen again.

The room fell quiet while they watched Craig thinking. What good would it have done for Liam to tell him? He was a good operational officer who hadn't lost sight of Leighton from the moment that he'd hit London on Wednesday. Craig couldn't have done any better himself.

And Bob Leighton wasn't on bail; they didn't even believe that he'd harmed his wife, so how could they have prevented him from going anywhere, even if he had seen the list last night? The truth was that they couldn't have. Leighton could go to Timbuktu and they would be powerless to stop him.

Craig shot Liam a quick look without the others noticing and they both knew what it meant. 'Keep me informed.' Liam nodded imperceptibly in reply, knowing that it was a minor slip that could have been much bigger. Annette was still talking in the background.

"But, sir. Where can he get to from Donegal? He has to fly from somewhere and they've no airport."

"Oh yes they do, Cutty. There are domestic flights to Dublin and Glasgow from Donegal Airport, near Carrickfin."

Craig looked at Liam surprised, he'd never heard of it. Liam's local knowledge was impressive. He nodded in respect, and continued. "He wouldn't get far from there, Annette. But once he's in the Republic he can travel around anywhere by road or train, and then fly from any one of nine airports."

"But s...sir, we have an extradition agreement with

the Republic." Davy's face said that he didn't think it was fair.

"We do Davy, but Bob Leighton isn't a criminal. And even if he was, any border transfer would take time. No, I think we've seen the last of Mr Leighton. He intends to get as far away from here as possible."

Annette was surprised at Craig's apparent lack of concern.

"But that will destroy our case, sir. We'll never find Irene Leighton's killer without him. And what about Kaisa? We haven't ruled her out. She has no alibi for two days."

Craig smiled quietly. "Leighton didn't kill her, Annette. And we've plenty of other roads to our killer. The bullet, the print, D.N.A, tattoos...we're a long way from running out of leads. And call it a hunch, but I don't think we've seen the last of Ms Moldeau. She doesn't sound the type to suit exile. My bet is that she'll be bored with Bob Leighton long before he leaves Ireland."

Chapter Twelve

Portsalon. Donegal. The Republic of Ireland. Friday.

Kaisa propped herself up on one elbow and watched her lover. He slept like a child, curled up on his right side, with his left arm across his chest, as if he was guarding his heart. She'd decided months ago that he was quite good-looking, in a pale skinny way. His red-brown hair curled up at the base of his neck, just above the top of his spine, revealing the soft, vulnerable space in between. He was so unlike her Stevan, but not completely repulsive.

She watched and waited, her face expressionless, ready to morph into a facsimile of love as soon as he awoke. She knew what love was supposed to look like, God knows she'd been force-fed enough romantic movies by men over the years. Dragging her along to see them, as if it was hard-wired into the female psyche to like dreary stories of love and loss. All they did was make her yawn and long for a Wesley Snipes DVD.

But enduring them had served its purpose. She'd sat through them all, hugging their arms, looking up at the big strong men, sucking them into her net, to protect and adore her. Just long enough to give her what she needed.

In return, they'd taught her how people in love were supposed to behave. She knew exactly what was expected of her. That had always been her talent; she always knew what was expected of her. She'd never felt romantic love, but who cared, they could keep it. The only thing she loved, apart from Stevan, was money. And she took any currency.

Kaisa saw his eyelids flicker and she composed her face, leaning in to kiss his cheek, in what she thought was a nice touch. "Good morning sleepy–boy" whispered in her husky voice should have the desired effect. She'd been told that her voice made men weak; it definitely worked on this one.

114

Bob Leighton opened his eyes and thought that he'd died and gone to heaven. She was still there. Gorgeous, smiling, pretty and pliable, the perfect woman. And he was going to have her for good; he didn't give a shit what anyone thought. So what if she wasn't educated, or rich. He didn't care, she was all his. He couldn't believe that they'd only met five months before.

What if they hadn't met? What if she hadn't been their neighbours' nanny? He'd never understood how they'd let her go. The wife was jealous, he supposed. He didn't care; their loss had been his gain. He shuddered, thinking of what he might have missed and she saw the movement, covering him quickly with the duvet in feigned concern.

"Are you cold, my love? Shall I make breakfast?"

He kissed her gently, pushing her soft white-blonde hair back from her face. Her eyes were soft and liquid, a light strong green, and her clear skin tanned so easily in the sun that she looked like a berry, even in December. She was beautiful, but not in the over-the-top, Essex way that lots of young women were. She was quietly, softly beautiful and she was perfect for him.

He looked past her at the clock on the bedside table, ten a.m.! Oh shit. He would be late for his meeting. He pushed her arm down gently and looked reluctantly at the pert brown breast that had escaped its wrapping, nearly lying back down again. Fighting the urge hard he leapt up, heading quickly across the weathered maple floor to the ensuite. He looked at his bleary eyes in the fluorescent mirror, he looked sixty. They'd arrived late last night and he'd had a skin-full, but she'd been drinking too, yet she still looked as fresh as a flower.

"Sorry pet, I have to run. I've a meeting that'll be very important for both our futures."

The future again. He smiled at the surprise that she'd get later, once everything was settled. Kaisa knew what was expected of her and obliged, faking a disappointed pout.

"But when you be back? I want cook something special."

115

"Don't worry. I'll be back around four, plenty of time. Let's go out. I could take you to the new place in Rathmullan?"

Such sophistication. But she had other plans. "No, I have all planned, you will see. We have romantic dinner here. "

Her broken English did things to him that no Irish accent ever had, and he had visions of a naked feast in front of the large, open fire downstairs.

"That sounds like a plan. Excellent. What time do you want me home?"

"Only at seven, all will be ready." She smiled up at him coyly. "I will be ready..."

The promise was implicit and he reached over and kissed her on the forehead, lingering for a longer time on her lips. "I'll see you at seven then, and I'll bring some champagne. If all goes well today we'll have plenty to celebrate."

Ten minutes later, they walked down the open Scandinavian staircase to the front room., with its wall of windows over-looking the North Atlantic inlet with the second most beautiful beach in the world. Then she stood like a good little girlfriend, waving him off, as he drove out of the private driveway of their rented villa, and disappeared quickly at the end of the lane.

Kaisa looked around the luxurious home. He had a lot of Euro, this Bob. And she'd take some of them with her, just for having to put up with his pale, weak hands on her last night. She'd been avoiding his touch for months.

But his money wasn't her reason for being there. She looked out at the ocean, thinking. The sunshine was hitting the rocks immediately below the window, and in the distance she could just make out a horse and rider cantering along the smooth, white sand. So many pretty places in this little country. It was very beautiful, yes, but too cold for her in winter, maybe they could head for Dubai when this was all over.

She'd played the part of the lonely little Estonian for six months now, breaking her perfect English just enough to make people feel protective, but not

116

frustrated. And always sticking to the rules that Stevan had taught her. Always give people what they expected. It didn't do to confuse them too much. And always say that you came from some Eastern European or Nordic country. Most people in Britain couldn't tell them apart, believing whatever they were told. So she had become Estonian Kaisa Moldeau and now she was Bob's little Kaisa.

She'd played it well. She'd got the job she needed, au pair to the Leighton's boring neighbours. And then she'd tempted the husband just enough for the frosty wife to pass her on to the Leightons. She felt a sudden sadness about Irene Leighton. The emotion was unexpected because she so rarely felt anything, but Irene had been kind to her, genuinely kind. She was genuinely sad that she'd gone, and for her part in it.

The feeling passed as quickly as it came and she thought about Bob Leighton. Such a self-important little man, but then, weren't they all. She laughed aloud, amused by herself. She was glad that it would end tomorrow after the months of pretence; it would be time to leave soon. But it had been worth it all to give Stevan cover. All the smiling and last night's limp fucking, tolerating his wet weak hands. All worth it for the pleasure they would get when their job was done.

She lifted a cheap pink mobile from her handbag and slowly dialled the number to arrange next Monday's meeting. It rang only once, picked up quickly by the eager man at the other end. She inhaled, letting it out slowly in an old trick, a breathless quality in her voice the predictable outcome. "Hello, Jo-es-eph." Lingering very deliberately over the additional syllable.

Joe Watson's heart jumped with excitement at the sound of her voice and he stood-up quickly, closing the office door. It wouldn't do for Michael to overhear.

"Ausra...It's lovely to hear your voice. Where are you?"

"At my father house. He is not well today." There was silence as she counted to three, then spoke at exactly the right time for effect. "I mees you, Joe."

Watson almost shouted aloud with excitement. *This*

117

was what love felt like. He remembered it from Irene. Sadness overwhelmed him for a moment, rendering him silent, but nothing could completely kill his euphoria.

Her vulnerable voice pulled him back to the moment. "Joe, do you not love me?"

He stared at the phone forgetting the past and tripping over his words. "Of course I love you. I love you. I really love you, Ausra. What time will you be there on Monday?"

She smiled smugly to herself, completely in control. "At six, I think. And Joe..."

"Yes?"

"I maybe see you Tuesday also, would that be good?"

He gripped the phone hard, unable to believe his luck. Two days next week, they'd finally have time to talk. He had a lot to say.

"Yes, of course. And Wednesday too if you can. And Thursday."

She rewarded him with a pretty laugh and his heart sailed away, already thinking of next week.

****

The Ormeau Road, Belfast.

Stevan wiped the blue cloth over the table, gazing out through the coloured glass window of the saloon bar onto Belfast's busy Ormeau Road. The mahogany wall clock said that it was time to open up, so he took the heavy keys from his jeans pocket, musing.

Nineteen years ago, he'd lived in a forest. Seven months ago, they'd been playing the tables in Las Vegas. And now here he was, wiping up slops in a Belfast bar. Life was never predictable. He laughed loudly, showing his large, white teeth to the empty room.

He was a striking man, with tanned skin and hard muscles, and the strong high cheekbones of his home country. His laugh was so loud that it brought Teresa running-in from the back bar.

"What're you laughing at Stevan? Go 'awn, tell me the joke."

He looked down at her, eighteen and pretty, thinking that she knew all about life. The things I could tell you, little girl.

"I laugh only at myself." Then, looking down at the wet cloth in his hand. "It is such a glamorous life we have - no?"

"No! You're right there. Just think about it, for the float in that till we could be lying on a beach, instead of serving booze to a pack of drunken students."

She looked reluctantly at the clock. "Aye well. That's that dream over. We'd better open up soon or my Da' will be chasing us."

Stevan smiled to himself. Poor little Teresa, she tried so hard to be a street girl. When really her father owned this and many other bars, dotted around Belfast and the outlying towns. It pleased her to pretend that she was 'cool', when her natural accent had been ironed-out years before by expensive elocution lessons. Only descending to street level when her father left the premises, to give her 'cred' with her friends.

She even talked about students as if she wasn't one of them, and all to impress him. Dropping her vocabulary to a level that she thought would make him feel easy. If only she knew.

Of course, she had a crush on him, which was always useful. She thought that he was exotic and exciting, and asked him constantly what Romania was like. How the fuck would he know? He was from Serbia! But he made up stories of nameless mountain streams anyway, to keep her happy. He hated disappointing women.

He was safe saying that he came from anywhere east of Italy. They couldn't tell one Slavic country from another in Belfast; we all look the same to them.

He thought fleetingly of Kaisa. She would be leaving Donegal soon for her next appointment, setting the scene for his part. He wished desperately that she didn't have to. That he didn't either.

He turned back to the moment and looked down at the girl's high, firm breasts pushing through her tight t-shirt. It had got incrementally tighter by the month, since he'd arrived. She wasn't bad to look at, in that slightly gauche, student way. His taste usually ran more to more angular beauties, but she passed the time, and kept him safe from her father's prying eyes. He could cope with screwing her a bit longer, and they would leave very soon now. After he had done his final job.

****

Port Salon. Donegal.

Kaisa lifted the bag that she had concealed behind the wardrobe and withdrew the items that she needed for the evening. Her seduction outfit, well, she might as well give him a good time. The glass phial full of clear fluid. She held it up towards the late afternoon light. It was beautiful; clear and sparkling, just like Cristal.

And of course, she mustn't forget the most important item of all, the piece de résistance that would finally end Robert Leighton's dishonest existence. The syringe with its nine-centimetre needle. Long enough to reach straight through his pale little nipple, through the fat and muscle of his weak chest wall and skewer his shrivelled little heart.

Even if she'd been capable of feeling remorse, she wouldn't have wasted any on Bob Leighton. Not after the way he'd forgotten his kind wife so quickly and screwed her last night. And much more importantly than any of that, he had outlived his value.

Chapter Thirteen

John Winter adjusted his tie nervously and looked in the mirror. Not bad. He hadn't worn one for a while and he'd thought that he might have forgotten how to tie the knot. But it had come back to him. It was like driving; arriving at your destination without remembering the route you'd taken, but knowing that if you actually thought too much about it then you'd get lost.

Natalie gazed up at him, knowing exactly what he was thinking and smiling wryly. She shook her head fondly at her genius boyfriend, knowing that in the thirty seconds it had taken him to fix his tie he'd have had more ideas than the average person had in a week. But he'd still forget to tie his laces and fall over at the end of the hall.

"And don't worry about Mirella, she's lovely, just a bit full-on at first meeting."

The comment came out of the blue but John's tone said that it was a continued conversation, and Natalie knew that the first part had just taken place inside his head.

She shrugged gently. "I'm not worried about her; she sounds just like my mum. She'll have your bank account details out of you by the end of a handshake."

John swallowed nervously, that was next weekend's treat. He looked down at Natalie, taking in her softly tousled dark hair and bright emerald-green dress, making her visible from half a street away. The colour scheme was coupled with a wide white grin that wrinkled up her snub nose and pale blue eyes. The whole effect was 'friendly leprechaun' instead of fiercely intelligent surgeon. She reminded him of his mother and he smiled. But more importantly this evening, she was just as eccentric as Mirella Craig. They would get on fine.

****

Donegal.

Kaisa smiled down at her lover coldly but Bob Leighton completely missed the change in temperature, focusing on the moonlight outlining the curve of her tanned smooth waist and the treasures that it bordered. He had a momentary twinge of guilt about Irene and Kaisa saw it passing rapidly, hating him even more for his quick rejection of the one genuine emotion that he'd probably ever felt.

She'd liked his wife, really liked her, and as far as she could feel regret, she regretted the pain of her last few days. Neither of them had understood the need for her painful markings, or the public theatricality of her death. Stevan promised he would ask when they got back to London.

Leighton yawned widely and fell from his side onto his back, beckoning her to lie above him, with her feet to his, bringing her head barely to his chin. He liked the way the size difference made him feel; male and female, and him with all the power. He yawned widely and stretched his arms overhead. "I'm tired, pet. Let's sleep for a bit, OK?"

Older man, longer recovery. But her thoughts stayed silent and she nodded up at him submissively, and then climbed off the bed, walking to the wardrobe to put on her robe. He smiled sleepily and star-fished across the bed, teasing her. Then he moved to one side, lying back with his arms behind his head, and started to doze. Kaisa smiled wryly at his sleeping position, how convenient; at least she didn't have to turn him over for access.

His breathing was gentle at first, deepening quickly into a rasping sleep. She knelt down urgently at the change in sound, reaching into her ready prepared bag and withdrawing the clear phial of fluid, and its delivery system. She moved slowly to the bed and nudged his knee to test his sleep, first gently and then more roughly. Then finally, she slapped his face hard with her open hand, eliciting no response. The drugs disguised in dinner had finally rendered him helpless.

She looked down at him contemptuously, feeling no pity or hesitation, and drew the liquid ceremoniously into the syringe, flicking the barrel repeatedly as she'd been taught. As if he would worry about an air bubble, when the liquid itself would have already killed him. She climbed onto the bed and straddled him, her hands trembling with anticipation and revenge. All the wet kisses and the wet hands that he'd touched her with, when he should have been mourning his kind wife. He hadn't even been there to stop them killing her, too busy with his big job.

She clasped both small white hands tightly around the barrel of the syringe, and pressed the needle-tip against his left breast, finding the nipple with its point. Then she pushed straight through it, down hard, through the skin and fat and muscle, and into the bony space beneath. Then on, even further, into the thick muscled wall of the organ that life depended on.

He didn't move, and didn't wake and Kaisa felt cheated, even though she'd known that he wouldn't. She liked them to see her face last.

His breath was still warm and his body still moved with each pulse, and she knew that if she withdrew the needle now, he would still live. But she wouldn't.

She lay down on him for a moment, feeling his heartbeats through her hands and thighs, and watching their rhythm through the needle's regular sway. She smiled gleefully, imagining his face if he woke at that instant. But he wouldn't. Shrugging her disappointment away she rested one hand casually on the plunger, savouring her power. Then finally, after a long moment watching, she gave the plunger a single hard push, watching as the clear fluid drained from the syringe.

Kaisa waited, thighs tight around his flanks, feeling their warmth, as the needle stopped swaying, and he slowly paled and died. Then she coolly climbed off his body and dressed, packing without a single backward glance. She walked downstairs, made the call and left, lifting the keys of the hire-car from the hall table and leaving the door ajar behind her, heading for Belfast for her final task.

****

The Craigs' House. Holywood, County Down. Friday evening.

Craig smiled at the two female heads huddled conspiratorially in the living-room corner and caught John's eye, knowing that he was beginning to relax. He'd managed to avoid Mirella's conversation on 'Natalie's intentions' all evening and it was almost coffee time. Soon they would be leaving and he would be home free.

Tom Craig smiled at his son's friends from his well-worn armchair, and stroked their Labrador's head absentmindedly as he fiddled with the radio. Craig could hear his mother clattering noisily around the kitchen, knowing that any minute she would call out. "Marco, come help with coffee."

He stood up in anticipation and John caught his move, panicking. "Don't leave that chair free, or your mum will sit down and grill me."

Tom Craig heard the remark and laughed. "It's like the dentist, son. There's no way to avoid it. My advice is to give in gracefully. It'll be over a lot quicker."

Just then, Craig's anticipated call came and he left dutifully for the kitchen, just as Lucia and Natalie wandered across to the two men. John smiled at them both. Lucia was a ten years younger, fairer version of Craig, in high heels. She felt like his kid sister as well.

She removed her father's elbow unceremoniously from the arm of his chair and plonked herself down beside him, while Natalie did the same to John. It made John feel part of something, and he liked the feeling after years of bachelorhood.

"Where's Richard tonight, Lucia?"

Her hand waved dismissively in the air, implying a casualness that he knew she didn't feel about her boyfriend of three months. "Touring. He's in Cardiff this week."

124

Richard was a pianist with the London City Orchestra and Mirella loved him for it, failing to instill her own piano virtuosity into her children. Although John had heard Craig play the Blues, and he was good. Lucia smiled wistfully, missing Richard but not admitting it. "I just hope he likes the snow they're getting!"

Natalie interrupted the exchange deliberately, covering Lucia's loneliness. "Lucia suggested that we go shopping together, to get new outfits for the N.S.P.C.C. Ball."

"That's just what you need, Nat, more clothes. Imelda Marcos was starting to worry."

Tom Craig looked over at John surprised, admiring the courage that Natalie rewarded two seconds later with a fond clip over the head, just as the others re-entered with the coffee. Mirella Craig caught the exchange and smiled, taking the radio firmly from her husband and turning it to Classic FM, determined to educate them while she had a captive audience. Then she lifted a chair very deliberately and sat beside Natalie, still perched on the arm of John's chair, and leaned in pointedly.

"Now, Natalie. John, he is my nice boy..." And she started the conversation on 'intentions' that John had been studiously avoiding all evening.

Chapter Fourteen

Craig's Apartment. Saturday Morning.

"Here, boss. No one has seen Leighton since yesterday. He went to a solicitor's in Rathmullan, left there at five-thirty and headed back to the house. But there's been no sign of him or the girl since."

Craig yawned over his mobile and reached across the bed to check the clock. It was nearly eleven! He sat bolt upright, lying-down again immediately when his head throbbed violently. The week had caught up with him in one night, aided by his father's red wine.

"Sorry, Liam. I was a bit distracted for a moment, say that again."

"Not a sign of Leighton for eighteen hours, boss. What do you want me to do?"

Liam could hear the fatigue in Craig's voice and almost volunteered to go to Donegal to check on Leighton. But a sudden vision of Danni standing in front of him, arms folded in a snit at the mention of any trip before the baby was born, made discretion the better part of everything, so he stayed silent.

Craig was sitting on the edge of the bed, rubbing his eyes hard. He raked his hands roughly through his thick dark hair and yawned again, finally managing to focus.

"OK, no-one has seen him for eighteen hours. Have the Irish Police been round to check?"

"Aye, well...they weren't too keen to make contact. Didn't mind knowing that he was there, but didn't want to question him 'cos he's our man."

"They can knock the door, for God's sake." He could hear himself getting exasperated, but not with Liam, so he reigned it in. "Sorry Liam, I'm just tired."

Liam knew that he had to be wrecked even to admit that.

"I'll drive up there later and see what's happening."

Liam immediately felt guilty for making him take the trip and was about to volunteer, Danni or no

Danni, when Craig continued. "You can't go, the baby's too close."

Liam smiled gratefully but he still wasn't happy. "Here, I've a better idea."

"What?"

"Give that smart-ass Inspector up in Limavady a call and get her to nip up to Portsalon, it's only sixty miles away."

Liam smiled to himself, waiting to see if Craig would rise to the bait. They all knew that he liked Julia McNulty, but wondered if he knew he did.

"That smart-ass Inspector?"

The way Liam had said it convinced Craig that no one in the office had the vaguest idea that he liked Julia McNulty. He didn't know whether to be pleased at the privacy or critical of Liam's description. He opted for the latter. "She's very nice you know."

Liam snorted derisively, intent on winding him up some more. "Nice to look at maybe, but she'd chew your head off as soon as she'd look at you."

Craig nodded, not spotting Liam's bait. He had to agree. "Yes, she is a bit challenging. It's a great idea anyway, Liam. I'll call her now and ask her to check on Leighton's whereabouts. I'll meet you in the office in an hour."

Liam smiled, clicking the phone off without a word. Craig fell back heavily on the bed for a moment, dreading the call, but excited by the excuse for contact as well. He reached for the phone and then put it down again, bouncing to his feet instead. He needed to be awake to call Julia McNulty and that would take a cold shower and a whole cafetiere of coffee today.

****

The C.C.U.

"Here, did you see today's Chronicle, boss? There was a sudden death in Donegal last night. Since when did the Chronicle report out of town? Maybe we could export Maggie Clarke."

127

Liam said it deliberately loudly, so that Davy could hear him. Davy didn't even look up, just raised his middle finger, smiling. It was the weekend and Liam was on the wind-up. His long legs were propped up on a desk at an angle, so that his feet deliberately obscured half of Annette's computer screen, and she gave them a hard shove that made him swing around in his chair. Nicky watched them from her corner, smiling; her twelve-year-old niece did exactly the same thing to her brothers.

"Will you get your big feet out of the way, Liam? I'm writing a report for the prosecution service. If you're having a slow day, I can easily find you some work."

She gave him her best threatening look. No one had the heart to tell her it made her look like an angry toddler.

"Here, missy, I'm your boss. You're supposed to worship me. It was in your contract."

Just at that moment, Craig entered the squad room. "Actually, I think you'll find that I'm your boss, and I haven't noticed much worshipping in my direction lately."

Nicky stifled a laugh at Liam being put in his box, but the reprimand by-passed Liam completely.

"Here, boss. There's been a sudden death in Donegal, some forty-year-old from Belfast. Can we investigate it?"

The vision of a Saturday road–trip perked Annette up; just then Craig surprised them all by urgently seizing the paper from Liam's desk.

"God, I was only joking, boss. It was natural causes."

But something about the death made Craig uneasy. "Liam, get onto the Chronicle and find out more about this, please. We need a name and cause of death. And put John onto their pathologist if necessary."

Annette realised what he was thinking. "You think it's a murder, sir?"

Liam sat bolt upright, annoyed that she'd joined the dots before him.

"It's not murder, boss. The article says the father

128

died of the same thing around forty. It's called sudden heart disease or something. And anyway, it's out of our jurisdiction."

"It's called S.A.D.S, Liam. Sudden adult death syndrome. And humour me; my instinct says this is something. Bob Leighton's forty and as you told me earlier he hasn't been seen for eighteen hours. By the way, D.I. McNulty's on her way up there."

"He was seen in Rathmullan yesterday afternoon, sir."

Annette interjected. "But that was yesterday, Nicky"

Nicky looked at her grumpily for jumping on the bandwagon. "They promised us an update if he left the house." Her tone was peevish and all that was missing was her tongue sticking out.

"And he hasn't left the house since yesterday afternoon, Cutty? Aye, right."

Craig raised his hand calmly to stop the childish exchange. They were all getting tired.

He turned to Annette kindly. "He hasn't been seen since yesterday, Annette, and after what happened to his wife...Well, D.I. McNulty's heading up there now to check the situation out. Call her in an hour and get an update please. She's liaising with the Derry police before she crosses the border."

Derry-stroke-Londonderry was commonly known as 'Stroke City'. And its name historically depended on which side of the political divide you belonged, although sheer laziness made 'Derry' more commonly used by everyone. Craig had been so confused by the nickname that he'd spent his first year back from London thinking that 'stroke' referred to the illness!

It had been the capital of the Northwest since the sixth century and was the only completely walled city in the British Isles. It was a pretty place; full of charm and surrounded by beautiful countryside, but its proximity to the Irish border had always made it an easy run, the few miles into a different country.

Craig jumped at a tap on his shoulder, not noticing Nicky moving to stand beside him. "What can I do for you, Nicky?"

129

"D.C.I. White would still like that word when you have time. Would this afternoon at two suit you?" She looked meaningfully at him. "Because of course, you'll be too busy doing your letters until then."

"Nicky, don't be mean. It's the w...weekend."

She shot Davy a cold look and Craig sighed heavily; he preferred a crime-scene to an office any day. It made taking rank a real challenge.

"It's OK, Davy. We're all in until this is solved, so I might as well do them. I tried Andy on Thursday, Nicky, but he'd been called out. Two's fine. Do you know what he wants?"

"Something about your work in London. He'd like to pick your brains."

And before Liam could form the words, Craig swung around. "No cracks from you and a bit more worshipping. Unless you want to be doing those letters for me?"

****

2 p.m.

Andy White was slim and quick, like a bantamweight boxer. He hailed from Dungiven, punctuating every other sentence with 'hey', as per the local habit, in the same way that a lot of Belfast people said 'like'.

He wore exactly the same colour of blue shirt every day, and even men noticed that it matched his eyes perfectly. Everyone thought that his wife had bought him a job lot, either that or he washed the same one every night. He took a lot of amiable flak for it, and he took it well.

He couldn't sit in a chair without fidgeting, and was propped against the edge of his desk reading a file when Craig entered.

"Hi Marc. Great day, hey?" Craig smiled. He had a lot of time for Andy.

"What's so great about it?"

"Another one bites the dust. That bastard O'Brien's snuffed it, hey."

"Did you have dealings with him?"

"Sure. He was heavily involved in the drugs traffic across the border. Probably using it to fund the 'armed struggle'. We got close to making something stick last year, then a junior player gave himself up instead."

Craig nodded. It often happened when the heat got too close to the big boys. They'd throw a small fish at the police to deflect them. It was known as 'playing your pawn'. All in the game.

Craig instantly thought of something. "What age was he?"

"Twenty-eight. Why?"

"Oh, nothing. Just that there was a forty-year-old sudden death in Donegal yesterday."

White shook his head. "Yes, I saw that. Not our boy."

"Anyway, what can I do for you, Andy? Nicky said you wanted to pick my brains on something?"

"I did surely. Did you ever come across Ketamine when you worked in London?"

"Yes. More than once. Nasty stuff. John Winter's your man for the detail, and Des Marsham in Forensics, but he's on holiday. They used to call it special K. A bad overdose was known as being in the K-hole. Is there much of a market for it here?"

"Well. And keep this to yourself, hey. But the Donegal Coroner got onto us two days ago. They think O'Brien was a suspicious death."

"Murder?"

"Well, they're not saying murder just yet, but they're pretty sure he was high on a regular basis. Well God, you'd have to be, wouldn't you? Nipping across the border with a bomb in your bag."

"Fair enough." Craig had never thought of it like that.

"They found Ket, coke and roofies in his system on the P.M, and gave us the nod in the spirit of cooperation. Just in case they'd added Ketamine to the shit they're smuggling to our side. I remembered you'd been in London, and everything London has, we get eventually."

131

Craig nodded, unfortunately it was true. "Ketamine's nasty, especially in high doses, and nearly undetectable by the victim until it's too late."

White shrugged. "The odds are that it's not murder and he was just using it. He had a shed load of coke in him as well, so his heart probably just gave up the ghost. I just don't want more shit being added to the stuff we're already trying to get rid of. I'll give the Doc a call."

A sudden thought came to him. "I say it wasn't murder, but..."

Craig looked at him sharply. "What?"

"Well it might be nothing, hey. But we're hearing rumblings about some new bunch of eejits crawling out of the woodwork. I think they're called the NIF." He laughed. "Or the naff, more likely."

"Never heard of them."

"No one has. Ach, it's probably nothing. Just the usual tripe. Hey, maybe they'll start a gang war and kill each other off. Save us some work."

Craig smiled wryly, turning to leave. Then he thought of something and turned back quickly. "We might be taking a trip up there later, Andy. Let me know if you need us to pick up on anything. And John would probably offer you a second P.M. if you wanted it? It might be an idea, just in case they missed something."

"Good thought, but we'd never get permission. The dissidents won't want their glory boy being seen as a junkie, hey. They'll want a hero's funeral."

Craig raised his eyes, knowing exactly what that would entail, and wondering how many pictures of it the Sunday Chronicle would have.

****

When Craig returned to the squad-room Davy was pacing the floor excitedly.

"I talked to London again, s... sir. They've more on the Lapua."

Craig nodded him on, perching on a nearby desk.

132

"They think there w...was definitely an accomplice in both murders."

"An accomplice? Take it from the beginning, Davy."

"You know how there were two s...shootings in London?"

"Yes."

"They believe that it's an international killer, based on the Paris connection. And in both London cases there w...were reports of another person, at the s... scene."

"When you say at the scene, do you mean near the victims, or at the shooter's location?"

"The victims. Both times."

Two people. The second person who'd walked Irene Leighton into Stormont.

"Any description or I.D.?" Craig knew it was a long shot.

"Female, s...sir. Both reported a young w...woman."

There was silence in the room, but not shock. Six months ago they would have been shocked at a woman's involvement, but not after the Jessica Adams' case. Craig nodded. The lad in the baseball cap could have been a woman. The guard might have been mistaken, and the dark winter morning would have helped. Good planning by the killer.

"S...She was noticed around both the London jobs, but there's nothing concrete yet, and everyone described her differently."

Liam sniffed. Witnesses were hopeless. The only decent one he'd had in the past year had been Ida Foster, an eighty something!

"Let's pull the witness descriptions anyway, Davy."

"OK, s... sir. And they think they might have a gangland connection in London. With a known big player. But there's nothing on an accomplice in Paris."

"Crap, we're looking at an overseas hit here, boss. None of our muppets could muster that sort of armour, not even back in their glory days."

Craig nodded at Liam, agreeing, this was way out of the local terrorists' league. But it still brought him back to the same question. Why would international players

133

want to kill a Northern Irish housewife like Irene Leighton? And the answer was still the same. Bob.

****

Love and Death Inc. Restaurant. Ann Street, Belfast. Saturday Evening.

Davy pulled at his jacket collar nervously, feeling uncomfortable. He normally wore T-shirts and jeans, but even his brother had said that he should make an effort on a first date. He smiled to himself, imagining Nicky's dating advice. She'd probably have just locked him in his bedroom.

It occurred randomly to him that it was time to move out of his parent's house. He could hardly bring a girl back there; his mum would never let them upstairs! And he could just imagine the conversations with his granny; she'd be passing on her cake recipe in a minute flat.

He told himself off quickly. He loved them all dearly and he shouldn't even be thinking of taking Maggie upstairs yet, she was a nice girl and this was only a first date. He smiled naughtily; maybe on the third.

His thoughts were interrupted by Maggie returning to the table, and he stood up hastily, remembering his manners. He looked at her smiling; she looked gorgeous, and well worth the jacket.

Maggie looked up at him, blushing. She hadn't felt nervous about anyone for ages and she really liked the feeling. She really liked him. She sat down, looking around curiously at their venue. When Davy had called and said that he was taking her somewhere cool, she'd racked her brains, guessing at all the mainstream venues that Belfast had to offer. She'd come up with a shortlist of three, but 'Love and Death Inc.' hadn't been on it. Now she knew why. It was far cooler than she was.

It had opened in two thousand and ten, elegantly placed in Ann Street on two floors of a long terrace. Known only to the uber-cool few at the beginning, it was really popular now, and she could see why. It was a world full of fabulous food, skulls and angels, with a cocktail menu that she'd only dreamed of.

She gazed around enquiringly, her eye falling on a poster that made her squeal with excitement. It was her favourite Belfast singer, Duke Special! The 'hobo-chic' piano-based songwriter had just finished playing lunchtime concerts there! The place really couldn't get any cooler.

She grinned across at Davy, as impressed by his choice of restaurant as she was by him offering to take her clubbing afterwards. The older men that she'd dated had to be dragged to clubs, and once there, they lurked around the peripheries, leching while the girls gyrated. But Davy had actually promised to dance with her, and she was praying that his cool choice of restaurant would be echoed by his cool moves on the floor.

If it was, she'd have found the perfect man. Arty looking but scientific, cool enough to choose the restaurant, but responsible enough to collect her from home. And best of all, mature, but five years younger than her. Her very own beautiful toy-boy.

Chapter Fifteen

Port Salon. Donegal.

"The house was empty when I got here, but the neighbours didn't see anyone leave. It seems that the last sighting of Leighton was yesterday afternoon in Rathmullan."

"What about the girl?"

"No one even saw her. Only Leighton."

"Are there any signs of a struggle?"

"None. There's nothing to indicate that anything untoward happened. Except..."

"Yes?"

"Well, all his clothes are still here. And not packed. So it doesn't look as if he's gone very far."

Something occurred to Craig. "Any sign of forced entry?"

"No, the door was shut when I arrived with the police. We had to smash the glass to get in. But no damage, other than that."

"Are the girl's things still there?"

Julia paused, realising that she hadn't noticed. She grudgingly said "No", reluctant to acknowledge that she'd missed it.

Craig thought quickly, no Kaisa Moldeau or her clothes. And no sign of Leighton. But his clothes said that he hadn't left. No forced entry and the police hadn't been called to the house during the past twenty-four hours. He snapped his fingers. Of course...

"Call the local hospitals and the coroner. She called him an ambulance and left the door open..."

****

The Castleton Hotel, County Antrim. Monday.

Joe Watson knew that he had to consider his position carefully; he was a government Minister for God's sake, and a good one. Even his political enemies admitted that he worked his ass off for the people of Newry. In fact, he was so good that they'd made him Enterprise Minister. No mean feat, considering that he was the only Commerce Party member in the Assembly. His years of success merchant-banking in London had finally made even the doughboys on the hill realise that he could do his sums.

The close protection officer standing outside his hotel-room door was a quiet indicator of his status. They were good lads. Well, except for that dickhead Sinclair who though he was Northern Ireland's version of Jack Bauer, scaring the bejeesus out of the airline staff with his glares. He'd have to go. But Drake was fine.

Very understanding of his little foibles they were too. And of his sudden changes of itinerary, especially the 'unofficial' ones. But those couldn't continue and he knew it. It was only a matter of time before the shit hit the fan, and some hack at the Chronicle door-stepped him somewhere very awkward.

Yes. He'd have to consider his position carefully. But right now, the only position he was considering, was lying on his back, looking up at the most beautiful girl he'd ever known.

"Your thoughts. They are not with me tonight, Jo-es-ph. Where are you?"

The tanned dark-blonde pouted as she pulled her jeans on. "You will get me in trouble with Madame if she thinks that you are not pleased. You must say to me if there is something that does not please you. Please do not tell her."

Joe looked into two black fringed green eyes that sat above the most perfect nose that he'd ever seen, and his heart flipped, several times. Then he noticed that the eyes were glistening with threatened tears and he shook himself out of his reverie.

"No, no pet. You're perfect, really perfect." He reached hurriedly for his briefcase, keen to please her. "Look what I've brought you."

He took out the largest bottle of perfume that he'd been able to find in duty-free and she smiled. A soft, sweet smile that dimpled her cheeks. He wanted to drink champagne from those dimples, amongst others. She seemed genuinely pleased with the gift and he loved to please her. There was nothing selfish about Joe, in his own mind at least.

He loved their little arrangement. He flew to London from the City Airport every Monday morning, telling Caitlin that he wouldn't be back until late that night. She was well used to his short political absences, although lately he'd noticed that she'd been a lot less reasonable. Then he flew back into Belfast International in the afternoon. And, after 'considering his position' for a few hours in the Castleton hotel in Antrim, he had a regular boys-only poker game alibi, before heading home to Helen's Bay at two a.m. It worked perfectly.

The game was full of rich men lying to their wives so it was the perfect cover story if anything leaked. And everyone would forgive him playing poker with the boys; it might even make voters think that he was exciting. It was the perfect arrangement, and it had been working for two years with different girls from Lilith's, until he'd met Ausra three months before.

It was decent of the Madam to let her come to the hotel, not that Lilith's wasn't perfectly pleasant; it had always suited him before. But he was a Minister now, and well, you couldn't be too careful, could you.

Lilith's brothel was located in a Victorian detached house three miles from the International Airport, in a narrow anonymous lane set well back from the road. It provided every service that a businessman could possibly need, and some that he hadn't even imagined. Joe had used it happily for years. But once he'd seen Ausra, he'd known that no other girl would do. And it would always have been hard to explain emerging from Lilith's to some hack, the four-star Castleton was much more anonymous.

His single gripe was that she could only manage Monday nights because of her elderly father, only managing a sitter one night a week. It elevated her in his opinion of course, such a kind girl looking after her

138

father. And it boded well for the future, when he was so much older than her.

And now that he was her only client, it allowed him to believe that they were really lovers, and that she actually had feelings for him. It was a little self - deception that was helped by no money ever changing hands. He'd convinced himself that making the large cash payments straight to Lilith protected her too. He wasn't selfish.

Joe shook himself from his thoughts and watched her stretch out across the bed, playing with her perfume bottle like a small child, her tiny hands dwarfed by its girth. She was tanned and bare-footed, and her low-slung jeans revealed a sliver of flat brown stomach beneath her white t-shirt. He could feel his position being reconsidered again and she smiled up at him, laughing knowingly.

"You have no time; already your friends wait for the poker. We will meet again tomorrow, I promise."

Tomorrow. His heart soared. Two nights this week, she was keeping to her promise. She was still talking, but he couldn't hear her words now, full of love, and listening instead to the music in her voice. Her accent was a soft mystery, somewhere east of the Alps for sure, but it could have been from any number of places. Hungary, Latvia...Who cared? She was here now and she was stunning.

She bounced up from the bed and leapt off deftly, avoiding his impending lunge, and danced away from him, giggling. Then, putting on her ridiculously high-heeled shoes, she grabbed her huge shoulder-bag and stepped quickly to the bedroom door.

Joe leapt off the bed after her and pulled her against his bare chest. He couldn't bear to let her go, and in that split second, he knew he was in trouble. He was in love. She looked up at him gently as if she had some sixth sense, and stroked the grey hair at his temple with a single finger. "Until tomorrow, Joe. Yes?"

"Yes."

Then she wriggled expertly through his arms, pulling her dark glasses from her bag. No one knew how she earned her money and her father would die from the shame, so she needed to protect her identity, and the glasses were perfect for that. The bedroom door opened and closed quickly, leaving him standing alone.

The nicer protection officer was sitting outside the room tonight, with his arms folded. He yawned tiredly as she emerged and she smiled at him sympathetically, with her full red pout. Then she wiggled quickly past him to the lift, catching his admiring look in the reflecting wall. She liked this one; the other man looked at her far too suspiciously. She hurried through the lobby, head-down avoiding the cameras, and left quickly for her destination.

Joe lay back on the bed looking at the clock. She'd only been gone ten minutes and already he felt bereft. Get a fucking grip, man. He had to shower and change to meet the others in the bar at nine otherwise his alibi would be blown. Normally he enjoyed the game, but the realisation that he'd fallen for her wasn't adding to his mood tonight.

Now started the 'tearing lumps off his heart' bit. Falling in love with Ausra but still loving Caitlin and his kids, knowing that he should be sensible, but feeling his skin raw at the thought of giving her up. He'd been here once before, sixteen years ago, with his first wife after Gemma had been born. It was painful, but simpler then. He was still idealistic about marriage and they had a new baby, the other girl had been no contest. But nowadays, he was rarely home, and Caitlin spent seventy-percent of her time angry with him. Plus he'd already cast Ausra in the role of 'self-sacrificing daughter who needed rescuing'. All of a sudden divorce seemed very possible.

****

The blonde walked quickly across the hotel forecourt, heading for the car. It would be dark soon, so there were only two hours left to do the trial run. She resisted the urge to gun the small Ford's engine. It

140

wasn't her usual calibre of ride but the aim was not to draw attention, and a flashy car would have attracted far too many looks. She cleared the long driveway from the hotel sedately; heading left onto the Antrim Road, and driving until she reached a small copse of Birch trees, pulling in.

The evening's sunset was bright, and the sky was warm, streaked with red lights. She remembered a rhyme that Bob had quoted at her; 'red sky at night, shepherd's delight.' How many shepherds did you know, Bob? She gave a wry laugh and then chastised herself. Focus, you can laugh later.

She scanned her surroundings quickly, it was isolated. Then she climbed out and opened the boot, reaching behind the spare wheel for the black bag. It was heavy and she struggled to pull it out. Stevan had wedged it in so tightly. Typical boy, not remembering how strong they are...or not realising how weak we are. She smiled to herself. Stevan had always over-tightened the jars at home, she remembered Mama chiding him for it. Oh, Mama...that was so long ago, and such a different time.

She shrugged the bag out of the boot, dragging it along the driver's side, using the car for support. Until it rested on the seat, hidden from prying eyes by the open door. Pulling at the metal zipper, she opened it, reaching inside quickly to finger the magazine, while Stevan wasn't there to stop her. Her only jobs were to check that the bullet was there, the scope was spotless and the mechanism was smooth. And then to drive to Stevan's chosen point and make the call. Just to test, one last time.

Over the next thirty minutes, she worked coolly and efficiently, then zipped the bag and returned it to its hiding place. Then she sealed the boot with a special fail-safe locking mechanism that would resist even her opening it again. Stevan was clever with the gadgets, his little toys...And of course, he wasn't a virgin at this. She snorted to herself; her big brother wasn't a virgin at anything.

She gunned the car now, with nothing but a few

141

birds to disturb, and crossed the gravel track from the copse back to the main road. Then she followed her sat-nav to the exact position that they'd chosen carefully, many weeks before.

She reached her destination at the old bridge within ten minutes. It was only a mile across country from the Castleton, but she'd had to cross the motorway to get there. She stopped the car at some fields to the rear of the hotel and stepped out, taking the binoculars from the glove compartment and looking down. The view was unobstructed. Excellent.

The sunglasses that she rarely removed clouded her eyes, and the evening light was dimming, but even so, she could see everything for miles around. And Stevan could use his night-sights. There would be no problem.

She watched Joe Watson for a moment, wandering around the bedroom that she'd just left, and she smiled. He wasn't in bad shape for an old man. Then she pulled the cheap pink 'pay-as-you-go' mobile from her pocket. It was hideous, but exactly what Ausra would use, to go along with the cut-off t-shirts and over-tight jeans that got Joes' motor running. She couldn't wait to reclaim her fifth generation phone and designer suits.

She made the call and waited for him to answer. Three rings and he picked up, just as she'd expected, pathetically predictable like all men. Still, she gave him credit for being an honest prick at least; even in front of his poker buddies there was no embarrassment when she called.

"Hi, Joe."

She could hear him leaving the room and entering the bathroom to speak to her, watching him as he went. Perhaps his armed-guard overhearing was too much to expect, even for her.

"Hello darling. I am here with my Papa and I come outside to call you. It is such a beautiful evening ...no?"

"I can't see it. I'm inside this dark room and I'd much rather be back in bed with you."

She raised her eyes to heaven, and mimicked making herself vomit.

"Of course, also would I, darling. But I think, as we cannot be together, why not we look at the same sky. Go look at the sky for me, as we do every week. No?"

Her husky voice had taken on the girlish wheedling tone that she knew he couldn't resist. *Sucker.*

She knew exactly what he would do next, and he did. Just as he had done it last week, and for the two weeks before. He walked and talked to her as he left the room, and then stood in the hotel forecourt looking up at the sky. Then she whispered sex and sweet nothings to him, with his dark protector standing just far enough away to allow for privacy.

She could see them both now, through the binoculars that she held to her eyes, the lens already adjusted to the exact distance that Stevan had calculated. Joe was so close that she could see the pores in his skin, and the trendy two-day growth on his armed guard's cheeks. Perfect. Stevan had calculated the perfect distance, the perfect position and the perfect angle.

Tomorrow evening would be her last performance for the Honourable's Member... and his last performance of anything at all. She wouldn't miss the work, but at least his conversation had been better than Bob Leighton's. She laughed at her own wit. Everything would be perfect. And by this time tomorrow, Joe Watson, Enterprise Minister would be perfectly dead.

****

Ten Square Hotel, Belfast City Centre. Monday. 7 p.m.

It was seven o'clock when Craig pulled up a stool at the end of the long bar in Ten Square, waiting for John to appear. His only concession to being off-duty was to remove his tie and loosen the collar of his white shirt. The look worked on him.

A slim, twenty-something barman approached him, wiping a tray as he walked. "What can I get for you,

143

sir?"

"Lager please. Whatever sort you have."

"Will you be wanting to eat? The restaurant menu's there."

He indicated a laminated menu perched on the counter, and then decided to bring it over, handing it to Craig.

"Maybe later, thanks. Just the drink for now."

The barman smiled and nodded, pulling a bottle from the freezer and reaching for a glass.

"The bottle's fine, thanks. Cheers."

Craig took a long drink of the icy liquid, even the action of tipping it back making him feel more relaxed. He closed his eyes for a moment, savouring the taste, and then cast a casual look around the quickly filling venue. It was early yet and the Monday evening occupants were mostly workers from nearby offices, postponing the inevitable trip home. To cook or be cooked for.

A few small groups of women were gathering, already glammed-up for the evening's hunt. Larger crowds of men milled around the peripheries, talking to their mates about work or football. The brave ones shot occasional looks at the women, hiding it from their friends, to avoid the inevitable ruthless slagging that men subjected each other to, in the name of friendship. The first sign of a repeat glance and the 'pack' would eat its own.

Girlfriends were different. Once they joined, the conversation changed, sanitised, and then slowed. Until the male crowd broke apart and drifted off to their separate destinations. Craig had seen it, been it, a million times. From eighteen, to...when? Death? Did they still do it in retirement homes? Fewer men by then, smaller packs.

John stood by the street-door watching his friend. Craig was completely blind to the two women staring at him, while he watched others, ever the observer. Was it any wonder that he was single? But that was only partly true, Camille really deserved the blame.

At school, Craig's half-Italian charm had been the

144

perfect foil for John's nerdiness. Girls had followed them around, worshipping Craig from afar. But he hadn't even noticed it, much more interested in his sport, while John sat on the touchline comforting them. They'd both scored, in entirely different ways.

He wandered over and rested his elbow on the bar, neither of them saying a word. Craig had seen him watching and John knew it, so any planned dating lecture would be redundant. Craig broke the amicable silence just as the barman approached.

"What do you fancy, John? Do you want to have a drink and go on, or stay here and eat?"

He handed him the menu and John peered at it vainly, then caved in and took his glasses from his pocket. The food looked really good, but he fancied Japanese, so he ordered a beer and turned around to check out the room. Craig laughed.

"How's Natalie then - still seeing her?"

John smiled wryly. "Yes, we haven't split up, despite your mum's grilling on Friday." Craig smiled at the quick retort. John was more confident than he'd been in years.

"And thanks for the reminder to behave. Nat's great, but I can still look, you know. She certainly does. By the way, she told me to ask why you aren't taking Julia to the N.S.P.C.C. ball."

Craig blushed deep-red, and John instantly felt bad about his jibe. Craig had blushed a lot when he was at school, but it was only ever over women now. The rest of the time, he was almost effortlessly cool.

"Are you going to give me a hard time, John? And if so, can I get something to eat first? I hate being bollocked on an empty stomach."

"I just thought that you really liked her. I was surprised when you told me you weren't seeing each other anymore."

"We only had one dinner together! And I do really like her, it's just that..."

Camille. He didn't need to say it, Camille had broken his heart, or as near as damn it. It hadn't helped that she'd reappeared after a five-year absence, expecting to pick up where they'd left off. He had been a mess ever since and there was zero point in giving him any grief about it.

"OK. I'll tell Natalie to mind her own business, and then duck."

They laughed loudly and a group of women by the front door looked over quickly at the sound, checking them out. They were high-maintenance beauties, but beauties nonetheless.

John motioned toward the window. "Do you know where the Wheel's gone to?"

The Wheel, Belfast's miniature version of the London Eye, had left two years before, and John was just noticing it now!

"It went to Dublin in twenty-ten but it's left there now. I heard a rumour that it might be going to Derry for the City of Culture next year. I've never been up in it, have you?"

"Yes. Natalie dragged me up one day when I had a bugger of a hangover. I nearly threw up. It would have served her right. Typical surgeon that girl, no finesse."

"I thought you only met her recently, at a conference?"

"I did, properly. But we were in a crowd together a few times, years back. When she was teaching anatomy to the medical students."

Craig nodded and they fell into ten minutes of amicable silence. Then the crowd began to grow, drowning out their thoughts, so they finished their beers quickly and headed to Zen for sushi. Much to the disappointment of the beauties by the door.

Chapter Sixteen

The C.C.U. Tuesday Morning.

Craig walked across the open-plan office, and stood looking out of the window nearest Davy's desk. It was early yet and no one else was in, so he gifted himself five minutes to think. He gazed at the modern buildings of Clarendon Dock, watching as their fluorescent lights flickered on, one by one, throwing the dust on the high, square windows into stark relief. Below them the morning commuters were parking their cars neatly in named slots. He'd always hated allocated parking, rebelling by parking randomly whenever possible, in some small measure of civic defiance.

He quickly ordered his thoughts. Irene Leighton had been killed professionally in a way linked with three other hits and the Vory v Zakone. Her husband had panicked more at the number ten than at any of the other symbolism attached to her death. But he seemed to have loved her. None of that stopped him preparing to skip the U.K. for a non-extradition country, and taking their beautiful nanny with him. The nanny had disappeared and so had Leighton, the difference being that she had packed her clothes. Or been packed for, and taken by force?

He paused for a moment, admiring the pale-blue cloudless sky and for the first time the air really felt like December, cold and crisp. It conjured up visions of ski-trips with Camille and warm Italian Christmases when they'd been happy together. He pulled his thoughts reluctantly back to the present.

OK, no one had seen the girl or Leighton since Friday and, so far, Julia had struck out with the hospitals in Donegal. But that didn't mean that Bob Leighton wasn't lying in one unidentified; he might have changed his name for his new life. But then, how did he leave the house at all without the neighbours seeing? It was a small cul-de-sac. Craig shrugged; it

147

wouldn't be the first time that people had ignored their neighbours.

Neither Leighton nor Kaisa had been back to the house in Stranmillis, and the boy was still with his grandparents. No one had heard from either of them. So where the hell were they? He raked his hair impatiently, wanting to kick something. He was focussing on the sky, looking hard for inspiration, when a light tap on his shoulder brought him abruptly back to earth. He turned to see Nicky smiling at him, pointing at the percolator bubbling by her desk so he smiled gratefully and followed her across the floor, pressing 'Julia' on his mobile as he walked.

****

The call to Julia McNulty had yielded nothing but earache, so after five minutes of her ranting about the unhelpful neighbours and bloody bureaucracy, Craig left her to it. He spent the remainder of his morning weighed down by paperwork on two other cases until finally, at twelve, he gave notice that it was Lucia's birthday and he'd be at Cayenne having lunch if anyone wanted him. The restaurant's name prompted Davy to ask what it was like for a date, nearly resulting in his assault by Nicky.

Craig had been there for less than thirty minutes when John paged him and he left the restaurant to take the call. After five minutes he returned, avoiding his mother's eye, and slowly lifted his jacket to leave, trying hard to look as if he wasn't. This wouldn't be popular.

"Sorry, Mum, but I did tell you that I was on duty. I really have to go. Lucia, I'm sorry. I'll send you shopping on Saturday to make it up to you. Here's my credit card, just pay the bill at the end."

She snapped it out of his hand, grinning. "You realise that I'm ordering Dom Perignon as soon as you leave. And that you're never getting this back!"

"Don't you worry, son. Just you do your job, and pay no attention to these two." His mother mock-

148

strangled his father, and he laughed.

"Luce, will you take the folks home in a taxi please?" He looked at her eyes, gleaming from an earlier bottle of bubbly. "I need my car. Besides, you're well over the limit."

She grinned up at him. "And I intend to be even more over it in five minutes time."

****

He reached the lab in fifteen minutes and headed straight for the mortuary, curious about John's page. All it had said was that he needed to see him urgently, and John was rarely urgent about anything. When he reached the freezing-cold room, John was standing in scrubs, re-arranging some files on a bench. A covered body was lying in an extended open drawer; the size indicated a man.

"What was so urgent? I left Lucia drunk in charge of my credit card at her birthday lunch."

John half-smiled, then looked puzzled. "It's not her birthday, is it?" A panicked look shot across his face as he realised that he'd forgotten to get her a present.

"Don't panic, it's her second birthday on the thirteenth. But she's away on a course so we held it today."

John relaxed, smiling as he remembered the Italian custom of 'Onomastico' or 'Name Day' when people had a second birthday on the day of their namesake saint. Mirella had brought her children up with all the Italian customs.

His expression suddenly became grim. "Sorry I had to drag you away, Marc. But I thought that you'd like to hear this before Harrison...or the press."

Craig tensed, knowing that whoever was in the drawer was linked with his case.

John opened the file in his hand and spoke quietly. "There was a death in Donegal on Friday night. A man from Belfast."

"Yes, I heard. Liam looked into it, but he couldn't get a name. A forty-year-old, from S.A.D.S, wasn't it?"

149

John nodded.

"But why are you involved? Didn't they handle the P.M in Donegal?" As Craig asked the question he went cold, already knowing the answer.

"They did, and normally that would be fine, but the police there weren't happy. It wasn't natural causes, despite what the Chronicle reported. So, because he was from here, they asked me to take a look." He paused for a moment, looking down at the body. "It's Robert Leighton, Marc."

Craig looked blankly at him for a moment, before the name registered. Then he nodded. Robert, Bob. Of course... He'd tried to run, not from them, but from someone much more dangerous. Well, he hadn't run far enough, and now whoever had killed his wife had killed him.

John was still talking. "They initially thought his death was natural causes. He had a family history of heart disease. It's called sudden adult death syndrome. S.A.D.S."

He beckoned Craig over to the drawer and pulled back the sheet to reveal Bob Leighton's narrow face. It was peaceful, even innocent looking, much more innocent in death than he'd ever been in life. John moved the sheet down to waist level, lifting a sharp probe, then he waved Craig closer and they leaned over the man's pale body.

"Have a look... just here. Can you see that red mark?"

John was indicating a tiny red dot on the man's left nipple. It was so tiny that anyone else would have dismissed it. Craig looked at him the same way he had in their science class at twelve, with a mixture of awe and 'what the hell?'

"It just looks like part of the nipple to me, John. What's the significance?"

"Let's go upstairs and discuss it. And I saw that look by the way. You used to give it to me when we were kids, when you thought I was some sort of brainiac."

"You were!"

They laughed. The twelve-year-old Craig hadn't

hidden his emotions well.

"I'll be honest with you. I did notice the dot, but I didn't actually realise its significance until I opened him up. And I wasn't sure even then, not until I got his blood results."

They got the lift the three floors up to John's office, grabbing a coffee before he started.

"OK. The doctor who did the first P.M. missed two signs that this was a murder. Actually, I can't believe that he ever thought it was natural causes. What I showed you downstairs was a small red dot on Leighton's left nipple."

Craig nodded.

"But what you would've seen if I'd opened him up, was that the dot was directly above his heart. There was a track right through the chest wall with a matching hole and track through the wall of the heart. Whatever made the dot went straight through the nipple into the heart."

"What was it?"

"An intracardiac needle." He reached into a small sample cabinet by the door, pulling out a needle so long that Craig shuddered.

"It's nine-centimetres long and used to inject drugs straight into the heart from the outside, through the chest wall. It's mostly used in cardiac arrests and some surgery. I'm checking for the exact match but they're pretty standard needles. They have to be very strong, to penetrate skin, fat, muscle, and sometimes cartilage, without breaking. You wouldn't want one snapping off in the middle of surgery."

Craig could picture it clearly. The needle went right through Bob Leighton's chest wall into his heart. "Surely the needle wouldn't have killed him?"

"You're right, it wouldn't. But whatever it injected would, and that was the second sign that the doctor missed. Leighton's blood screen showed a potassium level that was dismissed as normal post-mortem elevation. But there's no way that this was a simple P.M rise; the level is far too high. I believe that potassium, probably in the chloride form, was deliberately injected into his heart, stopping it immediately."

He paused for a second.

"We've got the preliminary tox-screen back and there's also evidence of significant Rohypnol, as well as some low level cocaine. That's backed up by the state of his nasal membranes. He'd obviously been using coke for a while, but the level wasn't high enough to kill him."

Craig nodded. "He was on it when we went to tell him about his wife." He paused, thinking. "Rohypnol. That was used to sedate Irene Leighton too."

"Yes. In a high enough dose it can subdue someone very effectively."

"Enough for someone to kill Leighton with the potassium?"

John nodded. "And a Potassium death looks natural, so it's hard to detect."

"OK. So roofies to subdue him, potassium to kill. They wanted this to look like a natural death."

"And with the family history of S.A.D.S they managed it for a few days. Long enough to cover their escape?"

Craig shook his head. "I don't think they're worried about escaping. They can get away whenever they want to. And if all they'd wanted was Leighton dead, they would have just shot him, like his wife, and then disappeared immediately. They took the time to research his family history and tailored the murder to look like natural causes, to delay us. They needed time for something."

He thought for a moment and then nodded. "They're planning something else, John. They haven't left Northern Ireland yet."

"There are two more things, Marc. And they might give you a clue to the killer."

"Yes?"

"Lividity shows that Bob Leighton was horizontal when he died, and he had unprotected sex immediately beforehand."

****

152

The Castleton Hotel. Tuesday 5 p.m.

It was five o' clock on Tuesday and Joe Watson felt excited. The last time he remembered being this excited was when he was a kid. Back then, one of his favourite TV catch phrases had encapsulated the mood. "It's Friday, It's five o' clock and it's Crackerjack!"

They'd all sat watching the black and white TV at his cousin's Deidre's house, cheering along loudly with the invisible studio audience. Then his Aunt had brought in Sukie orange juice and Jammy Dodgers, and school was over for the weekend. There'd been no feeling quite like it. Even his frustration at not understanding how the man got inside the little box couldn't detract from it. And that excitement was exactly what he was feeling now, sitting in the back of his staff-car being driven towards the Castleton.

He loved her. He'd thought about it all week and he really loved her. And he was going to tell her tonight. He smiled at the thought of the diamond bracelet lying inside his briefcase, and imagined fastening it onto her slim brown wrist. She would love it. She would love it, and...he felt a second's nervous hope...she would love him? Oh God, please let her love me back. It'll give me the strength to do what I have to, to be with her.

Even if she didn't love him now, he'd convince her to love him in the future. But it would help so much if she already did. Help him deal with the fallout at home, with the kids, with the press. Of course she'd love him back.

He didn't even notice that the car had stopped, until Ryan Drake, his bodyguard, opened the door for him. "Thanks. Could you check me in, Ryan. I'm going to shower, and then do some work."

The tall protection officer resisted the urge to raise his eyebrow like Roger Moore. 'Do some work'...Yeah right.

"Of course Minister. One of us will be outside if you need us."

Watson headed to the lift and then straight for room

153

five-one-seven. He had the same room every time; end of the corridor, large window, beside the fire escape, with no-one facing. Complete privacy, and no neighbours to complain about their noisy lovemaking.

He dumped his briefcase and jacket quickly, and ran the bath, reaching for the phone to order room service and champagne for six pm. She'd be here soon and everything had to be perfect.

He opened his standard ministerial briefcase and withdrew the unmistakable pale-blue Tiffany box from its resting place, laughing to himself. He'd spent the budget of a small country on this little trinket, mentally thanking Goldbergs for all those years of lovely bonuses.

Opening the box gently, he looked down at the white-gold circle studded with twenty square-cut diamonds. What was money for, except to spoil people you loved? He knew that it would fit her slim wrist perfectly; he'd measured her watch when she was in the shower the week before. He locked it back in the case, not wanting anyone to see his folly. Then he laid out fresh clothes and sank slowly into the bath, crooning to himself.

Ryan Drake was sitting outside the room, with his long legs stretched across the doorway, and his bulky arms folded. He heard the Sinatra number being murdered and smiled wryly; Joe was going to have a big night. Yes, he was.

****

Stevan packed his bag in his small bedroom in Fitzroy Avenue, a wide street in Belfast's Holyland district, just off the Ormeau Road. The area was terraced and studenty, and he'd been too old for it ten years before.

He looked around the cosy room, smiling and wishing it goodbye. Last night had been his final one at the bar and he'd had the pleasure of Teresa's strong young body until an hour ago. She wasn't half-bad. He'd been pleasantly surprised the first time, and he'd almost be sorry to stop now.

154

He hadn't told her that he was leaving of course, she would only have cried, and he couldn't bear to hear women crying. Kaisa never cried. Not healthily anyway. But that was a bad thing, she hadn't cried healthily since she was seven...

Teresa had left for work, and he'd lied, saying that he'd meet her there at seven. It was a pity that they couldn't say goodbye, but he was used to that, and it certainly wasn't worth another night of grubby students pouring in for Happy Hour.

He didn't have much to pack, that was one of his rules. Travel light, easier to burn. He looked down ruefully at the scruffy Levis and t-shirt that had been his uniform for months. He really missed his Armani suits, and somewhere to wear them that he wouldn't be arrested.

The heavy equipment was already in the car - Kaisa had sorted everything. She was a good girl, his little sister. He loathed what she had to do to prepare his targets, but her beauty was just as strong a weapon as his rifle.

Stevan thought reluctantly back to the day that had made them both who they were. And of the men who had taken whatever they wanted, and destroyed the rest. His face hardened with tension, remembering. He wouldn't let himself go there, to the memories, the images. It had taken him years to bury them and Kaisa never had. Thirty minutes, that was all it had taken to destroy five lives. Since then they'd both fought to survive in different ways, earning their livings the only way they knew how.

Someday he would find the men again, when he had enough money, enough to get Kaisa the help she needed and make her safe. And when he found them he would do to them what they had done. Make them watch helpless, while he destroyed everything good in their lives.

He shook himself, angry that he'd gone there; he needed to focus on tonight's work. He scanned the room for any debris that might trace him, and then ran down the two flights of stairs to his landlady's rooms, knocking gently on her door.

Jeanie Rogan looked through the peephole and then answered the door quickly, smiling. Her greying brown hair curled neatly to her shoulders and her floral dress fell demurely below her knees. Her round face wrinkled softly into fine lines as she smiled up at him. She was a motherly sort and Stevan liked motherly women, there was something fitting about them.

"Hello, Stevan, nice to see you. Is anything wrong, pet?"

He smiled his huge white smile and saw its immediate softening effect on her. She genuinely liked him, and it was mutual. Time for the broken English.

"No wrong, nothing wrong, Madam. I have this for you." He handed her a brown envelope containing three month's rent and more.

"What's this?"

"It is rent for next month. I have go home for one week and rent fall when I am away, so I pay you now."

She beamed up at him; he was such a kind boy. Her husband was disabled, and he often helped her out, putting up shelves and changing the oil in her car. Whatever she asked of him he did, without an excuse.

"Is everything OK at home? I hope nothing's wrong that you have to go so quickly?"

"Yes, nothing wrong. I have Grandfather - he is ninety. Big family party. I am back next week."

"Oh, that's lovely. Ninety, what a great age. Please take some photographs; I'd love to see them when you get back. Have a lovely time, Stevan, and thank you again for the rent."

She reached up and kissed him gently on the cheek. "Goodbye, pet."

He loved the local endearment 'pet' and he smiled at her again, unexpected tears filling his eyes. She reminded him of his mother. They were both proof that there was goodness in the world. Part of him wanted to hug her tight, and stay living this simple life, just to feel her kindness. But there could be no peace like that for him.

He looked down at her sadly, imprinting her image

to memory. Then he reluctantly walked out of the front door onto the street, leaving behind another kind woman that he would never see again.

****

The Castleton Hotel.

"Oh Joe, it so beautiful. I never had such a thing."

Joe looked down at her protectively. She was so petite, barely reaching his chin. Long strands of dark-blonde hair had fallen delicately across her cheek, and he stroked them back gently as she held her slim brown wrist up to the light, totally absorbed. She turned the bracelet round and round, entranced, the diamonds' lights reflecting in her green eyes.

She adored it, and she said that she adored him. He hadn't been this excited by anyone for years and he told her so. He wanted to leave Caitlin and be with her, even if it meant losing his political career. He didn't care. He had plenty of money and he wanted her, and he usually got what he wanted.

Kaisa smiled to herself. It was a beautiful bracelet and for one quick moment she almost regretted that he'd be dead soon. In a few more weeks she'd probably have got the necklace to match.

"Joe, I am so sorry, but my father he is not well today. I cannot stay long. I must go in only thirty minutes."

His face fell, and she reached over and stroked it affectionately, smiling at him seductively until he forgot his disappointment. She decided to be charitable, and give the condemned man his last wish.

"But...we have time..."

Thirty minutes later she dressed, while he watched her, totally content. This would be the last time that she'd ever leave him. She'd agreed to live with him, as long as they could have her father as well. A granny flat was no problem.

His kids would come round eventually and they'd love her too. How could anyone not love her? She lifted

157

her handbag, ready to go. It was cheap and glittery, but he'd buy her Gucci, a beauty like her should be dressed up.

"Will you call me later, Ausra, so that we can see the same sky?"

She mentally vomited, but turned, smiling sweetly. "Of course. I get home later, I will call. It will be very soon, not so late tonight." Before the light fades for Stevan.

She sat on his knee stroking his grey hair with her tiny fingers and then kissed him sympathetically, at length. She didn't hate him nearly as much as Bob Leighton; but he would still die. Then she left quickly, sunglasses on, and smiled at the 'man in black' outside as she sashayed past him for the last time. She climbed into her battered Ford and drove out of the hotel car-park, carefully observing the speed limit, and followed the sat-nav to the designated spot across the fields.

The evening was bright and clear and there were no strong crosswinds, but as Stevan always said, 'conditions mightn't be so good in thirty minutes'. The call had to be made soon. When she arrived, she was shocked and pleased to see her big brother already there. He was packing something large into a bag and he turned as she drove up, smiling quickly.

Stevan knew she was going to be angry and he prepared himself for the onslaught. She jumped out of the old car and hugged her handsome brother. They hadn't seen each other for weeks.

"Stevan, Stevan...Nedostajao si mi."(I've missed you so much)

It was so good to be able to speak their native Serbian again. Stevan looked down at his little sister, hugging her tight. He was sorry for what she wore and he was sorry for every man that she'd ever had to endure. But soon they would have enough money for her never to suffer their touches again.

"Nedostajala si mi." (I've missed you)

"Volim te puno! Ali Požuri, Stevan" (I love you so much. But hurry, Stevan)

Kaisa quickly opened the car boot for him to

158

retrieve the rifle. Then she handed him a pair of high-powered binoculars, readying herself to phone Joe Watson and entice him out of the hotel, into Stevan's sights. Stevan didn't move, and she looked at him, puzzled.

"Stevan, you must hurry. I told him I would call soon. He will get suspicious."

He stared at the bright new bracelet glittering on her arm; it was expensive. This man cared for her. Then he looked at his sister sadly, pained by her eagerness to kill the man who had given it to her less than an hour before. He shook his head quietly.

"There will be no shooting today, Draga. Get ready to leave."

She looked up at him, totally uncomprehending and he slowly lifted the bag that he'd been fastening when she'd arrived, unzipping it for her to see its contents. Inside, lay a DSLR camera with a zoom lens, powerful enough to reach the hotel. She'd seen him use one before, and in an instant she knew what he'd done, throwing herself at him hysterically.

"You have to kill him, you promised to kill him for me. You promised."

She screamed at him like a wounded animal, lacerating the rural silence, and his heart broke again, knowing that her childhood memories had never disappeared. Then she cried, for long, cruel minutes like a widow keening at a funeral, mourning for the life that she'd lost and the life she now had.

Finally her raw cries weakened until she stopped, exhausted by her efforts, and she sobbed softly, like the child that she'd been before they came. He held her close, rocking her gently until the sky darkened and her eyes dried, explaining that blackmail was their only task this time, unless it didn't work. He'd been grateful for the news; he was sick of killing now.

But why hadn't he told her, why Stevan? Told you that I would take pictures of you with a man, Draga? But how could I?

Eventually she fell quiet, exhausted, and they changed silently into the universal uniform of youth;

jeans and leather jackets. They emptied their pockets, bags and every other possession onto the ground beside the field, and set them alight. Then he drove the old car with its false I.D., down the motorway to the City Airport, abandoning it in the long-term car-park.

They walked casually to the ticket machine and through security, boarding the last flight to Heathrow. It had gone beautifully again. They were home free.

Chapter Seventeen

"What the hell have you done, Joanne? When is all this supposed to happen? I can't be any part of it, you've gone too far now. And have you even thought about the girls? What do you think it will do to them if their mother ends up in prison? You selfish, stupid cow."

Joanne watched her husband rant, looking him up and down in absent distain. He'd always been weak; she'd been the man in their marriage for years. Her face twisted in disgust and her next words came spitting out.

"You're pathetic, Declan! You've *always* been pathetic. I've been carrying you for years. With your gambling, and your stupid friends from school. You haven't taken off that bloody uniform since you were ten; you still need them to like you. Who cares if they bloody well like you? They're nothing, just another incestuous little Northern Ireland clique. And don't you dare bring my daughters into this; it's their future I'm doing this for. To give them the life they would already have, if you'd ever stepped up."

She turned her back, catching his reflection in the wall mirror, and then spun round again, venomously. "I even make more money than you - what a man!"

Then she walked towards him and stood with her face perilously close to his. "And, if you even think about telling the girls anything...anything negative about me, even by a hint or a look, then Daddy's little girls will get these."

She leaned forward into her Chanel shopper and pulled out some folded sheets. "They'll find out exactly what the man they worship is really like. You can keep these for your office wall, I have plenty of copies."

He grabbed the sheets from her and pulled them open, tearing at the edges. They were pictures of him with a woman. In the car, the street, at the races, and...Oh shit, in bed, in every position. And he'd no idea who she was! Joanne had faked the pictures somehow but they looked real, and the idea of his

161

young daughters seeing them, made him want to vomit.

"How did you make these? I'll get them looked at, it'll be easy to prove they're fakes." Then he looked at her murderously. "You cold bitch, how could you even think of hurting your children like this."

He threw the pages on the floor and reached for her arm, grabbing it with his left hand and clenching his right into a fist. He stood above her, his face so red that it was almost purple. They stood locked in position, silently, his left hand grasped around his wife's slim upper arm, his right fist poised one inch from breaking her perfect fucking nose. He hated that nose, it sneered without even trying.

After a moment's anger he threw her to the ground dismissively, like the soiled rubbish that he thought she was. She fell back against the Louis Quinze card table that she'd been given on leaving chambers in London, breaking a corner off it in her fall. But only her pride was hurt. She sat on the floor leaning back on her hands and laughed tauntingly up at him. "You can't even beat me up like a man..."

Declan turned on his heel abruptly and walked out, heading for the car before he killed her. His kids were all that mattered now. Her silver Aston was parked across the broad driveway, deliberately blocking him in. He pulled at its door angrily. Locked.

He looked inside it, disgusted. It was immaculate. Not a single sign of the kids, or anything human. She was a cold bitch. Why hadn't he noticed it before?

He climbed into his own BMW, pushing Izzy's CDs off the seat, and gunned the engine, ramming it directly into her car. Back and forth, back and forth, until he'd shunted it right off the path and onto the lawn, virtually destroying it in the process.

He saw her standing at the window watching and she waved sarcastically at him, then he raked out into the avenue and turned left onto the Malone Road. Heading for the outer ring-road and the countryside, where he could drive and think.

His mobile rang immediately and he glanced at the

screen. It was her, probably bitching about the state of her car. He ignored it and knocked the phone off, driving at eighty mph past Newforge Lane and on through the lights, heading for the back roads past the Giant's Ring. He drove and drove until the evening had changed into night and his boiling blood had finally dropped to simmering point.

Then he vaguely recognised a road. Where was he? The area looked familiar. He searched around for a signpost, and then realised that he'd driven the forty miles to his parent's small house near Armagh. Homing instinct. He stopped the car outside their immaculate semi and rested his head back on the seat support. How had he let Joanne get them into this mess, and how the fuck did he get out of it?

The car clock said nine-thirty. He'd lost time driving and thinking. But it hadn't been wasted, he'd made a decision. He felt better instantly and looked through the windscreen. His father was leaning against the gatepost, arms folded, watching his eldest son wisely.

Declan held up a spread palm, indicating that he'd be five minutes. He switched on his mobile, ignoring the answerphone ringing back; it would only be Joanne. And he started to make the call that he'd decided on. He would phone Caitlin Watson, she would be the quickest route to Joe and his minders.

He already knew how insane it would all sound, 'my wife's intending to blackmail and possibly kill your husband, and I think she's already killed other people'. He knew that it would be the end of his peaceful existence, and he also knew that it was exactly the right thing to do.

But before he could do anything, his father walked towards the car. He lowered the driver's window out of respect. "I'll be there in five minutes, Dad. Tell Mum to put the kettle on."

"Have you and Joanne been fighting again, son? It's just...she's been ringing here for the last hour, really frantic about you."

Yeah...Frantic, but not for the reasons his father thought. His father was still talking and Declan half

163

heard him say 'Bob Leighton'.

"What did you say, Dad?"

"Joanne was worried that you were upset about Bob Leighton dying. She said that you two were friends?"

"Leighton?"

Declan heard himself saying the name but he still didn't believe it. The urge to vomit hit him and he opened the car door, throwing up on the grass verge and narrowly missing his father's feet. Fuck, he was already too late. She'd already done it! She'd actually killed someone and she wanted him to know that she had. She was warning him to keep quiet.

"Sorry, son. I've upset you now. I should have waited until you were in the house. It was over the weekend, apparently. He was found up in Donegal. They think it was natural causes. Probably grief...after his poor wife died..."

Declan knew that tears were running down his cheeks because he could feel them. But they weren't tears of grief for Bob Leighton; he'd hardly known the man. They were tears for himself. Leighton hadn't died of natural causes, he would bet a fortune on it. Somehow, Joanne had killed him.

He had no idea what to do next.

****

Declan genuinely had no idea what to do, or where to go. He couldn't go home and he couldn't stay with his elderly parents. If Joanne was capable of killing Leighton, she was capable of anything and he had to protect them now.

After a cup of tea to pass himself he left his parent's small house, with a promise to return for Sunday dinner with the girls. His father walked him to the door. He was getting greyer and more stooped now; more vulnerable somehow. Was this the point where the child noticed that they had become the parent? All he knew was that he had to protect them, they were good people. He'd been brought up by good people to be a good person; but he'd taken a long detour.

Yes, he knew he was a snob and vain, and that money mattered far too much to him. But never as much as it had, and did, to Joanne. God, how could he not have seen what she was like? What she must always have been like. It slotted into place slowly as he turned over the car and drove away, waving at his mother smiling out the window.

All at once he could see the signs that he'd missed. Joanne defending criminals and always justifying their actions. Preferring dinner with them to a night at home with the girls. Back then, he'd thought she was just being a zealous young defence barrister, ambitious and excited by the law. But now, he could remember the secret smiles with her dark looking clients. Smiles that said 'you're only guilty if they can prove it'. Morality didn't even come into it.

He'd been blind then, but he could see it all now. She hadn't just loved criminal law, she'd loved criminals, admired them somehow. The secret smiles had said 'we're smarter than the rest. Sexier, more powerful somehow'. How had he missed it for so long?

Should he go to the police? But what about his parents, what about the girls? He couldn't leave them with Joanne; they couldn't be allowed to turn out like her. Carina was only fourteen, still malleable. The thought of what might happened to them made him shudder hard.

Joanne would be in prison soon; he'd make damn sure of it. Then he'd get custody and he'd make sure that she never saw them again. It wouldn't be much of a loss - they'd thought their nanny was their mother for years. He'd been their only consistent carer.

He made a sudden decision and quickly threw a U-turn, heading back towards Belfast. He would book in somewhere and do some serious thinking. He couldn't tell Caitlin Watson now; it might put her in danger. This had to be planned in a way that blind-sided Joanne. No, he'd think first and then call the police...

The charity race meet was on at Antrim on Thursday...maybe he would go to that to settle his mind. Fuck! He couldn't believe that he was thinking of

165

gambling at a time like this. Once an addict…

But then again…it might help him think, clear his head. Yes, that was what he'd do. He'd clear his head and the answer would come to him in couple of days, without Joanne's shrill voice shouting in his ear.

His thoughts were broken suddenly by his mobile ringing; Joanne again. He ignored it. He'd call her when he was ready. He was clearer now about what he had to do. He would let her know that her days were numbered before he went to the police. He owed the mother of his children that much.

****

Teresa filled the pint glass with draught Guinness, splashing it carelessly on the floor, and whole-heartedly resenting the skinny T-shirted lad waiting in front of her. She gazed forlornly past him at the bar's front door, willing Stevan to appear. But it was his night off and she was stuck here serving these boys.

Then it came to her: these were boys and Stevan was a man. Maybe not so different in years, but there was a world behind his eyes. She thought of his strong brown arms and his wide smile, her thoughts taking her much further. They'd shared feelings that she'd never had before, and she couldn't bear being without him now. She sighed and looked at the wall clock with its sloth of an hour-hand. Eighteen long hours until she saw him again. Except that she never would.

****

The young driver stood at the waiting area in Terminal One carrying a sign for 'Armstrong' and Stevan wondered again why Alik always gave them such English names. He shrugged and gestured Kaisa towards the man, smiling widely.

"Armstrong?"

The look was Delhi but the accent was pure 'Sarf London' and Kaisa laughed, happy to be back. She gave the boy her full wattage smile and Stevan watched him

166

melt into a puddle. She knew her power well.

"We have no bags. Where are we going?"

He loved the anonymity of London. You could be whoever you wanted to be and no one gave a shit. It was just one big theatre.

"To the Randle Hotel, sir. Your uncle insisted on it. It's a five star in Kensington." The driver started to describe it in detail, as if they couldn't possibly know the place. Then Stevan looked down at his scruffy jeans and Kaisa's woollen hat, acknowledging that they looked like mature students, at best.

They walked down the single flight of stairs leading to the short-term car-park, and soon they were in the back of a quietly elegant Jaguar, driving swiftly through the Heathrow tunnel and onto the M4 motorway, towards London. Kaisa was tired from her earlier tears and she curled up against him, just as she had always done as a little girl. He stroked her hair gently. Sleep, pet. She looked so innocent. But the things that she had seen, and the things that she had done...

****

Parliament Buildings.

Joe Watson yawned loudly without covering his mouth and Michael tutted mentally, disapproving. He'd have disapproved even more if he'd known why he was so tired. Joe smiled at his secret life that would soon be in the open, when Ausra was with him twenty-four-seven. He couldn't wait. But for now, he needed to focus on the work piled-up in front of him. He lifted the top file, and read the summary. 'Roads'. Boring.

A better idea struck him. "Have we heard anything back from the Conduct Commissioner yet?"

Michael sighed. Joe had the attention span of a goldfish at the best of times but he was worse than usual today, jumping topic every five minutes.

"No, Minister. Nothing yet."

"Well, there must be something better to do than

this lot." He gestured to the files. "Go and find it for me."

He waved the young man out impatiently, and two minutes later he was back with an envelope marked 'Urgent and confidential.'

"This just arrived by courier, Minister. I thought that you should see it."

He handed Watson the large buff envelope and waited expectantly for him to open it. Watson turned it over in his hand uneasily, not quite sure what he was uneasy about, then he looked up at his advisor coolly. "Is there some reason that you're still here, Michael?"

The young man was taken aback momentarily. It was dismissive, even for Joe.

"Oh. No Minister, not at all."

He left, face flaming, and stormed down the hall to chastise one of his subordinates, for natural balance.

Watson considered the envelope for a moment and then opened it tentatively, removing the sheaf of paper inside. His first reaction was relief; it was just another boring brief. Then he turned over the top sheet and gasped at what was behind it. It was a colour photograph, close-up and detailed, with every landmark of his body and Ausra's highlighted. His face was clearly visible and easily recognised. He thumbed quickly through the following sheets. Him and Ausra in the shower, on the floor, on the bed. His face clear in every one, but never hers. Even through his shock, he registered that none of them identified her. Very clever.

He could feel a cold sweat dripping down his face and his chest tightened urgently. He reached quickly into his briefcase and grabbed at the small spray, pumping it twice under his tongue and then sitting back until the pain in his chest had passed, but not the one in his heart. Blackmail. She didn't love him at all. She'd been playing him all along. But what did she want?

He turned back to the sheaf of paper, flicking furiously through it for a note, a highlight, something to tell him her demands. But there was nothing. For one happy moment, he thought that the pictures might have been sent by a journalist, warning him of an impending story. She might be innocent after all. She might still love him.

He was reaching for his phone when the landline beeped, and Michael knocked lightly at the door. "There's a call for you Minister, line one. It sounds important, something to do with the Strategic Finance Foundation."

Oh bugger, he wasn't interested in that today, but he knew that he had to pretend. He grabbed rudely at the phone and Michael retreated hastily, listening outside the door.

"Joe Watson."

"Hello, Joe." The woman's voice was familiar but he couldn't place it immediately. He ran quickly through a list, landing on the name confirmed two seconds later.

"It's Joanne Greer."

He didn't like her, and he was convinced that she was up to her eyes in the Horizon fiasco. His cool tone reflected his conviction.

"Hello, Joanne. What can I do for you?"

"I hope you liked the pictures, Joe. There are plenty more where they came from."

Her words confused him for a moment. What was the connection between her and the photographs in front of him? He was about to ask when she saved him the bother.

"So, here's the thing, Joe. You've been a naughty boy. And unless you do what I ask, I'll make sure that your wife, children and the whole of Northern Ireland has evidence of just what a naughty boy you've been."

"What? What are you talking about?" His tone was still cool but he could feel the fist in his chest tightening again.

"I'm talking about the Horizon project. If you don't stop asking awkward questions and cooperate with me, I have couriers ready to take those photographs straight to your wife and the Belfast Chronicle. And that's just for a start."

He spat down the phone at her. "You stupid bitch.

169

Do you really think that will stop me exposing you? Until now, I wasn't one hundred percent sure that there was a fraud, but you've just confirmed it. And as soon as you get off this line, I'm calling the police. You'll spend the next ten years resting your skinny Malone Road ass in jail, you embezzling cow!"

Instead of the fear that he'd expected to hear, her voice became colder, and the calmness of her next words surprised him. "You sad old man. Did you really think that a girl like that could love you? With your flab and grey hair. Oh, please." Bitch. She knew exactly where to hit him. "You go to the police then, Joe. But be sure you have the evidence to back-up your accusations, or you'll spend years in court for slandering me. If I were you, I'd take blackmail as a gift, because if you don't, you'll find that there's a lot worse coming in the future. Back off Horizon."

Before Watson could say anything more, the line went dead, and he was left wondering who it was safe to call next.

****

The C.C.U. Wednesday.

Craig skipped the gym and was in the office by seven-thirty. He'd finished his last phone-call just as Nicky arrived and bounded out of his office and past her to the lift, heading for the twelfth floor.

"I'll be back in ten minutes, Nick. Could you get everyone together for nine please?

She nodded quickly after him as the lift-door closed, wondering what he was so energised about. He was always quick but not as quick as that. She smiled to herself at the certainty that something new had happened in the case, and meandered into the kitchen to fill the percolators with water. The chief would need extra caffeine after a meeting with Harrison.

Craig emerged from the lift two floors above and walked straight over to Susan Butler, Terry Harrison's sedate P.A., especially chosen by his wife for her non-

170

romantic potential.

"Good morning Mrs Butler. Is the D.C. S. in?"

She looked at him over her glasses; in a way that he felt sure she'd practiced in the mirror, and nodded, slowly. She was a beige woman. Beige suit, beige shoes, beige hair, set against the beige carpeted background of the twelfth floor, the superintendents' domain. He'd insist on staying on the tenth if he ever took promotion. The quiet up here would kill him within a week.

She pursed her lips tightly and looked at her screen. "Detective Chief Superintendent Harrison could see you for five minutes, D.C.I. Craig. But only five."

She gestured him to a seat and he perched on it restlessly while she murmured quietly into the phone. Then she nodded him in, to tell Terry Harrison the details of Bob Leighton's death and ruin his day.

****

Craig re-entered the squad cheerfully at eight-thirty, remembering Harrison's face at the news, and Nicky handed him the first brew of the day. Everyone was there so he pulled up a chair and started the briefing early. Davy and Liam rode their wheeled chairs into the centre and Annette demurely lifted a high desk chair, sitting beside Craig with her neat notes resting on her knee. He linked his hands above his head and stretched. Then he began.

"OK, I need to bring you all up to speed on Bob Leighton. He's dead."

Liam leaned forward to interject but Craig held a hand up to halt him. "I'll answer questions in a minute, Liam. Let me brief you first."

He updated them on the unpleasantness of Bob Leighton's demise and Liam let out a low whistle. "Boyso, that's clever. These boys are professionals."

Annette nodded to herself. "A man died of high potassium when I was nursing. It was nearly missed."

"So was this, Annette. And it would have been, but for John."

171

"The Doc rides again. He's clever, right enough."

"We'll come back to Leighton in a moment. What does everyone else have? Annette?"

Annette lifted the top sheet from her pile and squinted at it. She refused to wear glasses, despite Davy's heavy hints, and the writing on the sheet was already in fourteen font.

"Kaisa Moldeau doesn't exist." They looked at her curiously. "There's no record of anyone from Estonia bearing that name, or from any of the other Baltic States. I've got feelers out to Croatia, Serbia, Romania and other countries in the region, but there are no hits yet."

"You might be out of luck, Annette. There were thousands of displaced people in eastern Europe after the various conflicts, and few surviving records."

She nodded at Craig, agreeing. "She dropped Ben off at his grandparents last Thursday and we thought she'd taken off permanently, to Donegal with Leighton. But apparently, she told the grandparents that she'd be back on Monday. It's Wednesday now and they haven't seen her, sir."

"What about her things?"

"Some of them are still at the Leighton's house, but not Kaisa. She could be hurt, sir."

He smiled at her mildly. "Or she could be guilty, Annette. OK, let's step up the hunt for her please. Get uniform to check any of her known haunts. Liam?"

"Aye, well. I'm still waiting for McNulty to contact me. She went back up to Portsalon to see if there was anything left after the ambulance took Leighton, but I wouldn't hold your breath, boss."

"Don't underestimate her, she's good." He turned immediately to Davy, ignoring Liam's quick grin.

"Davy?"

Davy sat forward eagerly and Craig knew that he had something.

"There are two things, s...sir. London mailed through the description of the woman, but I'm not sure how much good it will do us."

"Why?"

172

"It's very vague. Late twenties. Light complexion, fair-hair, thin and w...wearing modern dress. It could be anyone. One w...witness thought he heard her saying something in another language. 'Draga'. It means 'darling' or 'dear' in some eastern European languages. But s...she didn't say it to the victims, and she definitely w...wasn't a relative of either of the men who died."

"That doesn't make sense, lad."

"I know."

"Unless..." Craig thought for a moment. "Unless she was referring to the shooter. They could be a couple."

"It would go along with two people killing Irene Leighton, sir."

Liam nodded. "I'll get onto terrorism and see if there are any 'tag-teams' working."

Craig nodded Davy on.

"The other thing is that we've just got a hit on the prints, about ten minutes ago. But..." He looked uneasy and Craig was immediately curious.

"Something wrong with the hit?"

"Yes s...sir. It's a bit too convenient. It came in as a tip-off. The prints were identified in a note delivered to Jack Harris at High S...Street."

He handed each of them a sheet of paper as he spoke. It was a photocopy of a typed note.

'For the attention of the Belfast Murder Squad, working the murder of Irene Leighton. The prints you found belong to Joe Watson. Enterprise Minister. They had a past.'

How convenient. But what if they were Joe Watson's prints? An M.P. dead and a Minister implicated, Craig could already picture Harrison shooting himself in the head...after he'd checked his hair.

"I didn't know how to proceed. Do we take this s...seriously or not?"

Craig sat forward urgently. "Yes we do, but not because I believe that he killed her, although I've no doubt that the prints and probably the D.N.A on the cigarette, are his. We take it seriously because someone badly wants us to believe that he killed her, and that means that Watson might be able to tell us something useful about the Leightons' deaths."

He stood up. "Liam, Annette, go to High Street. Find out anything you can about who delivered the note, or who ordered it delivered, anything. Then visit Joe Watson. Don't tell him about the tip-off but invite him in for interview, to help with enquiries into the death of Irene Leighton. Just tell him that we've uncovered a past connection between them."

"Do we tell him anything about Bob Leighton, boss?"

"Or the prints and D.N.A., sir?"

Craig shook his head, firmly. "Nothing. Tell him as little as possible. Just ask him about his connection with Irene Leighton until I see him."

He turned to Davy. "Brilliant work, Davy. Now, as Liam is going to be busy with Watson, could you dig a little further with terrorism on the 'tag-team' please? And look into Bob Leighton's life; habits, past, finances, everything. We'll meet back here at three."

He turned to see Nicky tapping a pile of paper with her pen and sighed heavily. "Because I'm going to be locked in my office until then, signing forms."

Liam guffawed. "Who said rank doesn't have any privileges?"

****

London.

Kaisa woke up late and gazed around her, uncertain of where she was. Then she remembered. She was at The Randle. By the time they'd checked in the night before it had been midnight, and she'd fallen into bed un-showered, make-up still on. Her skin really needed a holiday.

She pulled herself upright and took in her surroundings slowly. Alik had done them proud. The door of her bedroom was open, and she could see the sitting-room with its glass walls and expensive rugs

174

from where she lay. Stevan's familiar voice was speaking very quietly so as not to waken her; he must have been up for hours. Just then, he entered from the adjoining room and she called-out to him, dramatically.

"Coffee – urgently."

She flopped back down, laughing as she realised that she was still wearing her t-shirt and jeans from the day before. She didn't care, there were no men to seduce her or hog her duvet and she wrapped it around her, curling-up so that only her head was exposed. At least she'd remembered to take her hat off.

Stevan reappeared, holding a large mug of steaming coffee just as she liked it. He put it into the small hand popping out from under the duvet, and sat down at the end of the bed, still talking on his mobile. Eventually he said goodbye, in Russian, and clicked his phone shut. Alik. He only spoke Russian to Alik.

"Good morning, dozy. Sleep well?"

"Like the dead." She laughed at her own cruel wit. "Oops sorry - bad taste"

He looked at her, shaking his head. Sometimes her complete lack of conscience scared even him. Ever since that day years before, he'd watched her, as she scanned other people's faces, learning their expressions of sadness, or kindness, or concern. She could mimic emotions perfectly now, but she couldn't feel them.

She felt some kindness for women and children. Always kind to the chambermaids, and beggars in the street. And unfailingly good to children. He'd seen her look at mothers and babies with tears welling up. But for men under seventy she felt nothing, worse than nothing. Hatred, and a complete lack of remorse.

More than that. She enjoyed using them, hurting them and killing them, even when they were kind to her. And of course, God had fashioned her into the perfect murder weapon. Wherever Kaisa walked, men looked and then followed. Then they died.

He shook himself from the sad thoughts of their past. He'd loved them all so much and yet he couldn't

175

protect any of them.

"Kaisa - get up. Alik wants a de-brief, and you look like a dirty fairy. I have calls to make, so meet me downstairs in thirty minutes for some lunch."

"Lunch? But it's only...Oh, it's twelve-thirty...shit. OK." She sank back down on the bed, as if going to sleep again.

"Move."

"OK, bossy...this is me, moving."

She stretched out both arms towards him and they laughed as they had as children, at her lazy-girl signal to pull her out of bed. He obligingly pulled her to the bathroom door, shutting it behind her. Then he walked out, heading for the lobby, yelling 'thirty minutes' over his shoulder.

Kaisa was already washing off the dirt, and erasing all memory of Bob Leighton and Joe Watson. Who were they again? She washed her hair three times to get rid of the dark-blonde rinse, and then wrapped herself in the heavy white-towelling robe hanging behind the door. She grabbed her bag, ready to repair her face. Oh, God. I need the beauty salon quickly. She pictured herself emerging two hours later a completely new woman and quickly picked up the phone, organising the appointment for the next day. Makeup would have to be enough today.

By the time she reached the lobby, she was transformed. Her hair fell in a glossy white-blonde bell just reaching the nape of her tanned neck. A white t-shirt and butter-soft leather jacket combined with a pair of tight jeans and stilettos, to complete her transformation from scruffy hooker to chic London girl. Stevan was talking impatiently in Ukrainian on the mobile and he ended the call abruptly as she sat down.

"Is something wrong?"

"Nothing to worry you, Draga. I may have some unfinished business. Alik asked Josyp to call me and you know I hate talking to that arrogant shit. He acts like he's in line for the throne. I'll sort it out with Alik when we meet. Speaking of which, he wants to see me

176

at two, so I need to get a move on, and you need to eat something. You're even skinnier than usual."

****

Parliament Buildings.

As Joe Watson walked back from his eleven-thirty meeting, he was still undecided about what to do. What proof did he really have that the S.F.F. was dirty, except his gut instinct? Horizon had cleared the approval stage without a blip, and that meant three subcommittees had checked it out. He'd sat on subcommittees in the past and they were rigorous, so if it really was crooked, how had they managed to hide it?

He walked into his office and threw a file at the wall in frustration. Bollocks. He'd had plenty of bad days in banking and not a few as a politician, but this had to rank as the crappiest to date.

He kicked the door shut with his heel and had just clamped his mobile to his ear, trying Ausra's number again, when his door re-opened, abruptly. Michael Irwin stood there, looking alarmed. Watson hit 'end call' and readied himself to shout about the interruption, when he saw the reason for his advisor's alarm.

Looming in the doorway behind him was one of the tallest, palest men that he had ever seen. When he opened his mouth, a voice of matching volume and size boomed out. "Good afternoon, Minister."

Before either man had time to speak, Liam and Annette had whipped out their badges. And Michael Irwin, who had a healthy wariness for the police, had already slipped out the door, closing it firmly behind him.

He positioned himself outside, at a safe distance. But not so far that he didn't overhear the name 'Irene Leighton' and see Joe Watson leaving five minutes later in an unmarked car, helping the police with their enquiries.

177

Chapter Eighteen

"Oh, so you've decided to talk to me now? To what do I owe this honour, you spineless bastard?"

"I don't care what you call me, Joanne. You're in deep trouble, and there's no way out but for you to confess."

"Really?"

Declan couldn't believe it; she was being smug, even now.

"I have no idea what you're talking about."

"You have no what?" Then he realised. She thought that he was taping her, and there was no way that she would fall for that one.

"You think I'm recording this? Do you think I'm bloody double-o-seven? Get a grip, Joanne. I'm not trying to catch you, you're already caught. All I'm doing is warning you that I'm going to the police." He paused, waiting for a reply, but none came. "Why did you tell Dad that Bob Leighton was dead? There's been nothing on the news, except that he's left the country."

Her tone was quiet, giving nothing away. "I heard that he was dead."

"If he is dead you could only know because you killed him! Did you kill Irene too? I wouldn't put anything past you nowadays."

There was a long silence which each thought the other would fill, then she started sobbing, none of her drama classes going to waste.

"All I know is that you've left me and your children, Declan. What possible interest could the police have in me?" Her voice dropped to absolute zero. "All our business contracts were signed by you, so I won't get a penny."

"What?"

He realised instantly that he'd been set up. He'd left the running of the business to her over the past few years and he'd just signed anything she put in front of him. He must have signed things on Horizon. She'd set a trap and he'd walked straight into it! How long had

178

she been planning this?

But he wasn't backing down now. "Catch yourself on woman. Do you really think anyone will believe that? That you allowed me to control everything, a business woman like you!"

Her voice became tearful again for any potential audience. She was playing it just like a woman scorned.

"Who do you think people will believe, Declan? The hardworking abandoned mother of two, or her unfaithful, compulsive gambler of a husband? What are your chances there do you think? Especially when they see those photographs."

Before he could answer her the line went dead, and he was left staring at his mobile. No closer to calling the police, but even more certain that his loving wife had murdered at least one person, and probably two.

****

The Randle Hotel. London.

"Draga - Alik doesn't need you. You stay here and relax."

Stevan reached into the top pocket of his perfectly tailored jacket, and pulled out a discrete black credit card and a silver bill holder, peeling off a wad of notes.

"Enjoy yourself this afternoon. Buy something to wear and then meet me here at five. We'll go to dinner, or the theatre. You choose. Anything you like."

He kissed Kaisa quickly on both cheeks and walked out of the hotel dining-room, through the white-carpeted foyer and into the waiting dark limousine. He rested his head back against the long leather seat and closed his eyes tiredly. The driver lowered the glass partition and spoke to him, respectfully.

"Mr Armstrong, your uncle requests that we travel to Essex today, so it may be a long journey. Would you like a DVD, or something to drink perhaps?"

Stevan roused himself long enough to acknowledge the query, declining both, then he sank back, grateful for a longer silence than he'd expected.

179

He liked silence. There was far too much noise in the world, and too many screams inside his head. His thoughts flitted briefly to Teresa. She would be looking for him now, turning excitedly every time the bar door opened and disappointed every time it closed. He hadn't wanted to hurt her, but she had just been a character in the play. He tried never to hurt people, unless it was his job, and now he even had limits there.

****

The Greers' Home. Belfast.

"That's all I can tell you, pet. Your father has left us. All I know is that he just rang me and announced that he wasn't coming home. That our twenty year marriage..."

Joanne Greer sobbed a little for effect, rubbing at her already puffy eyes. It had taken her an hour of exfoliation to mimic the rawness of crying. That, plus a few well-placed artificial tears purchased from the chemists, in anticipation of just such an occasion. They completed the abandoned wife look perfectly she thought. And from the concerned expressions of her teenage daughters, they seemed to agree.

Carina spoke first, her dark fourteen-year-old gangliness not yet reaching the raven sexuality of her older sister. Declan had said that she was like a beautiful colt and even Joanne had to smile at the analogy.

"But Mummy, Daddy wouldn't leave us, he just wouldn't. He loves all of us. He said he'd take me riding next week. He can't have left us, he just can't." Her breaking voice and bewildered expression almost made Joanne cry for real, but not quite.

Isabella was cooler, her voice more even. "I'm going to phone him, and ask what he thinks he's playing at!"

Joanne rushed to object, and then thought better of it. "Well darling...if you must, but he might say hurtful things, and I couldn't bear for you to hear that." She was thinking quickly now. "I think...if we give Daddy space for a few days...then he might come back. I'd

180

hate angry words to stop that."

Joanne could see doubt, and hope, and pain all rushing across Isabella's young face, as she backed down, hesitating. "Do you think so, Mum? Do you really think he could come back, if...if we give him some space? I read that in Cosmo, that men need space."

"I'm sure that's all it is, Daddy needs space. Let's give him some quiet time and he'll come back to us. I'm sure of it."

Carina rushed to give her suddenly-needy mother a hug. They'd never seen her cry; she was always so self-contained. But now she really needed them both, and they would look after her, they really would. Joanne smiled to herself; men really didn't stand a chance.

****

Epping. England.

The limousine pulled down the narrow leaf-strewn lane, shadowed on either side by elderly trees so bent that they were nearly entwined. The winter sunshine dappled the tinted windows as Stevan looked though them, into the pollarded black-green of Epping Forest. It was such pretty countryside, but cold, always cold. He longed for the summer heat of his childhood home, and days spent wriggling his toes in the stream, watching the bright whitefish swimming.

The driver pulled into an apparently invisible gateway that opened smoothly to the clicked remote. He drove swiftly onwards through two high, dark gates into the driveway of an imposing house. It looked as if it had been there forever, with its sixteenth Century wattle walls marked with crooked dark beams, and a long roof that sloped precipitously towards the ground.

Stevan had never been there before and he admitted to some curiosity. The driver said that it was Alik's daughter's birthday and they had a huge party planned for this evening. The reason he couldn't make it into town. As they pulled-up in front of the wide, low mansion, Alik Ershov came out to greet them. He pulled open the car door and welcomed Stevan warmly as he emerged.

He was a small man, slim and muscular, with the lightly tanned handsomeness that some men retain into their sixties. His grey hair and sharp blue eyes gave him an Aryan quality that belied his Jewish heritage. It had saved his father's life many times. The Dukh around his neck added to the illusion of Christianity, but it was only there as a symbol of his real religion, the Vory v Zakone.

Stevan noticed the bright pink sixteenth-birthday balloons pinned to the front door. Alik had many children by many different women and he loved them all, if not their mothers. He always retained custody. His control was absolute and nothing was too good for his children, natural and adopted, so long as they obeyed him.

He reached a strong hand up around the back of Stevan's neck, pulling him down forcefully to be kissed on both cheeks. "Welcome, welcome, come inside. But where is my lovely Kaisa?" He looked quickly behind him.

Stevan lied. "She was so tired. I let her sleep." He wasn't having Kaisa become wife number four; he would kill Alik at her first tears.

"No matter. Come, have a drink, tell me everything. Then I will tell you."

They walked through the large white main hall, full of toys and 'sweet sixteen' banners, then down a narrow corridor and into a quiet back study, opened by a secure key pad. Alik's office was not for prying eyes. The room was a warm dark-red with heavy leather couches, and chairs set around a large mahogany desk. Everything was dark and secretive, like the business inside.

Alik spoke English with the heavy Russian accent of his parents. He'd spotted Perestroika for the business opportunity that it was, and made his fortune providing whatever people wanted; women, drugs, booze. And of course, the very special services of

182

Stevan and Kaisa. He poured two glasses of vodka and set them on the desk, then sat down behind it, relaxing. Stevan knew better than to refuse to toast.

"You have done well Stevan, very well. The police are chasing their tails just as we'd hoped, and soon the confusion will grow even more." Stevan shot him a questioning look but Alik ignored it, continuing. "The client is very pleased."

Stevan could hear the 'but' coming. "But ...?"

Alik laughed. "Quick as usual, boy. Yes, there is a 'but'. You are not finished yet, you go back tonight."

"But we removed the problem and blackmailed the other. Was that not the plan?"

"Of course, of course. The M.P. caused trouble financially and the other was blocking progress on a project. But my friend is also interested in running trade to the North of Ireland; girls and drugs mainly. And now that they have no conflict it is too peaceful over there. The police have too much time to catch criminals; it is bad for business. They needed some false political unrest created. That is why I chose Stormont and the M.P's wife to kill. Turn one side against the other and create fear. Make them believe that there is still much terrorism, when there is very little. It provides cover, a distraction. You understand."

He laughed sarcastically and Stevan nodded. Terrorism provided a smokescreen for ordinary crime; he knew that well enough from his past. He also knew that his next question would be greeted with anger, but he asked it anyway, in a cold voice.

"Is that why we had to mark the wife and mother? To create fear?"

Alik's blue eyes narrowed sharply and he leaned forward, growling. "That is not for you to ask, boy. Be careful." He looked at Stevan angrily and then smiled coldly, resting back in his leather chair. "But...I will answer your question because it pleases me to." He drank the shot of vodka in one swallow and poured himself another one before starting.

"The Vory v Zakone is my religion and my father's before me. It will not be dishonoured, especially not by a Petukhi, an insect. Robert Leighton was such an insect, a man who took money for doing nothing and then stole more of mine to feed his habit. He was warned many times, yet still he continued. But he might still have been useful, so we needed to make him afraid. The death of his wife was for that."

He shrugged. "The location and markings were to make people believe that terrorism might be the cause. That the Vor worked with local terrorists to kill her. Also my little indulgence if you like, to mark her as my territory. This I can do. You understand?"

Stevan understood, and it made him despise the man in front of him. He stored the feeling away for the future and nodded, returning to the job ahead.

"Who is the target?"

Alik smiled like an amiable uncle "Patience boy, I will get to that. The young are so impatient. Be careful, it breeds mistakes. If I hadn't been so hasty I would never have married my wives. In the old code it was not allowed." He laughed loudly at his own joke and even Stevan smiled at the thought.

"But then you wouldn't have your children."

Alik reached over and slapped his arm hard. "You're right, you're right. No action is one hundred percent wasted."

He fell silent and reached forward into a drawer, lifting out a small black box. It contained a delicate mesh of platinum laced with thirty diamonds, each at least half a carat. Stevan swallowed hard. It was amazing, and worth at least a million.

"For Alexa's birthday. You think she will like it?"

Stevan laughed at the thought of any sixteen-year-old girl not liking it. "It's stunning, but she'll need a body-guard to wear it."

Alik smiled, pleased by his reaction.

"To business then. The client has another problem. Her husband, who is her business partner, is not happy about the death of Robert Leighton. He knows nothing of her part in the wife's death, but she foolishly told him of the M.P. Now it seems that he has trouble with his conscience and means to talk to the police.

Conscience is such a burden to some people."

Stevan was shocked, surprised that the client was a woman, although why should he be? Kaisa was proof of how lethal women could be; but her murders came from trauma, not from money. But the honesty of their client's husband was unexpected and it pleased him somehow. Alik read his mind, but not completely.

"I see what you are thinking, and you are right of course. But only she was the client, the husband knew nothing. And even worse than telling the police, he is trying to alienate her from her daughters."

An angry darkness crossed his face at the idea. "That, I cannot allow. This client and I have knowledge of each other for many years. She helped me many times as my barrister and...she was someone to me."

Stevan understood. Every man had a woman who was special to him. He had yet to meet his.

"So you see, we need a quick remedy for this husband. Can you do this, Stevan? I know that you are tired and just returned, but this is two days work at most."

Stevan nodded slowly. "Of course, I will. But not Kaisa please. She's tired and must rest."

Alik smiled avuncularly. "Agreed. Not Kaisa. She stays in London."

He reached into the drawer again and pulled out a white padded-envelope. Stevan knew exactly what it would contain. False I.D, tickets, a burn phone, money and a legend. He opened it to see who he would be this time, and where he would get his weapon. He couldn't return to the gun they'd left at the airport. The police would find it eventually, but without a single print.

He read quietly for a minute. He was to be a Nordic businessman on a trip, arriving in Belfast for an imaginary meeting. He would stay in a hotel this time, 'The Lagan Warehouse' - not too high, not too low. He was to meet a man in the bar, exchanging money for information - the key to an unmarked weapon and the wherewithal to destroy it. So many guns still at liberty in that conflict-weathered country. But it would be only two more days and one more death. Then rest, and never again.

They talked on about the target, about life, about the birthday girl. Then Stevan waved good-bye and climbed into the car, for the journey back to his shortened evening with Kaisa. An early dinner and then she would have to amuse herself. He had a plane to catch at eight o'clock. She would fret about him, but they both knew the life. The more work, the more money, and the more money the sooner they would leave it behind forever.

****

High Street Station. Belfast.

Joe Watson was either a bloody good actor or he really had no idea that Bob Leighton was dead. And he was like no politician that Craig had ever met. There was none of the usual arrogance and bluster, or apparent belief in his own infallibility. The man in front of him sagged like a deflated balloon.

Joe slumped in his chair, observing the scene in an 'out of body' way. This had to be happening to someone else. Three hours ago, he'd been at work in Stormont and now he was being interrogated about murder. He remembered the Chinese curse, 'May you live in interesting times' and smiled. His life was certainly that.

Craig clicked on the tape-machine and relaxed back in his seat, mimicking the other man's posture. He stared hard across the table, trying to work him out. There was something exhausted about him; but not physical tiredness, more a sense of futility with the world.

"Mr Watson. Do you know why you're here?"

Watson looked at him blankly, either not hearing him or not caring what he'd said. Craig repeated himself more firmly, and was rewarded with a nod.

"It's something to do with Irene."

"Yes, it is. Did you know Mrs Leighton well?"

His eyes immediately said yes, and Craig wondered

186

if his mouth would do the same. It did.

"I knew her very well."

Then unprompted, Joe Watson gave them enough information to close a gap in their case.

****

The C.C.U. Counter-terrorism.

Ross Ellis was a medium bloke in every way. Medium height, medium weight and medium-brown colouring. In fact, the only things that stood out about him were his overly large feet, which were size thirteen. He joked that some six-foot-five man was running around with his size nines, and he wanted them back.

Pretty much everybody liked him, except his ex-wife, and that was only because he'd asked his lads to tail her on the 'front and follow' to catch her with her boyfriend, hence the divorce proceedings. Davy didn't know what he'd expected a Chief Inspector in counter-terrorism to look like, but it was definitely more James Bond than Ricky Gervais.

Ellis was hunched down behind his desk when they arrived at his glass-doored office, so Davy knocked tentatively and waited, Craig letting him take the lead. He knocked deliberately lightly so as not to anger the room's occupant. Davy had a healthy respect for the cloak and dagger boys and you never knew what spooks would do if they were roused.

Ellis looked up and they suddenly saw why he'd been hunching. One hand was covering a half-smoked cigarette, in a 'smoking forbidden' force. He laughed and waved them in, grinning at the younger man's floppy hair and black nails.

"Hi, Marc. Come on in, son. I don't bite."

He stubbed the cigarette out slowly in a cup as he talked; walking to the wall sink to rinse it. Then he lifted a can of air-freshener from his desk drawer and sprayed it around liberally to mask the smell.

"Are you Murder's new analyst?"

Davy nodded, half-smiling. He liked this man

187

already for his rule-breaking, convinced that people needed the occasional rebellion. Ellis was still talking, quickly and with a vague north-coast twang.

"You lot on the tenth put us all to shame, with your fashion sense. What with Craig and his London suits, and you with your Goth chic. I tell you, when the force makes a 'boys of the police' calendar for charity, there you'll be, Mr June and July. Posing with your Armani jackets strategically draped over your designer bits."

He laughed loudly at his own joke and Craig and Davy laughed along. When the laughing finally stopped, Davy spoke.

"EMO."

"EMO?"

"I'm an EMO, not a Goth, just for accuracy."

"Ooh, that's me told." He smiled and waved them to two chairs. "Right then, Emu. What can I do for you?"

Craig made the introductions and then excused himself, leaving Davy to fill Ellis in on the bullet, the gun, the Vors and Liam's earlier conversation with Geoff Hamill. Ellis' eyes widened as Davy first picked his brains and then buried him in information, leaving him with a huge headache that would get bigger very soon.

****

The Watsons' Home.

Caitlin Watson was a slim, glossy dark-blonde who looked just like the Miss Northern Ireland that she'd once been. She'd been married to Joe for fifteen years and they'd each brought children from their previous lives, to form the perfect modern family. So perfect in fact that Annette remembered them being photographed 'en famille' in the glossy pages of the Ulster Bazaar. 'Here is my lovely over-styled wife, reclining on our over-styled bed, in our incredibly over-styled and expensive bedroom.'

Craig had tasked Annette with interviewing her about the Leighton's, without alerting her to the fact

188

that Bob Leighton was dead. Or that her husband Joe was helping them with their enquiries into Irene Leighton's death. When she'd complained about the impossible task, Craig had said that he had 'every faith' in her powers of diplomacy. She only wished that she had.

Caitlin had opened the door smiling five minutes before, and now she was pouring coffee from an exquisite porcelain pot into minuscule matching cups. As she poured, Annette looked around the modern room admiringly. Whoever had chosen the colour scheme had matched it perfectly to Caitlin's own and the effect was striking.

She took the proffered cup tentatively, smiling at its size. Even Liam's little finger wouldn't have fitted through the handle. She balanced it on her knee with her left hand and opened her notebook with her right, turning to the purpose of her visit.

"If you could just tell me anything that you know about the Leightons generally, Mrs Watson. Did you socialise with them? Or did your husband ever talk about them, for instance?"

Caitlin Watson stared into space, recalling. Then she spoke, in a strangely still voice, so monochromatic and quiet that Annette strained to hear.

"We didn't socialise with them, but I met them both at functions, of course."

"Government functions?"

She nodded. "Yes. But others too. Irene was involved in lots of charities. She was always throwing fund-raisers. She was a very nice woman."

"Did you know her well?"

"No." She looked down at her perfectly manicured nails, sadly. "I don't mean it unkindly, but she wasn't into fashion really, and most of my friends are. But I liked her very much, everyone did."

Her expression changed to one of disgust. "Which is more than I can say for her husband." She shuddered slightly. "A nasty man. Joe doesn't like him much either, I can tell you that."

Annette leaned forward and placed her cup on the

too-low coffee table between them, trying not to ask her next question too eagerly. "Do you know why your husband dislikes him?"

"I think loathes him would be a better word, sergeant. Joe loathes him. He's lazy, hardly does any work in his constituency, and Joe says that he's crooked."

Annette was writing furiously in her small notebook and looked up sharply at her last word, echoing it. "Crooked?"

"Yes. I'm not sure of the details but Joe says he fiddles everything, even his expenses. The man's loaded and he fiddles his expenses. And his father was honest to a fault."

"His father?"

"Yes, Robert Leighton senior, his father. He was high up in government here for years. Everyone knew him, and respected him."

Annette's interest in local politics was zero, so she sincerely hoped that someone's back at the ranch was higher. She swallowed, forming her next question as diplomatically as possible.

"Did your husband have any direct dealings with Mrs Leighton? Perhaps in her charity work?"

Caitlin Watson just stared at her uncomprehending, and then laughed lightly. "Joe? Charity work! He's a good man, but not a saint. No, I don't think he ever met Irene except at functions. Why?"

Annette closed her notebook and slipped it into her handbag, standing to go. The woman in front of her obviously knew nothing that could help them.

"Just general background questions, Mrs Watson. That's been very helpful, thank you. I'll leave you now." She extended her hand and the other woman shook it without rising. "I'll be in touch if we have any more questions."

Then, without giving Caitlin Watson time to ask 'what questions', she was out of the door and into her car, heading back to Docklands.

****

The C.C.U.

The briefing had been called for three and everyone was gathered ready, apart from Davy. Craig nodded Annette on and she'd just started reporting when Davy hurtled in, raising a hand in apology and sliding his chair in beside Liam's.

"I did my best not to give Mrs Watson any clues, sir. And she didn't seem to pick up on anything." Annette paused for a moment, looking wistful. "You should see the house. My whole downstairs could fit into the living room. And the decor..."

"How the other half live, eh, boss."

"You mean how the other five-percent live nowadays, Liam."

Annette smiled at Craig, continuing. "The only contact they had with Irene Leighton was at charity functions; Mrs Leighton ran a number of fund-raisers."

"Did Joe ever see her separately, Annette?"

"Not as far as Mrs Watson was aware. And I think she was being truthful, sir."

"The wives are always the last to know..."

Annette turned on Liam angrily. "God, Liam. Do you have to drag everything into the gutter? There's no sign that Joe Watson was having an affair with Irene Leighton."

Craig looked at her ruefully. "I'll come back to that in a minute, Annette. Carry on."

"You mean he was?"

Craig shook his head sadly, not answering, and waved her on.

"Apparently Bob Leighton is crooked. Everyone knows that he fiddles his expenses and maybe more."

"Did she give you any details?"

"No. But she did say that Joe hated him. No, sorry, she said he loathed him."

"That's worse, isn't it, boss?"

"It's certainly sounds like it. Anything else?"

"No. Nothing, sir. I didn't get any sense that there was animosity between Mrs Watson and Irene Leighton at all."

"OK, thanks. Davy?"

"Yes, s...sir. As you know I've been downstairs with Ross Ellis, from counterterrorism." Davy laughed. "He w...was having a cig when we arrived."

Craig smiled. Ellis had been addicted to nicotine since university. One of the last surviving smokers. Him and Julia McNulty.

"Who's we, lad?"

"I introduced Davy and then left them to it. Did Ross throw any light on the bullet, Davy? Or the Vors?"

"None. And he looked really w...worried when I left. He was already calling D.I. Hamill."

It was just as Craig had thought; the Vors had no presence in Northern Ireland. If they were here now it was for a specific reason.

"Liam?"

"Nothing much, boss. The prints match Watson and we're waiting for the D.N.A. to come back. When we lifted him, either he did a good imitation of knowing nothing about Bob Leighton's murder, or he was telling the truth. We've sent his prints to London, on a long shot, but I doubt they'll match anything else. Oh, and Bob Leighton was playing golf in Scotland on the lost weekend before he went to Dublin. Innocent enough but he obviously didn't want the wife to know."

Craig nodded. "Detachment rules."

"What?"

"It's a military expression. It refers to when you are away playing and tell no one the details. OK, then. As you all know, Liam and Annette picked Joe Watson up at Stormont at lunchtime and brought him in for interview on a voluntary basis. That has now been made more formal since his prints matched. But I still don't think that he had anything to do with Irene Leighton's murder. In fact, I'm sure that he didn't, although I'm certain that his D.N.A will match that found on the cigarette. By the way Annette, did his wife confirm that he smoked?"

Annette nodded. "Yes, then went into a rant about how awful it made the house smell."

Liam leaned forward, looking serious. "Why so sure

he's innocent, boss? The prints look pretty convincing."

Craig shook his head. "Too convincing. I was convinced that he didn't do it before the interview, and I'm positive of it now."

"What did he say, sir?"

"First of all, he was devastated by Irene Leighton's death and he had no idea that Bob Leighton was dead until I told him." Craig was like a lie detector and they knew that he wouldn't have been fooled.

"W...why devastated?"

Craig looked down sadly, and what he said next surprised them all. "Because he loved her, Davy."

Liam opened his mouth ready with cynicism, but Craig kept going. "Twenty-two years ago."

"What?"

"But she was only eighteen, sir"

Craig nodded. "And he was thirty."

"Dirty old man."

"Here Davy, don't you be too quick to say thirty's old, you're only five years off."

"I meant the age-gap."

Annette was nodding furiously in the background as Craig continued. "Yes, that was an issue, but it seems to have been a genuine relationship."

He paused and looked down, his next words quiet. "Irene Leighton, or Irene Hannigan as she was known then, became pregnant. Watson wanted them to get married, so they went to England."

Davy leaned forward, innocence written all over him. "W...Why didn't they stay here?"

Annette turned to him gently. "It was nineteen-ninety, Davy. You were only three. But a girl who got pregnant and wasn't married in Northern Ireland back then, would have got a very hard time from her family."

Liam nodded. "Even worse if she lived in the country."

"And the man?"

"A bit, but not as much, lad."

"That's disgusting."

Craig nodded, agreeing. "But it's the truth, Davy. Equality wasn't always what it is now. Anyway, they left for London and the baby was born, a little girl called Rebecca." The 'R' on the baby bracelet.

"They were planning to marry and return home afterwards, when..." He hesitated. "The baby died at three months from S.I.D.S."

Liam and Davy looked at him blankly, and Annette nodded. "Cot-death."

The room fell silent, until eventually Craig broke it. "Watson wanted them to get married, but Irene Leighton was grieving so badly that she pushed him away and flew home to be with her family. He stayed in London and joined Goldbergs' Bank. The rest is history."

"She married Bob Leighton two years later, sir."

"Yes. And Watson married wife number one, and then Caitlin fifteen years ago. But that's not all he told me."

"I bet that he and Irene Leighton were seeing each other again."

Annette glared at Liam and then looked at Craig for denial. He shook his head and she smiled. "You see, Liam, not everyone's unfaithful to their wives. Caitlin Watson has a good marriage."

The way Craig shook his head again told her that she was wrong.

"Sorry Annette. Liam's half-right. Watson was having an affair."

Liam's smug look annoyed even Davy, and he knocked Liam's elbow away, making him fall forward.

"But not with Irene Leighton, Liam."

A shocked Davy stared at him. "God, are you over forties always at it?"

Craig smiled ruefully, understanding his twenty-five-year-old perspective.

"I can see where you're coming from, Davy. Watson has been seeing a girl for a few months, and by all accounts he's fallen hard for her."

"Girl?"

"Sorry, woman. Late twenties."

"Even dirtier old man."

"Was seeing her?"

"She hasn't returned his calls since yesterday."

"That's a convenient disappearing act."

"I know, but I still believe him. He's not helping himself though; he won't say anything about her."

"Hoping that she'll come back, sir?"

"Something like that. He says he loves her."

Craig shrugged; men were good at deluding themselves. He'd believed Camille was coming back for years. And just when he'd finally stopped hoping, she'd reappeared.

"He was planning to leave his wife for her." He turned to Annette quickly. "Do you think Caitlin knew, Annette?"

Annette shook her head slowly. "I honestly don't think so. But I could be wrong. I'll question her again."

"Watson won't give me a name or a description for the girl."

"But she would have been in the perfect position to get his prints and frame him, sir. So would his wife."

"She'd have plenty of access to his D.N.A., boss."

Annette shot Liam a warning look to keep it clean, as Craig continued.

"I agree with both of you. And if Watson won't tell us about her, we'll interview his bodyguards. They'll definitely describe her."

****

Port Salon. Donegal.

Julia McNulty was secretly pleased that Craig had asked her to help, especially after her coolness during his last visit. It showed that he trusted her professionally, as she did him, but only professionally now. She pulled out her badge and showed it to the blue-uniformed Garda guarding the white villa. They'd sealed it off at Dr Winter's request, once it became clear that Bob Leighton hadn't died naturally. Two men had been guarding it day and night since then,

195

preserving what little evidence might be left.

She lifted the crime-scene tape and walked slowly up the path, looking at the expensive house set in its private ocean driveway, where Bob Leighton had breathed his last. She stood on the elevated front step for a minute, looking out at the view. Portsalon beach stretched out below them for half a mile, sweeping towards the Atlantic Ocean inlet. It was a bright, dry day and there were crowds of people milling across the white sand, making it feel like summer.

She could just make-out a rider ready to mount a black horse, and a kite-flyer with his bright red charge, his finger pointing high in the air looking for the wind. A little family, the mother laden down with clothes and beach toys, was walking towards a shaded area just north of the house. Her toddlers running behind her like baby ducks. It was idyllic and she wished that Craig were here to see it.

Just then a small, uniformed officer tapped her on the back, waking her from her daydream and she shook Marc Craig from her head, turning to enter the house

"We're ready for you now, Inspector." His accent was lilting and soft and Julia could feel her own softening in reply. "That's grand. Thank you."

She ducked as she walked through the low front door and was immediately surprised. The ceiling rose spectacularly into a wide open-plan living area. It was enormous; one thousand feet of cream-carpeted luxury. Two squashed-leather sofas were angled in front of a wide, open fireplace, with an imitation animal rug lying in front of it. At least she hoped that it was imitation. She had a sudden vision of Bob Leighton frolicking naked on it and shuddered.

She wandered through the rooms slowly, the luxury growing with every high-ceilinged bedroom, and marbled ensuite. Finally she returned to the living room and sat down on a sofa, reaching into her pocket for the list that Annette had e-mailed through. Bob Leighton had been murdered, which meant that his murderer had definitely been here. Was it his son's

196

nanny? Was she capable of murder? Or was she a victim as well? She'd certainly disappeared.

No one but police and ambulance staff had entered since his death, so any forensics that they found should link to Leighton's killer. But they'd be here for days finger-printing the place, unless they narrowed it down somehow.

He'd died in bed after recent intercourse and Julia knew that Annette was right. The only person that he would have let close enough to kill him in bed was his lover. And he'd left Belfast with Kaisa Moldeau - although it was unlikely that was her real name.

She looked at the list closely. Annette had identified all of the places that a woman might have touched. Julia smiled at some of them. In the kitchen: sink, cooker, fridge door. Dishwasher door, low cupboards more likely than high, cleaning materials and the bin. In the bathroom: mirrors, bath-taps etc.

But it was the bedroom that was the best. Apart from the expected mirrors and wardrobe doors, Annette had added one that really made her laugh; bed headboard, top and front. Naughty, naughty, Annette.

As she watched the C.S.I.s working, she thought of every boring regulation possible to stop herself wondering whose prints would show up on Marc Craig's headboard. Definitely not hers.

****

Joe Watson had two close protection officers, as they called bodyguards in polite circles, Ryan Drake and Ian Sinclair. They took it in twelve-hour shifts to guard him. Craig had finished interviewing Drake and was waiting for Sinclair's version, but if it was as bland as Drake's was then they'd strike out completely.

One of them was always with Watson, travelling with him. Sitting outside the hotel room while 'the girl' was with him. And watching him play poker for hours. They were even with him when Watson received her weekly romantic call, outside the hotel's front door. Standing just far enough away to be politely deaf, while he had phone sex, or phone love, or whatever it was called. He was never out of their reach or sight for one minute.

They'd checked Drake out and he seemed as clean as they came. Fifteen years police, tactical support, firearms trained, one of only four guarding Watson since he'd become an M.L.A. There'd been a few threats against him in his early days as a politician, but they'd settled. Now there were only two of them on the detail, Watson insisting on the counter-intuitive reduction when he became a Minister.

Drake liked Watson. He was a bit too fond of the ladies, and could be a spoilt dickhead when he was under pressure, but mostly it was an easy gig. Well, compared to guarding a judge during a terrorist enquiry, which had been his last one. But he had told Craig to ask Ian Sinclair's opinion.

"Ian's more conscientious than me, always putting himself out more than he has to. You know the type. 'Gives a fuck even when it isn't his turn.'"

Craig had smiled; it was one of John's favourite quotes from 'The Wire'.

Sinclair was waiting for him now at High Street, and Craig took up Liam's offer of a joint interview, driving them both there. As they walked in the door, he recognised the unmistakably fit shape of a protection officer perched on the hard bench in reception, and nodded to him. "We'll be with you in five minutes, Officer Sinclair."

"No problem, sir."

Ian Sinclair folded his bulky arms and closed his eyes, resting his head back against the cold magnolia wall.

Just at that moment Jack Harris, the station's long-time desk sergeant, came ambling out amiably. "Ah. Hello sir. And so nice to see you too, Inspector Cullen." He bowed in mock-respect to Liam. They'd known each other since college and Jack never let Liam forget that he'd taken rank.

They went into the back office and Liam helped himself to coffee, ready for a gossip but they were interrupted almost immediately by a female constable, introduced as Sandi.

"Shall I take the coffee straight into the interview room, sir?"

Craig roused himself quickly. "Thanks. That would be great." And they followed her quickly into the small neon-lit interview room. She placed the tray on a bench to one side, and left.

Ian Sinclair was already seated in the room, his arms resting over a chair-back, relaxed. He'd sat in too many of these rooms to be anything else but. He stood up as they entered and Craig extended his hand. Sinclair shook it firmly, no fat visible, even on his hands. He removed his jacket and draped it over the back of the chair, every muscle on his torso etched out through his shirt.

"I signed my gun in at the desk, sir." His accent was from England somewhere but Craig could only narrow it to somewhere in the southeast. "I'd like it back when I leave; I hope that's in order? I've been temporarily reassigned while the Minister helps you with enquiries, and I'm on duty at six."

"Of course. Who are you guarding next?"

"A Judge. He's ruffled a few people's feathers and they're making threatening noises."

Craig nodded. "This shouldn't take us too long, Officer Sinclair."

"Ian, please."

"Right, Ian. We've already interviewed Officer Drake, but any information you have about Mr Watson would be useful. Particularly about the girl that he was seeing?"

"OK, sir. First, you need to know that I didn't get on particularly well with Mr Watson."

Liam sat forward and boomed ominously. "Well now, why was that?" Craig signalled him to back off and Liam sat back again, disgruntled.

"Well frankly, he's a careless prat and a bloody nightmare to guard. He didn't want us there at all, and if he could have slipped the leash, he would have done. He kept changing his schedule, making unplanned and unwarranted stops, and was far too familiar with everyone; from the aircrew to the hotel staff. He was a typical politician, so desperate to be popular that he would have told you the combination of his safe if you'd vote for him."

He sat back abruptly, shocked at his own candour.

"Here, did he have a safe?"

"Yes, probably." Sinclair laughed and relaxed again "My point is…He couldn't or wouldn't keep himself safe, and he resisted most of our efforts to do so. I think he was going to ask for me to be moved, because he thought I was restricting him."

Craig nodded; Watson had already put the request in. But it seemed to Craig that Sinclair was just a conscientious officer being driven mad by an irresponsible charge. There'd been occasions at The Met, during the run-up to the Iraq War, when he'd protected M.P.s visiting public protests. They were a nightmare to guard, seeing every request for their cooperation as some dictat from the fascist police, instead of realising that they were just bloody trying to keep them alive.

"I know that some charges rail against the restrictions of having protection. It's not easy keeping them safe when they won't help you. Just tell us anything that you think might help."

"Well, I didn't trust the girl that Watson was seeing. It was bad enough and a possible media nightmare when he insisted on visiting Lilith's - that's a brothel out at Antrim."

"Here, a brothel? A real one?"

Sinclair nodded and Craig looked at Liam, astounded at his naiveté. Then he remembered that brothels weren't as common in Northern Ireland as they were in London, where they'd been in every house on some streets. He made a mental note to catch up with the local police about Lilith's and nodded Sinclair on.

"He took a shine to one particular girl and started bringing her to the hotel. I tried to talk to him about it, so did Ryan, but he wouldn't listen. He was too busy

200

thinking with his dick."

They all nodded, understanding.

"She was a stunner, I'll give her that. Well, none of us except Joe ever saw her face, but you can always tell. Petite, slim, curvy. A pocket-rocket."

They understood Joe Watson's behaviour perfectly now.

"Dark-blonde hair, shoe size three or four, five feet one. Size eight, thirty-six inch chest, no visible tattoos or scars."

"You're good."

"It's my job to see things. I can also tell you that she wasn't naturally dark blonde."

"How do you know?"

"Her sunglasses wiped off some of her eyebrow pencil once, and the end of her eyebrow was white-blonde. In my experience only white-blonde girls have white-blonde eyebrows."

"White-blonde hair is attractive, so why would she dye it darker?"

"Exactly my thoughts. She was disguising her natural colouring for a reason. I saw a bit at the back of her hair that was white too, as if she'd missed a bit. I'd say she was a natural white-blonde and was tinting it dark-blonde for Joe."

"Anything else you noticed?"

"She liked to wind us up, wiggle past, stand close, that sort of thing. We were both there one day, handing over, when she deliberately leaned in close to Ryan, and I could see her eyes though the side of the glasses. They were green and the colour looked natural. It's harder to cover darker eyes with a believable lighter lens, so I reckon that maybe green or blue was her natural eye colour."

"White-blonde, with blue or green eyes. Northern European?"

"Yep. But there was no point saying anything critical about her to Joe, he was daft about her." Sinclair paused for a moment, thinking, and Liam noticed that even his clenched jaw looked muscled, lifting his own chin in reflex.

"Our routine never varied, which was another mistake and I said so. But Watson wouldn't listen. We'd get back from London and check in at The Castleton at about five on a Monday. Then she arrived about six and Joe's poker game was at eight or nine. We got him the same room, five-one-seven, end of the corridor, no access other than past us, the usual safety rules. She'd arrive, there'd be some chat and giggling between them, and then, regular as clockwork, the shower would start to run at about six-fifteen – six-twenty. Every week, same routine, so we reckoned that they nipped into the shower together and got to it."

He took a sip of coffee and looked at Craig, in a way that instantly told Craig that his next revelation had meant going slightly 'off piste'

"I was suspicious of her from the start. So eventually, one evening about two months ago, I asked Ryan to stay for a ninety-minute overlap. Normally we just do a ten-minute handover and then the outgoing officer goes home, but this time I asked him to cover me. As soon as I heard the shower running I nipped into the room."

He paused again as if expecting a bollocking, but Craig said nothing.

"I bugged the room so that I could hear a bit, not gratuitously; just for Joe's safety. And I had a quick look in her bag. There was nothing much, a few mints and the car keys to an old Ford - she drove it every week."

"Did you get the registration plate?"

"Already checked. It was registered to Lilith's and insured in their name. Anyway, she also had a can of spray-on bandage, but no I.D. No licence, no cards, nothing. Nothing else except a handbag mirror and a lip-gloss. So..."

He reached into his pocket and pulled out two small evidence bags, sealed and dated fifteenth October twenty-twelve.

"I finger-printed the mirror and took off the end of the lipstick for D.N.A. traces, then re-blunted the lipstick and returned the bag before they left the

202

shower. I knew they'd be in there for twenty minutes."

Liam smiled lasciviously. "Tight squeeze."

"Not really. The room had a double shower, deliberately chosen for it."

Craig looked at Liam in warning. "I'm sure Liam was referring to your timing. I'm impressed."

"Don't be too impressed. If I'd been really effective she would never have been in there."

His jaw clenched again and there was silence for a minute while he regrouped.

"The bug in the room only gave up three useful bits of information, and some of it might be false of course. She said that she lived with her father who she cared for - that's why she could only get away to meet Joe on a Monday. She said she'd given up working at Lilith's after she met him, you know, the whole 'you're so special Joe' routine. But you could check that easily enough."

"Yeh, it ranks up there with 'you're the first' "

Craig rolled his eyes at the things Liam came out with, and then they all laughed.

"She also said that her name was Ausra and that she was Lithuanian."

"Yes?"

"Well, Joe might've believed her, but there's no way that she was Lithuanian. I was in the army and worked with N.A.T.O for a while."

Craig nodded; he'd already known about it from Sinclair's background check.

"I was out in Yugoslavia, and I can tell you, she wasn't from Lithuania or any other Baltic state. That accent was pure Serbian."

"Phew...that's a hell of a lot of information."

"Yes well, like I said, it wasn't enough to stop him."

Craig could see Sinclair beating himself up and he leaned in firmly. "Listen, you did your best. If someone wanted him tricked this badly, then it was always going to happen. It could have been a lot worse."

He updated Sinclair broadly on their suspicions about the Leighton's' fates and he nodded. He'd known the girl was dirty and it wouldn't surprise him if she was involved in their killings.

"I'm not sure about gathering the prints and D.N.A. without her knowledge, sir."

"We'll keep it under the radar. If she's innocent then nothing will show up, and if she's not, well then, you've helped the enquiry." He turned to Liam. "Have the hotel room sealed off and printed please, Liam. And get any close circuit TV that the hotel has...I'll see what D.I. McNulty got from the house. "

"Just one last thing, sir. The car key was to an older Ford, before remote locking. If you show me some pictures of keys I can pick it out for you."

"That's great. Davy will get in touch on that. Thanks again."

They stood up and shook hands. Then Sinclair twisted to slip on his jacket, outlining his enviable torso again and reminding Liam just how long it had been since he'd been to the gym. He looked down at his paunch balefully.

Craig called Sandi to escort Sinclair out. He'd seen her eye him up earlier, and if she couldn't engineer a dinner date in the ten minutes that it could take her to find his gun and do the paperwork, then he'd very much underestimated her.

"Drake was right about Sinclair."

"Why? What'd he say?"

"He gives a damn even when it isn't his turn."

****

The C.C.U.

Davy was daydreaming happily about Maggie when he was rudely interrupted by a ding from his right hand screen, indicating that he had mail. He'd meant to turn the noise down after Nicky's scolding for disturbing her, and he could already see her tutting across the room. He leaned forward to his skull's-head computer mouse and clicked – it was from The Met, probably just some boring UK-wide circular. Then he opened it and immediately took a copy to Craig's office.

Nicky was sitting at her desk outside, checking her Christmas-red lipstick in the mirror, and re-applying it with such concentration, that he was loath to interrupt. It looked like a delicate operation, one slip and she'd look like a vampire. He decided to be brave.

"Boss around, Nicky?"

She looked around exaggeratedly in every direction and then back at him, expertly finishing her lipstick during the sweep. "Nope, I can't see him."

He smiled down at her, knowing that it was her last gasp of disapproval at Maggie. He didn't mind, his mother was just the same. "Very funny. Everyone round here's a comedian. Could you tell me where he is then? I have an important memo for him."

She smiled cheekily and pointed towards the door. "He'll be coming through that door in five...four...three...two..."

All of a sudden, Marc Craig walked across the floor towards them, and Davy stared at her as if she was psychic. Then he said it, in a way that risked his own death.

"Are you like one of those dogs who knows when its master is about to get home?" He moved quickly to stand beside Craig before she could grab him.

"Hi, Davy. Do you need me? Come on in. Coffee? Thanks, Nicky."

They entered Craig's corner office before Nicky could answer, but Davy knew she would get her revenge later. Craig's office was summer-bright even in December. It was full of long slim windows that only opened slightly, in case anyone decided to commit suicide. Hadn't anyone ever told architects that you could commit suicide with a paperclip if you wanted to?

From the room's tenth-floor height, the view over the river and East Belfast was panoramic; Davy could look at it all day. Which is probably why he'd never be allowed a view – he would get no work done.

If he hadn't worked here, he would never have known the history of Sailortown, the river and the docks, with its war scars and old churches. Centuries of stories of life and death.

He thought that it hadn't been made enough of. School kids should meet the people who'd worked the area, before the generation that had lived there died out. It was like a living history exhibition.

"What can I do for you, Davy?" Craig sat down at his desk and lounged back in his chair, loosening his tie - it was the most relaxed they ever saw him. He gestured Davy to the chair opposite.

"I thought you should see this, s…sir. It's just come through from London marked urgent, in response to my flag on the 338 Lapua. I'll give them a call now."

It was from a D.C.S Rajiv Chandak at headquarters, requesting a contact, and suggesting a call to La préfecture de police in Paris, if it hadn't already been done.

"Great. I'll give London a call if you chase up the Paris connection."

"I passed the details to Interpol two days ago but nothing more came back from them, or from the Home Office Large Major Enquiry System. H.O.L.M.E.S.2. I've s…searches running on the other international databases."

"I'll ask about Paris when I call. Maybe we're finally catching a break."

Davy smiled shyly, still in awe of his boss. Craig always reminded him of a TV detective, all London suits and interesting back-story. And a bit deep, unlike Liam. He smiled quietly to himself, but none of his thoughts made it into speech.

"The labs have been trying to narrow the gun down and w…we're sure that it was a TR-42 now. I'm on to firearms to find out about dealers and trafficking."

"Thanks." Craig nodded him out and picked the phone up, just as Nicky entered the room holding two cups of coffee. He took the sweet black one gratefully.

"Thanks. Davy's just gone back to his desk, Nicky. Would you mind taking it over to him?"

He pretended to miss her glare, and threw her a wide smile instead. "And would you mind closing the door? I'm going to call London. Thanks."

She gave up glaring after a few seconds; it never worked with him anyway. Either he saw it and ignored it, or he really didn't see it. She'd never quite managed to work out which.

Craig dialled and waited to be put through. A strong Birmingham accent came on the other end; he loved English accents, there were so many of them.

"Could I speak to chief superintendent Chandak, please?"

"You're speaking to him, son. Who's that?"

The brummie twang almost made him laugh, it was such a change. He didn't know why people voted brummie an unpopular accent, he loved it. It was Geordie that he had a hard time with, rarely understanding the words, although he could still appreciate the melody.

"Good afternoon, Detective Chief Superintendent Chandak."

"God, that's a mouthful. Super will do."

The accent laughed in a deep bass and Craig continued, smiling. "It's Marc Craig from the Belfast Murder Squad, sir. I'm calling about your e-mail to our analyst."

"That was quick, what can I tell you then?"

"Well. We've had a recent high profile killing, the wife of a member of parliament, and it looks like a professional job. We have the bullet, but no gun."

"I saw your bulletin. Single shot, 338 Lapua. No trace of the shooter?"

"That's about the size of it, except that we believe they had an accomplice."

The superintendent's voice became urgent. "A woman?"

"We think it might be. Your shootings had the same pairing, didn't they?"

"Yes. We've had two over the past thirteen months; both single shots, both Lapua Magnums, no sign of the guns. And we've got nothing on the shooter at all. There was a vague sighting of a girl around the same time, but nothing concrete. What we do believe we have, is some hint of a gangland connection; with a

207

pretty senior player over here that's well known to us."

"That could help us. At the moment, we've no idea of who commissioned the killing or why. What was the Paris reference?"

"They had a similar killing in Paris two years back. 338 Lapua, no gun, but nothing on the shooter or a girl. The Lapua's not one that we come across in the average gun crime. That's why your bulletin flagged up."

"Is there anything further back that you know of, anywhere?"

"Paris is the only one we've heard of outside the U.K. This could be a new shooter, or someone who's graduated to it from other things."

Chandak paused, considering. "How would you feel about a quick trip over to put our heads together? I'm not a great one for doing business over the phone. I prefer to see the whites of your eyes."

He laughed a big booming laugh and Craig already liked the man. He'd love a trip to London, even an overnighter; it had been his world for so many years. And he thought he could justify it now that they had two deaths.

"That would be great; I used to be at The Met."

"Even better, I won't have to warn you about the canteens then. Where were you based?"

"Fulham when I was in uniform, then I did the high potential scheme and worked in Kensington. Usually in Earls Court Road, with D.C.S. Merton."

"Trevor Merton? He's just retired, but he's still knocking around the building somewhere. Hates to leave us. We'll get you two together for a coffee. That sounds like a plan, D.C.I. Craig, leave it with me. Let's say tomorrow then. I'll contact your Super and clear it with him now, Terry Harrison, isn't it?"

"Yes, sir. I can transfer you."

"Fine. I'll smooth the way and you bring us whatever you have. If it's the same shooter then maybe between us we can catch a break. See you tomorrow."

Craig went to the office door and asked Nicky to transfer the call, then gathered whatever he needed.

Five minutes later Harrison called, giving permission for the trip. Emphasising that it was costing public money and expenses were to be kept to a minimum. Craig had no intention of living it large, and he'd happily spend his own money. It would be well worth it to see London again.

Chapter Nineteen

"Sorry Marc. The print that your guy pulled from the mirror was Joe Watson's. There's nothing there from the girl at all. Maybe the lipstick will give us a hit. Come down and have a look at the bullet."

"I'll be there in twenty, John. Just let me move some things."

Craig was disappointed and John Winter could hear it. They needed to catch a break. It took volumes of evidence to prove someone guilty, when all the guilty ever had to do was be smart enough not to leave a clue. He tried to help Craig solve his cases, although he shouldn't have been on the shop-floor half as much as he was. But he loved getting involved - it was the closest adults ever got to playing cops and robbers.

Craig drove fast and accurately through the late afternoon traffic, up the Ormeau Road, towards the Saintfield Road. The road was full of new bars and restaurants and luxury urban living, once you'd got past the untidy-looking student quarter. Students made everything look scruffy; he'd been the same when he was one. It must be in the jeans.

Within ten minutes, he was holding a coffee and staring at John's computer screen open-mouthed. John was right; it was like no bullet he'd ever seen before.

"So that's a Lapua."

"A 338 Lapua Magnum to be precise. Des is back from holiday. I'll see if he's free to join us. He's working on a court case for Monday."

As they waited for Des Marsham, John pulled-up a print on the screen.

"The print Sinclair found was from Joe Watson."

"It was too much to hope that we'd get the girl from it."

"Yes, but it does tell us something."

Craig looked at him questioningly.

"Watson may have touched the mirror, but what sort of woman doesn't leave a single print on her own

210

handbag mirror?"

"One completely without vanity?"

John laughed. "How many of those do you know?" He didn't wait for a reply. "Didn't you say Sinclair found a spray bandage in her bag as well?"

"Sure. He assumed she'd cut herself."

"I think she was using it for something much more interesting. There was a presentation on it at last year's Forensic conference. If it's sprayed on the fingertips it covers up prints."

"God. If she was doing that then she was definitely up to something. Sinclair's instincts were right on the money."

John flicked back to the image of the bullet and a minute later the bearded figure of Des Marsham came bouncing in, excited.

"I've never seen one of these rounds and I've just been reading up on them. Amazing little things, wait till you hear this."

He pulled out an A4 sheet and started to read. "The only calibre designed specifically for sniping, designed to penetrate five layers...."

Craig raised a hand gently to stop him. "Sorry Des, I've already heard it all from Davy and he was as excited as you are. You should ring him for a chat."

He turned to John. "Thanks, both of you. Watson's girl is up to her ears in this. Liam's pulling the tapes from the Castleton and we've Keith Ericson at Antrim, chasing the brothel where Watson met her, so we'll get something on her. I may need to call you to a late briefing, John."

"No problem. I'll be here until six and at Natalie's after that if you need me."

Craig grinned. He was already writing his best man speech.

****

The C.C.U.

"OK. As you can see we're being joined by Dr Winter,

D.C.I. Ellis from counter-terrorism and Sergeant Ericson from Antrim. Annette's had to go home early, to take Jordan to the orthodontists. And Nicky's kindly taking notes."

Craig nodded at Ross Ellis and the larger rounder figure of Keith Ericson, bringing them up to date. There was nothing much new, until Keith Ericson made his contribution.

Ericson was in his last year before retirement and if he'd had his way, he'd have gone years before. There was a slightly wistful air about him, as if he was longing to be playing golf somewhere hot. His faraway look was amplified by the long shape of his lugubrious face, which reminded everybody who met him of Deputy Dog - it had been his nickname for as long as Liam had known him. Ericson spoke painfully slowly, and nothing, neither person nor natural disaster, could ever speed him up.

"Well now...There are a few things, sir."

Everyone's hearts sank; it would take him an hour to report at least. They couldn't spare the time so Craig interjected, pleasantly. "Just the most important thing please, Keith." Ericson looked a bit put-out, but he continued undeterred, and Liam mentally went to sleep.

"Joe Watson went to London every Monday morning for business, Westminster stuff. Then he'd slip back early that evening via the International Airport. He'd meet the girl at the Castleton Hotel, play poker with his mates and then go home to the missus later, with her believing that he'd been in London all day. Apparently it had been going on for months."

"Thanks Keith, we've been appraised of that. Do you have anything on the girl?"

Ericson sniffed, annoyed, and deliberately slowed his speech to a drawl. "Mystery woman...all we know so far is that he met her at Lilith's."

"Lilith's? What's that, sir? A bar?"

"No..." Craig smiled at Nicky benignly. "During the Troubles some of the more enterprising boyos spotted a gap in the market, providing 'services for tired business men'. So they decided to set up a pleasure-dome out near the airport. They stocked it with high-class call girls and ran a pretty clean shop apparently. No drugs, no trafficking etc. But they certainly gave the tabloids plenty of photos of well-known men. Anyway, the boys running it were put away for their other little enterprises during the Troubles', and a woman took it over. She's called Lilith I presume?"

He looked around for confirmation and Keith answered. "Actually no, not Lilith. Megan McHenry. She called it Lilith's because it has some sort of mysterious connotation. Seems Lilith was supposed to be the first witch and the first sexually assertive woman. A lot of medieval witches took the name."

Craig looked at him, surprised, and Liam laughed. "You've been at the Readers' Digest again, Keith."

Ericson rewarded Liam with a sarcastic nod and Ross Ellis leaned forward, interested. From the amount of fiddling and oral gratification he was getting from his pen, Craig knew that he was dying for a cigarette.

"Anyway...the place has been running well for years. We drop in now and again to make sure she knows that she shouldn't be doing it. But to be honest, it's quiet, clean, they pay their taxes and, well sure it keeps the girls off the streets of Antrim. And it stops the businessmen kerb-crawling."

Ellis grinned broadly. "Dear God, can you just imagine that picture...The shame of it, streetwalkers in Antrim. It would be like having strippers in Camberwick Green." They all laughed and Keith continued, warming to his theme.

"You see loads of well-known men out there. She said last month that they had enough men there from the council one night to hold a meeting. God knows what the female leaders do for their entertainment."

Craig wondered where Ericson had been for the past few years.

"Anyhow, Watson met the girl there, took a shine to her and made her exclusive. He paid Lilith enough to make sure no one else touched her."

213

"The bodyguards echoed that when we interviewed them, boss. She arrived at about six every Monday and left about eight. Then Joe would go and play poker with a bunch of his mates in a room downstairs. The description we have of her could be anyone: five-feet-one, slim, curvy."

Nicky snorted. "Typical man description, I'm surprised they didn't just say 34.23.34."

"Aye well, it could be worse, Cutty. When it comes to distinguishing features he could have said 'had a brain'."

That was too much for Nicky and Liam got a heavy thump on the arm. Craig looked at him despairingly.

"Settle down, Liam." He turned back to the others. "They said that she always wore sunglasses."

Ellis leaned forward urgently. "Indoors? Didn't they think that was a bit strange, Marc?"

"Apparently she didn't want to be identified. Watson said that it wasn't exactly her dream-job, so you could understand that. The only other information Drake gave us was that she wore fashionable but not high-end clothes, and no jewellery. Although he did say that he'd noticed her wearing an expensive looking bracelet when she left the room last night. He saw a Tiffany box in Joe's luggage and thought that he must have given it to her."

"He must have liked her a lot."

"Drake said he did. Joe confided to him that he intended to leave his wife for her."

"Phew... Now there's a motive for Mrs W to frame him."

"If she knew, Liam."

"She knew...never underestimate a woman, boss. They spot the clues. And God gave them a heightened sense of smell, especially for other women's perfume."

Nicky looked at him despairingly and Davy nodded sympathetically, agreeing with her.

"Do w...we have anything on the girl's voice?"

"Drake said that she never spoke, never. It was strange, lad. But she always smiled at them as she walked past. He described her as 'sex on legs.' That should make her easy enough to find in Northern Ireland." Craig shot him another warning look.

"She'd got in the habit of calling Watson after she left. He'd go outside to the front of the hotel and they'd talk to each other looking at the same sky."

Ellis stuck two fingers down his throat and was joined by Keith.

"You've got to be joking. How old is this man, Marc?"

"I'm pretty sure that's why he won't discuss her. One, he hopes that she's coming back, and two; he knows he was set-up and made a fool of himself. Ian Sinclair said that he heard her voice, and it didn't sound like any Northern Ireland accent he'd ever heard."

"Where then?"

"He thought maybe Serbia. Liam, what about the tapes from the Castleton? Anything there on the girl?"

"Aye. Well she's a real little weapon of mass destruction all right, never seen a wiggle like it. But as far as identifying her, there's nothing useful, boss. She kept her face covered the whole time. All we have is her build, height and facial outline. If we do find her, it could be useful for matching, but not enough for a straight I.D. But short of actually having cameras in Watson's rooms there's nothing else that would have done."

Keith Ericson piped up. "I might be able to help a bit there. Lilith said the girl came to her four months ago, with a story about how she needed to make money for her sick father - the usual stuff. Anyway, they have a reputation to uphold, if there is such a thing in the brothel business. So she insists that all her girls are H.I.V tested and seen by a doctor before they meet customers, so at least we have a name for the girl. Ausra Mitic. I've checked it out and no one with that name exists. But we have two more people now who can identify her if we find her. Lilith and the doctor."

"Get them both to do photo-fits please, Keith. Or better still get any photographs that Lilith might have. Let's see if we can get an I.D. on this girl."

Ericson had come to a natural halt and Craig quickly grasped the opportunity to move on. "Ross?"

"OK, Irene Leighton was killed by an ace sniper - just the single bullet, no mess, lovely job." He nodded to himself half-admiringly. Ellis was a good shot and not adverse to a spot of hunting, something that he and Craig had argued about a few times. Craig's limit was clay pigeons.

"Or maybe he's just spent too much time playing computer games?"

Ellis ignored Liam's comment. "So let's say, hypothetically, that Watson's girl was something to do with the Leighton killings."

Davy sat forward, surprised. "W...why make that leap?"

"Because she had the opportunity to get Watson's prints and D.N.A. And they were dropped off at High Street with a convenient note linking him to Irene Leighton, a relationship which Watson has now admitted. Humour me, just for a minute."

Davy shrugged and Craig nodded Ellis on.

"So, on Mondays, Watson is at the Castleton with his little dark-blonde hooker Ausra who was really white-blonde. It would explain why Sinclair noticed the patch of white-blonde hair at the back."

"She must have missed a spot, sir. It's easy to miss a bit at the back of your head if you're dying your hair yourself."

Liam looked nosily at Nicky's hair and she firmly ignored him. "There are loads of wash-in wash-out hair rinses and gels on the market. She could easily have changed her colour and look, just with different clothes and a pair of cheap sunglasses from any supermarket."

"We don't know what she really looks like, Ross."

"True, but we can have a fair guess that she's involved with a professional killer, Marc. If she knew about the death of Irene Leighton or was working for someone who did, then the best we can say about her was that she was a honey-trap. And that they've been planning this for months."

"More like a Venus fly-trap."

"She didn't do this alone."

John leaned forward, interjecting. "Irene Leighton was shot, Marc."

"And she was walked into Stormont by someone, John; it could have been a woman. The London killings indicate the possibility of a couple working together."

Ellis interjected again. "OK, so whoever framed Watson for the Irene Leighton murder had his D.N.A. on the cigarette and identified his prints. It must have been someone close to him, probably a woman? But the killing of the two Leightons must be linked, so maybe the woman who got close to Watson was somehow also involved with Bob Leighton?"

Liam shook his head. "The girl involved with Leighton was their nanny, Kaisa; we have nothing to show that it's the same girl. And just say that it was Caitlin Watson who got Joe's prints and D.N.A, and then linked him to Irene Leighton's death, what would she have to do with Bob Leighton?"

John added. "Bob Leighton's killer knew all about his family history of heart disease, and chose a method of killing that mimicked that. This Ausra is a complete stranger. Although..."

Craig leaned forward urgently. "What, John?"

"The information about the heart disease was probably available from newspaper reports or death records. His father died of S.A.D.S. and he was a prominent politician, so his cause of death would have been reported. Once she knew who her target was, it would have been an easy matter for any professional killer to do their homework and work their way into Leighton's life. So I suppose..."

Nicky interjected. "Sir, I know that Annette had another chat with Caitlin Watson. She was more fed-up with Joe than she let on." She caught Liam's smug look and scowled, continuing. "But not enough to frame him, Liam. She spoke to a divorce lawyer a few weeks ago but said that she just wanted to put the wind up him. She didn't really want a divorce. And without Annette actually mentioning the girl Ausra, she said that she was convinced that Caitlin knew nothing

217

about Irene Leighton, or the other woman."

Craig trusted Annette's instincts. "Thanks Nicky, but if it is the same girl then we need to prove it. Liam, chase up McNulty again on the prints, and work with Annette to dig a bit deeper into Caitlin Watson. If she knew about Joe's relationships with Irene Leighton and Ausra, then we need to find out.

Davy, keep going on the databases, let's see if Ausra Mitic's D.N.A. is anywhere in the system, and find out who she is." He turned back to Ellis. "But it still doesn't get us any closer to finding out who ordered these killings, and why, Ross. Anything on the terrorism front?"

"Only that a group called the N.I.F. have claimed Bob and Irene Leighton's deaths."

"The who?" Craig thought quickly of his conversation with Andy White.

"The Northern Ireland Freedom Brigade. They say they're a new dissident group, except no-one has ever heard of them! It's complete bollocks, Marc. They don't exist. There's no intelligence on them, nothing. Someone's just invented a new acronym to stir things up. Claiming the killing of an M.P and his wife, and leaving her body at Stormont; that'll work. Especially once the Chronicle gets hold of it.

But I can tell you that the real guys are bloody annoyed about it, and they're already looking for someone to blame. With a bit of luck they'll bump each other off."

Liam muttered. "Here, here."

Craig rubbed his face tiredly, half-agreeing, but trying to keep a grip of the meeting. "I'm sure D.C.I. Ellis didn't mean that."

Ellis just shrugged, he believed in the wild-west school of policing. Craig let the banter fly for a moment and then called them back to order. "OK, funny as they are, enough vigilante jokes. But this isn't the first N.I.F. runour that I've heard." He updated them on White's comments.

Ellis chewed thoughtfully at his pen. "The rumour-mill's working overtime then. OK, real life. This is someone covering themselves on the Leighton's killings, and they're digging themselves a deep hole in the process. Either that or they're deliberately trying to stir up the terrorism angle to cover-up something else; violent crime, drugs, girls, something."

Craig nodded, the terrorism angle felt right. The room fell silent until Craig broke it, bringing everyone up to speed on the bullet.

Ellis interjected. "We're looking at an overseas hit here, Marc. I've done a bit more digging and none of our guys could muster that sort of armour, not even back in their glory days. It's too high-level. This was a professional job. What exactly were the Leightons involved in, that someone wanted them dead?"

"I think the wife was sacrificed to get at the husband. No one has anything but good to say about her."

Craig paused for breath and Liam was about to jump in, but Ellis was quicker. "Davy, have you found anything on known contract killers?"

"The Met are looking, and Interpol, but nothing s...similar yet."

"What about the gambling, Davy? Is Watson in trouble there?"

"No, he's just a recreational gambler, the odd game of poker. Mrs Watson gave us permission to look at their accounts and there are no problems. W...Watson made a load of money at Goldbergs and more from investments here."

"Liam, any other reason why someone would frame him for murder?"

"Not a thing, he's well liked, boss. I've been onto Newry and the people down there say Watson did a lot of work for poorer people, and built a lot of community bridges. Everyone says the same thing. Even his first wife likes him and that's a miracle. They should canonise him just for that."

"But it doesn't tell us who framed him and why. Davy, go back to his wife and dig a bit more. Any private business interests, investments, and people he hacked off in the past. Unless he was Santa Claus someone is bound to hate him."

"What about quangos, committees and s...special interest groups, s...sir?"

"Good point. Liam, work with Davy to cover those. There's a reason someone framed Joe Watson. People don't bother to do that unless there's something in it for them. So follow the trail backwards. Who does he have power over? And whose life is he disrupting, or about to disrupt? We'll brief here at two every day unless you hear otherwise. Liam will be leading some of the briefings - I'm heading over to London tomorrow for a day or two, to follow up on some new leads."

****

Stevan took his room-card politely from the girl at reception, nodding as she smiled and handed him the receipt. She was really very cute, and he'd never seen so many freckles. For one brief moment, he thought that it might be fun to count them.

"That's room four-o-seven, Mr..." She looked down at her desk computer. "Mr Marberg. It's a deluxe room. I do hope that you enjoy your stay with us."

Sven Marberg smiled down at her, nodding a polite 'thank you.' Then he turned and headed towards the back stairway, taking the lift to the fourth floor. He checked his watch quickly. The flight had been slightly delayed but it was still only nine-thirty. He had time to shower and change before he went to his imaginary business meeting, with his imaginary client. With the very real agenda of accessing his weapon and target.

He opened and closed the room door quickly, keeping to his habit of staying low key. Then he threw his Mulberry travel-bag onto the bed, running the shower until it was hot. The plumbing in this country had proved a bit variable, and he didn't want to step into freezing needles. Leave that to the real Nords. He looked at his newly blonde hair in the steel bathroom mirror; it went well with his tanned skin. He looked every inch the prosperous Nordic executive.

He had stuck to the rules and kept the pretence of coming from an eastern European or Nordic country. People would take their cues from his height and colouring, and he was fluent in most languages. It was a good cover.

He stood under the warm shower, letting the water flow over his dark muscular back, and he felt his mind drift. A holiday was definitely in order, somewhere very warm. Kaisa needed a bit of colour. He laughed to himself; she'd looked like 'Casper the friendly ghost' that morning.

And he really needed a woman. Properly this time. Not the scripted groping of his character legends. Although Teresa had been pleasant enough; and the receptionist might provide a nice little diversion later tonight. He had a sudden vision of 'joining the dots' of her freckles with fresh cream and it made him smile.

No, he needed a real relationship soon, someone to talk to and maybe even settle down with. Kaisa would try to sabotage it of course, but he knew that it was up to him to breed; she would never overcome her hatred of any man long enough. Yes, he would leave the life behind soon and marry, but he had to choose the girl well. And she would have to understand that he could never ever leave his little sister.

****

"Here, boss. Does that mean I'm in charge 'til you're back? Annette and Davy will need supervising."

Craig was at his parent's house in Holywood saying hello, and Liam had just called him, talking about his trip. He excused himself from the noisy family kitchen, ignoring his mother's finger wagging at his phone, and stood outside in the cool December evening continuing the call.

"Annette can cope very well, Liam, and you know it. And Davy has plenty to get on with. Besides which, I'll only be a couple of days."

"Aren't you staying the weekend to catch up with your mates?"

"Maybe next time. I just want to see if they can help us. If it looks like extending beyond two days then I'll let you know."

"Aye well...All right then...I suppose."

"Can you nip out to Lilith's with Keith and see if they can do a sketch of the girl. And try Joe Watson again for a sketch, he had the best view of her face of anyone."

Liam gave a lecherous laugh. "And the rest."

"And you can knock comments like that on the head right now, especially at Harrison's briefing."

"What? Ach, boss. Do I have to go to that?"

"Yes. It's the only way to find out what's happening elsewhere. One of the privileges of rank you're so fond of mentioning. I bet you won't feel so privileged after you've been to it. Davy is working with Des on the bullet."

"Is Des back then?"

"Yes, on Monday. And D.I. McNulty is finishing up in Donegal this evening. She's sent all the prints they found over to John, so follow up on those with her please."

"I'll put Kevlar on before I go near her."

Craig laughed, more relaxed about Julia McNulty than he had been in months. "I'd better get back inside; I'm getting dirty looks through the kitchen window. And don't worry, I'll be on the phone every hour, trust me, if only to stop Annette and Nicky strangling you."

They cut the call and he went back into the warmth, sitting on the wide kitchen bench beside his sister. She smiled, and he noticed that she was looking tired. "What's tiring you out, Luce? Partying?"

"I wish! No, just work unfortunately."

She worked for a charity helping the growing immigrant population in Northern Ireland, and there'd been a recent spate of racism causing people to leave their homes. Uniform had told him that they'd seen her there trying to help.

She brightened up quickly, grinning at him. "We're planning a big rally at the City Hall next month. We've got people coming from all over the E.U."

Craig groaned loudly. That meant the tactical support group would get involved and he'd get ripped about her for weeks.

"Don't you moan at me. If you were in those people's positions, you'd be glad we were doing it. Anyway, freedom of speech and all that, aren't your lot supposed to uphold it?"

"My lot! Listen miss, I must caution you that anything you say…"

Tom Craig sat in the middle of the kitchen ignoring everything around him, reading his Scientific American while Murphy barked loudly at his feet. It was a technique that he'd perfected many years before when he'd had to write scientific papers in a house filled with two noisy children. And a pianist wife who was constantly practicing for some or other concert. He could tune out every single sound now.

Of course, it had its dangers. Especially when he didn't hear Mirella saying, "dinner's ready" for the third time. Then it was likely to result in a bread roll thrown at his head, followed by a stream of incomprehensible Italian, the only safe response to which was a weak smile and next-day flowers.

Both of their children spoke Italian but he'd never managed to get further than 'amore'. Still, it kept the mystery alive. His reverie was rudely interrupted by a loud banging on the worktop.

"Stop doing that, now."

They all turned, puzzled, towards the small dark-haired figure of Mirella Craig, unsure which one of them she was talking to.

"All stop everything, now. You stop reading, you stop torturing your sister, and you stop up-winding your brother. Now eat!" So they did.

223

Chapter Twenty

Declan hadn't slept all night from disbelief that Joanne was capable of killing someone, anyone...and especially for money. Could he ever kill? Perhaps to defend his kids or parents. Yes, he could definitely kill for them, but for money? No. That was a whole different type of cold.

He shuddered. He couldn't believe that he'd ever made love to Joanne now. Worse still, that his lovely daughters were fifty-percent from the evil bitch. Nature versus nurture. He just prayed to God that his genes were stronger.

He looked towards the window, and the quality of the morning light told him that it was about eight. He should have gone into the office yesterday but there was no way that was happening; he needed time to think. And he needed to be far enough away from Joanne not to hit her. He'd never hit a woman, but he thought that he could make an exception for her.

He'd driven around for hours after he left his parent's house on Tuesday, not even noticing where he was, until he'd found himself back on the familiar ground of the Upper Malone. He'd pulled into Newforge lane to think and had found Virginia Apartments; private, self-contained and rentable by the week. There was no way that she would find him here.

He couldn't go home, he couldn't go back to his parents and he couldn't go to any of his usual haunts. She would find him at any hotel in the city. God's knows he'd slept in most of them during their volatile marriage, when he'd had enough of listening to her shit.

The apartments were a bit close to home but Joanne never walked anywhere, smug in her hermetically-sealed little world. That would all change soon. He idly wondered how prison would suit her; it would be hard even for her to accessorise there.

The image made him laugh, and suddenly he had

224

the energy to bounce out of bed and wonder what to do next, over a hot, white coffee. He knew that he should go to the police, but how could he prove that it had only been Joanne responsible for the Leighton's deaths? And that he'd known nothing about them? And what about Horizon? She stitched him up completely there and innocence was pretty hard to prove when you'd signed a contract.

He flicked the local news on mute and watched the headlines sailing across the bottom of the screen. All of a sudden 'Leighton's Murder Claimed' appeared and he clicked the sound on urgently, watching as the middle-aged newsman told the world that Bob Leighton's killing had been claimed. What the fuck?

"A new dissident splinter group, the N.I.F. the Northern Ireland Freedom Brigade, has claimed the killings of Robert Leighton M.P. and his wife Irene. There is some dispute about this claim..."

The N.I.F.? He'd never heard of them and he bet that nobody else had. That would hack the big boys off.

The screen changed to a view of Donegal and the sight of crime scene investigators outside a house, but Declan ignored it, thinking frantically. He was totally confused now. Had he been wrong about Joanne's involvement?

No...Definitely not. Joanne had known that Leighton was dead before anyone else. She'd done it. But she was even smarter than he'd realised, managing to give someone else the blame. How the hell had she managed it? Did the N.I.F. even exist?

If they did, either they were in cahoots and they'd done the job for her, or she'd framed them. In which case she was playing an even more dangerous game than he'd realised. The real boyos would be none too pleased.

But it changed things. If he told the girls that Joanne was involved now they'd never believe him. And what if he told the police? They might think that he was involved in terrorism, and that would bring him a whole world of pain.

He thought for a minute longer, and then decided to

do what he'd always done, and what had always driven Joanne mad about him. He'd just wait and see. The news would change over the next few days, and when it did, he'd be ready to head for High Street station.

In the meantime...well, he might as well take in a race or two. The charity race meeting was on at Antrim this afternoon. He looked at his watch; six hours until it started, plenty of time for breakfast and another little reward. He lifted his mobile and scanned for 'bookie', smiling as it dialled.

****

London. Thursday Morning.

Craig disembarked at Heathrow and headed quickly for the Express train, and the short fifteen-minute journey to Paddington. It had all changed from the fifty-minute tube ride on the cramped Piccadilly line, when he'd first been there in ninety-eight. Stopping and starting, dropping and picking up. He almost missed it.

The occupants on the tube covered the whole range of Londoners, mixing with the newly-arrived from every country. They covered all age-groups, from excited kids to tired pensioners. But the Express was more like a mobile morning office, with businessmen stroking at their phones desperately, as if they were lovers. One or two hopefuls even tried to log-on or make calls, aborted mid-sentence at every tunnel.

He sat back and relaxed, remembering the city that he'd lived in for so many years. He loved London; it was constantly changing. People had too much variety here to divide themselves with arbitrary doctrinal differences. If only Northern Ireland could learn the same trick.

The journey ended too quickly and he disembarked, walking slowly along platform seven towards the coffee stand. The smell soon reminded him that his plane ticket hadn't extended to breakfast and he'd just bought a coffee and croissant when he felt a light tap

226

on his back.

He turned to apologise, assuming that he was blocking the way, only to come face to face with the tight muscular build and wide white grin of Yemi Idowu. A grin that he hadn't seen for nearly five years.

"What the...? Yemi!"

Craig smiled broadly and put out his hand. It was grasped quickly by the other man's and followed by an arm around his shoulder. "Marc, it is good to see you, my friend."

"How did you know I was coming? Are you working the shootings?"

"Chandak is my boss. He didn't know we knew each other, but when I heard that you were coming I insisted on picking you up. We need to catch up."

"How are you? You look well. And how's Bunmi?"

"She is well, but there are two more of us now. We had twin boys just last month."

He reached into his pocket and produced a photo of a smiling Bunmi holding two tiny bundles.

"You know, Marc. Breeding is a habit, once you start."

"I'll take your word for it, Yemi. Congratulations. So are you involved in the cases?"

"Yes, yes. But we will talk about that in the office. The next twenty minutes are for gossip only."

Without Craig even noticing, they'd reached the back slope towards Praed Street where Yemi had parked his car, using his charm and badge to stop them towing it away. He reversed rapidly up the hill and then headed the three miles towards headquarters, as they talked over each other and laughed the whole way.

As they approached the underground car-park, he paused and looked at Craig seriously. "You look well my friend, but too thin. You need a woman and a good meal." He hesitated and Craig knew that there was something else.

"Bunmi will truly kill me for telling you this. She wants you at dinner tonight to relax. But I think it would be wrong not to."

"Is something wrong?"

"Camille is in London."

Craig didn't react in the shocked way that his friend had anticipated, and Yemi looked puzzled. "I know. We're in touch." He explained her contact after five years and their long lunch in November.

Yemi relaxed visibly. "Do you know that she's in a play here?"

Without waiting for an answer, he reached into his pocket and withdrew a ticket, handing it to Craig. Then he said nothing more. Craig put it in his top pocket nodding thanks, and they parked, walking towards the lift in companionable silence.

By the time the lift-door opened at the fifth-floor murder unit, the topic was snipers. And Craig had shifted back into his forty-two-year-old D.C.I. self, intent on ignoring the ticket for at least eight hours.

He walked confidently through the familiar neon-lit floor full of computers and shirt-sleeved men, feeling instantly at home. It could have been a newspaper office, but one where the news was always deadly.

Yemi led him to the door of the corner-office and knocked, leaving him there. A shouted 'yes' was his cue to push the door open, to be greeted with a more sophisticated and darker-skinned version of Terry Harrison. He wondered briefly if D.C.S.s were cloned, but any similarity vanished at the warmth of the man's greeting.

Rajiv Chandak stood up smiling, with his hand held out. "D.C.I. Craig?"

They shook and Craig confirmed his identity "Yes, sir. Thanks for arranging to have me picked up."

The tall D.C.S laughed, showing large teeth. "I would have had a fight on my hands if I'd tried to stop Yemi. I believe that you two know each other?"

"Very well, sir. We started out in Fulham together, as youngsters."

"Good, very good. Nice to have hands across the Irish Sea, especially as we're getting more crime back and forth. I know your new Chief well from the Association of Chief Police Officers. He'll do OK for you. He made a good fist of it in his last post. Take a

228

seat."

He gestured Craig to a comfortable, high, armchair set beside a small coffee table, leaving his desk to join him.

"It seems as if we're dealing with the same shooter here. We've had two over the past year using the 338 Lapuas and now you've had one. A Mrs Irene Leighton, wasn't it?"

Craig nodded.

"Our victims were both men, but very different backgrounds. Both in business, but nothing in common apart from that. We've been back and forth through everything and we can't find any link. Yemi's looking for anything that could tie them to your victim, and so far, there's nothing there either. We have to assume that these are three separate hits.

What we do have is intelligence that leads us to these being professional hits, real 'guns for hire' stuff. One of our informants is linked-in to the Russians in east London."

Craig nodded. When he'd lived there east London had been the home of decent immigrants, and less decent 'gangs and geezers'. They'd moved into old commercial sites, and then out to towns around the M25, once they'd made their money and wanted to look legit.

Most of the original cockneys had left east London now, only kept alive in episodes of 'East Enders.' Their communities destroyed by developers, just like Sailortown. At least the Olympic legacy might improve things here.

"Any names yet, sir?"

"Not on the shooter. But there's a nasty piece of work called Alik Ershov that we've been trying to link to organised crime for years. The word is that he's mixed-up in this somewhere, although why he'd be involved in Northern Ireland is anyone's guess."

"There are a lot of people back and forth here for business every week, sir. So hiring a hit from here would draw less attention than using our local boys. And whoever hired them might have contacts here?

229

Can you tie anything firm to Ershov?"

"You know what it's like. We get two layers below him and then no one knows who they're reporting to. He's very well insulated. And every penny of his legitimate earnings is declared. They all got wise when Capone got nailed on his taxes."

Craig laughed hollowly; the stereotypes of dumb crooks couldn't be farther from the truth. At the top level, these guys were bright. The police had to keep up, or give up.

"He's first-generation Russian, and into drugs, people trafficking, guns and gangs."

The word gang made the hairs on Craig's neck stand-up and he interrupted urgently.

"Gangs? Any particular sort?"

Chandak looked at him curiously. "Not sure that you'll have heard of them, Ireland's been lucky enough to miss this bunch. They're called the Vory v Zakone. Mostly Russian and other ex-soviet republic. Ruthless bastards."

"Is Ershov a Vor?"

Chandak was surprised by Craig's urgent tone. He thought that the Vors had skipped Ireland, but maybe they had found it, now that there was peace. He nodded.

"There's been talk of it, but they're very secretive. You probably know as much about them as we do."

"I know that they obey some sort of 'Thieves' Code' and there are estimates of about ten thousand of them dotted around the world. I heard Obama had to deal with some a few years back. The leaders are called 'Thieves-in-law' and have to show a long criminal record. Their trades and ranks are shown by tattoos."

He filled Chandak in on the markings found on Irene Leighton. Chandak gave a low whistle.

"Ershov fits the Thief-in-law part for sure. Right, you only have a couple of days here, so I'm going to force-feed you with everything we have. Then we'll get our teams working together. I'm hoping that someone got careless in your killing, and it might give us some fresh leads on ours. Whoever ordered your hit might be

230

feeling twitchy by now."

"Yes. Especially as the dissidents got blamed." Then Craig brought Rajiv Chandak up to date with the latest twist in their crime.

****

Joanne Greer had made up her mind long before dawn. At first she'd just intended to get rid of the Leightons, but Declan's parochial morality had taken things out of her hands. So what happened next was his own stupid fault. If she could be sure that he'd keep his mouth shut, he wouldn't be dying in a few hours' time. But he couldn't do that. He insisted on saying that he would call the police on her, so he had to go.

She'd set him up nicely as the gambling swine that he was. Not that she'd ever given a shit about his gambling, as long as he didn't use her money. And she knew that he'd never been unfaithful to her, although she often wished that he had, it would have kept him away from her bed. Then she could have just hired a photographer, instead of having to pay a fortune on photo-shopping.

The photographs had cost a fortune to mock-up, but they would serve their purpose when he died. She would look betrayed and vulnerable in every one's eyes, the wronged wife and mother. She yawned and kicked off the duvet, none of it would matter in a few hours anyway. Declan would be dealt with by the end of the day; Alik had assured her of it.

It had been exciting speaking to Alik again last year, after all that time. Her mind drifted back to fifteen years before, when they'd still lived in London. She wished she'd never left it, but Declan and her parents were to blame for that. With their chorus of 'it'll be better for the girls Joanne, better schools Joanne, safer streets, Joanne'...yap, yap yap, whine bloody whine.

Eventually she caved in, but she'd regretted it immediately. And hated them all for it ever since, even the girls. Although no one would ever have guessed.

She'd been the consummate actor, throwing herself

231

into the endless round of fashion-shows and charity events that passed for Northern Ireland's middle-class social life. London had been so much more exciting. The anonymity and variety, the people you met, the endless surprising opportunities. The men.

She'd thought about Alik often. Fifteen years before, he'd gone from just being a client that she was defending, to something more. Much more really; it had surprised her. They couldn't have been more different. Her, with her well-bred, long tanned legs. And him with his Slavic rawness. Muscular, brutal and strong.

The sex had been fucking amazing, literally. She'd never had anything like it before, and definitely not since. She thought of Declan's clammy, limp hands and shuddered. Alik was so male by comparison. Brave, fearless, dominant. He'd fought all his life to survive and she admired him for it. He was exactly what she needed.

All her life she had been stronger than the men around her. Sharper, quicker, braver, more successful. She'd despised them all for it, ridiculed them for it. But with Alik, she found her soft side, with him she could leave the warrior at the bedroom door. He was far more of a man than she would ever be.

And when she'd got him acquitted, his admiration had flowed even further. Out of the bedroom and into her bank balance, her jewellery drawer, her wardrobe. He was a provider and she wanted him.

Since they'd been in contact, she'd followed all of his instructions unquestioningly. The disposable phones and never calling him, always waiting for his call. And she loved it, she was being dominated and controlled by him and she really loved it. He had made her feel female for the first time in years.

It had only taken a few weeks of contact for Joanne to realise that she didn't want to be here. She wanted to be there, with him, for the rest of her life. The girls didn't need her now, and she didn't care if they did, they already had two sets of grandparents at their beck and call. And Isabella looked too much like Declan to

232

feel comfortable with her gaze now.

She would go to Alik soon. They'd discussed it many times, he'd wanted her to leave Declan fifteen years ago, and he wanted her just as much now. . She was already packed - things were getting too hot in Belfast. Joe Watson's big mouth had already earned her one police phone-call, and although she'd managed to wriggle out of it, they were getting far too close.

She just had to play the grieving widow for a few days after Declan died. Cooperate with the inevitable stupid questions from the plods, and then she could leave next week without suspicion. She didn't know how she was going to survive the next few days, but she would keep her cool; it was one of her biggest talents.

And then...well, she was a widow after all. Her husband had just been murdered ...sob...and she was so distressed that she needed to go to the Priory Clinic in London, to recover from Declan's death. Such a discrete venue was justified of course, to avoid the embarrassment for the girls, and the prying eyes at the Belfast Chronicle.

She rolled her eyes. That bloody rag would make a meal of the whole thing - she'd just seen their reporting of Bob's death. Very undignified. She smiled sarcastically at the image of his last moments – killed in bed, after sex. He should have been grateful.

Of course she had to leave and recuperate after Declan died, everyone would understand, of course they would. And she might take the odd trip back, to see the girls, just for appearance sake. Before she eventually announced that she'd met Alik and found happiness. And who would begrudge her that, after Declan's affair came out? She turned-on the shower and languorously washed her thick dark hair. It was all settled. Just a few days more.

****

Declan stared at the phone as his call dialled out again. The girls were refusing to pick-up and he was slowly getting the message. They thought that he was a

233

scumbag because Joanne had got to them first. Shit, shit, shit.

Well, there was nothing he could do about it today, so he was going to see his first love, his racehorse Wandsworth. Deliberately named to remind Joanne where they'd really lived in London.

The meet was for charity, so he was going to blow a packet from their joint account, betting on every nag that he took a fancy to, and she could do nothing to stop him.

Chapter Twenty-One

Stevan had concluded his meeting the previous evening very satisfactorily indeed. The other party had had an endless supply of goods, available on very short notice: even his personal favourite. Perhaps there was more to this little country than he'd thought. He would take possession, complete the job and be on a plane home tonight.

The arrangements had left him with the evening before free and unable to leave the hotel - it wouldn't have done to bump into Teresa or Jeanie. So he'd had to find another little diversion... It was amazing how many freckles that receptionist had had, and they were everywhere. Absolutely everywhere.

He shook himself from the pleasant image and got ready for his trip. He disposed of his detritus, dissolving his suit in the sink with the solution they'd brought. All he needed now was his twenty-something uniform, cap, sunglasses, money, and a couple of small bottles and gloves.

He'd paid the bill the night before, including a huge tip for 'Freckles', so he left the room quickly now, taking the lift to the ground and bypassing reception discreetly. Then out to the front, where the taxi was already waiting. He got in and nodded, handing the driver a slip of paper with an address written on it. Pretending not to speak English limited conversations, which limited leaving any clues.

They stuttered out through the busy Saturday traffic and onto the M1 motorway, driving towards the quaint town of Hillsborough and an open-house day at a luxurious new development. The show-house was waiting, ready for viewers, with others in various stages of growth, ranging from staked-out plots to half-built shells.

Stevan gave the driver another note that instructed him to wait for fifteen minutes, and then walked nonchalantly through the gates of the development. He turned left towards the show-house for the cabbie to see him, and then sharp left again, into plot fourteen and the half-finished shell built there.

Entering the empty kitchen, he reached urgently under the sink, feeling for the package. It was there. He swiftly unzipped his rucksack and pushed it in. Then he walked casually into the show-house for a quick alibi tour, exiting back to the taxi exactly on time.

As they sped down the Ballyrobin Road, eight kilometres from Antrim Racecourse, Stevan gazed out at the pretty winter countryside, gearing himself up for the kill. The car dropped him at the main gate, under instruction to return at two-forty-five precisely. Plenty of time for his return flight to Heathrow.

He pulled down his baseball cap and walked inconspicuously past the glamorous race-goers, ignoring their laughter. Part of him wished that he could be part of it, that he was really here for the races. An unexpected sadness surprised him, and he knew then that if he listened to their chatter for too long, he would walk away from today's kill, and the life, for good.

He walked on hurriedly and then stopped again, abruptly, watching the crowds milling past him. For a moment he heard nothing but silence, only seeing the women's brightly coloured dresses fluttering past him like petals. He felt completely at peace without knowing why. And then he did. In that split second he realised that he'd already walked away from the life, and that this would be his last job ever.

****

Antrim Racecourse.

It was a clear, soft day and Declan was convinced that his luck was in, he could feel it. Standing in the VIP tent, wearing Ralph Lauren and drinking champagne, how could it not be? He looked around at Northern Ireland's great and good, and not so good, and laughed to himself. All the characters were there, it would be an entertaining afternoon.

His next thought surprised him. He felt happy for the first time in years, genuinely happy. He hadn't loved Joanne for a long time, he realised that now, so why had it taken him so long to leave? The answer came immediately and with it a hint of sadness, the girls, they were why he hadn't left. But he still felt happy.

Bob Leighton's death was a tragedy of course, and one that everyone in the tent was talking about, but at least it had brought him a final chance at life. Without it, he would never have had the balls to leave – Joanne had stolen those years ago. But now, here he was, drinking champagne under a cloudless winter sky, and growing a new pair.

He could feel the eyes of the other VIPs on him, noticing Joanne's absence, a mixture of curiosity and smiles. She'd gone to school with most of the women, and they'd married the weak men that he'd known at school. Sad enough in itself, except that their kids would probably do the same. Northern Ireland needed some new blood.

He raised the glass to his lips and smiled ironically at the gathering. They voted for each other in the best-dressed lists, praised each other's businesses, and even slept with each other, afraid of diluting the gene pool with the 'wrong sort'.

There were some salvageable people amongst them, but mostly they just did what they did best, survived in the shark pool. So today, he was going to do what he did best. Gamble, and not just on the horses.

He walked to the bar along the back wall of the tent and turned to face the room, full of fat-faced men and over-tanned women, looking and whispering. A few noted his move curiously, still talking. His best friend Neil, who had always hated Joanne, leaned over and asked the bartender to turn the music down.

It took a moment for people to notice the background quiet, and then another for the chatter to die away, until finally, the majority were silent, and the ones that weren't drew sharp looks. Then Declan spoke, without a single care what the fat frauds thought of him.

"Most of you know that I'm married to Joanne, and most of you can see that she's not here today. And those of you who matter will be happy for me on that. I'm don't love her and I'm going to divorce her, and frankly I don't give a toss what you think about that, or me. But you will stop looking at me as if I'm an exhibit, or..." his voice took on a hard edge "any of you that I do business with, will be losing your contracts with Greer's. Which, despite what Joanne may have told you, is my company. So be good." He raised his glass to the room. "And enjoy your day. I know I will."

Neil nodded and the bartender turned the music on again, grinning into his glasses. As Declan left the tent to check out the runners and riders, he noticed a pretty redhead in a mini-dress smiling widely at him and he smiled back shyly, feeling free for the first time in years.

****

Stevan had found a near perfect vantage-point at the back of the hospitality pavilion, lining up perfectly with the VIP marquee, and he could see his target clearly now through his scope. He was walking casually towards the tent, head down, studying some papers, and marking them forcefully with a pen.

Stevan knew exactly what he was doing. He was marking his 'picks' for the day, and he could see the man's slight smile through his sights. He recognised that smile well; he'd worn it himself at the Dubai Racing Club many times. There was no feeling quite like watching your horse ride home a winner. Declan Greer was a betting man and he liked him for that.

The marquee was sponsored by a French champagne company. It had one whole side open to the outside world, and its floor was laid out in an artificial grass lawn. He could see a long linen table laden with flute glasses, each ones' gleam picked out clearly by his scope. There was a long bar behind them serving cold drinks. His mouth suddenly felt tinder-dry; he could do with a glass himself. Maybe at the airport, he had work to do first.

His target lifted two glasses and walked over to a red-haired girl in a short green dress. She looked pleased to see him and she looked nice; she wasn't his wife. Stevan could tell it even from this distance, and it made him sorrier for what he had to do. That was his curse, he was always sorry for his targets.

He was sick of the killing now. At the start, it had been about hatred, pure and unalloyed, each guilty death bringing him an almost visceral pleasure. Then anger, anger for murdering their innocence, and for the loss of warmth that no one now living could replace. No number of dead could warm them now.

Then survival; to eat and live, and wear and smile. Only two things had guaranteed that. The ability to kill. And money. The first bringing enough of the second to insulate them forever. And his skill had found plenty of interested buyers.

He took the black stealth TR-42 from his rucksack and stroked its twenty-inch barrel. It was his favourite weapon. There were other, newer models, and plenty more expensive. But it was like a thoroughbred horse; elegant and reliable, and accurate as hell. He wasn't going to change just because fashion dictated. Whatever else he was, he was loyal, even to his guns.

He set-up, aligning the scope sights perfectly with the open side of the tent, adjusting his stance and waiting. It was a still afternoon and the wind had dropped completely now. The air was cold and still, perfect shooting conditions, like Serbia in the winter.

This time would be more public than the last, and the woman would be witness to the kill, very unfortunate. It went against his rules of decency to involve women, even as a witness. He hated Alik for Irene Leighton. He had made them trap her and mark her, and then lead her trustingly to her freedom. Only to kill her somewhere that no one could ignore, hoping to stir up political unrest.

It had turned his stomach in the way that no other kill ever had, and it was turned against killing permanently now. Even Kaisa felt remorse for the death of such a good woman. Now this man's foolish, honest, open urge to tell the police was precipitating his own death.

Stevan knew that he was the best at what he did. It wasn't a boast, he just was. Most others in the business used two shots to the chest and one to the head. It wasn't necessary and it was cruel to those left behind. A single head shot was all he ever needed. Years of practice.

The scope was perfectly aligned and he looked at his watch. Not just yet, there were three minutes left. He stood up and watched them through his binoculars. A man with binoculars, a normal sight at the racecourse. Who would question it? The target was facing the red-haired girl now, smiling and pointing out something on the paper to her. It would be the odds and form for the next race, Stevan knew that it would. He'd done it himself to impress some nymphet. The things men do.

He watched them, musing. As ways to die went, it was a great one. Think about it; sunny day, pretty girl, champagne-soaked chatter and looking forward to watching your horse win, with no idea that you were about to die. Could you really ask for more? Life would only be disappointing after this.

Stevan watched as the horses lined up for the off, and Declan Greer turned towards the line, raising his right hand to point out something to the girl. He was almost facing him now and he looked nice, like the girl, another innocent victim. He was repulsed by more killing, not for survival, not for food or warmth, but for money.

Stevan thanked God that he couldn't see him, he was much too intent on the horses. For once, he would be spared that instinctive glance towards his gun, he knew it. He lined up his sights ready to press the trigger, and felt a sudden vibration at his waist. He dropped the barrel instinctively and reached urgently for his phone. It was his one constant connection to Kaisa and she only ever rang it in an emergency. Something was very wrong.

"Draga, what is it? Why are you ringing?"

Her sobs came raw and fast as if she was gasping for breath, and his mind went back through the years, to another time when she'd been hurt. There was only one thing that would make her cry like this, and he would kill the man who had done it.

"Who did this? Who is he?"

She was crying so hard that she choked and coughed, and the sound almost drowned-out the one word that she managed to say. But he heard it. He soothed her gently with kind words, until he could hear her breath calming and her tears flow more quietly. Then he gave her instructions to meet him and gently closed the phone.

As the horses left the gate and the crowd roared out, he lined up his sights again, in anger now. He pressed the trigger down lightly, launching the sleek bullet that broke through the air, twisting and curving perfectly, until it reached its intended destination.

It split the air six inches from Declan Greer's temporal bone. And then, with one soft deliberate thud, it skewered straight through the marquee's central pole with just enough momentum to lodge undamaged in the wood, and provide the police with another clue to Irene Leighton's death. It was a perfect shot, even by Stevan's standards.

The cheering crowd covered the sound, but the man felt something skim past his ear, casting around for its final resting place. Stevan watched, pleased, as the redheaded woman smiled and teased him, as if he was searching around to make her laugh. And then at his male friend's expression when they saw the hole in the tent's support, realisation finally dawning, and with it the urgent grab for telephones.

He reached quickly for his rucksack, urgently removing the bottle and heavy gloves. Then he stripped the rifle down quickly into the scope, frame and stock, laying the pieces on the ground, and emptying the contents of the bottle onto the small pile. He watched calmly as the costly piece of equipment dissolved in front of his eyes, the small price for their freedom.

Moving swiftly, Stevan pulled on his sunglasses and joined the throng of race-goers queuing up for last minute spaces. He stood casually against the Course's white outer wall, waiting for his taxi, and chatting on his mobile to an imaginary girlfriend, completely ignored by the others around him.

He was at City Airport with forty minutes to spare and he used it well; ditching the bag, phone and SIM separately, and then covering his dyed-blonde hair with a brown gel that worked so well that he made a note to tell Kaisa about it; she hated dying her beautiful hair. Then he smiled, realising that she would never have to dye her hair again, or pretend to be anyone else, or sleep with any man that she didn't choose.

He smiled again, remembering Declan Greer and his lovely companion, glad not to have made her cry. He hoped that they would be happy together. Then he gave a final smile, just for himself. There would be no more jobs and no more pretence. It was over. He had only one thing left to do.

****

Port Salon. Donegal.

Julia was standing on the steps of Leighton's rented villa when Craig called her for an update, admiring the view and having a cigarette while the suited C.S.I.s., completed their work.

The London office line showed up as 'private', so she answered the call brightly, unaware that it was him. "Julia McNulty. Can I help you?"

She took a last silent pull on her cigarette and exhaled slowly, waiting for the caller to speak. Craig hesitated, certain that her tone would be colder when she heard his voice, and preferring the silence.

Her tone became more insistent. "D.I McNulty. Who's calling, please?"

There was a fine line between hesitation and stalking and he decided not to cross it, so he spoke quietly. "It's Marc Craig, D.I. McNulty. Just looking for an update."

Her voice cooled predictably and he sighed. He liked her and really wanted to get past this, he just didn't know how.

"We've nearly finished the sweep of the house, D.C.I. Craig." Again with the formality. "The C. S.I.s are wrapping up, and the prints have already gone to Dr Winter. I spoke to the neighbours and they remember Leighton, but none of them saw anyone else. But there were some Chinese takeaway boxes in the kitchen. I called the restaurant and they open in an hour, so I'll go down there then. There's nothing else."

He said nothing for a moment, and then decided to behave as if she'd been cordial, and do the same. "That's great, thank you. I'm back at The Met." He deliberately implied a permanent emigration just to gauge her reaction, and wasn't disappointed by her sharp intake of breath. She did give a damn, and her next word confirmed it.

"What!" As soon as she'd said it, she wanted to bite it back. Then she shrugged to herself. There was no point pretending that she didn't care for him, she did and he knew it.

Craig was annoyed with himself for the trick, but smiled anyway. "Just for a couple of days, to follow up a lead on the case. Maybe...?"

"Yes?" Her tone showed defeat, but he didn't want her defeated. She sensed him disengaging and added quickly. "Maybe...?"

He took her cue bravely. "We could have coffee when I'm back at the weekend?"

Julia paused and took a fresh cigarette from her bag, clicking her lighter slowly. He heard it and held his breath; she hadn't said no. Then she sighed, gently but kindly, afraid of what she was agreeing to, but powerless to refuse. "Yes, coffee would be nice."

****

The C.C.U.

Joe Watson had reluctantly agreed to do a sketch, and Annette took it as a good sign. Maybe he was finally seeing his lover for what she was, instead of romanticising their financial arrangement. They would need to confirm the image with Lilith's of course, but Liam could do that.

She left him with the sketch artist and went back to the squad-room to tidy her desk. It was getting so cluttered that she'd found a sandwich from last week earlier, and she dreaded to think what was in the drawers. She was tidying away when Nicky stood up at her desk, beckoning her over.

"Annette, can you take this call? It's Dr Winter and he says it's important. I can't call Marc unless it's urgent, and Liam's disappeared as usual."

Annette nodded to transfer it and lifted the receiver cheerfully, feeling important. "Hello, Dr Winter. How can I help? You know that D.C.I. Craig is away in London today?"

John's soft baritone flowed down the line, enveloping her. She loved his cultured, newsreader's voice and his old-fashioned language. "Ah hello, Annette. So lovely to speak to you. Yes, I know that Marc's away, but I thought that I should alert you to this, as soon as possible."

She could see Davy at his desk straining to hear, so she beckoned him over. "Dr Winter, would you mind if I put you on speaker? So that Davy can listen?"

"Not at all, good idea. Right, well. You'll know that we didn't get any prints at the hotel except Watson's, from the girl's handbag mirror?"

"Yes."

"Well, we've just had a break-through. There were some prints on the bathroom mirror. Her spray bandage must have washed off in the shower. We've eliminated the staff and room-cleaners, and no one else has stayed in that room for three weeks. Luckily, it's the quiet season. So we were optimistic that they would belong to her. That's just been confirmed."

"How?" She leaned forward excitedly and Nicky could see that something was up. She strolled over to join them, leaning on Annette's cubicle-wall.

"D.I. McNulty has been in Portsalon and they finished printing the house. Some fingerprints were found on the mirrors and..." He hesitated, embarrassed. "Well, they were also found on the headboard in the bedroom, so..."

He didn't need to finish the sentence, they all had imaginations. "Anyway, they match the ones found in the Castleton. Joe Watson and Bob Leighton were involved with the same girl."

Annette stayed silent, thinking, so Nicky jumped in. "That's brilliant, Dr Winter, really brilliant."

"Yes, but there's more. We have D.N.A. from the lipstick belonging to Joe Watson's lover and we have D.N.A. from Bob Leighton's body, his last sexual contact."

Davy could hear him getting shy again and jumped in to the rescue. "It confirms that W...Watson's lover was also Bob Leighton's"

"Yes. And the piece de resistance is that D.I. McNulty had struck out completely for witnesses in Portsalon – no one had seen anyone with Bob Leighton. But there were some old takeaway boxes from lunchtime on Friday, so she went to the restaurant an hour ago and they said that a young woman with white-blonde hair had signed for the delivery."

"W...Why would she do that? She was trying to keep a low profile."

"Hunger I suppose, Davy. They probably had no food in the house if they arrived late on Thursday night. The delivery man is doing a sketch so we should have that this afternoon."

"Joe Watson is doing one now, and then Liam is getting onto Lilith's. We should be able to confirm that it's the same girl by later today. That's brilliant, Dr Winter." Kaisa Moldeau and Ausra Mitic could be the same woman.

Davy interjected. "This matches with the sighting of

245

a fair-haired woman at the two London shootings, and I've a call out to La Prefecture of police in Paris too."

"Dr Winter, do you want to call D.C.I. Craig with this information..." Annette hesitated, hoping. "Or shall I?"

John smiled to himself generously. "You do it, Annette; I've got to get back to the print. We're running it in every database we have, but no hits yet."

He was hardly off the line when Annette phoned Craig.

****

"Here, Joe Watson is a busy wee boy. There's hardly a committee up at Stormont that he isn't on."

"He's Enterprise Minister, Liam. Every department will want him at their meetings to squeeze money out of him. But he can't have attended them all personally. He would have sent his advisors to most of them, to report back."

"How do you know all that?"

"Have you never watched 'Yes Minister'? It's really funny."

Liam looked at her kindly. Annette found the Telly-Tubbies funny.

She caught the look. "No honestly, it is. They're making a new series too. It tells you all you need to know about government. They spend all day in committees, and I can't imagine Stormont's much different."

"Aye well. His name's on a lot of stuff up there, that's all I'm saying. He sat on a few outside boards as well. Mostly dealing with public funds. There's the Q.I.X., the F.I.W. and the S.F.F. Why do none of these things have a proper name? Why not just call them Fred or Mavis, it'd be a lot easier to remember." Then he grinned lasciviously. "I can think of a few names that they'd never forget."

Annette tutted at him impatiently. "Give me the list and I'll get Davy onto it. We need to find what was worth framing Watson for murder. He must have been about to lose someone money, or he'd already lost them money. Or...he was up to no good with someone else's money. Agreed?"

"That's fair enough, but it'd be a damn sight easier if he'd just tell us, instead of clamming up. By every report on the man, he's two things that point away from him being up to no good personally. He's honest and he's loaded. He didn't need to do anything criminal to make money."

Annette nodded. Liam was right. "His wife says he gives a lot away secretly and doesn't tell anyone, and he doesn't even take his M.L.A.'s salary. So let's concentrate on him losing someone else money. All these boards are involved in bringing contracts here, either building something or manufacturing something."

"Mostly building developments and I.T. projects, Cutty. Here, that fits with the Vors being into land development."

"Big land projects are a licence to steal. Let's focus on land projects that Watson might have recently interfered with, or was about to. I'll give Mrs Watson a call and see if he'd mentioned anything to her. And let's get the kettle on; this is going to take a while."

Liam cast a covert look at his watch and Annette leapt at him immediately.

"Don't you dare think that you're leaving all this to me, Liam Cullen. There's far too much to get through."

"Sorry, but I'll have to leave you to it for an hour. I've to go to Harrison's briefings while the boss is away."

She snorted. "Well, if you want to play the big boss then you're taking me..." she saw Nicky winking at her behind his back, "and all of us, to The James for dinner when you get back."

He bowed mockingly. "No problem. Or as the boss and Doc Winter would say 'that will be entirely my pleasure.'"

****

247

Liam was late, so he ran up the stairs to the twelfth floor, taking them three at a time, an advantage of being six-feet-six. The door to Terry Harrison's office was closed and he could just make out the short, round shape of Eric Jenner propped against its glass panels. Good, Ross Ellis was delegating to his Inspector as well. He didn't feel so out of place now.

He knocked the door quietly, half-hoping that he would go unheard and could nip away, when the high thin voice of Terry Harrison came through the glass. "Eric, could you just open the door for Liam, please. Thanks."

Liam had forgotten that his huge frame and noisy entrances announced him long before he spoke. Jenner opened the door and looked slowly up at Liam, as the rest of the room's occupants smiled. They looked like Morecombe and Wise.

"Come in and find a surface to lean on, Liam. Sorry, we're out of chairs. We haven't started yet."

"Sorry, sir. I forgot all about it."

Harrison smiled, sardonically. "Now, that's how to make me feel important." The room collapsed in sycophantic laughter, then settled again quickly as Liam's face reddened.

"OK. Each section read through your reports quickly, please. Then I'll summarise."

There were ten people in the office and it was going to take a while to get to Liam, so he drifted off into a daydream, trying to solve the case. Eventually, he heard something that made him listen.

"338 Lapua, sir. Very unusual."

He looked around quickly and saw that Derek Cantor, the D.C.I. covering the Lisburn and Antrim areas was talking.

"It happened at the Antrim charity race meeting earlier this afternoon. The intended victim was a Mr Declan Greer; he's a partner in Greer L.L.P. He was watching the races from the VIP tent."

"Yes, I know of the Greers. They have the tallest office building in Belfast, the glass pyramid in the city centre. I met the man and his wife once, at some

248

function."

"They're both heavily involved in land development, sir. And he does a lot of charity work. "

Harrison nodded approvingly at the charity work, more so because he could claim association with the man.

"Right. Go on."

"The attempted shooting took place at the start of the two-forty p.m. race. Mr Greer had been off to check the runners and riders and had just come back to the marquee five minutes before, to watch the race. Apparently there'd been a bit of a scandal in the tent earlier, when he announced to everyone that he intended to divorce his wife, Joanne. It seems it was the first that anyone had heard of it, and the announcement created a bit of an uproar, according to his friend, Neil Hurtham, who was there as well."

He flicked-open his notebook at the relevant page and quoted. "I couldn't have been happier for Declan. Joanne's a selfish, nasty bitch."

"No love lost there then. I have to say that I didn't warm to the woman." Of course you didn't, sir.

"It seems not, sir. Anyway, as Greer was watching the race start he heard something passing his left temple, near the ear. It was a single shot and the bullet lodged in the central pole of the marquee, that's where we retrieved it. If it had hit him, he would have died instantly. He was pretty shocked so the medical examiner checked him out, but he's fine now. And, as I mentioned, the bullet is a 338 Lapua Magnum. It's very unusual, a sniper round..."

"Usually shot from a SAKO TR-42 or an A.I." Liam immediately realised that he'd just finished Derek Cantor's sentence, and that everyone was looking at him.

"Liam, can you help us on this?"

"Sir, our case used the same bullet. Irene Leighton, the M.P's wife."

Harrison nodded. Craig had briefed him but the name of the bullet had slipped his mind.

"Wasn't that a dissident murder, Liam?"

Liam went to answer Cantor's question, then hesitated politely. Harrison nodded him on.

"It wasn't the dissidents, sir. I'll keep it short, but we now have reasons to think that Irene Leighton, and probably her husband Bob, were killed by professional contractors from overseas."

"But I thought Bob Leighton died of natural causes. Didn't he have a family history of heart disease? S.A.D.S or something?"

"He did, but Dr Winter did a second P.M for us and he was definitely murdered."

"Yes, I authorised that P.M. Good help?"

"Very much, thank you, sir." Craig would've been proud of his diplomacy.

"Irene Leighton was killed using the same type of bullet that D.C.I. Cantor has just described, so what are the odds of them not being related somehow?" Liam had forgotten the 'sir' and considered going back for it, but Harrison didn't seem to have noticed.

"I agree. They were both professional killings, although thankfully he missed Greer. Still, damn close. To judge the distance and velocity of a bullet like that so accurately, this man is very talented."

Cantor spoke up. "We did a sweep of the likely shooter-site and found a lump of metal lying on the hilly ground, to the back of the hospitality pavilion. Forensics thinks that it could be the gun, and the shooter destroyed it deliberately."

Liam interrupted eagerly, forgetting where he was. "Who's your forensic guy? I'll get Des Marsham onto him."

Harrison nodded them on, interested in the exchange. "Tim Norris, I'll send you his number, Liam. Anyway, I think that we have to look at the wife, Joanne Greer, as a possible killer, sir. She was dumped very publically about thirty minutes earlier. A woman in the tent, Phoebe Murtagh, admits that she got straight on the phone to Mrs Greer, as soon as her husband made the announcement that he was divorcing her."

What a friend.

Harrison shook his head. "There may be a connection in there somewhere, Derek, but a professional hit couldn't have been arranged that quickly. You said that everyone was shocked by the announcement about divorce, so Mrs Greer may not even have believed that he meant it." It was said hopefully, and everyone in the room knew that Harrison was thinking of his own rocky marriage. "By all means work up the 'woman scorned' angle, but look for other reasons why someone wanted Declan Greer dead too. And see if there are any links with Liam's case.

Liam, continue with your investigation of the Leighton killings, with this new information and a possible link between the two in mind. Just bring D.C.I. Craig up to speed in London."

Harrison noticed the quizzical looks from others. "Marc's in London on something else related to his case. The Met's had two deaths using the Lapua, and there was a third one in Paris two years ago. The feeling is that we have an international hit man at work, and unfortunately he decided to pay us a visit."

****

Annette gawped at the two sketches in front of her, kicking herself again for not making the connection earlier. The charcoal likenesses had all the detail of photographs. One was of the dark-blonde woman that Joe Watson had described, and the second had the white-blonde hair that Ian Sinclair was convinced of, the colouring just confirmed by the takeaway boy's sketch of Bob Leighton's companion. There was no question, they were the same woman. It was Kaisa Moldeau.

****

Liam left Harrison's office already pulling-out his phone to make the call. It rang five times and he was just about to give up when Craig finally answered.

251

Liam could hear from the echo that he was in a stairwell too.

"Hi. Is everything all right? Annette's just been on."

"What for? No, don't worry, I'll ask her. I've just been to Harrison's briefing, boss."

"Thanks for picking that up, sorry to lumber you."

"Actually it was good. Long story short, there was another Lapua shooting. Yesterday."

"Damn. Give me the details."

Liam filled him in, outlining what they'd agreed.

"That's great. E-mail the details to D.C.S. Chandak's office."

"How do you spell that?"

Craig laughed. Liam had trouble enough with Northern Irish names.

"Nicky has the address. Send it over as soon as you can please, Liam. I'll give John a call; you just get on with working Joe Watson. Is it Derek Cantor's case?"

"Yes."

"Right, I'll give him a call as well then. That's great. Thanks, Liam."

"Aye well, it's not that great. We're playing catch-up."

"Only by a few hours, don't worry. They've just been doing the basics. We've picked it up at just the right time. I'll call you later."

He clicked the call off and redialled immediately, getting John Winter's secretary, Marcie. "He's down with Dr Marsham, Mr Craig. I'll just put you through."

Des answered the phone quickly, handing it over to John.

"Hi, John. Do you know Tim Norris?"

"Yes, I taught him on a training course last year. He's from Glasgow. What about him?"

Craig filled him in quickly. "Can you pick up that side of it with Derek Cantor's team, and the ballistics on the bullet? We need to get all five shootings lined up for comparison. And could you send everything over to D.C.S. Chandak. Nicky can give you the details."

"I can, but the bullets might not give us anything, Marc. The ballistics won't match if they're from

252

different rifles. But if we're lucky, they might have a lot number that will show if they came from the same batch. Hang on for a second." There was silence for a moment then John spoke again.

"Des was just telling me that Norris has already been on. It seems that there was a metallic remnant at the possible shooter-site and they're pretty sure that it's the gun. But we'll confirm that with the residue. I'll put it all in my report."

"Thanks, John."

Craig rang off quickly and swiped into the bright open-plan office, where Yemi was sifting through The Met's two cold cases. He sat down on the edge of the desk.

"We've had another attempted killing. Using a 338 Lapua Magnum."

"When? Was it in Belfast as well?"

"Today, twenty miles away at Antrim race course. At a charity fixture. Thankfully, they missed, but it would have been a single head shot to the left temple. This guy can really shoot. They managed to distance it so accurately that it had just enough momentum to lodge in the tent pole."

"Definitely the same calibre?"

"Yes. The intended victim was a businessman. The team that picked it up are playing it as a wife's revenge killing. But it can't be totally unrelated to the others, there has to be a link. The odds of such an unusual round being used in two shootings in a small place like Northern Ireland are miniscule.

We think that they might have destroyed the gun and left it at the scene. It just looks like a lump of metal now but it might still give us something. Our Director of Pathology will send over his findings later this afternoon. "

Yemi looked at him shocked. "Man, that's quick. We would be waiting a whole week here." Craig laughed.

"It would be four days for us normally, but he's a friend. One of the benefits of a small place. Is the D.C.S. free? I need to bring him up to date, and then we can sit down with all five reports and see what they have in common."

As he approached the glass office Craig could see that Rajiv Chandak was alone. He knocked the glass door gently and was waved in.

"Anything new?"

"Yes, sir. I've just had a call from my D.I. There's been another shooting outside Belfast using the Lapua. It happened earlier today and another area's team picked it up, so we've just caught it. They're following it through as a wronged wife murdering her husband, but it has the hallmark of our man. The reports are being compared and they'll be with us later. So I thought Yemi and I could spend an hour or so then, comparing all five murders to see what we can connect. If that's ok?"

The D.C.S. nodded thoughtfully and Craig leapt into the silence. "The sniper missed this time."

Chandak sat forward urgently. "A miss. Explain please."

Craig filled him in on Declan Greer's narrow escape and Chandak looked pensive.

"We've no evidence of them ever failing before, Marc. Are you sure that it was a Lapua?"

Craig nodded. "Definitely, sir." He paused for a second. "It's just a thought, but I think that he might have missed deliberately." Chandak nodded him on.

"The conditions and line of sight should have been perfect, so we're stuck for another explanation."

"Why deliberate?"

"I don't know yet, it's just a hunch, sir." Then Craig told him about Annette's call on Kaisa Moldeau.

"I believe that she masqueraded as the Leighton's nanny, walked Irene Leighton into position to be shot, and then took Bob Leighton as a lover and killed him. She also set Joe Watson up and framed him for murder to get him out of the way. And now Declan Greer has a near miss. We need to find out what connects these people to each other, and hopefully what connects the shooter to all five hits.

They're sending the sketches of the girl through later and we should get them to the witnesses to your

254

two shootings, and to Paris. She was definitely working with the shooter. There must be a connection, sir, and we'll find it. But I wanted to ask you more about Alik Ershov."

"What do you need to know?"

"I've been looking at his file and I know that I'm probably missing something, but it doesn't look as if he's ever been questioned on your two killings. Was he?"

"You mean, why wasn't he brought into a dark room with a bright light?"

"Something like that."

"We didn't have enough grounds. And..." He hesitated, and Craig could feel a deal coming. "The drugs squad warned us off at the time. They were planning some big bust on imported heroin."

"Did it ever happen?" Chandak smiled ruefully, knowing what Craig was hinting at.

"They got some stuff, but too far away from Ershov to tie anything to him. By that stage, our trail had gone cold on the murders. What we do have is a lot of observation footage, mostly up at his house in Essex. And we keep a very close eye on his right hand men; who they mix with, where they go, any trips they take to the docks and airports particularly. But so far we have nothing, they're bloody careful."

"Could I have a look at the footage, sir? The recent stuff for the past fortnight maybe? Our killers might have been lying low in Northern Ireland this whole time, but we think they left, after they framed Watson, perhaps on Tuesday or Wednesday. If it's the same pair of killers, they must have gone back almost immediately to shoot Declan Greer.

At that speed, it would probably have had to be by plane. At a pinch, the boat to Liverpool or Scotland. We're pretty stuck for photos if it's the ferry routes, but if they flew, then your airport footage could be very useful. It's a long shot, but I've a couple of hours to kill. Would you mind?"

"Be my guest."

Chandak reached over and hit the intercom. It

brought his comfortable looking P.A. Rita rushing into the room, so shocked at being buzzed that she expected to find him dead. Her florid face crinkled into a smile, visibly relieved to see him upright.

"Yes, sir. What's wrong?"

"Rita's shocked at me using the intercom, Marc, because I mostly just yell through the glass for her." He turned to the small, round woman, who was still puffing for breath.

"Rita, would you mind taking D.C.I. Craig into the bowels of the earth? Sit him down with a nice cup of tea and the last two weeks footage and reports for Alik Ershov's little gang. And then contact the London airports for me."

He shot her a dazzling white smile and she flushed even more. Then she bustled out, leading Craig five floors down to the rabbit warren of surveillance and storage, and left him drinking coffee in peace.

****

The C.C.U.

"Liam, do you have that list of Joe Watson's board memberships?"

"Nah. I gave it to Davy earlier on. He's doing that one."

Annette frowned. "So which one are you doing?"

"Stormont committees, and they're driving me mad. Never did a man sit around in as many boring meetings as this one." Paperwork was Liam's private hell.

"I told you. *He* didn't, his team did. He was probably off at Lilith's most of the time."

She laughed at her own joke. Her wit had definitely improved working here. She stretched her arms above her head tiredly and then looked at her wristwatch, going into prefect mode.

"Look it's five o' clock now. How do you fancy another hour with all three of us blitzing this stuff, then over to The James for an early drink and dinner?

Davy? Nicky? We can come back to it fresh afterwards. Can everyone keep going until then?"

She looked around at Nicky typing away with her earphones in, and Davy talking on the phone, and realised that she didn't need to persuade anyone but herself and Liam to keep going.

Then, completely without warning, Davy stood up and shouted "Yes!" loudly. Liam saw him rising and played a dramatic drum roll on his desk. Davy had had eureka moments like this before and they were usually pretty impressive.

"Ladies and Gentleman, I think that we've got our connection."

Nicky saw him standing-up and took her earphones off. "What'd you say?"

Before Davy could answer her, Annette leapt in excitedly "You mean a connection between Watson and Greer?"

He nodded and paused smugly for effect.

"Davy, if you don't tell us right now I'm going to deck you. Get on with it."

Davy looked over at Liam nervously and got on with it. "They were both members of S.F.F., the S…Strategic Finance Foundation. It's the body that makes decisions about allocating public money to business and developments. Part of their job is attracting inward investment from the Republic, UK, E.U and America. In the past three years, they've put five billion pounds through the books in grants, loans, and joint initiatives. Things like that.

Every Enterprise Minister has to be on the board, but the reason that it wasn't obvious at first was that Joe W…Watson only took over as Minister in February. His predecessor was that old buffer, Ron Burgess. You remember. He was on that TV debate last year about the effect of the Euro on cross-border retail margins."

Liam raised his eyes to heaven. So that was who watched those things. "Was that on at Croke Park or Ravenhill, lad?"

Nicky laughed loudly. When he was being funny she really fancied Liam, except Gary would kill her if she even thought that way. He was the jealous type and she quite liked it; it was a good way to keep him in line.

Annette looked at her, chastising. "Oh God, don't laugh and encourage him, Nicky. He's been running amok with the boss away. Go on, Davy."

"I'll ignore that philistine remark, Liam. Anyway, Ron Burgess was the old Enterprise Minister and he retired nine months ago, so Joe W...Watson only joined the foundation in February for a months' overlap. But Declan Greer and his wife Joanne have been members since two-thousand and eight. They practically founded the thing.

To be fair, it's done lots of good things. Helped create eight thousand jobs, built three housing estates for the over sixty-fives. That type of thing."

"I know Greer's an accountant, but why is his wife on the board?"

"The word is she's the real high-flyer, Annette. S...She's a lawyer, commercial and contract law mostly, and w...was a highly paid criminal barrister in London years back. I've phoned around a bit and Declan Greer is very well liked, an affable type, but apparently s... she's a bit of a bitch."

Nicky wagged her finger disapprovingly at Davy's language and he turned his head away shyly. "Anyway, it s...seems that they're quite the little Bill and Hilary'."

"That's brilliant, Davy. Can you get hold of the notes and minutes for the board meetings since Watson joined, please? I'll start digging into Joanne Greer's background. If Liam..." Annette turned to look pointedly at him. "Will look at Declan's?"

From Liam's pleased look, Annette realised that she'd just given him a free pass.

"Aye, sure. That'll be no problem at all, Cutty, seeing as Derek Cantor's lot have already done it for me."

Liam pulled himself up to his full height and boomed across the section. "Now, as your acting D.C.I." Annette snorted.

"I'll ignore that. As your boss, I think that Davy's mental exertion should be rewarded with a drink now.

Then you two can return to the hard work at six. I'll be heading out to Lilith's, but only to meet Keith Ericson, of course."

Nicky needed no encouragement, already pulling her handbag out of the drawer, and Davy was on his feet instantly. Annette knew when she was beaten and grudgingly logged-off.

****

The meal at 'The James' on Princes' Dock Street was like a school outing. It wasn't that Craig's presence had ever inhibited them exactly, but they were like all teams when the leader was away, immediately saying the one thing that they might think twice about in their presence. Which meant that Liam got ruder, Nicky put him down harder, Davy laughed more at both their antics, and Annette became the disapproving 'head girl', calling them all to order. And that was just what she was going to do, when she'd finished her chips.

Liam had just suggested a second drink when she overruled him ruthlessly. She stood up and headed for the door, throwing. "Well, I've work to do," over her shoulder, successfully hitting everyone's guilt and duty buttons with one short sentence. They knew she was right, but that didn't mean that she was getting away with it scot-free. Liam waited deliberately until she was at the door and then shouted across the crowded saloon. "And another thing, Annette. I'll be home when I've finished at the brothel, and not before."

****

The Met. London.

Craig stretched out his right arm and rubbed his wrist. It ached from the strangely shaped computer mouse that he'd been clicking at for an hour: London issue. He squinted at the dim desk-light and rubbed his eyes hard. The tape room was typical of its type, small and dark. He thought that there must be a standard U.K.

259

uncomfortable design, to discourage loitering, as if anyone would get a thrill out of watching traffic-cam CCTV.

He turned back to the screen tiredly, and clicked on the video file for the evening of Tuesday, eleventh of December, Joe Watson's final evening with the girl. The tape cut to Alik Ershov's house in Essex. There was nothing much to see, except for a dark Jaguar leaving at seven and returning again at eleven. The windows were tinted so there was no way of seeing inside. And the only view that the long-range-lens could get was of the suited driver, a young Asian man, climbing in at seven, before he drove off.

The next file in the sequence was labelled "Heathrow Airport Terminal One" at eight-thirty, about ninety minutes later. The same driver, caught as he parked in the short-term car-park, and then walking alone towards the Terminal building. He was collecting someone!

Craig tensed, hoping, no, knowing what he would see next. The surveillance camera followed the man through international arrivals on the ground floor where he entered the lift. The next view caught him emerging one floor up and walking to domestic arrivals, to stand in the greeting area by the doors. He was holding a name-card, but the camera couldn't pick out the detail. It didn't matter, what came next was worth far more.

The automatic doors opened and a trail of people started coming through, some carrying briefcases and some with hand luggage. Craig knew from experience that the trolleys would come last. He leaned forward and turned-up the tape's resolution, staring at the man closely. The driver was watching everyone. He didn't know what his pick-up looked like!

Just then a tall, tanned man walked towards him smiling, sunglasses obscuring the upper half of his face. It didn't matter, the girl who walked alongside him identified them both well enough for Craig. It was her. She was wearing a hat and sunglasses, but the build, curves and the description of her face-shape and

260

smile were enough to identify her.

She looked just like the Donegal photo-fit that Nicky had e-mailed across, as soon Joe Watson had corroborated the dark blonde, green-eyed version of it. Kaisa Moldeau was Ausra Mitic, and she was part of a couple.

The cameras followed them through international arrivals and out into the short-term car-park, where a final shot caught them entering the car. The registration was caught entering the Earls' Court Road, and traffic-cams followed them, eventually parking in Sloane Crescent. Craig looked at the file; the accompanying notes said that there were hotels there. An hour later, the car was sighted heading towards Essex with only the driver exiting at Alik Ershov's house. He'd dropped the others at a hotel!

Craig turned the page. The car had been sighted again the next day, doing the journey in reverse. Then back to Ershov's house in Essex with only the man, returning again to London a few hours later. There had been something on at Ershov's that day, with lots of young girls in party dresses climbing out of ritzy cars. But Craig doubted that the man was a party guest. Perhaps Ershov thought the party provided them with some sort of cover. One thing was clear; the man must matter for Ershov to send his driver for him two days in a row.

The surveillance team lost the passenger after the return journey to the hotel, but it didn't matter, Craig knew exactly where he'd gone next. Back to Antrim to kill Declan Greer. Or not.

He called Nicky hurriedly to request Heathrow and Belfast Airports' footage on all Wednesday's and Thursday's arrivals and departures from London, plus the passenger lists. Even aliases might help them in some way. Then he printed out the best images of the pair and left the room quickly, sprinting up the five flights of stairs to Chandak's office. Yemi came out of the office just as he arrived.

"Ah, Marc. I was just coming to see you. This came through from your office. From a Dr Winter."

"Thanks, but come back in with me. I've got something to show you both."

They listened patiently as Craig outlined the evidence, and then compared the girl from the tape to the photo-fit of Kaisa Moldeau. It was close enough. Chandak called Earl's Court quickly, sending officers to every hotel in Sloane Crescent with copies of the images, without holding out any real hope of still finding them there.

"If they're the professionals that we think they are, they'll be in the wind by now."

"At least it gives us a definite link between Ershov and the two shootings in Northern Ireland, sir. The information John has sent will stand comparison to your cases, I'm sure of it. And probably Paris' as well.

It must be the same shooter in all five cases. The 338 Lapua isn't a commonly used round and we've got metallic residue at the racecourse now, which I'm certain will be a sniper rifle. The two main rifles to use that ammo are the SAKO and A.I. and it's likely that he sticks to the same type, the SAKO. Maybe the guns will lead the firearms team somewhere. But whatever else, we must have enough to get Ershov in for questioning now, sir. Surely?"

Chandak nodded. "We can have a go anyway. His driver picking up your pair, and the male visiting him at the house the following day was very careless of him. But there's no way Ershov will have taken that risk without having a good story prepared, so I doubt we'll make the murders stick to him directly. Although...it might give us some leverage. We might get something on your two." He smiled broadly. "And I'd like to give this bastard a few uncomfortable hours."

Chandak gave the order to lift Ershov the next morning at seven. Allowing for London traffic he would be in the interrogation room by ten-thirty a.m. at the latest. Plenty of time to gather their thoughts for the interview.

"Right, now, he's not coming in under arrest. We don't have enough for a warrant, and I don't want to shoot our bolt too soon. He'll lawyer-up of course, uses a bunch of slick bastards at Montgomery and Windsor in Hyde Park. But we'll get him for a day at least, so see what we can get out of him. In the meantime, I'm going to get his phone records reverse-checked. Let's see if he's been a careless little Russian…"

Chapter Twenty-Two

Heathrow Airport.

Stevan disembarked with his hand luggage and moved quickly to the Terminal One exit he'd walked through with Kaisa just two days before. He pressed the lift's call button impatiently, with one eye on the three armed airport police officers who were wandering casually past the waiting relatives at domestic arrivals.

He was being paranoid; they weren't interested in him. It was confirmed as they strolled past him and he entered the lift unimpeded, feeling relaxed enough to hold the doors open for an elderly man.

The lift descended to the trains' floor and he walked rapidly down the long neon concourse, past the electronic hoardings and ticket machines until he reached the Express platform. He stood to one side, scanning the emerging crowd for Kaisa's familiar white-blonde hair.

A small hand waved frantically through the crowd at him, and she ran towards him, hurling herself at his chest for a hug, as if she hadn't just seen him the day before. It was her child-like trust and constant need for his presence that made him adamant never to leave her. He would be her protector forever, at any cost.

"Stevan, are you OK? Was it OK? Why are we leaving so quickly?"

He smiled down at his baby sister, remembering her chubby little legs when she first started to walk. Not so chubby now, she was far too thin. It was beyond fashionable. He had to get her away from all this death.

"We will not talk of these things now, Draga. I will explain later. You have the luggage?"

"Yes, I left it at the Terminal ready. The taxi-man was so kind, he helped me with everything, for a big tip of course." He smiled wryly; not that big if he knew her.

"Good."

He looked at his watch; five-thirty and their flight

was at seven. Only ninety minutes to get through security. She opened her bag and handed him the fresh passports. For once, the pictures looked vaguely like them, although the names were still false. It didn't really matter. After all, what evidence did they have on them? They wouldn't find them, and if they ever did, what could they prove?

Alik had diverted their payments through so many laundering rings that it would be impossible to unpick them before they disappeared again. And it was in his interest to help them disappear, until he needed them again. But he wouldn't find them even then. This had been their last ever job, but neither Kaisa nor Alik knew that yet.

He would tell her it was all over when they were safely in Egypt, a country with no extradition treaty with the UK. He had bought a villa on the edge of the Red Sea where they could sunbathe, go sightseeing, and she would put on weight.

He smiled down at her and kissed her hair softly, putting his arm around her thin shoulder. He had enough money now to care for her, and get her the help that she needed. And to live off for the rest of their lives. Alik had always paid well, and very soon, he would pay Stevan again.

****

Lilith's. County Antrim.

The house looked innocent enough, just like any family detached. Set back off the Seven Mile Straight, in a sharp cul-de-sac. Its neat flower beds were newly weeded, and its shiny black gate was painted to match the front door. There were no red lights shining, no foaming Jacuzzis in the garden. Not even any half-dressed women sitting in the window displaying their wares, in an attempt to turn demure Antrim, into Amsterdam by the River Maine. Just a trio of gnomes, all clothed, fishing in an imaginary pond by the gate, and a neat set of net curtains, making the windows

265

proud to be seen. Liam was disappointed. He wasn't sure what he'd expected of a rural brothel, but this certainly wasn't it. He'd hoped for some jokes to tell about the visit at least. What an anti-climax.

Keith Ericson drove them sedately to the end of the cul-de-sac and parked, not at all put-out by the house's boring aspect. He had been here before.

Liam undid his seat-belt and made to get out of the car, turning to grab the sketches from the back seat. Then he noticed Ericson putting his seat-back down and slowly closing his eyes, as if he was about to snooze.

"Here. What're you doing, Keith? We've to go in with these. Come on."

Ericson yawned, with a half-open mouth. "Look Liam, would you mind doing it yourself? I was up half the night with our John's wee girl. She's with us for a few days and she's teething, so we didn't get a wink of sleep. I've been in there loads of times, there's nothing very exciting. I phoned Lilith to expect you.

He pulled his peaked cap down over his eyes and waved Liam away. "It'll only take you five minutes."

Liam looked at him annoyed, then shrugged and slammed the door hard behind him. He ambled towards the house waving his warrant-card ostentatiously, trying hard not to look like a punter, and reached the front door without seeing any neighbours watching.

There were no other cars parked on the short road. Still, it was only six-thirty, probably their quiet time. Liam laughed at the images in his head, searching the front door for a bell.

It was discretely hidden behind a hanging basket and he pressed it hard, half-expecting to hear a chorus of 'Je t'aime'. A disappointingly weak ding-dong rang out instead. Another anti-climax.

After thirty seconds the door opened sharply inwards and a tall, slim brunette in her thirties was standing there, wearing a business suit and black Elvis Costello glasses. He sneaked a look past her down the short wainscoted hall. Still no naked women.

266

"Can I help you?"

"Yes." He produced his I.D. and tried for gravitas. "I'm from the police. I'm here to meet Megan McHenry. She was contacted by Inspector Ericson, about a sketch we'd like her to look at."

The brunette scanned him briefly and sceptically, and then led the way down the hall, into a small chintz sitting room. Liam grew more disappointed by the minute; it was just like his Mother-in-law's. Leaving him there with a cup of tea and the promise of someone coming to help him, she dismissed him with a haughty look. Liam looked around the room while he waited, straining to see the polished china ornaments and over-plump velvet cushions as sex–aids, and failing badly.

A minute went by before the door re-opened, and a small red-haired twenty-something walked in, also wearing a suit. They all looked like accountants. She looked at him disapprovingly and then beckoned him to follow her.

"Where am I going now? I just need to get these sketches looked at."

The young woman peered crossly at him over her glasses, admonishing him with a glance. "I'm taking you to your appointment. Have some patience." He shut-up quickly. She reminded him of Annette in 'head-girl' mode.

They walked through another door and down two flights of stairs, into a long straight corridor with rooms on either side. The place was like a Tardis. Finally, she knocked on a door at the end of the corridor and was answered by a muffled. "Come in."

She pointed him forward and turned on her heel, walking away briskly. Liam walked into the room cautiously. It was totally dark and his fight or flight instincts reared, until a low red light flickered on, accompanied by dark music with a heavy baseline.

His eyes quickly adjusted to the sight of the brunette and a blonde sitting at a table in front of him, clad in identical suits. It was like an accountant's cult.

"Here now. This is very interesting and all that, but

which one of you two ladies is Lilith?"

Without warning a key turned in the lock behind him, and they answered him in unison by standing up. Then he noticed that the dim light was masking walls of ceiling to floor leather with an assortment of cuffs and manacles built into the fabric. And that the ceiling above him was completely covered in mirrors.

The women reached for the necks of their jackets and with one tug, their whole outfits came off, revealing stockings and black satin basques. The brunette lifted a whip from behind the desk, while the blonde reached over and grabbed Liam firmly by the lapel.

"Inspector Ericson said that you have to be punished severely, for being a very naughty boy."

The next sound heard by Keith Ericson, standing outside the door, and probably by half of Antrim, was. "Keith, I'm bloody well going to kill you, get me out of here..." He only hoped that his camera had caught it all.

****

Annette was still in the office when the phone rang, and Liam's deep voice boomed hoarsely down the line, informing her that he wouldn't be back for a while.

"What's happened at Lilith's? And when are you coming back, you skiver? I'm buried under paper here."

"Oh, Lilith's. Aye, well, I'm sure Keith will fill you in. Sorry about the paper but I've got to head to St Mary's, Cutty. Danni's gone into labour."

She felt immediately guilty for giving him a hard time. "But she's not due for weeks yet, is she?"

"No. The baby's coming early. The same thing happened with Erin. Sure, it'll all be fine, but she's up to High Do, so I really need to be there. Sorry."

"Don't worry; I'll keep on with things here. I'll call the chief or Dr Winter if I need help. You forget everything and just go and see Danni. And tell her good-luck. Let me know how it goes, will you?"

268

"Aye, I will. But it'll come out kicking and screaming like they all do, deciding it doesn't like the view already. Give the Doc a call for me and say sorry. I said I'd drop down."

She dropped the phone softly, then thought for a minute and picked it up again, dialling the lab. John Winter answered in three rings.

"Hello, Dr Winter."

John looked at the receiver, puzzled. Annette never rang him direct, although she always could. "Hello Annette, anything wrong?"

"Liam says that he can't make your meeting, Danni's gone into early labour."

"How early?"

"About three weeks I think, so not too bad. She may settle, and if not the baby should be ok anyway, shouldn't it?"

"The dates might be wrong. I'm sure she'll be fine."

"It happened with Erin too, so he's not too worried."

"He might not be worried, but if he's got any tact he'll try to look as if he is. Looking casual while Danni's in labour won't score him any points."

"And we all know Liam's got zero tact, so it'll be 'nul points' for him."

****

London.

Craig lay back on the bed in his small hotel room and looked at his watch; seven p.m. They'd made good headway today, and he was certain they would catch a real break tomorrow. It was still light outside and he wondered what to do with his evening. He had a few options. There was a standing invitation to Yemi's; Trevor Merton was in town, and...

He looked reluctantly at the theatre-ticket sitting beside his suitcase, instantly feeling less relaxed. It lay there as if it was expecting him to use it, and he knew that he should. He felt like a coward for even thinking about not going, but he was.

He didn't need any more pain in his life. He'd finally reached a place where Camille could only hurt him when he accidentally opened an old photo-album. And Lucia had managed to hide most of those away. And he didn't think about her every day now, just once in a while, when certain music was played, by someone else's choice. Or when it was a special day; an anniversary, Christmas, birthdays, holidays. He smiled to himself ruefully. OK, there were still a lot of special days.

No one else had stood a chance since her, he knew that. He'd been too badly burnt. It wasn't that he hadn't met women he liked, or even liked to date over the past five years. It was that, when it got beyond the liking, to them caring for him, or to when he started to care about them, he guillotined every relationship. Kindly he hoped, but quickly.

There was no point. He'd invested everything once, for nine years, and she had shredded his heart, putting her acting career above everything. He relented slightly, remembering her pretty smile and soft blue eyes, stepping back slightly from his harsh judgement of her. OK, she hadn't just shredded his heart; he'd done the same to hers. His career in The Met had pulled him away just as hard as hers had.

His next thought stung hard and he closed his eyes, trying to push the pain down but failing. She hadn't just left him, she'd left him for another man, and the pain had nearly killed him, attacking him on every level.

Craig tried to close out the images of a stranger's hands on her soft skin, his mouth on her body, and more, worse... But he couldn't. He'd tried for years and he still couldn't. What did that make him? Chauvinistic? Neanderthal? Insanely jealous? Male? Or just so in love that he couldn't bear the thoughts or the images of her with someone else.

She'd said that the man could help her career, as if that was any excuse. And, although she'd never say it, he knew that he couldn't. He felt as if he couldn't look after her on any level: in her career or in bed. Shred,

270

shred, shred, Camille. Now he had no heart left to shred.

Except maybe he did, or he'd be able to go along tonight, watch her acting and enjoy it. Applaud, maybe even have a drink with her afterwards, and then leave the bar alone.

His mobile phone rang noisily, jerking him out of two-thousand and seven. 'Annette'. It wasn't like her to call him twice in one day. "Hi Annette, good to hear from you. Is everything ok?"

"Yes."

She was slightly breathless. Not the running type of breathless, the excited type.

"Sir, I'm sorry to bother you, I hope I didn't..." came tumbling out, as she went on without waiting for his reply. "Danni's gone into labour, so Liam's had to go."

"Is she OK?"

"Yes, fine. Although I'm sure Liam will manage to make things worse."

Craig laughed and she hurried on. "Did Liam tell you that Watson, Bob Leighton and both the Greers were on the Strategic Finance Foundation?"

"Yes, he mentioned that you'd found a link there. He said you were working it up, what did you find?"

"Lots. One of the main projects the S.F.F. is working on is called Horizon. It's a huge capital-building programme with millions invested already. A joint initiative with some developer called Derek Tucker based down in Waterford. Anyway, the minutes of the last meeting showed that Joe Watson - he'd only been on the board for nine months since the outgoing Minster Ron Burgess left. Anyway, it shows that although the programme approval and some major investment had already occurred, Watson was talking about pulling the public funds out of it." Craig was sitting up now, this was something, he was sure of it.

"He'd commissioned a separate report looking at the 'Return on Investment' for the project and it came through two weeks ago. It basically said that Horizon wasn't good value. The word was that Watson intended to shut the whole project down. The decision has to be

271

announced formally at the next board meeting for it to be valid, and the board's due to meet next week, on the eighteenth.

Watson has the final veto on all projects involving public money and he was definitely going to pull the plug on it next week, I've just confirmed it with both him and with Mrs Watson. He told her."

"Right." Craig knew that she was onto something but he had to play devil's advocate. "Surely they stop projects all the time, Annette?"

"Yes. That's why I did a bit more digging. Tucker told me that a lot of the contracts and money for the build had already been awarded to companies. They weren't his, but he gave me the names of three and I chased them up. It turns out they're all dummies, set up very recently, out in the Cayman Islands.

I haven't got behind the names yet, but I bet you that someone on the Foundation's board was going to make money out of this whole Horizon thing. And they wanted Joe Watson stopped before he gave the veto.

My first thought was that Declan Greer had something to do with it, but everyone Davy has spoken to about him says that he's a nice man. Bit of a gambling habit but honest. They also said that he wouldn't dare make a move without his wife's say-so. So I dug a bit deeper on Joanne Greer."

She paused for breath and Craig smiled to himself. She was becoming as good at the deskwork as Liam was on the street. They made a great team, even if they didn't always realise it.

"Anyway, I went digging and got more on her, so D.C.I. Cantor and I are going to interview her tomorrow. But my bet is that Declan Greer wasn't the one involved here, and..."

Craig inhaled as if to interrupt, Annette sensed it and kept talking, very quickly.

"I think that maybe he's innocent, and expendable. And that it wasn't only Watson and Bob Leighton who were in the way."

She paused then to allow Craig to contradict her, but he wasn't going to. This was leading somewhere.

He stayed quiet and she went on again.

"There's a bit more too, sir. I looked up Joanne Greer; well to be honest she's the only one I suspect now. She's the only one on S.F.F. who hasn't been threatened or killed, apart from a couple of retired execs who live in Guernsey. And they don't get involved in the day-to-day work; they just seem to be on the board to make up the numbers. So I looked into her background.

The Greers lived in London for seventeen years, until thirteen years ago in fact. She trained as a barrister over there and practiced criminal law, always as a defence barrister. And she defended some nasty buggers too. They make our lots' worst efforts look like bloody ASBOs."

Craig could see why she was agitated. Enough to swear, always a no-no for Annette. He decided to interrupt her now for real, partly to calm her down.

"Annette..."

"Sir...but."

He insisted, gently. "I need to say something. Firstly, this is brilliant work, really excellent. And secondly, do you have a list of the criminal clients that Joanne Greer defended in London?"

"Yes, sir. Here in front of me, that's what I really rang about. But I haven't had a chance to check them all yet."

"You can fax the list over to me tomorrow, but at the moment just look carefully. Is there an Alik Ershov on there?"

They descended into silence. The only sound audible was her quiet breathing, as she searched the list. Craig willed her intensely to say 'yes'. Then she answered him excitedly.

"Yes, yes, sir. He's here! He's here. She successfully defended him on three occasions between nineteen-ninety-two and ninety-nine. She got him off a fraud charge, a living-off immoral earnings ...and a murder! Sir, she got him off the murder of a man who worked for him. Lev Chopiak."

Yes! They had a link between Joanne Greer and Alik

Ershov. But there was something else that he wanted.

"Annette, this is great stuff. Go home now, or Pete will think that you've left him. But I want you in early tomorrow morning to follow-up that connection. The money trail will take a while to come through - Davy can dig a bit deeper on that. And Nicky's already pulling airplane passenger lists and CCTV to run through. She'll tell you about all that. But what I want you to do tomorrow morning is find anything that links Joanne Greer and Ershov recently, over the past twelve months, and particularly since Watson joined S.F.F.

That means any money changing hands, or any big withdrawals from Joanne Greer's accounts. She'll have separate accounts from her husband; I'm certain she will, so check them all.

Get her phone records, home, mobile, office, everything. Go to Judge Standish for any warrants that you need, he's quick and he'll see you anytime, twenty-four-seven. Do your interview with Derek in the afternoon, please; I need those connections by lunchtime. Tell Davy to drop everything else and help you with it. We've got Ershov coming in about ten-thirty tomorrow morning and I want to have something up my sleeve for leverage."

"I'll be on it at seven, sir. There's one last thing. Did Dr Winter call you again?"

"No. What about?"

"He got a match on the D.N.A. from Bob Leighton and the lipstick Officer Sinclair got, and it's been backed up by the prints."

"That's great; Kaisa's in the system then. What was the crime?"

"That's the thing, sir. She wasn't a criminal, she was a victim."

She paused, speaking more slowly. "She was a war crimes victim, sir. She was only seven when her fingerprints were taken. I don't know any more about it, Dr Winter has everything."

Craig was puzzled. He needed to call John.

"OK, thanks Annette. Go home now, and send that information over to D.C.S. Chandak's office tomorrow if you would. I think you've just broken our case for us. Great job."

****

The Greers' Home. Belfast.

Joanne Greer wasn't exactly panicking. No, not panic, that wasn't a word in her vocabulary, but she certainly felt an urgent need to talk to Alik. The police had appeared thirty minutes after Declan's botched shooting, and questioned her all bloody afternoon. There were still two of them outside, just in case. Just in case of what? She'd spent the time since they'd left thinking hard, retracing her actions and words, looking for mistakes, but there were none.

It was only six-thirty and the evening was still bright, but she'd closed the curtains on the arched sitting-room window. She couldn't bear to see them standing in her driveway, talking on their echoing radios. They'd acted as if they knew more than they said. Maybe she'd underestimated the Northern Ireland plods. She'd always known that they were good at the terrorist stuff, but their basic policing must surely have slipped during the Troubles. They couldn't possibly be as good as The Met, could they? And she'd tied them in knots in court often enough in the past.

And then that phone-call five minutes ago, from some woman. Asking sneaky little questions about her barrister work, and naming criminals that she'd defended. Thank God, they hadn't mentioned Alik. But she'd had a long list; he must have been in there somewhere. And she was coming here, to her home, tomorrow! This was getting too close for comfort; she needed to talk to Alik, now. Sod his stupid pay-as-you-go rules. She was fed-up waiting to be contacted, waiting to be told when she could and couldn't talk to him. His control-freakery was getting very old.

She picked up the faux nineteen-forties phone sitting in the window bay, and quickly made the call. The ring-tone said that he was in the U.K, although you

275

never knew with Alik. He picked-up quickly and she had a fleeting thought that calling his mobile would be expensive, she told the girls off about every bill. The thought disappeared as soon as he spoke.

"Yes." His dark voice made the line vibrate, and her as well.

"Alik, darling, I need to talk."

"Why are you calling me?" He hung up abruptly and tears sprung to her eyes, a mixture of hurt feelings and pride. Almost immediately, her handbag vibrated. She grabbed at it, pulling the cheap pay-as-you-go phone out and fumbling with the controls.

"You stupid bitch." He was shouting at her so loudly that the only thing shaking now was her hand. "What are you doing? You have no idea what you have done. Why are you so stupid?"

Then Joanne did something completely out of character that shocked them both. She cried. Not the manufactured wronged-wife's tears of the past few days, or the useful business tears that she kept for difficult meetings. Not even her tears of frustration at Declan's constant stupidity. But the genuine tears of a frightened woman, looking for comfort from the only man that she'd ever really loved.

Chapter Twenty-Three

London.

Craig knew that he'd missed curtain-up, but he'd already made his choice. He couldn't sit through a performance watching her like a normal punter. Besides which, he had paperwork to do for tomorrow. He immediately felt like a coward, then he defended himself against his own accusation. He would go backstage after the play and see her face-to-face. It would be private, and it was all he could handle.

There was no point beating himself up about something that he couldn't do. His job brought him enough challenges; he didn't need to test himself in his leisure time as well. He nodded to himself, only half-convinced, but felt better for making the choice. The indecision had been killing him ever since Yemi had handed him the ticket.

Curtain down was nine-thirty. Plenty of time to work, and then change into a few years older and slightly more expensive version of the man that she'd first met. He brightened up, like a man who'd just received a stay of execution, and decided to call John. He needed some details on the rifle, and on the girl's mysterious past.

John didn't answer the phone for what seemed like ages, and he was puffing like the Portrush Flyer when he did. Craig was curious.

"Don't tell me. You've taken up jogging?"

For a moment all he could hear was John inhaling deeply. It was starting to worry him, when he finally spoke in a wheeze. "You fit people can mock all you like, but I'm determined to get in shape. If you saw the inside of people's arteries like I do, you'd understand why."

My God! He was jogging.

"Natalie's persuaded me to do the half-marathon at Forfar, and it's only seven weeks away "

It was worse than jogging, he was running. Craig

277

was normally the athletic one; he didn't think John even possessed a pair of trainers.

"You're kidding! You, running? Where are you at the moment?"

"Half way down Annadale Embankment on an eight-mile route. And it's only my first day, in fact it's my first ever run, so don't take the piss."

Craig laughed, disbelievingly. "I have to; you know that. That's what mates are for. Don't you think you should have tried something shorter than eight miles, after forty years of inertia?"

Craig could hear him sitting down. His breathing gradually quietened to the point where it didn't drown out the background noise, and the sounds of traffic and birds were finally audible. He talked on while John couldn't.

"Listen, I agree with Natalie. You need to get fit. But you can't go from nought to one hundred in your first run, John! You'll kill yourself. And there's no way she told you to do eight miles straight off. "

"You're right, she didn't. But I can't be bothered building things up slowly. I get bored. So I thought I'd just go for it."

Craig raised his eyes to heaven. "For a man with a big brain you're really thick sometimes, John. When I get back, we'll do some weights and cardio at the gym, before you kill yourself. Besides which, Natalie loves you for your mind."

They both laughed. "Well, she'd better. I look like the weed in the Mr Muscle adverts in this outfit. And I don't think that I love anyone enough for this. Where are you, by the way?"

"In my hotel room." Craig looked around the small, overheated room, lying. "It's not too bad. I'll ring you back when you can talk without gasping."

"I can talk now. And if I can help you, I'll feel less of a useless dick, knowing that I'm good at something. What can I do for you?"

"We're bringing in a suspect tomorrow morning for interview. So I'd like a bit of background on the rifle, and on the D.N.A. hit that Annette said you got."

278

"Right, yes. Did you get my report today?"

"Sorry, I haven't had time to look at it in detail yet. I've spent most of the day staring at surveillance tapes and sketches. Can you give me the quick version?"

"OK. Well, you know both rounds were 338 Lapuas?"

"Yes."

"And you know there are two main rifles used for that round, but I'll get onto that in a minute. I checked with Norris and they followed the trajectory back from Declan Greer's position. They found aluminium residue at a site about one-and-a-half kilometres from where he was shot. Up in Dublin Road, near the back of the course's hospitality pavilion. Do you know it?"

"Yes. Could the metal be identified as a rifle?"

"No, just a heap of metal. It had high concentration Sodium Hydroxide residue on it."

"You think it was used to melt the rifle down?"

"Definitely, it's nasty stuff, burn a hold in nearly anything. The shooter dissolved the rifle and left, probably ditching the gloves and containers elsewhere. If they search around there'll be a PVC container with some Sodium Hydroxide residue, I'm sure of it. I've asked Derek Cantor to have a check, just in case a child accidentally lifts it.

Anyway, it wasn't completely dissolved so Des has done the calculations. He thinks the aluminium weighed about 5.5 kg, which makes it most likely it was a SAKO, rather than the A.I. They're both aluminium but the A.I. is about a kilo heavier."

"You're quite the expert on rifles nowadays."

"It's exciting stuff."

Craig smiled. John had always wanted to be the cowboy when they were kids.

"In fact, I was thinking of taking up shooting, just targets. Fancy joining me?"

"Sure, I'll take you to the range. Targets are fine, but nothing living."

"Agreed. Ross Ellis shoots, doesn't he?"

"He goes deer hunting. We've had a few arguments on it. What about the D.N.A.?"

John was silent for a moment, and Craig could feel his sadness before he said anything. His voice confirmed it.

"Marc, I know this girl is probably, well, almost certainly a killer. And I know your sympathy always lies with the victims. But I have to tell you, after what she went through, I don't think anyone would be normal."

"Tell me." Craig knew that whatever he heard next would be terrible.

"The D.N.A. went back to a War Crime's database, compiled after the Bosnian conflict in ninety-two to ninety-five. It belonged to a seven-year-old Serbian girl called Kaisa Mitic."

Not Moldeau. "Both the D.N.A. and the prints match her."

Craig's voice was gentle. "What happened to her, John?"

He hesitated for a moment, and then started. "She was living in a small village in Serbia with her family; parents, an older brother and a baby sister. The older brother was fourteen. They were poor, just making enough to live on. They had a smallholding near some woods, beside the river Sava." His voice became angry. "They had absolutely nothing to do with the war, or the army." He paused for breath again, and then went on.

"One day the Serbian army came through. It was nineteen-ninety-one. Just before they went into Bosnia and before the worst of the atrocities against the Bosnians started. They came to the house looking for food and refreshments, but the family only had a few cattle and chickens - you can imagine the poverty. Anyway...they saw the little girl, and..."

He stopped again and Craig's blood chilled, the hairs standing-up on his neck. He knew what was coming next. It was like some bad horror movie where the plot is inevitable, and you want to shout at the screen and warn the victim, but you're powerless to help.

"The soldiers took it in turns to rape her, Marc. Grown men, five of them. The records said there were five of them. They raped a seven-year-old girl, in front of her parents and brother. When they'd finished, they stood the parents back to back and shot them through the head with a single bullet - they died instantly. Then they turned to do the same to the children. They stamped the baby to death first, presumably to keep it quiet, but the older boy managed to grab Kaisa and drag her off into the woods.

They managed to lose themselves. The soldiers shot after them but they missed, then the bastards torched the farm and the bodies and just walked away. Probably to do the same thing to the Bosnians. In fact, definitely to do the same."

Craig started to ask him questions quickly. Mainly to take his mind off what John had said, because to dwell on it would have generated such a murderous rage in him that he'd have put his fist straight through his flimsy wardrobe door.

"What did the children do next, John?"

"The boy got her to a doctor and reported what had been done, brave little thing. He was able to identify the soldiers. He knew them, Marc. They were men from the next village, men that would have said hello to their family at local events. They were just animals who saw an opportunity to take something that they'd probably already seen and wanted, the little girl. The boy testified against them after the war. His name was Stevan."

Craig nodded to himself. Of course. "He's our shooter, John. They aren't a romantic couple, they're brother and sister. The war destroyed them and now they destroy other people."

"You're certain they're both involved?"

Craig told him about the surveillance tapes.

"That makes sense. Look, I know what they did here was completely wrong, and there's no excuse. But dear God, Marc, where does all that anger go if it's not dealt with? And the girl, how much damage did they do to her?"

They were quiet for a moment, thinking. She was only seven. Craig thought about how he'd have reacted if it had been Lucia, and his parents. He'd love to believe that he'd have been as brave as Stevan the boy, and that he'd be better now than Stevan the man. But he couldn't be sure of it. War created a lot of killers, and not just at the time.

The phone-call ended itself. There was nowhere else to go with it, just a quiet 'thanks' and 'talk tomorrow' and then, click. Each of them left trying to work out who the real victims were.

****

Craig paid the black–cab driver and stepped out into the cool night air of Shaftesbury Avenue .The faces of people walking past were dappled with light from the bright overhead signs, announcing that 'Chariots of Fire' was on at The Gielgud Theatre, and 'Les Miserables' at Queen's.

He looked around, feeling the excitement of the West End, and smiling despite his tiredness. The three glasses of wine he'd drunk in the hotel bar helped. As John often said, 'fatigue is directly soluble in alcohol', and who was he to argue with a doctor.

A small group of teenagers walked past him on the narrow pavement, laughing. Young and unburdened. They reminded him of Davy, and he hoped that he'd stay that way; that Maggie Clarke was kind to him.

He picked his way past the pavement detritus, not remembering it as bad five years before, but still loving London anyway. For its noise and life and variety; and its rainbow of people. He hoped that Belfast would be as cosmopolitan too someday, on a smaller scale.

He reached his destination and gazed-up at the overhead sign. The red and green lights announced her loudly. Camille Kennedy, gifted actress. The lead in 'The Cold Stone' by Stephen Maray. The play that she'd performed in the festival in Belfast, now in the West End. The photograph on the billboard showed her as a nineteen-thirties siren, and he remembered watching her in the Grand Opera House. The role suited her.

He glanced at his watch. Nine-twenty-five. The play

ended in five minutes. He'd timed it perfectly. He walked quickly to the stage door and gave his name. It opened inwards immediately, the manager briefed to admit him and show him to her dressing room.

He entered the large warm room with the star on its door, impressed, and happy for her. For years she'd shared cold storage-cupboards with five others. He was pleased that she finally had the star status that her talent warranted. No matter what it had cost them both.

Craig looked around while he waited, at the flower-bouquets and good-luck cards, some from well-known names. And then he saw his own. Not one that he'd sent her for this show, because he hadn't, but one from years before. Ten years before when she'd played Rosalie, the maid in an Oscar Wilde play called Lady Windermere's Fan. She'd been so nervous that he remembered her shaking in the wings and gripping his hand tightly. He'd left the card and a present for her to find when she came off.

He picked it up, smiling at the words that he'd written all those years ago. He'd been a different man then, and they'd had a different relationship. He felt torn between leaving immediately, preserving the past as it was, and staying for five more minutes, to discover if they had a future.

Just then the door opened wide and she rushed in. Slight and blonde, red-lipped and Marcel-waved, in a sheath of gold lame, looking exactly like the screen siren she was supposed to be. She looked stunning, and he couldn't breathe for a moment. She was even more beautiful than he remembered.

She saw immediately what was running through his mind, looking up into his dark eyes while he looked down into hers. She stepped slowly towards him, lifting her hand to his cheek. He didn't retreat and she moved nearer, so that his breath stopped still, making the air between them silent.

They were so close now that only the colours that they wore said where she began and he ended. She reached her other hand to his hair stroking its thick dark strands seductively, rhythmically. Until he pulled her to his chest, his arms around her waist and his thighs tight against hers, and their lips met, for the first time in years.

Softly and tentatively at first, exploring each other gently. Then he pressed down harder and her lips parted in submission, opening to his taste and feel. She sank into his arms so entirely, that she felt as if she was falling backwards and him with her. He whispered her name softly. "Camille," as if all the years had fallen away, back to when they first met. They were young again, when they would make love for hours and then name the stars from the balcony of their small flat.

He moved swiftly to the door and locked it, cutting off the light outside and leaving only the faint glow of the table-lamp to highlight her beauty. In one smooth movement he lifted her onto the couch and caressed her lips with his, forgetting time, until she begged him hoarsely to make love to her. In a memory and movement as natural as breathing he slipped her dress straps down one by one. Until her lame sheath fell to the floor, and her bare, tanned perfection lay in front of him, unchanged and just as he remembered her.

He stood, pulling off his jacket, and knelt down before her, reaching forward to stroke her smooth thighs gently. Her skin was like gossamer, even softer than he remembered and she moaned quietly and went to speak. He placed a finger on her lips, stilling all conversation, and started to kiss her slowly, from her feet, through her thighs and beyond. Taking time and patience, never hurrying, never stopping. Bringing her gently to ecstasy once, and then turning her over and caressing her again. Using first his tongue and then his hands, losing himself in her scents and sighs. Then stronger strokes, arousing her again, until she cried out for mercy.

He stood for a moment, looking down at her, watching her gentle, quick recovery. He looked at her shining eyes and at the sweat dripping off her sleek, tanned skin. And more than anything, at her longing. Her parted lips and languid eyes begged him for more

284

and he drew her firmly to her feet, and to him. Then he lifted her further, and entered her with one hard thrust, to give them both what they had wanted for hours.

He stopped and looked lovingly into her eyes, and then thrust again and watched as she submitted to him. Stroking her hair and nipples unhurriedly, and tenderly caressing her skin, he moved rhythmically, again and again, until finally they thrust in time with each other.

He finally felt her body tense and arch, signalling his own longed-for release, in a fire of warmth and sensation between their thighs that neither had ever felt before. He held her close for minutes, as if she was fragile and could break, until finally her breathing slowed and his own matched hers, and finally, their bodies pulled apart. Then without a word, they dressed and left, walking slowly to her apartment, and a night that neither of them would ever forget.

Chapter Twenty-Four

The Met. London. Friday.

"I have no idea why you bring me here. I say nothing without my lawyer."

Craig was in a much brighter interview room than the C.C.U.'s; London obviously had better interior design than they could afford. The table had no scorch marks from abandoned or stubbed cigarettes, and the sign on the wall, bearing testament to 'no smoking or mobile phones' hadn't been defaced at all. Even the tape-machine was more high-tech than he'd used before. But none of that altered the facts - he was looking at a criminal, and they were the same whatever the decor.

True, Ershov hadn't been caught with stolen goods, or bloody hands. And no one was waiting on the other side of the wall to identify him. They didn't even have a charge. But he knew a criminal when he saw one. No matter how hard they scrubbed, and covered their bodies in expensive cologne, they couldn't wash away the stench of what they'd done. It was always there, like some indefinable shadow, darkening the room.

He much preferred the street villain, the obvious crook. Who 'f'ed and blinded' when you arrested them, called you a pig and took a swing. There was a kind of honesty about that approach. In your face. It was this type that he couldn't stomach, the type who never got their own hands bloody.

He wanted to reach across the table and grab Ershov by his scrawny, be-jewelled throat. But they had to deal with this filth to get to the ones who did the killing. They all knew it. But it still made him want to throw up.

The lawyer was taking his time in appearing, so they left Ershov alone in the room, with a cup of coffee and his requested newspaper. The Financial Times - ever the respectable businessman. Then they headed back upstairs, where Rajiv Chandak was waiting for them at

286

his office door.

"What's happening down there?"

"Nothing yet, sir. He's lawyered-up and saying nothing until they get here."

Chandak shrugged, too long in the tooth to let it bother him. Just the games people played.

"Right. Marc, something has come through from Belfast, Rita has it. RITA..."

The round, comfortable figure of Rita came ambling into the office with a transparent plastic folder in her hand. She followed it with a ready-prepared tray of coffee and biscuits. Chandak smiled down at her warmly. "If I didn't know better I'd swear my mother had moved down from Birmingham to take care of me. Thank you, Rita."

Yemi needed a quick word on another case, so Craig drank his black coffee pulling out the sheets of A4 that Annette had faxed over. She'd done just as he'd asked, and she'd got a result. He punched the air. Yes!

Yemi caught his friend's familiar gesture, and looked over at him, smiling. "You've got leverage on Ershov?"

"We have. Annette's worked the oracle. We haven't got the money trail yet, but we do have something that'll make him pretty damn uncomfortable."

"Well, are you going to tell us? Or do I have to get Yemi here to torture you?"

Craig laughed. He wished he could take this double act back with him, Liam would love them. He pulled a page from the pile and put it in front of them on the desk. Then he pointed to the line that he'd circled heavily in pen...

****

Belfast.

Joanne Greer had had enough. She'd had police all over her home, her business and her life since yesterday and she was sick of it. She was even more tired of acting like 'the wronged wife'. There were only

287

so many facial scrubs that a woman could take.

She was finally alone in the house. Carina had been dispatched to school and Isabella to Uni. She couldn't stand them moping around anymore, saying 'poor Daddy, someone tried to shoot him'. Pity they missed the bastard.

She would be looking into that, it wasn't what she'd paid for. But at least Declan had kept his mouth shut about Joe Watson so far. She knew it was only for the girls' sake but she would take anything she could get. The worst thing was that he had gone from gambling waster to Nelson Mandela in five seconds, just because he'd been shot at! She'd completely forgotten that it would elevate him to sainthood in the girls' eyes. Damn, damn, damn. Still, at least he was out of her life now.

Now she had another problem, the plods had hinted at it yesterday but they'd actually stated it today. She was a suspect in his shooting! And for all the wrong reasons, that was almost what annoyed her most. Stupid fucking man, why did he have to announce his plans to divorce her in front of a tent full of people? Now everyone thought that she was some sort of pathetic woman who'd ordered him shot out of love.

She unfolded her long brown legs and stood up, strolling over to the window and staring-out at the drive absent-mindedly. There they are, like insects, crawling all over my Aston, staring at every dent Declan inflicted, as if they're an indicator of motive. As if I would have killed him over those. Mind you...

There was a soft knock on the door behind her, and without looking she impatiently said. "Oh, come in, for God's sake."

She immediately heard heavy feet entering, and then a second lighter pair. They stopped abruptly behind her, as if expecting her to acknowledge their presence. Well they'd be waiting until hell froze over. Eventually the man spoke.

"Mrs Greer. We need to ask you a few more questions. Could you take a seat please?"

Could I take a seat? In my own house. Could I take a

seat? How about, 'I own the fucking seats'. But she bit her tongue and said nothing, turning and smiling, ever the charming host.

The fat balding one was standing there, Canter or Cantor, or something like that. He was accompanied by a smallish slim woman with a boring brown bob, and boring brown shoes. I bet they have flat heels, she just looks the type.

"Of course, D.C.I. Cantor. And may I ask who this is?"

"Detective Sergeant McElroy, from the Docklands Coordinated Crime Unit."

Joanne disliked her immediately, self-important little thing.

"Yes, well. I'm quite sure that all crime is terrible. Do sit down."

She sat back down in her armchair, folding her long legs up again. She reminded Annette of an elegant flick-knife, and every bit as sharp.

"I'm very tired. Must we have more tedious questions? Is it really necessary?"

"I appreciate that, and I'm very sorry Mrs Greer, but we do need to ask you a few last questions. Or rather sergeant McElroy does."

He nodded to Annette and she opened her handbag, removing a small tape recorder. Joanne thought that the bag was small and cheap, like the woman.

"Do you mind Mrs Greer? It saves me writing everything down, and with my handwriting that makes it much easy to transcribe later."

She looked at Annette as if she was a tiresome child, and waved her hand dismissively. "Whatever you wish, just get on with it."

Annette had spent ninety minutes that morning digging into the Strategic Finance Foundation and into Joanne Greer, and she was very sure of her ground. Now that she'd met her, she knew that it wasn't just her duty to interview her as an attempted murder suspect; she was positively going to enjoy it. This acidic creature couldn't have been more different from Caitlin Watson, who still loved her husband even

289

though he'd been planning to leave her for an Eastern European hooker.

"Thank you Mrs Greer. I only have a few questions. Firstly, could you please tell me how long you and your husband have worked with Mr Joe Watson, on the Strategic Finance Foundation? And could you also please tell me what you know about the Horizon Project?"

Joanne tensed imperceptibly but Annette saw it, knowing immediately that they were on the right track. "My final question is about your time spent as a criminal barrister in London..."

****

The Met. London.

The newly-painted white door of the interview room opened, and a young man entered arrogantly, wearing a suit with a vulgar pin-stripe, and a badly ironed shirt. He thumped his briefcase down on the table; barely missing Yemi's calmly clasped hands, and sat down heavily in the chair beside Alik Ershov with a sigh.

He folded his arms lazily, shooting his cuffs to display a pair of white metal cufflinks bearing a family crest. Within one moment, he'd firmly established his origins in the English upper classes and Craig just knew that an affected drawl would emerge from his mouth next.

"Good day to you, officers. I am Harry Montgomery of Montgomery and Windsor Solicitors, Hyde Park Corner, and I'm here to tell you that you have absolutely no business with my client. And that he only came with you this morning to be of assistance, because he is a law-abiding citizen. So I insist that you conclude your business with him.

Furthermore...as you dragged my client here at an unearthly hour, without giving him time to organise his affairs for the day, I've a mind to bill the police for his loss of earnings and inconvenience."

"That would be the police in Northern Ireland."

"What?" The word stretched out into a drawl.

Ershov looked away quickly at the words 'Northern Ireland', and they all saw it.

"What business do you have in London then, and with my client? You have no jurisdiction here."

He turned to Ershov. "We're leaving now, Mr Ershov. They have no right to even question you."

To his solicitors' surprise, but not Craig's, Alik Ershov didn't move a sinew. Instead, he remained immobile, staring straight ahead and past them, focussing on the wall at their back. To a novice it might have looked like a complete absence of movement, but to Craig and Yemi, it looked like rapid calculations going on inside Ershov's head. A gambler calculating the odds.

If Northern Ireland was involved, what did they know? How had it happened, and just how exposed was he? Ershov needed the answers to several questions, and they knew that he did.

Craig leaned forward and placed an A4 sheet on the table in front of him, watching the Vor's face closely as he strained to read the circled detail upside down. Then watching even more closely as his recognition of the number dawned. The twenty-second call that Joanne Greer had made to him the evening before.

Ershov's poker face changed to one of murderous rage in an instant, and even Montgomery saw it. That stupid bitch, she had ruined him. He would kill her with his own bare hands now, and enjoy it.

Harry Montgomery looked at the paper, not understanding the significance of what lay in front of them. "This is nothing, just some phone records. My client has no comment to make."

He pulled back his chair and lifted his briefcase, moving to take Ershov's coat from the stand. Then Ershov finally spoke, his carefully broken English instantly improving as he turned to his brief. "We need five minutes." It was an order, not a request.

Craig and Yemi left dutifully and stood outside in the corridor, while client privilege gave the room's occupant's time to concoct a fairy-tale. One designed to save Alik Ershov from whatever they knew; if they could. Eventually, the door reopened and Montgomery beckoned them back in.

"My client would like to be helpful to your investigation, because he is a law-abiding citizen. He will be as forthcoming as he can, for certain considerations. Otherwise he is saying nothing." Game over, Mrs Greer.

Chapter Twenty-Five

Belfast. Friday.

Liam watched Joanne Greer walk confidently through security at Belfast City Airport. Once her bag, belt and shoes had cleared, he nodded to the searcher to let her pass without any further checks, following at a safe distance. If she saw him it wouldn't matter. They'd never even met.

She looked every inch the casual traveller, off to London for business, or for shopping and shows. Her large tortoiseshell sunglasses set off a brown leather jacket, that's cost could have fed a small family for years. She pulled up the collar in a pretentiously chic way, slipped on her Gucci loafers and headed for the stairs to the business lounge, where Annette was already seated, watching quietly from behind a screen.

She sailed past the greeting hostess and threw her bag down on the lounge's carpeted floor with an exaggerated sigh. Then she strolled over to the coffee-machine for a cafe-au-lait, looking around her while she waited. Good, there was no one here that she knew - Friday was always good for outward travel.

It was quiet in the lounge. Just a few pairs of women eagerly anticipating their weekend away from the kids, and a tired-looking businessman, heading home for two more days overworking, hammering on the keys of his laptop like some desperate final act. Annette wondered how his work had become so much more important than his life and then she laughed, realising their whole team had been working late all week. People in glass-houses.

Joanne lifted a copy of the Ulster Bazaar from the rack, and sat flicking idly through it. Her top half looked completely relaxed, but the rapidly tapping foot below gave away her true level of stress. She calmed herself with the reminder that should she would soon be safe with Alik. That police sergeant had been a real cow, with her double-edged comments and her snide little looks; she'd felt uneasy since she'd left. How the hell had they latched on to Horizon? Why that specific project? And how had they managed to connect Joe and Declan?

Then all of a sudden, Sergeant Frumpy had left her a message to say 'thank you for helping with our enquiries and there'll be no further action'. No explanation at all! But she hadn't needed to be told twice. Her next call had been to an airline.

She didn't believe in God, it was just an invention to keep children well-behaved, but if she had done, then she would have thanked him for getting away with everything. Even to her it seemed slightly churlish to take all the credit herself. She was still smiling as the lounge tannoy announced the departure of her flight to London Heathrow.

Annette watched from her vantage point as Joanne Greer rose, drew herself up to her full height and then cast a last contemptuous look at the lounge and Belfast. As she walked unsmilingly through the tunnel and into her window-seat in row one, Annette rang through to the two plain-clothes officers in rows six and eight, handing over the observation. Then she walked downstairs to meet Liam in the foyer, and they settled down to wait for the last few hours as the game played out.

****

Heathrow Airport.

Alik Ershov and his driver waited at Terminal One arrivals for Joanne Greer, as if he was ready to whisk her away to safety. He smiled, as if he was meeting the woman he loved, which he was. But their reunion would be short-lived. He was a survivor and Joanne was much too dangerous to him now; she had to be sacrificed. She really should understand. After all it was exactly what she would do to anyone who got in her way, she had already proved that.

Besides, he'd offered her a life once before and she'd

294

rejected him, and he had a long memory. Maybe he'd never really forgiven her. He thought not, otherwise surely he would have found another way to appease the police? Even he thought that he'd jumped at their proposed solution a little too quickly.

He knew one thing for sure. When he'd been given the choice of giving up Stevan and Kaisa, or Joanne, the choice had only taken him a moment. True, they were all killers. But in the moral hierarchy of murderers, he respected Stevan's quest to give his wounded sister a future, much more than he respected Joanne's endless greed. He fingered the Dukh around his neck unconsciously, he had the Vor code and Stevan had his. He respected that.

Stevan was like the son he should have had. He loved his little sister more than the world and Alik admired that too: family was everything. Besides which, he was a supremely practical man. Stevan could be useful again, and Kaisa was beautiful, and he loved beauty.

He looked at his watch, yawning. Two-thirty. Not long now. He was quite looking forward to seeing Joanne's face when they arrested her, her arrogance had always been one of her least endearing qualities.

Craig and Yemi watched him from their seats in the cafe, listening to the voices of the Belfast officers, narrating Joanne Greer's journey. She'd just collected her bag from the carousel, and was heading for the automatic doors. Craig could see them opening and closing from where they sat, and he signalled, alerting the officer posing as Ershov's driver.

They didn't have the money trail confirmed yet. It would take time to strip the front companies back far enough to tie them to Joanne, so they needed a confession on tape to get her back to Belfast. They needed Ershov to greet her by name, and get her to say something that implicated her in the murders of Bob and Irene Leighton. And the attempted murder of her husband. Ershov had been confident that he could get it from her within five minutes; after all, she trusted him.

The plan was to give Joanne's bag to the driver and then for Ershov to take her to the airport's main cafe for coffee, for as long as it took her to talk. They couldn't let her get into a car with him; the risk of her disappearing was far too great. He might kill her now for implicating him.

The automatic doors opened again, and Craig finally saw the chic middle-aged woman, pictured in the photographs that Annette had sent. Walking behind her at a safe distance were the two plain-clothes-officers, dressed as tourists. They peeled off to sit in the smoker's area, making moves to light their cigarettes just as Alik Ershov moved forward, with his arms wide-open and a broad smile on his cold, tanned face. He drew Joanne Greer's face towards him with both hands, for a kiss. Judas.

She smiled at him happily. Yes, he looked older, greyer, maybe a bit softer around the edges, but he was still the man that she had loved fifteen years before. The man she would love again now. Her smile widened and she kissed him properly, full on the lips. It surprised Ershov for a second and he looked into her eyes, confused: she'd changed. She seemed softer somehow, and a moment's doubt entered his mind. Maybe there was another way. Maybe he could get her out of the airport.

Craig watched Ershov's resolve crumble in moments while they embraced, and he moved quickly towards the exit doors. He mingled with the emerging travellers and stood just far enough behind Joanne Greer for Ershov to see him clearly. He stood there completely still, as people created a path around him, and stared intensely at the Russian, willing him to look at him. Finally he did. The implication was clear. You and the life you've built up, or Joanne Greer. You choose. Right now.

Craig watched the calculations being done and the answer quickly becoming obvious. Ershov was back on track; his self-preservation was much stronger than any love. He started talking gently to Joanne Greer, like a confiding lover, but with an inaudible subtext.

Sorry Joanne. Should have got me while I was young and trusting. Too late.

He relieved her of her bag like a gentleman and handed it off to the driver, leading her gently by the arm towards the cafe. "Let's have a coffee before we start our journey." She acquiesced, happy to be dominated by him now.

Craig followed at a reasonable distance but he could hear everything through Ershov's wire. The two smoking officers had stubbed out their cigarettes and were front and following now. Keeping Joanne in their sights at all times, and ready to move as soon as Craig gave the signal.

Joanne was relaxing by the minute. She'd got out of Belfast and he was here to greet her, it was all going beautifully.

"Alik darling, it's so good to see you. I can't believe we're together again."

"Neither can I, Dushyenka. It must have been a terrible strain for you, you must tell me everything."

"I'm so sorry I phoned you. It was really stupid of me, but I was at my wits end, the police were all over the house."

"I know. Don't worry. I forgive you." Adding, "you stupid bitch," silently. Without that phone-call, the police would have had nothing.

They arrived at the cafe, and stopped talking briefly while the waitress led them to a table, taking their order. Then he eased her smoothly back into the conversation, as if the gap had never existed.

"Tell me everything, Joanne. Why such steps? And the full background, I want us to share everything." Perfect, he'd walked her right into it without implicating himself.

She looked at him, confused for a moment. He already knew everything, so why go over it again? After all, he'd been involved since the start. He saw her doubt immediately and looked at her lovingly, taking her hand. She melted, humouring his need to savour their victory, and over the next ten minutes, Joanne Greer told the story that sealed her fate.

They couldn't have got any more from her if Craig had written her script. She talked about Horizon and the dummy companies, underlining why first Irene and then Bob Leighton had to die. Then about Watson's blackmail and her stupid husband finding out and threatening to tell the police. He'd had to go as well. Once she'd started she just kept talking. Ershov had done his bit well; they had the whole thing on tape. All that was left now were the account numbers, and they would come.

Craig was sitting alone at the table nearest the door. Officer one was at the table nearest Ershov, and Officer two, the female officer, was seated beside the ladies' toilets, just in case Joanne tried to escape that way.

Craig had heard enough, and he got ready to move. The arrest had to be Belfast's; otherwise Joanne Greer would end up in London's system for months. Rajiv Chandak and Terry Harrison had agreed everything and her arrest warrant had been issued in Northern Ireland. It was sitting in Officer one's top pocket right now.

Craig nodded quickly to the others and they stood up simultaneously, moving towards the table together. He took up position between Ershov and Joanne, and Yemi walked into the cafe to join them. The plan was to arrest them both to keep Ershov's cover. Ostensibly he was being investigated for fraud, but Yemi would take him back to the office. His oily solicitor was waiting there for the full debrief and release, in the full knowledge that they would be watching him very closely in the future. Joanne would be taken back to Belfast without ever know that it was Ershov who had betrayed her. Neat.

Craig and Yemi stood by the table and Joanne looked up at them as if they were annoying her. She stared at Yemi arrogantly. "Can I help you with something? This is a private conversation."

"Yes. I think you'll find that you can both help us, Mrs Greer."

She froze, her coffee-cup immobile in mid-air. Ershov pretended shock at their presence.

"Mr Ershov will be helping me in a fraud investigation, and I believe you will be helping D.C.I. Craig back in Belfast. Marc, would you like to do the honours."

Craig reached his hand out to Officer one, taking the warrant that he was holding. He opened it and read clearly.

"Mrs Joanne Greer, I have a warrant for your arrest for the murders of Mr Robert Leighton, Member of Parliament and his wife Mrs Irene Leighton. I also have a warrant for your arrest on the charge of the attempted murder of your husband, Mr Declan Greer." Shock flashed across Joanne's face and the coffee cup fell out of her hand, slowly breaking into pieces on the floor. A young waitress hovered nearby watching them, uncertain if she should clear it up.

Craig continued. "Please stand Mrs Greer. We will be taking the next plane back to Northern Ireland."

The two officers moved forward to read her rights and escort her, but Joanne just sat immobile, seeing everything that she had built in life falling apart. Ershov stood up protesting, and reached-out for her, led away shouting, by Yemi. Craig thought that he should get an Oscar.

Joanne Greer was still sitting, staring into space, and Craig could see her mind racing, trying to find an escape. He nodded Yemi good-bye and looked down at her, rigid and silent. He couldn't feel any sympathy for her. She'd killed two people and had planned to kill more.

Finally, he stepped away and called Annette. "Annette, we've got her and we'll be back on the sixteen-ten. Could you get a doctor to meet us, please? It looks like she's going to need some help."

Then they guided her, sleepwalking, to the departure gate, and boarded, returning Joanne Greer to Belfast four hours after she had left. The business woman stared through the window for the whole one-hour journey, watching her future disappear.

****

A triumphant Liam and Annette joined them in Belfast, as a doctor accompanied Joanne Greer to High Street. She would be held there until some slick lawyer got her out on bail, and then tried to unpick the case that they'd worked so hard to make watertight. It was all part of the game.

By six p.m. they'd completed the paperwork and briefly toasted the safe arrival of Liam's baby son, before he went back to the hospital, promising a much bigger celebration next week.

By nine o'clock Annette had gone home for a well-earned rest and Craig was lying on the sofa in his Stranmillis flat, flicking through the channels but not really seeing the screen. He was wrecked, but it was the tiredness of relief as much as anything. They had their guilty party and he'd finally ended a chapter in his life.

He and Camille had seen each other again for lunch that day, this time staying well away from her apartment. It had been easier somehow. They had kept it brief: she had a matinee performance, and he'd invented a meeting, in preparation for the operation at two.

Last night had confirmed what they'd both known; that they still loved each other. Their lovemaking had filled the night and early morning cathartically, breaking down the barriers of five years as it waned, and freeing them to talk.

It had helped him that she'd seemed hurt by the way it had ended years before as well. Not out of revenge, but because somehow it made their time together seem less worthless. She'd left him out of ambition, not because her love had died, but she'd left him just the same. She'd chosen her career, as had he, and nothing would change if they tried again now. They both knew that and they'd finally made their peace with it.

His life was the police, his parents were aging and he wouldn't leave them alone. And hers was acting, the theatre, movies, and for that she needed to be in London and America. If they were both being truthful, although they still loved each other they each loved other things more.

300

He was glad that they'd made love one last time. The ghosts of their relationship weren't laid to rest, but they were less restless now. And quiet enough to free them both to get on with life.

He smiled to himself, remembering her for the first time in five years without pain. He held on to the memory for a moment and then he clicked off the TV and set the alarm for an hour's time, closing his eyes. He had an important call to make.

Chapter Twenty-Six

Craig ushered her tentatively towards their seats, settling down in the century-old Abbey theatre, warm, although December winds were howling down Lower Abbey Street, freezing Dublin's fair city. As the lights dimmed and the pre-show 'phones off' announcement was made, he stole a secret look at her profile, tracing her pretty nose and pert chin slowly with his eyes.

Her soft green angora jumper contrasted warmly with her titian-red curls, rambling unbound across her shoulders and down her back, making her look like a pre-Raphaelite angel. He wanted to reach forward and touch them, but he held back shyly, still nervous in their fragile peace.

Julia turned towards him as if reading his thoughts, and reached slowly for his hand. She entwined her slim white fingers in his strong tanned ones, resting them between them with a smile, finally understanding his months of delay. But that was over now and there was everything to hope for.

As the lights dimmed she reached across quickly, kissing him impishly on the cheek. He smiled, pleased, as they settled back to watch Owen McCafferty's new play, 'Quietly' and Julia waited excitedly to see her favourite Irish actor, Patrick O'Kane, bring the character of Jimmy to life, in a way that no one else could hope to better.

She wondered how Craig had found the coveted last-night tickets so late, but she didn't want to ask him, preferring their secrets to emerge naturally, tired of interrogation in her daily life.

She sank down into the warm velvet seat and rested her head on his shoulder, curving her body towards him. And as the opening words flowed over them, they both thought of their first Christmas together, excited and nervous by what might lie ahead. Until eventually all thoughts of Christmas were forgotten as the performance in front of them carried them away, into Jimmy's world.

****

The C.C.U. Ten days later.

"Show me the pictures then. Who does he look like?"

Liam grinned proudly. "He's a fine big boy. Five kilos."

"Five Kilos! Poor Danni." Nicky and Annette winced in maternal solidarity, while Liam continued, unheeding.

"He'll cost us a fortune in clothes." Suddenly he realised what Annette had asked. "What do you mean who does he look like? He looks like a baby. Well... mind you... no, he doesn't actually. At the moment he looks like a squashed tomato; all red, and sort of like this."

He pulled a face intended to look like a squashed fruit and Craig laughed.

Annette hit his arm in mock-outrage. "That's your son you're talking about. Don't you let Danni hear you say that."

Liam shot her a martyred look. "She threw me out! Says I'm getting in the way and her Mother will help! So much for paternity leave."

Craig shrugged. "You can take it when he's sixteen and play football with him."

"Or teach him how to chase girls..."

Annette smacked him on the arm. "Liam!"

"I'm only joking."

"No, you aren't. That's the problem. Have you picked a name yet?"

"I like Danny, but the wife says that would cause chaos. So at the moment he's called Bruiser."

Craig and Davy laughed and Annette sighed despairingly. "He must have a real name, Liam. You can't call him Bruiser for life."

Craig gave her a wry look. "Oh yes, he could. If Danni would let him."

Liam grinned. "We've all sorts of names in the hat at the moment and I'm running a book on the top five. Fancy a bet, Davy? The leader at the moment is Rory.

303

Mind you, I like Micky myself."

Annette raised her eyes to heaven, looking for support from Nicky. But they all sided with Liam and made their bets. Even Nicky agreed that babies looked like squashed fruit for a few weeks. So much for maternal instinct.

Annette finally brought the conversation back to the case, to a chorus of 'kill-joy'.

"Kaisa must have done a lot of research on both men, sir. She tailored her looks to suit each of them. She was a dark-blonde, like Caitlin, for Joe Watson."

"And his first wife Jenny, she was dark-blonde as well."

"And apparently Leighton's mother and sisters all have light blonde hair and are very petite."

"But her hair was naturally w...white-blonde anyway, Annette."

She looked at Davy kindly. "Yes, but if Leighton had come from a family of brunettes she would probably have died it dark for him. She gave each of them what they wanted, and had them eating out of her hands. People often fancy the same type, or someone who looks like a family member. There's lots of research on it."

They paused and thought of the implications for their own lives. Craig smiled widely, thinking of John. Natalie was a ringer for his late mother Veronica, and every bit as eccentric. But had Kaisa Mitic really been that clever?

"It can't be that simple to get things out of people, Annette."

Annette smiled and started laughing to herself. "No disrespect, sir, but have you really no idea how stupid men are sometimes?"

He laughed. "Well, Lucia tells me often enough. Go on then."

"Kaisa was beautiful. Stunning in fact. She played vulnerable and completely pliable with both men. And she probably-"

"Bonked their brains out, Cutty?"

"God, Liam, do you *have* to be so basic? I was going

304

to say that she seduced them. She knew exactly how to get what she wanted from both of them. She got expensive perfume, jewellery, and money from Joe Watson. And she got the offer of a home and protection from Bob Leighton. From both of them in fact. She didn't need to 'get' anything out of them." She paused for effect. "They volunteered it, just to impress her."

The three men sat silent for a moment, while what she'd said sank in. She was absolutely right. Every one of them had told or given a woman something at some time, to impress her about how clever, rich or strong they were. It was all about sex, and it was powerful enough to bring down Presidents, mostly the male ones.

Craig conceded the point. "You're right. Some men really are that stupid."

Annette grinned. "I know. Great isn't it?" And she and Nicky smiled at one of the female sex's strongest, and most politically incorrect weapons. Lust.

Chapter Twenty-Seven

Sharm El Sheikh. Egypt.

Stevan yawned loudly and reached for his drink, relaxing in the sun's warmth. He had never seen winters like this in Serbia, or wealth. He lifted his sunglasses and looked around the hotel pool, eyeing the bikinied women with their long, glossy limbs. One of them had caught his eye in the bar the evening before. He could see her now, lean and edgy, her costume just that side of avant-garde, and her reading material matching. She was just his type. But she would have to wait; he had business to attend to.

He smiled at his sister happily. She was already turning brown and filling-out, after only a week of five-star meals. He'd made the right decision bringing them here first instead of the villa. The trail needed to cool before they reached their final home. It wouldn't do to be followed.

Besides, it was better for Kaisa to be here when he left. She could entertain herself with pampering and shopping, and make little friends. He watched as she threw a beach ball to the ten-year-olds she'd befriended. Splashing and smiling like the child she still was, in so many ways. He rose and wandered over to the water's edge, calling her. "Draga, I must go soon."

She pouted up at him, shielding her eyes with a hand. "Must you, Stevan?"

He nodded, kindly.

"For how many days?"

He held three fingers up and she pouted again. Then one of her small companions got water in their eyes and cried, and she rushed to care for them, Stevan all but forgotten. He smiled quietly and went his room to prepare, passing the edgy beauty with a long look, and a thought. Three days, then we'll see.

****

The C.C.U.

The murder squad office was quiet for once. Harrison had taken them off the rota for a few days, to give them time to tie up loose ends and tidy-up the case, before it went to the public prosecutors.

Two people were dead, but there could have been more; Declan Greer had had a near-miss. But Irene and Bob Leighton were definitely murdered, and Craig didn't want to leave any loopholes that Joanne Greer's slick legal team could wriggle her through later. She had the money to hire the best the U.K. had to offer.

He was confident that they would convict her. They had her motive. Horizon's money trail led straight back to her private accounts, not Declan's. The poor bugger had just been her patsy. She'd had a good go at hiding the funds, routing transactions through five banks around the world. But the forensic accountants were unpicking things nicely, and they had the added bonus of her husband giving evidence for them, finally standing up to her to save his children's future.

His daughters would be angry with him initially, but he had the time to make it better. And more importantly time without his wife manipulating them, which it sounded like he hadn't had for years. He'd given them everything that he knew about Joanne, and it wasn't pretty listening. Now they had her call to Ershov, the payments that she'd made through an intermediary for the hits, and Ershov turning against her.

Of course, her defence team would discredit Ershov without much difficulty, and say that the hit-team worked for him. But he'd been careful. They could show that he knew Stevan and Kaisa Mitic, but it would be difficult to tie him to directly commissioning the hits. And as no money from Horizon had entered his accounts yet, where was his motive? No, it would all stick to Joanne.

Ershov wasn't their problem now anyway. He'd struck a deal that meant they couldn't prosecute him

307

for the Northern Ireland killings. But Yemi and Rajiv Chandak were working hard to find Kaisa and Stevan, and nail them all for The Met's two unsolved cases. Paris was next in the queue. Realistically, they would be lucky if they got Ershov and might have to leave it at that. If Kaisa and Stevan had any sense, they'd be far away by now. The last sighting had them boarding a plane for Cairo on the thirteenth.

That's what he would have done, although he wasn't sure that they would be safe even there. Watson was still looking for Kaisa, even though they had advised him strongly against it. If he didn't stop looking, Craig's money was on Stevan finding him first.

His thoughts were interrupted by a knock on the office door. He was grateful for the interruption. "Come in." The door swung wide open and Liam was standing there, grinning broadly.

"Here, boss. It's twelve o'clock, legitimately lunchtime. And it's too nice a day to be hugging a desk, so we were thinking lunch...Maybe up at Cutter's Wharf? You could call it team-building, or some other management shite?"

Craig laughed. He could see three faces like something from of the cast of 'Oliver' hiding behind Liam. Davy, Nicky and Annette were in on the escape. He looked at the pile of paperwork in front of him with absolutely no inclination to do it, and then through one of his long glass windows and out over the Lagan. The sun was shining, highlighting a buoy in Belfast Lough, bobbing gently up and down with the water. And a faint boat horn was sounding, the sound echoing plaintively in the cold winter air, heralding Christmas and holidays.

He looked at the files again, calculating the shortest time it would take to write them up, and then struck a deal with himself. Leadership classes had their uses.

"OK, here's the deal, and the price. Liam, phone John and Des and invite them to meet us at Cutters at one. Annette, help me sort out these files. Nicky, you're going to take dictation directly from me now, instead of me having to tape it. And you're going to type up my letters by tomorrow lunchtime, please."

Nicky smiled at his uncharacteristic cheek. Craig looked at Davy realising that he'd run out of tasks, the smile on Davy's face showing that he'd realised it too. He searched for a moment longer, and then shrugged, defeated. Liam had already loped back to his desk to make the call, smug that he'd got off so lightly, when Craig remembered something else.

"Come back here, you're not getting off that easily." Liam slumped back, caught.

"If you're not taking paternity leave, you're going to write up the liaison reports with Derek Cantor's and Rick Ellis' teams, and..." Liam opened his mouth wide to object. "Over lunch you're going to tell us what really happened at Lilith's. And remember, I've already got Keith Ericson's version on tape..."

****

London.

Stevan walked quickly through arrivals and hailed a cab, collecting his unmarked car at Langley. He drove quickly around the M25 until he reached the M11, driving towards Ongar and deep into Epping Forest and then parked and switched off the engine, putting the seat-back down. He pulled his baseball cap over his eyes and snoozed, waiting. It wasn't long before a dark-blue Mercedes pulled off the main road, crushing the leaves and branches in its way. It came to an abrupt halt and parked close-by, but not too close. Stevan stayed very still, mimicking sleep.

The Mercedes' driver made no move, idling the engine, as if considering the wisdom of his choice. Finally he cut the engine, clicking open the boot remotely, silently inviting Stevan to come and look. Stevan moved swiftly from his false sleep and crossed to the car without speaking, fingering the Ruger at his waist, ready. He lifted the boot and touched its contents carefully, examining every inch. Then he stepped-back, and motioned the car's driver to emerge and come towards him.

The man who stepped out was no more than twenty-five: lean and dark. His head was shaved to two days growth, and a single silver earring hung from one lobe. He wore a dark metal Dukh around his neck.

He reached out a hand in greeting and Stevan saw the familiar eight-pointed star tattooed across his wrist. "Hello, Stevan."

The hand hung in the air for a moment, unshaken. Then he shrugged and lifted a cigarette from his pocket, lighting it, blowing the smoke skyward in the icy forest air.

"Let's get this over with, Josyp. The less time I spend with you the better."

Josyp smiled coldly and showed the whitest teeth that Stevan had ever seen. Alik had spared no expense on his young cousin's welfare. Following the code: 'Teach the criminal way of life to youth with potential.'

"So polite, Stevan. As always. Good thing I'm not sensitive."

Stevan pushed through his sarcasm, ignoring it. "Where is he?"

"At the house."

"When did they let him out?"

"Tuesday. He's under house arrest. They're watching him closely- two in the house and two in the grounds." He paused and continued sarcastically. "No problem for you though, surely?"

Stevan stared at the younger man, disgusted; even he couldn't kill a relative. But then, he'd never wanted power, and the man in front of him did, very much.

"He has brought trouble to us...for a...woman." Josyp spat out the word, in a way that made Stevan pity any future wife. "He breached Ponyatiya law trusting this Joanne. A true Vor cannot be brought down for a whore. He has to go."

There, he'd said it, the thing that they both wanted. Alik Ershov's death. But for two entirely different reasons.

Stevan jerked his head towards the boot. "SAKO."

"Your usual choice."

310

"Not this time, this time it must be face to face. He has to see me kill him."

"Don't be insane! The police will catch you."

"I'm touched that you care, Josyp."

"I don't give a shit about you, but I might need you when I'm Chief. You can't go near the house. Anyway, I thought you liked distance. Alik always said you didn't like it when they looked at you."

"I'll make an exception for him."

Josyp stared at him in realisation. "That's why you came so quickly when I called. You were already on your way, weren't you?"

Stevan nodded once, sharply. After a few seconds the other man nodded too, understanding. "He touched Kaisa, didn't he?"

Stevan spat the next words out. "When I was in Belfast. It's why I missed Declan Greer. Deliberately." His fists clenched white. "Alik laid his hands on her against her will, and now he'll die."

Bile filled his mouth as he remembered his sister's raw tears at the racecourse, and every night since then. He'd never stopped Kaisa sleeping with men on a job, if she chose. Although he hated it, she'd always felt in control. And mostly they'd died as payment, except Joe Watson, and she was still angry with him for that. But Ershov had visited The Randle on the night that he'd left, and what he'd done there had revived her childhood memories and set her back years. For that alone he deserved to die.

Josyp nodded in agreement. The rape of a woman after drinking with her wasn't considered wrong by a Vor. But Kaisa was deeply troubled, and Alik could have any woman that he chose. Even Josyp agreed that she was out of bounds.

"Get me into the house."

Josyp thought and nodded once, quickly, as Stevan continued. "Thanks for the gun, but I'll do without it."

"I'll open the back gate and keep the police at the front of the house for you. The only thing I ask is that you keep it away from the children."

Stevan looked at him, horrified at Josyp even

thinking that he would let children see. He nodded at him curtly. "Agreed. Get him in the study at six and I'll do the rest."

Both men walked quickly back to their cars, Josyp to leave for Ershov's mansion, and Stevan to doze for an hour before the call came.

At five-fifteen Stevan's alarm buzzed and he pressed a button, sliding the window down to let a blast of icy air wake him up. Why hadn't Josyp called yet? He pressed-on the radio and Radio Essex cut through the darkening December sky, bringing him up to date with traffic and weather in the area. It could prove useful when he headed for the airport. He yawned and lifted the armrest, pulling a sandwich from its interior and was just taking a bite when the car-phone rang.

He seized the handset urgently. "Yes"

The gruff voice that answered belonged to the heir apparent. "He's going in at five-fifty-five to take a call from Moscow. It will be ten minutes long at least. The back gate is open."

The call ended abruptly and Stevan knew that it the last time he'd ever hear that voice, although Josyp had no idea. He threw the sandwich quickly onto the passenger seat and gunned the engine, spraying a trail of grass and ice in his wake. Pulling left onto the High Road he followed its curves and slopes into Burial Park; one mile from Alik Ershov's expensive gated home. He drove the last mile slowly, lights dimmed, until he could make out the high, wide shape of the open back-gate into the grounds. Josyp had thoughtfully included a floor plan with the rifle, so he knew that the dimly-lit room beside the pool was the study that he'd been in only nine days before.

He parked the car in a nearby copse, and moved quickly and silently across the grass and through the open gate, stopping every few seconds to look around for police or family. There was no one. Josyp had kept to his word. They were all at the front. It was in both their interests to dispatch Alik quickly and anonymously.

He reached the window outside the room and

checked his watch. Five-fifty-five. As predicted, the door opened and the room's light brightened slightly, as he heard the heavy sounds of a man moving around inside. He gave Alik a moment to settle down and make the call.

As soon as he heard the familiar voice speaking Russian, he lifted the already open window a sliver and eased himself in silently. Alik was seated in his large leather chair behind the desk, with his back towards him.

Stevan hesitated for a moment, choosing between common sense and desire. Desire won. He grabbed quickly at the chair with one hand, swinging it around and cutting the call easily with his other, the look of shock in the Vor's eyes was worth the riskier face-on kill.

Before the older man could call out, he clamped both hands around his neck and squeezed. Squeezed the life out of him for Kaisa, the affectionate child who had hurt no one until they'd destroyed her. And for Irene Leighton, a helpless, innocent mother that he'd made them tattoo for the pathetic honour of the Vors. And then ordered them to kill, viciously and publically. Trying to stir up political unrest in a newly peaceful country, its war-torn-past too much like Stevan's own, to ever want it revived.

Stevan watched as Alik's eyes widened frantically, and then reddened more by the second, filling with small, bloody dots as he wrung his hands tightly around his neck. He could feel the sinews in the Vor's neck stretch and tighten, and the satisfying crack as his hyoid-bone broke. His search for air grew wilder, as he rasped and wheezed and finally quietened beneath his grip.

All at once the writhing and retching stopped, and Ershov's body fell back limply, against the expensive seat in his dark study. The only sound was the quiet ticking of the wall clock, beating in time with Stevan's softly exhaled breath.

Stevan looked down coldly at the man, feeling nothing but calm. Then he smiled once and slipped out of the room the same way that he came, disappearing quickly into the night. Back to Kaisa and out of the game forever.

****

The C.C.U. December 21st.

It was the Friday before Christmas and for the first time in five years Craig was really looking forward to the holiday. He swung his chair around to face the window, relaxing, and he gazed out at the Lagan, always reflecting the seasons in weather and activity.

The afternoon light was dimming and a soft snowfall had covered the Harland and Wolff cranes like icing. It made them look festive, like two giant yellow Christmas trees. The last shards of winter-sun shone across the river, and he could just make out Stormont in the distance, reminding him sadly of Irene Leighton and her orphaned son. His eyes were pulled back to the river by the happier sound of a party-boat starting early, its seasonal lights twinkling to the sound The Pogue's 'Fairy-tale of New York' and he smiled down at the giggling revellers dancing on the deck.

They'd completed the files for the prosecutors and they'd had a few days' rest; now he was getting bored. So bored that he'd just called Harrison's office and asked to be put back on the Rota. But not until New Year.

After a moment more spent staring at the water he wandered out onto the main floor, searching for some banter. Just then his phone rang and he gestured Nicky to transfer the call, answering it quickly. It was London. He clicked on the speaker and Yemi's deep, clear voice rang across the room.

"Hi Yemi, you're on speaker. Fire ahead."

"I thought you would all like to know, Alik Ershov is dead."

Craig looked at Liam, shocked. "What! How did it happen?"

"Like something out of the S.A.S. handbook, that's

314

how. They came in through an open back-window last night and strangled him, while our people were at the front. Clean get-away."

"Who wanted him dead?"

"Hundreds. It would be quicker to ask who didn't. Look, I have to go to a meeting, but I just thought you should know. Keep in touch, Marc. And Merry Christmas everyone."

The line cleared and Liam's next words earned him another human rights course. "Excellent job! Saved the courts a fortune."

THE END

Core Characters in the Craig Crime Novels

D.C.I. Marc (Marco) Craig: Craig is a sophisticated, single, forty-two-year-old. Born in Northern Ireland, he is of Northern Irish/Italian extraction, from a mixed religious background but agnostic. An ex-grammar schoolboy and Queen's University Law graduate, he went to London to join The Met (The Metropolitan Police) at twenty-two, rising in rank through its High Potential Development Training Scheme. He returned to Belfast in two-thousand and eight after more than fifteen years away.

He is a driven, very compassionate, workaholic, with an unfortunate temper that he struggles to control and a tendency to respond to problems with his fists. He lives alone in a modern apartment block in Stranmillis, near the university area of Belfast. His parents, his extrovert mother Mirella (an Italian pianist) and his quiet father Tom (an ex-university lecturer in Physics), both in their late sixties, live in Holywood town, six miles away. His rebellious sister, Lucia, his junior by ten years, works in a local charity and also lives in Belfast.

Craig is a Detective Chief Inspector heading up Belfast's Murder Squad, based in the Co-ordinated Crime Unit (C.C.U.) building in Pilot Street, in the Sailortown area of Belfast's Docklands. He loves the sea, sails when he has the time and is generally very sporty. He plays the piano, loves music by Snow Patrol and follows Manchester United and Northern Ireland football teams, and the Ulster Rugby team.

D.I. Liam Cullen: Craig's Detective Inspector. Liam is a forty-seven-year-old former RUC officer from Crossgar in Northern Ireland, who transferred into the PSNI in two-thousand and one following the Patton Reforms. He has lived and worked in Northern Ireland all his life and has spent almost thirty years in the police force, twenty of them policing Belfast, including during The Troubles.

He is married to the thirty-seven-year-old long suffering Danielle (Danni), a part-time nursery nurse, and they have a one-year-old daughter Erin and are expecting their second child. Liam is unsophisticated, indiscreet and hopelessly non-PC, but he's a hard worker with a great knowledge of the streets and has a sense of humour that makes everyone, even the Chief Constable, laugh.

D.S. Annette McElroy: Annette is Craig's detective sergeant and has lived and worked in Northern Ireland all her life. She is a forty-three-year-old ex-nurse who studied and worked as a nurse for thirteen years then, after a career break, retrained and has now been in the police for an equal length of time. She's is married to Pete, a P.E teacher at a state secondary school and they have two children, a boy and a girl (Jordan and Amy), both young teenagers. Annette is kind and conscientious with an especially good eye for detail. She also has very good people skills but can be a bit of a goody-two-shoes.

Nicky Morris: Nicky Morris is Craig's thirty-seven-year-old personal assistant. She used to be P.A. to Detective Chief Superintendent (D.C.S.) Terry 'Teflon' Harrison. Nicky is a glamorous Belfast mum, married to Gary, who owns a small garage, and is the mother of a young son, Jonny. She comes from a solidly working class area in East Belfast, just ten minutes' drive from Docklands.

She is bossy, motherly and street-wise and manages to organise a reluctantly-organised Craig very effectively. She has a very eclectic sense of style, and there is an ongoing innocent office flirtation between her and Liam.

Davy Walsh: The Murder Squad's twenty-four-year-old computer analyst. A brilliant but shy EMO, Davy's confidence has grown during his time on the team, making his lifelong stutter on 's' and 'w' diminish, unless he's under stress.

His father is deceased and Davy lives at home in Belfast with his mother and grandmother. He has an older sister, Emmie, who studied English at university.

Dr John Winter: John is the forty-one-year-old Director of Pathology for Northern Ireland, one of the youngest ever appointed. He's brilliant, eccentric, gentlemanly, and really likes the ladies.

He was Craig's best friend at school and university and remained in Northern Ireland to build his medical career when Craig left. He is now internationally respected in his field. John persuaded Craig that the newly peaceful Northern Ireland was a good place to return to and assists Craig's team with cases whenever he can. He is obsessed with crime in general and US police shows in particular.

D.C.S. Terry (Teflon) Harrison: Craig's boss. The fifty-three-year-old Detective Chief Superintendent is based half-time at the C.C.U., where he has an office on the twelfth floor, and half-time at the Headquarters building in Limavady in the North-West Irish countryside. He shares a converted farm house at Toomebridge with his homemaker wife Mandy and their daughter Sian, a marketing consultant. He has had a trail of mistresses, often younger than his daughter.

Harrison is tolerable as a boss as long as everything's going well, but he is acutely politically aware and a bit of a snob, and very quick to pass on any blame to his subordinates (hence the Teflon nickname). He sees Craig as a useful employee but resents his friendship with John Winter, who wields a great deal of power in Northern Ireland.

Key Background Locations

The majority of locations referenced in the book are real, with some exceptions.

Northern Ireland (real): Set in the north-east of the island of Ireland, Northern Ireland was created in nineteen-twenty-one by an act of British parliament. It forms part of the United Kingdom of Great Britain and Northern Ireland and shares a border to the south and west with the Republic of Ireland. The Northern Ireland Assembly, based at the Stormont Estate, holds responsibility for a range of devolved policy matters. It was established by the Northern Ireland Act 1998 as part of the Good Friday Agreement.

Belfast (real): Belfast is the capital and largest city of Northern Ireland, set on the flood plain of the River Lagan. The seventeenth largest city in the United Kingdom and the second largest in Ireland, it is the seat of the Northern Ireland Assembly.

The Dockland's Co-ordinated Crime Unit (The C.C.U. - fictitious): The modern high-rise headquarters building is situated in Pilot Street in Sailortown, a section of Belfast between the M1 and M2 undergoing massive investment and re-development. The C.C.U. hosts the police murder, gang crimes, vice and drug squad offices, amongst others.

Sailortown (real): An historic area of Belfast on the River Lagan that was a thriving area between the sixteenth and twentieth Centuries. Many large businesses developed in the area, ships docked for loading and unloading and their crews from far flung places such as China and Russia mixed with a local

Belfast population of ship's captains, chandlers, seamen and their families.

Sailortown was a lively area where churches and bars fought for the souls and attendance of the residents and where many languages were spoken each day. The basement of the Rotterdam Bar, at the bottom of Clarendon Dock, acted as the overnight lock-up to prisoners being deported to the Antipodes on boats the next morning, and the stocks which held the prisoners could still be seen until the nineteen-nineties.

During the years of World War Two the area was the most bombed area of the UK outside Central London, as the Germans tried to destroy Belfast's ship building capacity. Sadly the area fell into disrepair in the nineteen-seventies and eighties when the motorway extension led to compulsory purchases of many homes and businesses, and decimated the Sailortown community. The rebuilding of the community has now begun, with new families moving into starter homes and professionals into expensive dockside flats.

The Pathology Labs (fictitious): The labs, set on Belfast's Saintfield Road as part of a large science park, are where Dr John Winter, Northern Ireland's Head of Pathology, and his co-worker, Dr Des Marsham, Head of Forensic Science, carry out the post-mortem and forensic examinations that help Craig's team solve their cases.

St Mary's Healthcare Trust (fictitious): St Mary's is one of the largest hospital trusts in the UK. It is spread over several hospital sites across Belfast, including the main Royal St Mary's Hospital site off the motorway and the Maternity, Paediatric and Endocrine (M.P.E.) unit, a stand-alone site on Belfast's Lisburn Road, in the University Quarter of the city.

15082918R00172

Printed in Great Britain
by Amazon